Praise for *The Other Lover*

'A beautifully written and touching love story'
*Woman's Own*

'A sensitive tale of friendship, death and emotional need.
I'm championing her' Sarah Broadhurst, *Bookseller*

Praise for *Laughing as They Chased Us*

'Read it and sigh for the transitory beauty of youth and
first love' *Time Out*

'Sexy and heady' *Cosmopolitan*

'A super debut' *Daily Mirror*

Sarah Jackman was born in Berlin and has lived variously in the UK, France and Germany. She now lives in south Wales. She is the author of *Laughing as They Chased Us* and *The Other Lover*, also available in Pocket Books.

*Also by Sarah Jackman*

Laughing as They Chased Us

The Other Lover

# never stop looking

## Sarah Jackman

**POCKET BOOKS**

London · New York · Sydney · Toronto

A CBS COMPANY

First published in Great Britain by Pocket Books UK, 2009
An imprint of Simon & Schuster UK Ltd
A CBS COMPANY

3 5 7 9 10 8 6 4 2

Simon & Schuster UK Ltd
1st Floor, 222 Gray's Inn Road
London WC1V 8HB

www.simonsays.co.uk

Simon & Schuster Australia
Sydney

A CIP catalogue record for this book is available from the British Library

ISBN 978-1-84739-275-6

Typeset in Garamond by Ellipsis Books Limited, Glasgow

Printed and bound in Great Britain by
CPI Cox and Wyman, Reading, Berkshire RG1 8EX

*For my parents, Michael and Gwynneth*

## Acknowledgements

My thanks to Kate Lyall-Grant, Libby Vernon and the team at Simon & Schuster UK. To Teresa Chris, Jackie Ford and the Directors of Swansea Print Workshop for their support when writing this novel.

Thanks also to all family and friends, to Claire Ringrose, Dean Kayes, Diane Gallagher, Juliet Silburn for their constant encouragement and support.

The author wishes to acknowledge the award of a Writer's Bursary from the Academi for the purpose of completing this book.

Five black-suited bouncers, fidgety with testosterone, had come out of the club and were smoking and chatting at the exit. Like Abbie, they were waiting for the clubbers to leave. An illegal taxi, loitering in the badly lit part of the street a few metres away, attracted their attention and sped off at the sauntering approach of a couple of the men. A game of cat and mouse – the cabby would be back for the easy fares later. With barely a shifting of their heads, they clocked Abbie standing on the other side of the street and paused. She pulled down her hood and shook her hair free to show that she was just a woman and not worth bothering with. The men walked back to their posts.

She slid her cold fingers into the inside pocket of her jacket and fingered the pile of flyers there; this was her last call for the night and the most important. Hope and nerves stretched the waiting time. She paced about to keep warm but didn't take her eyes off the exit. She was waiting for that movement, that tremor that passed between the bouncers; a tightening of the shoulders as they pushed their chests forward, a clichéd tug at the cuffs of suit sleeves that told her it was time.

She was across the road by the time the doors had been secured open. First there was a trickle of those trying to beat the rush; soon she was immersed in the rapidly growing, slow-moving crowd. She worked her way from one person to the next, touching warm, bare arms, damp shirt backs, holding out a flyer, saying excuse me ... could you please ... sorry but ... have you seen this man? ... have you seen this man? ... have you seen this man?

She knew by now how to play it once she made eye-contact. Those high, those drunk, those whose night had dealt them a knock, the happy ones, the ones in love. She offered them whatever they wanted to see: desperation, hope, resignation, a little flirting if that's what it took to get a moment of their attention.

She recognized, too, the ones who were a waste of time, the ones who would always blank her, the others who were so wrapped up in themselves, their ears and brains buzzing that there was no point even trying.

'No.'

'Sorry, love.'

'Go away.'

'Piss off.'

She'd heard it all before.

'What kind of man you lookin' for, darlin'?' A short man wriggled his crotch at her. Egged on by the whoops which went up from his mates, he came closer. Abbie held the flyer out at arm's length to keep him from getting too close.

'Will I do ya?'

'He's my husband. He's missing,' she told him. She met his eyes and saw they were hard. There was real threat behind his swagger. Perhaps he'd been given the brush-off tonight by some girl. She stepped back but he caught her wrist. 'You haven't answered my question.'

His mates had quietened now and were beginning to shuffle away into the shadows. Abbie glanced around. Most of the crowd had dispersed and the bouncers had disappeared.

She tried to twist away but he gripped her wrist even tighter; she could feel his fingers pressing into the bone. He tugged her towards him so that their bodies were almost touching and thrust his face closer. 'I'm still fucking waiting.'

She let her body go limp. She called up the thought of Nick out here, somewhere; on his own, not knowing what to do, who he was, trying to make sense of it all and the tears came readily to her eyes.

The man dropped her arm as if he'd found himself holding the limb of a corpse. He spat on the ground before giving Abbie one last, blistering look. 'Oh, piss off, you sad cunt.'

Abbie ran to catch up with the tail end of the clubbers and followed a group into the late-night café. She went to the Ladies where a couple of girls were comforting their friend who was crouched in the corner by one of the sinks. No one paid Abbie any attention when she pushed her way into a free cubicle. She sank onto the toilet and sat there for a few minutes, shaking. The flyer was still in her hand. She had crumpled it in her agitation and a deep crease struck across Nick's face, straight through his eyes. She rested the flyer on her knees and attempted to flatten it out with the heel of her palm before putting it in the inside pocket of her jacket.

When Abbie returned to the dining area, the windows of

the café had misted up from the combined body heat of the clubbers. As she queued, her shaking began to subside.

She felt a nudge from the girl behind her. 'It's you,' she said to Abbie, who turned back to meet the angry eyes of a member of staff. 'Next!' they growled at her. 'Next!'

'Tea. A large tea,' she said, deliberately omitting the 'please'.

There was a very small table with a single chair squashed between a glass-fronted drinks fridge and another – occupied – table for four. Before she sat down, she scanned the room for Nick and then for the horrible man from outside the club, but saw neither.

She unzipped her jacket, her fingers automatically sliding inside to locate the flyers. She selected one which wasn't creased to place in front of her. She put her elbows on the table, held her mug of tea close to her face and steam condensed on her cheeks. Her eyes felt as naked and rubbery as hard-boiled eggs.

Over two hundred thousand people go missing in the UK every year. People liked to quote this fact to her every now and then. Some because they wanted to show her they were up to date on current issues; others – like the police – offered it as a kind of explanation, as if to say: we've got our work cut out, so don't get your hopes up. The well-meaning ones offered it so she wouldn't feel so alone.

Abbie knew there were a lot of people, like her, living this waking nightmare but whenever she heard that statistic all she could think was how tiny it seemed. There were over sixty million people in the UK, so searching for two hundred thousand among them was virtually impossible and looking for one of those missing thousands in London was like looking for a needle in a haystack.

When she next raised her eyes, the café had emptied out and the windows were clearing to reveal a drizzly dawn. Only misfits with nowhere to go remained. The night was over. She had done all she could; all that remained was for her to make her way home.

She walked quickly. With her purpose over, she always felt more vulnerable. The rain had dampened her hair before she thought of pulling up her hood. When she did, the warmth and anonymity inside it instantly made her feel better. The shadows were dissipating, the light from the street lamps was fading as night time retreated. The streets were quiet but Abbie had never known them in this part of the city to be empty. She felt compelled to check out every person that she passed or who approached, even those who couldn't possibly be Nick. Just in case, she told herself. Just in case.

It was cold as she came out by the Thames. The wind cut across the open bank straight through her clothes. She wished she was back in her flat. She wished for tiny wings to sprout at her ankles and propel her home. At Westminster Bridge, her wish came true in the form of the last night-bus. Inside and warm again, she looked out at the city. Grey light obscured the buildings in the distance and mist hovered like steam over the river.

The lamp through the curtains in her front window glowed in greeting but she kept her hope crouched low inside her belly as she unlocked the door, and felt it slink away as she entered the inert atmosphere of an empty home.

She went to check and collect the note she had propped up on the mantelpiece in the study next to Nick's framed photograph.

'Good morning, my love,' Abbie said, touching his face.

In the kitchen, the cooker clock radiated a green underwater tinge to the half-light. It was 4.19. She pulled out the note tucked under the kettle but left Nick's bottle of vodka and glass where it was. In the living room, everything seemed as neat and tidy as it had been when she went out over six hours ago but she couldn't help scanning the plump cushions for any dents and dips which might have been made by a relaxing body; a body glad to be home at last. She snatched up the final note from next to the telephone and screwed up all three and left them on the table. She took off her jacket, removed the flyers from the pocket and threw them next to the discarded notes.

Tiredness assaulted her.

In the bedroom, she sank, fully clothed, onto the bed. She slowly pulled up the duvet to her shoulders, as if it were filled with leaden fibre, before falling into sleep.

There was a picture in Owen's head of how it would be when he finally left the house. This picture had evolved over several months, usually at night – most nights – when he was struggling to get to sleep. He used it as a mental barrier, a shield against the physical proximity of Fliss lying next to him, otherwise another sickening round of questioning threatened to start up: was he doing the right thing? Had they made the right decision?

The picture marked the dividing line between the Before and the After and it always started at the point when he closed the front door; cutting himself off from the inside, leaving him to pause for a moment as the suffocating sensation lifted from his chest. Even as he lay in the bedroom, on his back with his eyes closed, he could feel his lungs inflating as if he was drawing in that first deep breath of fresh air before taking the first step towards the car.

A bag – actually his sports bag – was slung over his left shoulder. He held his car keys in his right hand. In the bag were a few clothes, toiletries, his iPod and a single book. He always skipped over the details of the clothes, preferring to linger instead over the choice of book. This was the only item in the image which he allowed to change – sometimes it was a hardback by Stephen Hawking or a new John Grisham. Once, it had been a biography of Bono with whom he felt an affinity ever since someone had remarked how alike they looked back in the eighties when he was a student and U2 were just starting out. More recently he had settled on *What am I Doing Here?* by Bruce Chatwin. He'd recently spotted it on 'his shelf' in the bookcase and remembered enjoying it years ago. It seemed like it might be one of those books which were good to reread at certain stages in your life.

The sound of the diesel car starting up three doors down distracted him and he instinctively looked towards the window. He was relieved to see the first signs of morning beginning to show. Fliss shifted in the bed and although he wondered briefly if she was awake too, he knew it barely made any difference if she was. They had reached that point where they had nothing left to say. Nothing but practicalities, anyway.

Tomorrow morning – this morning, in less than four hours, he realized – Fliss was taking the kids to stay overnight at her mother's so that he could concentrate on the final packing. By the time she returned on Sunday he would have gone.

Owen returned his attention once more to the bag. Whenever they were going away on a family trip, he'd find, when it was time to leave, that Fliss had added other things to his suitcase. It would be packed fit to burst with extras like her hairdryer perhaps, or a sweatshirt for Izzy, or a spare pair of trainers for Tom. It was important, therefore, that in his picture there remained plenty of space in his sports bag so that as he approached the car, he could grab hold of the bag and feel the fabric loose in his hand like the scruff of a dog's neck. He would throw it easily onto the car passenger seat where it would land with a soft thud. This was the only way – he wasn't sure why – that it was possible for Owen to envisage his future self with a lighter step and a clearer shape.

He clung to this picture even in the face of the growing evidence – the literally growing pile which had begun accumulating in the spare room over the last few weeks – that a single, half-empty bag was not going to be all that he took away from the house. He clung to this picture at night, even when, only a few hours earlier, he had been online buying the numerous items with which he needed to stock his flat: a TV, a laptop for the kids, a games console, not to mention all the kitchen equipment and towels and bed linen.

He felt it finally slip from his fingers later that morning as Fliss removed a couple of sheets of A4 paper from the kitchen drawer and handed them to him. He stared at the long list she'd written. He felt tension crawling up his back as he sensed her watching him.

'They're your things; or, you know, your share of things I thought you should have. I've tried to be fair.'

Upstairs Tom was thumping around in a last-minute packing frenzy. Owen, out of earshot of Fliss, had advised him to take plenty to do. Owen's mother-in-law's house was as uptightly pristine as the woman herself and there were very few concessions given to the presence of kids. Izzy had been ready to leave for ages. She was in the living room watching TV; elbows on knees, her face pushed forward as if she were in the process of being sucked inside the screen. She had been oblivious to Owen when he walked past just five minutes ago.

'All the Queen CDs?' he read out to Fliss. 'Are you sure about that?'

Fliss couldn't stand Freddie Mercury and his joke made her smile, which had been the aim of it.

'I think I can live without them.'

He also noticed, with some amusement – but he refrained from remarking on it – that she had tried to palm off on him Uncle Peter's badly made wooden model of the *Mary Rose*. He couldn't remember ever having expressed a liking for it and, since it was her uncle, he saw no reason to feel guilty about 'accidentally' leaving it behind.

'Is it OK?' she wanted to know. He rolled the sheets into a tube and stuck them in the back pocket of his jeans. 'Yes, great. Thanks. Very useful.'

'I knew you wouldn't get round to doing it.'

'No, I didn't,' he admitted but didn't let on that it had never crossed his mind to make such a list.

He watched Fliss clearing away the breakfast things; stacking the bowls into the dishwasher, returning the butter and milk and marmalade to the fridge, spritzing the table with something smelling strongly of lemon and bleach.

'Don't, please,' Fliss said. She stopped what she was doing and folded her arms across her front. It was one of Fliss's unfinished sentences which she excelled in and which never failed to infuriate him. This time, though, he got her meaning perfectly. For as long as he could remember, even before they began to have problems, she hated anyone watching her, particularly Owen.

He left the kitchen, deciding it was best to keep out of the way until he was called but Fliss had followed him out.

'Right,' she called. 'It's time we were off.'

He accompanied them to the front door. He saw a look of panic pass over Fliss's face; he felt Izzy's hand grip his for a second. Some half-arsed lyrics about 'words unspoken' kept spinning across his mind as the unsaid goodbyes blared out in the silence. He tried to settle his expression into something resembling a reassuring calm while the urge to pull them all close and never let go surged through him. Somehow he was able to watch them walk away; even Izzy with her pale, tearful face. The one who seemed least affected was Tom. Without Owen noticing, his son was already standing at the car, impatiently pulling at the door handle until Fliss bleeped off the central locking.

Owen couldn't bear to wave them off but he remained in the hall, his back leaning against the door until he was sure the car had gone. He walked slowly into the living room and over to the window and stared at the drive where Fliss's car had been.

According to the cooker clock it was 10.37. Abbie's bottom lip and tongue throbbed from the shock of hot coffee. She was dressed but she didn't remember doing it; she didn't remember putting Nick's vodka back into the freezer, she didn't remember making coffee either. The moments between waking and now were obscured by a fogged head and a milky film across her eyes. She blinked rapidly to try to clear her sight. She tipped the coffee down the sink and retraced her steps to the bedroom.

She had to switch on the lamp because the room received very little natural light. Its single window looked out onto the brick wall of the neighbouring house with only a narrow, deeply shaded alley separating them, making the bedroom the ideal place to display and keep Abbie's collection of costumes without fear of them getting sun damaged. Nick had screwed a wooden bar two-thirds up on two of the walls for Abbie to hang them from. He often said it was as if they were sharing the room with a dozen other people because, like now, as Abbie walked around the room, the dresses would sway gently on their hangers, the skirt hems would flutter as you passed them.

The muslin drapes were still hanging around the bed so Abbie set about looping each into a loose knot before fastening it to a bedpost. The unmade bed was a twist of white sheet and red duvet cover – like an old-fashioned candy stick – which she tidied hastily.

She remembered now coming back in the early hours, lying straight down without getting undressed, and was comforted with the recognition of what her disconnected actions and murmur of anxiety signified: just a bad day. She sat on the bed and picked up Nick's framed photograph from the bedside table. Her heart caught as it always did whenever she looked into his ice-blue eyes.

'Good morning, my love,' she said.

She headed to the living room where she opened the curtains and switched off the lamp she kept on overnight.

Hanging on the clothes rail was the delicate Victorian ball-gown she'd started to repair yesterday. Rather than attend to it now, she turned to the shelving. She took down twenty pairs of scarlet trousers which needed black stripes down the sides to emulate soldiers' uniforms. She had decided to use Velcro so that the stripes could be removed at a later date.

On a bad day it was better to concentrate on the simpler work, the most mundane alterations and repairs that she joked to herself she could do with her eyes closed: replacing buttons and lost sequins, sewing up seams, reattaching braid and trim that had come loose. She had learnt the hard way. One time she'd sliced the sleeve of a rare Elizabethan coat, another she drove a needle in so far behind her nail that she had dripped several beads of blood onto the pale blue silk of Madam Butterfly's dress. Luckily, these were rare mistakes, and ones that still remained undiscovered – the blood eased off with salt and brown paper; the cut – tiny and on the rear of the garment, painstakingly darned with a near-perfect match of embroidery thread she'd hunted down in Selfridges on Oxford Street.

She laid the trousers out on the table before remembering the bag of ladies' white gloves. She left the trousers and took the bag into the study along with her sewing box which she placed on the piano-stool beside her armchair. She checked for an ample supply of white thread before sitting down.

The air-tight bag opened with a swelling sigh, releasing a scent of powder and perfume. She tipped the contents into her lap. Women's hands were so much larger these days and the actresses were for ever popping the frail seams at the finger tips. A lot of theatre companies used cheaper replica gloves instead. Abbie had made several pairs of them herself but there was something special about the narrow cut and softness of age with the real ones that you couldn't copy.

She took a moment to focus her mind. Her eyes rested on Nick's armchair opposite her. She liked the way the morning sun was spilling onto it, setting it ablaze, keeping it warm. She took three deep breaths. Concentrate, she told herself. Concentrate.

We're allowed out to play – me and Becca – but only once we've done the washing-up. I wash as quickly as I can, placing the glasses and plates directly into the tea towel Becca holds out ready. She places everything on the work-surface behind her to put back in the cupboards at the end while I'm rinsing the bowl clean and wiping out the sink.

Afterwards, we stand in the living room doorway waiting for Mum to speak; half-afraid she'll find something else to delay our release into the warm, summer evening.

– Don't go too far, she warns.

We take our usual places sitting on the garden wall, facing the street. I bounce the heels of my trainers against the brick over and over again. Becca chews gum, blowing bubbles which burst with a crack.

The boys are playing football. I can't work out who's in which team but Becca keeps cheering Si who she started going out with a couple of weeks ago. I try shouting, – Come on, Jon! because I told Becca I fancied him but the words sound fake and feeble and I snap my mouth shut in embarrassment. The only reason I told Becca I liked Jon was so that we could talk about boys and because, sometimes, I think I might; that is until the next time I see him.

One minute there's nobody on the other side of the street, the next there's this boy, standing there, watching.

He has long, black hair, baggy, black trousers, and a white shirt half hanging out.

– Who's that? Becca asks and I shrug because I can't speak. I'm holding my breath.

For the first time in my life, I wish that I didn't have Becca next to me. Her prettiness, her liveliness, the way she draws everyone to her only emphasizes my skinny plainness. I fold my arms over my flat chest, I peer through my hair which hangs limply in front of my face, I press my fingers to my mouth to hide my teeth.

— Hey, Nick, Si shouts and the game of football stops.

Someone picks up the ball and everyone makes their way over to me and Becca.

— This is Nick, right, Si says and we all mutter hello.

Everyone seems on edge. Only Si keeps up the conversation. He tells us that he met Nick at a party his parents threw, while Nick gets out cigarettes, lights up and offers the packet to everybody in turn. Nobody dares take one. We all live round here and we'd soon be in trouble. You might think that the houses with their blank windows are empty, but secrets pass between them without you knowing and bad news gets home quicker than you can run.

I'm the last one Nick turns to. I'd love to take a cigarette. Not because I want to smoke but to prolong the connection, to maybe even touch his hand when he cups it over his lighter as I lean in towards him. Nick's eyes are amazing; blue like crystal, sharp enough to pierce your skin and leave a shard in your heart.

A car pulls up and everyone turns to watch as Mr Duncan gets out. I take my chance to look at Nick who is watching everyone watching Mr Duncan. My eyes are brown; as dark as a cave. They drag Nick's image in, down deep inside me.

Becca nudges me. The boys want to move onto somewhere else. She wants to know if we're going to go, too.

Si asks Nick the question I'm dying to ask.

— Are you coming?

— Sure, he says. — Why not?

And it isn't until weeks later that I realize I was and am, besides Si, the only one who is really happy about him tagging along. Nick isn't like the rest of the group. They put up with him because of Si's influence. Nick's always going to the cinema; he quotes lines from the films and acts out scenes from the plays he sees at the theatre, too. This, I discover, is considered by the rest of the group to be damning behaviour. No one else we know ever goes to the theatre unless they are made to with the school.

I defend him to Becca. – He's not weird. He wants to be an actor.

And then I'm forced to admit that I fancy Nick, while Becca looks at me as if I'm crazy.

Owen wasn't used to being on his own. Yesterday he'd been too busy and last night so knackered that he hadn't really noticed but this morning, the instant he woke up, the silence, even the temperature of the house, didn't feel right. He couldn't think of the last time he'd been in this position. There had been odd occasions when he was at home and Fliss and the kids were out of the house but these were usually brief periods of time – a short punctuation in his day – before he was due to be elsewhere to pick one of them up or before someone returned, bringing news and noise and demands.

The kitchen was considerably colder than they usually kept it as if the frost coating the lawn had taken swift advantage and settled inside, too. He remembered that he'd turned the heating thermostat right down when the house had become uncomfortably hot after several hours of humping boxes around. He decided to leave it on quite low for the time being; he'd soon warm up again once Steve arrived with the van. He ate some breakfast cereal and put the coffee machine on then wandered into the dining room where everything was stacked up in readiness.

At some point late in the evening, before he realized he hadn't eaten any dinner – when his blood sugar level must have been at an all time low – he'd thrown Fliss's list on the floor in a temper fit. Picking it up now, he saw that less than half of the items had been crossed off and that he had absolutely no interest in taking any of the rest with him. He would tell Fliss that he didn't have the room so she didn't make a fuss but, apart from his CDs, some books, his personal paperwork, laptop and iPod, he didn't actually feel that much else belonged to him, anyway. It was Fliss who had pored over interior design magazines and who had chosen the majority of what they owned and he honestly felt that she deserved to keep them.

He took a last, slow wander through the house to see if there was anything he'd missed, shutting the children's bedroom doors as he passed without looking inside.

Strangely, for the amount of boxes he had filled, the house didn't appear much emptier. This was rather a relief because the last thing he wanted was Izzy and Tom coming home to a place which looked like it had been burgled. Minimum disruption to the kids, that's what he and Fliss had agreed and, although he knew that kind of sentiment was freely thrown about when couples were getting divorced, he was determined to honour it in the best way he could.

The smell of coffee reached him so he took the phone handset into the kitchen and tried Steve's mobile a couple of times as he poured himself a mug. Steve's phone went straight to the answer service, which wasn't a good sign. He hoped he wasn't going to be late. He backed his car out of the drive to make way for the van and started carrying boxes out. Ten minutes later, he heard a van engine approaching. Steve bumped up the drive, arm slung casually out of the open window. He shouted a loud greeting down to Owen above the blare of Virgin Radio.

'This your lot?' he asked, jumping out. He indicated the five boxes Owen had brought outside.

'Not even half of it.'

'Mind if I have a coffee before we get started? I've got the hangover from hell and you look terrible, mate, too, if you don't mind me mentioning it.'

'Better make it quick. Fliss is going to be back at lunchtime and there's no way I want to be here and go through all that again.'

'Bit heavy was it?'

Steve, he knew, would be quick to get the wrong impression – he always did – where Fliss was concerned. A lot of people only saw the surface she offered; that almost dismissive confidence that put people's backs up. He had been fooled by it, too, all those years ago. Super-cool, she had seemed back then to him; others used to call her intimidating, aloof. Stuck-up, even. To discover the anxious, self-doubting side of her had intrigued Owen. Today, he felt compelled to do right by Fliss and at least attempt to keep the record straight.

'No, it wasn't like that; Fliss is being brilliant. It's me. It's just so final. It freaked me out a bit.'

'But it's what you want, right? You're not having second thoughts, are you?' Steve stopped in front of him.

'Nothing like that. It's the kids. That's the worst thing.'

Owen was only slightly shorter than his friend and yet Steve seemed to tower over him. Owen looked down at his feet – perhaps it was the camber of the drive; water sometimes lay after a steady downpour in the area where he was standing.

'You'll still see them, though. You and Fliss have sussed that all out.'

'I know. But it's not the same.' Steve didn't have kids, so he couldn't know what it was like.

Part of Owen wanted to tell him how bad he felt – as if he was doing something so terrible that he should be punished for the rest of his life – and part of him knew that no amount of explaining would make Steve understand. This was the part that won. He stepped forward and Steve turned aside to let Owen go first into the house.

Owen heated the cold coffee from the jug in the microwave and handed Steve a mug.

Steve sat down. He dumped in two sugars and then a third after a brief hesitation. 'Need the energy,' he said, a little guiltily.

Owen poured himself half a cup and joined him at the table.

'Fliss rang Julie last night.'

This took Owen by surprise. 'Was she OK? Did Jules say?'

'She went off to the bedroom to talk to her so I don't know. They're so secretive, women, aren't they?'

'So she didn't say anything at all to you?'

'Just that she couldn't believe that you were actually leaving.'

'Who couldn't? Julie or Fliss?' He felt panic rising.

'Jules,' Steve hesitated. 'I think.'

'It can't be Fliss, she wouldn't have said that. She wants this as much as I do.'

'Really? I always thought it was more you than her.'

'Why do you think that? Does Julie think that, too? Is that what Fliss is saying?'

'Don't get your knickers in a twist. It's just the impression I had. You know better than anyone, mate. It's your divorce.'

'Yes.' At least he had thought he knew but what if he'd got it all wrong? Fliss had said that she was unhappy but what if she had just agreed because she knew he wanted to go? What if everyone else knew this and he was the only one who didn't?

Next door were all those boxes, outside on the drive was a van. Opposite him, Steve had his nose in his coffee, red eyed, hair all over the place, a whiff of last night's alcohol coming off his skin.

No, Owen told himself, of course he was right. He'd seen it in Fliss, a mirror of his own bravery when they had both acknowledged that neither of them wanted to be together. They had cried together and comforted each other but the understanding had remained; it was the end. It had been ending for a long time.

He felt his head clear. 'Come on,' he said. 'Let's get on with it and get the fuck out of here.'

Noises in the flat above broke into Abbie's thoughts. Over the last twelve years since she and Nick first came to live here, she had lost count of the people who had lived above them. It seemed to be one of those transitory places where people paused for a short moment in their lives before moving on.

She had missed the sounds of the last tenants since they left a few weeks ago. There was something comforting about people's footsteps on the stairs, the washing machine rumbling, the sudden bursts of whatever music her neighbours favoured at the time. As long as they kept themselves to themselves.

In the past some neighbours had attempted to strike up friendships. Belinda, the South African woman, had been the worst for that, knocking on Abbie's door virtually every evening after she moved in, intent on making a drinking partner of Abbie. And she certainly didn't want to repeat an encounter like the one she had with the large-bellied, hairy bloke who demanded a mutual agreement for the use of her backyard for sunbathing and barbecues. She explained to him that there was no way of getting into the garden except through her flat.

'I don't mind that,' he'd said, staring intensely.

'No. Absolutely not,' she'd told him. Never in her life would she have allowed that man access to her home and let his clumsy brutishness stomp all over her home.

'Bitch,' he called her before she shut the door in his face.

Abbie placed her hands in her lap. She took three deep breaths. With each breath the man's angry face faded. She felt her shoulders relaxing.

– So, do you think about kissing Nick? Do you want to snog him? Becca asks and I know I do more than anything in the world.

I'm lying sideways on the settee. Becca is sitting cross-legged on the floor in front of me. Our parents are out somewhere so we've taken over the living room. The floor is covered with magazines; scrunched up and discarded crisp packets, Becca's manicure set, two empty glasses, the biscuit tin. The TV is on but the sound is off because we're playing CDs, which would infuriate Dad if he was here. I watch the characters on the TV mouth their words, mismatching the vocals from the song. Briefly – for a split second only – they coincide.

For the first time ever Becca is hungry for details from me. I turn on my back and fold my arms across my stomach hugging this fragile sense of power close.

– I think about him all the time, I tell Becca.

I can't stop thinking about him; I gobble up everything he says and does, the way he walks, the clothes he wears and hoard them for later. I love the way he brushes his hair away from his face when he's about to speak, revealing those amazing eyes. I have noticed that he doesn't care what the others think, that he is laughing at them when they think they are laughing at him. I want to know him as well as he knows himself.

Becca's long silence is alarming.

– But don't say anything to anyone. Promise. No one. Not even Si. I don't want Nick to know.

Becca picks at the flaking varnish on her toenails. She is so pretty with her hair tied up, her blue top on. She seems to get everything right, so easily.

– Why not? If you fancy him that bad, maybe Si could sort it out.

I panic because I know you can't do that with Nick; I don't know how I know but I do. He has to make the first move otherwise he'll be scared off, he has to choose me. There are times when I feel his eyes following me but if I look round, I never catch him.

I see it panning out before me: Becca will tell Si, who'll tell one of the other lads who'll tell the others and it will finally reach Nick as a joke, something to be ashamed of instead of something good.

– Please don't, Becca, please.

They were knocking on her door. Her new neighbours. She got up, moved quietly down the hall.

Abbie peered through the spyglass at the two men who stood the other side of the door. They both looked to be in their thirties; one had his head shaven and sweat decorated his temples, the other had a spiked-up fringe which was sagging a little with damp. The bald one was holding a cardboard box.

'Nobody home,' Spiky said.

'Probably at work,' the bald one added, pushing his face

closer. He had a meaty nose and a wide mouth. She shrank back from his proximity then leant forward again. Their voices were clear, echoing in the hall.

'Can't we just get on, then?'

'Oh, yes. I was only trying to be polite,' Spiky said. 'You know, introduce myself.'

Abbie studied her new neighbour and found him to be ordinary. Average height, not too fat, not too thin. Jeans and T-shirt. There were thousands like him.

'I wonder who lives there.'

'It's a single woman, the agent told me.'

It was a shock to hear herself being described in that way. She knew she shouldn't care but she was angry at the estate agent. She hadn't liked him on sight; he was a cocky young man who had tried to peer past her into the flat all the time he was talking as if he wanted to winkle her out of her home like a crab from its shell. People like that never got their facts right, they were too busy looking out for the next chance to line their pockets to listen properly.

She pressed her eye to the spyglass again.

'Read: batty old spinster,' the bald one said as he put down the box and pushed it across the floor with his foot. He nudged it in place against the outer door to prop it open.

Abbie returned to the study. She picked up the glove where she'd left it and stood for a moment facing Nick's chair. The sun had moved off, leaving it cold. She would have given anything to have opened the door wide and been able to say I'm sure my husband will help you when he gets home. Yes! She imagined herself responding lightly to their looks of surprise. I'm a married woman. I've been married for eleven years.

She sat down and the soft weight of the glove settled in her hand before she turned it inside out, threaded her needle and began to sew.

– It's perfect! Nick stands in the study. – This is where I'll read scripts and learn my lines.

– We'll take it then, I say, even though the rent is higher than the maximum we'd agreed on. It's the only flat that Nick has liked. My mind races to calculate how we'll afford it. Sod it; we'll manage. Somehow. The suburbs are stifling Nick. His job, cold-calling insurance, is killing him. We've been putting all our money aside so that we can move out and be together. I work in Woolworths on a Saturday and Thursday evening and babysit whenever I can. No one knows what we're planning. Not even Becca. Once we're settled in London, our real life will start. Nick will quit his job and take on part-time work until he gets his first acting job. I'll have finished school and will work in a shop until I start my fashion design course. We have it all planned out.

I hug Nick and imagine myself in here, drawing my designs. The tailor's dummy that my parents bought me will stand draped in the beautiful clothes I'm going to create. I'll need a table for the sewing machine. We'll spend more on this room than on any other in the flat. The first thing we'll buy even before a bed to put a mattress on are armchairs. In the evenings, we'll spend hours here together. I tell Nick how I see it. I tell him how cosy we'll be.

We move in. We don't have much. A few things begged, borrowed and – though I don't ask – judging by the newness of the TV, dinner set and fridge – some of them are possibly knocked off.

The flat looks shabbier and grimier than it had when we came to see it the first time. The wallpaper is peeling off, there are stains on the carpets and the bedroom is the darkest, dingiest room I've ever been in. I search Nick's face for disappointment but he is elated. He goes straight to the living room and starts ringing everyone we know.

— We're having a party. You've got to come, he says time and time again, a smile in his voice which comes from his heart. — It won't be the same without you.

I walk around the flat, trying every light, peering into boxes, opening and closing windows and cupboards. I check out every room then return to Nick who is sitting on the floor in the living room. I crouch beside him, close, just to feel him there. He puts the phone down and wraps his arm around my neck pulling my face towards him to plant a swift kiss on my lips.

— We've done it, he says. — We've finally done it.

I know from his voice that he, too, can hardly believe it. Since we signed the papers, paid our deposit and revealed our plans we have been bombarded with scepticism and hostility from everyone we know. Even my schoolmates think I'm crazy. For the last few weeks I have felt an outsider at home. It is as if, in some way, I have betrayed my family. My parents and even Becca throw objections and comments at me like handfuls of gravel. They think I'm being ridiculous, that I should be focusing on my future, on taking a place at university; that I underestimate what it takes to support yourself in the 'real world'; that I'm too young and stupid to know my own mind. That this is something Nick has forced me into.

I stand up and wander from room to room feeling my new

home settling around me. I wouldn't care if I never stepped outside the front door again.

Becca is the first to arrive for the party. She brings me flowers and a moving-in card. It says Home Sweet Home on the front and shows a house enclosed in a big, cerise, heart-shaped bubble. Inside, with her special silver pen in her careful calligraphy, she's written: 'Good Luck in your New Home and Life together. Love your big sis.' I have to put the flowers in a bucket found in the cupboard under the sink because I don't own a vase.

I feel nervous showing her round. I am ready to rush to the flat's defence and deny its faults but Becca doesn't say anything except that she can't believe I have my own home. Soon others arrive, filling it up with noise and music and I lose track of Becca. Later, each time I go looking for her, she's getting friendlier and friendlier with someone I don't know, so I don't interrupt them.

The next morning there are bodies crashed out all over the floor. Great party, they say as they gain consciousness. One by one, sickly skinned and red-eyed, they struggle to sit up.

I feel rotten with a hangover and when I go into the kitchen to get some water, I find vomit in the bucket and Becca's flowers lying trampled on the floor. I leave everything as it is, queasiness catching in my throat.

A cache of three cans of beer, which someone had secreted behind the curtain in the living room, is passed round for hair of the dog. Everyone begins to talk about last night; funny moments, crazy stuff people did that I don't remember any of. It's almost as if I'd been to a different party. I sit quietly on my own. Across the room, Nick hugs his knees to his chest and pulls hard on a cigarette.

The things I remember are: Becca leaving in a taxi with that bloke I'd never seen before; two of our best mates nearly having a fight and someone pretending that the police had arrived. But mostly I remember Nick finding me in the study where I thought there was a CD I wanted to play in one of the unpacked boxes.

He caught me by the waist, kicked the door shut behind him, pushed a box against it to stop anyone following us. He cleared a space in the middle of the room then took the glass I was still holding from me, put it on the mantelpiece and pulled me to the floor. I was trembling like the first time we ever had sex. I had to hold tight onto him as if I was going to fall apart, my nails biting into his skin so hard the crescent shaped marks remained there for days afterwards.

I feel a burning in the pit of my stomach and when I look at Nick, his eyes are fixed on me. I know he's remembering that moment, too, and while I'm impatient for everyone to go, he is savouring the slow wait, like a hungry animal hidden in the woods, biding his time until we'll be alone.

Steve tapped his fingers on the cheap kitchen work-top and Owen couldn't help comparing it with the marble ones at home that he'd paid an arm and a leg for. He reminded himself that he could no longer refer to the house as his home. Granted it was still his house but no, not his home. He paused to consider what that made him. Joint owner? Landlord? Absentee landlord? He was sure that there must be a legal term for it these days with one in three marriages ending in divorce but all he could think was that it made him a big fat failure. He caught the thought back before vocalizing anything to Steve. It hinted at misgivings which he didn't want to give body to. Instead, he comforted himself by calculating the amount the new kitchen would increase the property value of the house by.

Steve landed a sharp congratulatory punch on his arm which brought Owen back to his senses. He was glad to have kept quiet because Steve was almost garrulous with excitement.

'You've got yourself a proper, nice bachelor pad, mate. You've done us proud.'

'Us?'

'Need I remind you that things aren't great indoors for me either. I kind of, you know, need a bolt-hole, sometimes.' Steve grimaced as he always did when he talked about his home life. His troubles with his wife, Julie, and his descriptive detail of numerous affairs and one-night stands had been a constant theme since Owen had first become friendly with him at work over ten years ago. Owen used to think that it was inevitable the couple would split up but now he was more convinced, like Fliss, that they thrived on the weekly dramas, those and the making up. These days, Owen wasn't even sure that Steve had indulged in any extramarital activities at all; he had begun to take most of his friend's tales with a very large pinch of salt.

They wandered back into the living room and Steve continued his praise of all the things that Owen was trying hard not to look at: the shitty-brown three-piece suite, the mismatched curtains and garish carpet.

Steve folded his arms and nodded with approval. 'I can see us watching the footie in peace with a few drinks, some takeaways. Excellent.'

Owen didn't feel so happy about the brief but precise image he had of the living room with pizza delivery cartons and empty cans of lager scattered around. It seemed his life was in the process of doing a U-turn. At thirty-five he'd returned to living like a student.

He tried to shake off the looming self-pity by telling himself that it could be worse. Much worse. All the other flats for rent in this area and his price range that he'd been to see were claustrophobic boxes to which some moron had laughingly attached the word 'executive' just to be able to charge the earth in rent.

If he'd been ten years younger, if he'd really been the bachelor that Steve kept calling him, and if the reality was going to be anything like the kind of thing he allowed his mind to indulge in every now and then, then those places were ideal. Cool, impressive, the sort of place to bring women back to, a place perhaps where you can work out what you want from life. But Owen was already knee-deep in his life and there were no children allowed and even if they were, where would you put them? Under the executive bleached-beech bed?

He glanced around with a more benevolent eye. The house might be a bit run-down and rather old-fashioned but at least there was space in the flat. He walked over to the window. There was quite a good view of the bridge from the front and, he been surprised to see, some big leafy trees at the back screening the railway line. On the map, he'd worked out that it was only a short walk to the station which would take him directly into central London, saving him nearly an hour each way on his daily commute. He quickly skated over what he was going to do with this additional free time. He had all sorts of ideas.

Steve was still nosing about so Owen followed him into the main bedroom. This, like the living room, was at the front of the house looking on to the street but instead of the sash window it had a small, double-glazed window. Owen tapped a wall, deducing from its hollow sound that the bedroom, together with the bathroom next door, had probably been the other half of the living room before it was divided up.

'You're going to have this big one, right?'

'Saves the kids squabbling over it.'

He knew as soon as he said the word 'kids' that this was at the bottom of his disquiet. The flat was eerily devoid of any of their possessions. It would be much better when the kids came over; it would feel more like home.

As there were a few hours left before the van had to be returned to the hire firm, Steve hinted that the cost of his day's labour could be paid for by a large Chinese takeaway.

'Give us a chance to check out your new manor,' Steve said and Owen felt excitement spark in his belly, like the anticipation of the first night on holiday in a foreign country.

Outside, Owen looked up and down the road.

'Which way?' Steve asked.

Owen didn't have a clue. 'Left?'

Left took them up to the junction of another busier road where Owen took note of signs to the train station. They decided that another left turn seemed the most promising for shops but it quickly led them to a rather bleak area. On the opposite side of the road was a compound of dirty concrete flats and next to them was a row of Victorian houses with a very neglected appearance. On their side of the road, they passed a school which was surrounded by a three-metre-high chain-link fence. Shortly after this, at an intersection in the road, they came across a small area of unkempt, knobbly grass. It wasn't more than four metres long and two metres wide; there were no flowerbeds or trees but a big metal sign read 'Protect Your Green Spaces'.

By now, Owen was beginning to feel disheartened and daunted. He knew that SW8 was still a little run-down but he hadn't expected to feel intimidated. There were very few people around and those that were seemed to eye him and Steve warily. He had dismissed Fliss's concerns about the children living in London. They always loved coming here on family days out, he had reminded her, and he'd maintained that it would do the kids good to gain a little more street-wise experience than their suburban life offered. His reasoning now seemed questionable and rather risky.

He was about to suggest to Steve that they turn back and return to the flat when round the next bend in the road, they came across exactly what they were looking for. The shops were a mixture of smart and shabby. They passed an Italian delicatessen, a newsagent, travel agent, a second-hand furniture shop, an estate agent, an electrical store, a bistro with occupied tables under a tall metal patio heater, and separated by an antiques shop they discovered a Chinese and an Indian restaurant.

'This will do,' Steve said after glancing briefly at the menu in the window of the Chinese restaurant. There were only a couple of people waiting so even though they each ordered several dishes they were back out within fifteen minutes.

They decided to take a different route home which Steve was convinced would be more direct but they lost their bearings quickly. Before they had to retrace their steps, Steve flagged down a couple of community policemen on mopeds and explained that they were lost. It turned out that they were heading in the right direction after all.

'Continue down this street, past the park on your left and then take a right at the traffic lights by the Mandeville pub.'

'Is it far?' Steve asked.

'You'll be home before your food's cold, don't you worry,' the policeman joked.

'I hope that sad piece of grass we saw earlier, isn't what goes for a park round here,' Steve said once the mopeds were far enough away to speak. He caught Owen's eye and suddenly they were both laughing so uncontrollably they had to stop walking for a moment.

A short distance on, the park came into view. Floodlights towered above a row of tall, knobbly trees. Through the foliage growing up the fencing, Owen could just make out what looked like a large area of grass.

'There are basketball hoops over there,' Steve said, pointing. 'And tennis courts.'

Two male couples were heading towards the entrance with rackets. A woman jogged on the spot at the traffic lights ready to cross over to the park. Owen felt comforted by the proximity of tennis players and joggers near to his new home.

'I might take up running myself,' he said and Steve laughed rather too loudly Owen felt.

Back in the flat, they tuned in the new TV while they waited for the Chinese to warm up in the oven. They watched the BBC news and then flicked between the terrestrial channels before concluding it was better to turn it off. Steve shook his head. 'You're going to have to sort out Sky rapidly, mate. Jesus.'

They put all the containers of the Chinese food on the big table in the living room and sat either side of it. They helped themselves and ate without speaking. Owen was starving; he felt like he hadn't eaten for days.

'What about this bird downstairs?' Steve's eyes lit up. 'I mean what if she turns out to be OK, you know, a student, or a, I don't know, a nurse. Or even better, a student nurse. You could be in luck there.'

The last thing Owen wanted to think about was 'birds'. He found himself turning away from Steve and his lascivious expression which was made more alarming by the red sauce smeared around his mouth. Owen fetched a loo roll from the bathroom and placed it on the table within reach of them both.

'On second thoughts,' Steve went on, 'a bit too close to home if it all went tits up. Best not to go shitting on your own doorstep.' He yanked off several sheets of the roll and wiped his mouth.

'I'm steering clear of women for a while, thanks,' Owen replied. He was surprised at the bitter edge to his words. He glanced at Steve, ready to explain that he didn't really feel as fucked up as he sounded but was stopped by the concerned way his friend was looking at him.

'You'll be fine. It'll work out for the best, you know. It might feel a bit strange now, mate, because it's a big change. But it's a step forward.'

'Are you still talking?' Owen said, but he was touched. He spooned more food onto his plate. 'What about you and Julie, then?' The question had come out of nowhere. They stared at each other across the table as if neither of them could believe that Owen had just asked it.

Steve broke the silence. 'What about us?'

'You know. What's going on?'

'Same old, same old.'

'Are you going to do anything?'

Steve grabbed more loo roll, scrubbed it across his face, then threw the crumpled paper onto the table. 'Like what?'

'I don't know. Like . . . I don't know. Sort it out.' With

Steve's eyes fixed on his, Owen felt he'd gone much further than he was comfortable with. He remembered Fliss once telling him that Steve looked up to him. That he took what Owen said seriously. 'I'm not suggesting you should do anything as drastic as me,' he said. 'In fact . . . I wouldn't . . . Just . . . you know . . . like you said, you can bolt here anytime you need to.'

Steve leant back in his chair, belched and beamed at him. 'Thanks, mate.'

Owen wasn't sure whether he was being thanked for the meal, his offer or maybe even both.

As soon as he was alone, instead of being able to relax as he'd imagined he would, Owen found it hard to settle. He went from room to room checking everything out, paying greater attention this time to his new home. He surprised himself about how squeamish he was over the idea of sitting on a loo which had been used by God knew how many others before him and at the distaste he felt at the thought of sleeping on someone else's mattress. He made himself test the bed, which was a little saggy but otherwise OK.

He inspected the kids' rooms. He was going to put Izzy in the one with the low window. It opened wide, didn't have a child-proof lock and was directly above the felted roof of the extension below. Tom would be climbing out of there before you could say Xbox but he could trust Izzy to be more sensible. The window in the second bedroom faced the wall of the next house; just a little wider than the length of his arm. It made the room quite dark but Owen thought that Tom would probably appreciate that. He often kept his curtains closed so that the light didn't reflect onto the screen when he was playing his computer games.

Owen dragged his suitcases into his bedroom and started to unpack his clothes. The wardrobe was a rickety chipboard affair which swayed every time he approached it. It was small, too, and although he started off by hanging and folding everything neatly, he ended up wedging in the last clothes haphazardly, feeling dismal.

The living room stank of the Chinese meal so he scraped the plates into a plastic carrier bag along with all the containers and took everything into the kitchen. The pedal bin was too small to take the bag, so he tied it up and left it on the floor. Behind the unpacked set of saucepans, he spotted the four-pack of beer that he'd bought for himself and Steve to drink once they'd finished moving him in. He put one can in the freezer, two in the fridge and opened the fourth. He drank the beer in thirsty gulps while looking out of the living room window.

There was a yellow glow in the sky which he guessed to be the floodlights from the park but with the ceiling light on and the darkening evening outside it was difficult to focus on anything past his own reflection. He watched his arm move up and down as he drank the beer.

He picked up the handset of the phone and collected the second can from the freezer. The cold made his fingertips ache as he carried it into the bedroom. He snagged the top window open for some air, lay on the bed, propped himself up with a pillow and telephoned his parents.

'Oh Owen love, we wondered when we would hear from you.'

'Have you got a pen ready? I'll give you my new landline.' He listened to his mother rummaging in the telephone table drawer for a pen and the address book. The same cloth covered one they'd had for years. He continued talking. 'You can always get me on my mobile anyway. The reception here is fine.'

'It's OK, I've got it.'

He gave her the number and made her read it back to him to check that she'd written it down correctly.

'So, is everything OK with you and Dad?'

'We're fine. We want to know about you. How are you settling in?'

'I only got here today. Steve helped me move.'

'Are the children there?'

'Not yet. The day after tomorrow.'

'That's a Tuesday. What about school?'

'It's half-term, Mum. Remember. I'm having the kids for a couple of days so they can see, um, my new place.'

'How many bedrooms does it have?'

'Three.'

'Is there a garden?'

It felt like she was working her way through a checklist of questions, marking him up or down depending on the answers he gave.

'No. It's a first floor flat. There's a park. With tennis courts, basketball, lots of stuff, just down the road.' Zero for no garden. Six for the local leisure facilities.

'You'll have to go there with them. You can't let them go out in London on their own.'

'I wasn't planning to. I have looked after the children on my own before now.' He ended his sentence in a lot softer tone than he started it, reminding himself that his parents were only worried and were trying to be as supportive as they could in circumstances that were new to them. They had been married for nearly forty years and he was the first of their children to be divorcing.

'We were wondering what's going to happen to your lovely house?'

He guessed that was one of Dad's questions. 'We're not selling it, if that's what you mean. Fliss and the children are staying there.'

'How is Felicity?'

'I haven't spoken to her today, yet. But I'm sure she'll be fine.'

'I'm sorry, dear.'

'Why are you sorry?'

'You sound so upset and I keep asking the wrong things. We don't know what we're allowed to say.'

'I'm not upset. You can say or ask me whatever you want. Fliss. The house. The kids. Anything. Don't worry. I didn't mean to snap; I'm just tired. It's been a long day.'

'And how are the children?'

He took a deep breath. 'I'm going to ring them after I've spoken to you.'

'Be sure to give them our love.'

'I will.'

There was a pause and he felt compelled to provide more reassurance before he finished the call. 'Everything's going to be fine, Mum. I'll tell you what, I'll get the kids to give you a call when they're here and they can tell you all about it.'

He pulled the pillow out from behind him and lay flat on the bed. With only twice-yearly visits to his house, his parents had little idea of the way he and Fliss lived and now, he felt, he had moved even further out of their range of understanding. He couldn't imagine what they would think about his new home. He couldn't imagine them ever coming here to see him.

He fetched another beer in preparation for his next call. The phone in the house rang on and on and then went to answerphone. He tried it again. The same thing happened.

He tried not to panic. He entered Fliss's mobile number and pressed dial. She answered straight away.

'Hi there.'

'Where are you? I rang the house.'

'We decided to stay another night at Mum's. There didn't seem any need to rush back and it's company for me.'

'What about the kids?'

'They're fine. They're watching a DVD. Can you believe it? Mum's actually bought a DVD player.' He could hear Shelley protest lightly in the background. Fliss, away from the phone, called out: 'It's your Dad.'

He wondered which one would be the first to speak. His hands were sweating from nerves.

'Dad!'

Iz. 'Hello, sweetheart. Are you having a good time?'

'It's OK.'

'I'm sure it's better than OK. What's the DVD you're watching?'

'It's cartoons.' She whispered, 'It's more like for Tom's age, though.'

'Oh well, I'm sure there'll be something for you afterwards.'

'I think there's only one. Mum says we'll do something nice tomorrow.'

'Sounds good.'

'Tom wants to speak.'

'OK, I'll talk to you tomorrow. Bye, sweetheart.'

There were no niceties or preamble with Tom. 'I showed Grandma how to work the DVD. She didn't know *at all*.'

'Good job, well done.'

'We've got coke and Mum and Grandma are having wine.'

'Sounds like a bit of a party.'

'Not really. We're just watching cartoons.'

He smiled at Tom's literal take on the world. 'I'm watching TV, too.' A small white lie.

'Where are you? At home?'

'In the flat, yes.' There was a silence which Owen hurried to fill. 'I can't wait until you see it. In a couple of days' time.'

'OK.'

'So, I'd better let you get back to the DVD.'

'OK. Bye then.'

Before Owen could ask to be passed back to Fliss, Tom had ended the call. He waited a minute to see if she would call him, then it occurred to him that she was probably waiting for him to do the same. She answered after a couple of rings.

'Hello, again.'

'Sorry, Tom rang off before I was passed to you.'

'Oh, I thought we were done. Hang on, I'll just go into the kitchen.' The phone reception crackled; he could hear Fliss's breathing as if she was walking quickly. 'OK. What is it?'

'Nothing, really,' he said. 'I wanted to confirm that the arrangement's the same for me to come and get them on Tuesday.'

'Yes. We'll be there. Three o'clock as we agreed.'

'Fine. Good.' He paused. 'I suppose that's all then?'

'I suppose it is.'

'Well ... bye, then.'

'Bye, Owen. Take care.'

'You, too.'

He decided he needed a change of scenery for the fourth beer and chose the settee. He stretched out, the can on the floor beside him; switched the TV on, then placed the remote on his chest.

All these moments that he'd anticipated for so long were now happening: the moment of leaving, the first phone call to Fliss from his new place, his first night in the flat. These moments had towered over him; making him sweat, his heart race and his insides churn up but, in reality, they were all turning out rather flat.

He hadn't wanted drama and lots of I miss yous and tears or any of that from Izzy and Tom when he phoned. That they almost couldn't be bothered to speak to him was good – it meant that he and Fliss were making the situation as easy for them as they could. It was just that he hadn't expected to feel the emptiness spreading out from the centre of him; threatening to take him over.

In the study, Abbie picked up the shawl that she'd been in the middle of repairing. She regarded the stitches she'd already done – the march of neat thread across the material, hardly visible in the brown and orange brocade. She eased her needle into the material next to her thumbnail and gently pulled the thread through. Soon her breathing fell to the pace of her steady sewing and she let the memory rise.

Our first kiss.

Bone-melting, heart-thumping, sweet, sweet kiss. His hands on me. Finally on me. Burning my skin where they touch.

I have been wanting this to happen for such a long time but I'm still not expecting it. Not now, at this moment. Nick takes me by surprise. He is always surprising me.

We're coming back from the shopping centre, the usual gang. I've been walking alongside Becca and Si but we're approaching a short-cut between two houses where there's only room to go single file. I've been thinking about this path the whole time we've been out. I've been waiting for ever to have a chance to be near him and my skin prickles as the possibility arrives. The summer heat after the cold of the air-conditioned shops prevents us from talking. I push up the sleeves of my top and let the breeze tickle the hairs on my arms. The strong summer light presses down. It feels like everything is possible. I drop back by slowing my pace. I'm conscious of Nick directly behind me now. At the end of the passage, I'll turn, wait for him, walk side by side, on our own, even if it's only for a few steps.

He grabs my hand, pulls me round. He pushes me up against the fence and pins me there with his hips. He places his finger to my mouth. 'Ssssh.'

The others carry on. Oblivious.

It's dark in this passage. There's a smell like hot tar; the wood's rough, it grazes my elbows. He leans in closer. His chest is bumping against mine.

He puts his hand under my chin, slowly tilts my face up. Now that I am free to look at him openly, it scares me too much. I lower my eyes.

– I've been wanting to do this for a long time, he says.

His hands are on either side of my face; his head dips in. I'd never imagined a boy's lips to be so soft but they are. Soft and dry but playing hard. He presses down on my mouth so hard that I can feel the ridges of my teeth underneath my bottom lip.

When we emerge into the glaring light, they're all waiting for us. Nobody says anything. Nick, hands shoved deep in his pockets, heads for the boys, leaving me with Becca.

– God, she breathes into my ear. She links her arm through mine. I lean into her; my body suddenly weak. – What happened? Did he kiss you?

I nod, grin stupidly.

– What was it like? Was he good?

I run my tongue around my mouth, across my gums and bruised lips where Nick has left his mark.

Bone-melting, heart-thumping, sweet, sweet kiss. His hands on me. Finally on me. Burning my skin where they touch.

I rub the goose-pimples on my arms and nod. I know that my life has changed for ever.

Owen was woken suddenly by a noise somewhere in the flat. He listened for a minute but there was silence. He rubbed his stiff neck and wiped off drool which had crusted on the side of his face. It was dark outside. He checked the time on the teletext. He'd been asleep for a couple of hours. Another noise echoed up the stairwell then he heard what sounded like the exterior door closing. He got up and went to the window.

It was lighter outside than in the room. The sky was hardly dark at all; a shifting grey sludge above the city lights. He could clearly make out a slight figure of a woman standing on the pavement in front of the building. She was wearing dark jeans and a jacket with lighter coloured trainers. If that was his neighbour, then she appeared to be much younger than the estate agent had intimated. Her long dark hair was blowing about in the wind. She caught it in her hands and pulled up her hood. She pushed her hair inside it as if she was trying to contain some lively creature. This done, she set off walking to the left.

Now that he had seen his neighbour leave, he suddenly felt

absolutely alone. Behind him, silence seemed to climb through the building and crawl towards him. He wanted to act on his instinct and rush round, turning the TV up, putting the kettle on, switching every single light on in the flat but he couldn't seem to get his limbs to work. He battled the panic which had turned him to stone and once the feeling had subsided, he went straight to the bedroom, hurriedly undressed and pulled the duvet tight around him.

He woke hours later, the early light falling on him from the unpulled curtains. There was a hum and a thrumming vibration; the bed rocked beneath him. He sat up confused until he was able to place the noise to a train running on the line at the back of the house.

He spent the whole day cleaning the flat and unpacking. In the evening, he decided to get some air and explore a little more. He took a right from the flat this time and came to a local store only a short distance away. It was one of those great little shops, stocked to the ceiling with any food or household item you could run short of or need at the last minute as well as booze, DVDs for rent, a cash-point machine, newspapers and magazines. It reminded him of a more eclectic version of the little shop on the caravan site near St Ives where his family used to spend a fortnight every summer holiday. He had always come out with some treasure: a packet of Wagon Wheel biscuits, a penknife, the *Beano*.

He wandered through the aisles, knowing that there were half a dozen things he probably needed but which he couldn't bring to mind; instead he bought some Mars ice creams as a treat for the kids the next day.

Outside the shop he realized that because of his frozen purchases he would have to leave further exploring for another day. He walked slowly back, enjoying taking in his new surroundings. A full bus passed, followed by a near empty one; a woman across the road was picking up after her black Labrador, her jeans stretched taut on her bum as she bent over, a jogger emerged from a street higher up and headed in the direction of the park.

There was a light on in the downstairs flat but no sign of his neighbour. As he entered the building, he paused briefly but he couldn't hear any sound from the flat either. He trod carefully up the stairs so that he didn't make much noise. When he opened the front door his first thought was that the flat smelt unfamiliar. But, in the kitchen, a few minutes later, after he'd closed the freezer door and was stuffing the empty carrier bag in the drawer, he experienced a sudden sense of ease. As if, for the first time, he felt that he was really living there.

Izzy let him in the house, gave him a hug at his request, then disappeared upstairs. The children's belongings were packed up ready in the hall. Fliss appeared from the kitchen.

'Do you want a drink or something?'

He declined. 'We'd better get straight off,' he told her, following her, anyway. 'I'd like to get back so that they're not eating too late.'

Instead of her usual jeans and top, Fliss was wearing a skirt and blouse, and he was pretty sure that she'd had her hair done, too. It looked good, although Owen preferred it a darker blonde than it was now.

'You look nice.' The instant he said it, it occurred to him

that she might have dressed up for his benefit and he felt clumsy for drawing attention to it but Fliss seemed pleased.

'Thanks,' she said and passed a hand across her fringe. 'Maria's coming over for a drink this evening, so I thought I'd make an effort.'

'Anything else planned for the next couple of days?'

Fliss shook her head. 'It sounds silly but I couldn't really imagine Izzy and Tom not being here and having all that time on my own. Maria offered to come round otherwise I don't think I would have even thought about asking her.'

'It takes a bit of getting used to.'

'How have you been?'

'I don't think it's sunk in yet,' he told her.

'I feel terrified,' she blurted out and he could see in her eyes that the fear was real.

'You'll be fine.'

'I've relied on everyone too much.'

He could see tears were close. He looked behind him. The kitchen door, luckily, was pushed to and there was no sign of the children. 'I'm not sure I know what you mean.'

'For company, for keeping busy, for everything.'

His automatic reaction was to comfort her; he had been doing it for years except now, of course, everything was different. He was too far away from her to reach out and take her hand but to take a step forward seemed like offering too much. New boundaries had been set. He felt helpless as he watched her distress.

'It's not so bad,' he told her and added in an encouraging tone, 'You might actually enjoy it.'

She half-turned away from him. 'I know. I'm being stupid.'

'Not stupid. A parent.' He spoke gently. 'It's actually a lot easier in reality.' He could feel the swell of emotion gathering as he finished the sentence. Finally, she looked at him. 'Believe me. I know. OK?'

She nodded. 'OK.'

Izzy helped him carry out their stuff to the car but Tom had to be called several times before he'd come down from his room. He kicked up a fuss about bringing his bike.

'Next time,' Owen said, more to shut him up than as a promise but from the scowl Tom fixed on his face, Owen knew this was unlikely to be forgotten.

He watched Tom in the rear-view mirror. A tadpole of fury in the backseat, his son was curled towards the car door, his arms wrapped across his body, the earpieces of his mp3 stuck in defiantly.

A wanker in a van pulled in front of him. Owen hit the brakes.

'Fuck!'

'Dad!'

He mumbled his apologies to Izzy and glanced at Tom who was sitting up, trying to peer between the front seats.

'What happened?'

'Just some idiot, Tom.'

'Dad said the F word.'

'Thank you, Iz. Tom didn't need to know that.'

Izzy opened the handbag she'd been nursing on her knee and took out a tiny mirror. She studied her face from several angles and in that gesture looked unnervingly grown-up; and so much like Fliss.

Tom pulled out his earpieces. 'Are we nearly there?'

'Not long now.'

'My friend Jodie has two bedrooms,' Izzy said. 'And in her dad's house she's got a TV and DVD player in her room. She's got all the Olsen twins' films.'

'Well, Iz, I hope you're not going to be disappointed but that's not going to happen.'

'Oh, I know *that*. Jodie's dad is rich.'

He glanced at Izzy to gauge her reaction but his daughter's face was inscrutable. 'Well, good.'

'You have got a TV though, Dad, haven't you?'

'Yes, Tom. Don't panic.'

From the moment that he had set off from the house, the flat's failings had become magnified and now that he was only a few minutes away, Owen found that he was dreading the children's reaction.

'Well,' he said, as he took the final turning at the traffic lights. 'We're here. That one. Up there.'

The kids had gone quiet. He saw what a complete disaster it was. There was a trail of green slime descending from the guttering, flaking paint on the windowsills. He was glad that he'd managed to keep Fliss away from the place. 'Unsanitary' was one of her favourite words and he could just imagine her horror if she ever came near it.

The children seemed subdued as they got out of the car but by the time he was opening the front door, excitement had won them over. They pulled their trainers off at the door as they'd been told to do and set off skidding on the wooden hall floor in search of their rooms.

'Which one's mine?' Tom yelled.

'On the left. Izzy, yours is further up on the right.'

They disappeared. Owen hesitated over which child to follow. He chose Tom, who he found standing in the middle of his new room, his body quivering.

'Tom?'

'It's a cot.' Tom's voice was thick with tears.

Owen suddenly saw the bed with his son's eyes. The white painted spindles of the head and foot boards were vaguely reminiscent of a cot. He tried to mollify him. 'Don't be daft, Tom. A cot has bars on the sides. There aren't any bars on the sides.'

'It looks like a cot to me,' Tom repeated, spitting the words out.

Owen had to fight to control his own voice which betrayed the anger he felt towards his son at that moment. He reached out to touch him, to remind himself that he was a father, that he should be understanding. Tom pulled away.

Owen became aware of Izzy behind him in the doorway. He turned to her. Her eyes looked huge as she stared up at him.

'Go back to your room, honey-bunch, I'll be with you in a minute.'

'OK-Daddy-don't-be-horrible-Tom,' she said in one breath. 'Dad's doing his best.'

'I bet you've got a proper bed,' Tom hurled at his sister, spittle flying everywhere, a snot string dangling from his nose. He kicked out at the bed and his foot made contact. He sank to the floor, howling now with full force. Blood was seeping through the white sock; a strawberry red stain where his big toe was.

Tom's body became completely compliant as Owen helped him onto the bed.

'Fetch some loo roll, Iz, and a bowl of warm water.'

She was soon back holding a loo roll under her arm and a cereal bowl of water; it lapped and spilt over the sides in her rush to reach them. Owen carefully unpeeled Tom's sock. Izzy gasped, Tom whimpered.

Christ, Owen was thinking. This would be just great. First night I'm looking after them here and we end up in Casualty. With growing alarm, he realized he didn't even know where the nearest hospital was.

'Keep still.'

Cleaned up, he could see that the injury was only minor. The nail had split and torn but the plump tip was only superficially cut. 'You'll live.' He wound loo paper round the toe and then found some packing tape to secure it. Not exactly hygienic but it was all he had.

Now that the drama was over, the children settled to watch TV while he made beans on toast for supper. Everyone seemed a little subdued for the rest of the evening; Tom played on his PSP while he and Izzy watched a nature programme on the BBC. Owen was relieved that, apart from limping dramatically, Tom didn't make any fuss when it was time to go to bed.

Half an hour later when Owen went to kiss Izzy goodnight, she slid her arms round his neck and whispered in his ear, 'I love my room, Dad.'

'I'm glad, sweetheart. Sleep tight.'

He left the bathroom door ajar with the light on and then returned to the living room. He sat on the settee with the telephone in his hands; the news was on – quietly, so that he wouldn't miss any noises coming from the kids – but he wasn't paying much attention to it. It was a while later before he actually phoned Fliss.

She answered immediately. 'How did it go?'

'Fine,' he said. 'Everything's fine. The kids are in bed.' He thought he heard a voice in the background. 'Is that Maria?'

'Yes, she said she'd stay until you phoned.'

'Oh.' Now he felt guilty for keeping Fliss waiting. 'Sorry, I should have—'

'It's OK. I expect you've been busy.'

'Yes,' he lied. 'I've only just stopped.'

'And they like their rooms?'

'I think so. They can tell you themselves when they call tomorrow.'

'Tomorrow. Yes.'

Her muted response came as a surprise until Owen realized that Fliss had been expecting to speak to them this evening. He felt bad to have disappointed her, but relieved for himself. God knows what Tom would have told her and she would only have worried. 'And you? You're OK?'

'Yes. Maria's been great.'

He seized the opportunity to finish the call. 'Well, I guess I'll let you get back to her.'

'I better had,' Fliss said, sounding surprised. There was a short silence before she added, politely. 'Thanks for ringing, Owen.'

'No problem,' he told her overly cheerfully and rang off quickly before he made even more of a mess of saying goodbye.

Owen couldn't sleep. Tom's furious face together with Izzy's sorrowful eyes as she said, 'Dad's doing his best', kept circling his brain. A yowl outside set his nerves going. A long, tearing cry followed. What the fuck was that? It sounded like a child being murdered. He got up and crossed to the window. There was a fox on the street. The moonlight tipped its copper fur with silver. It raised its head, yapped twice before padding away, nose and tail hanging low. There were more foxes in London than in any other single place in the world, he'd read somewhere. Probably because people fed them instead of hunting them. This one certainly seemed confident as it padded down the path and stood for a minute, nose high, scenting the air.

Owen sat on his bed. The flat was quiet again.

This then was his new life. This was how it was going to be from now on. This was his place where his children would visit and the rest of the time he would be alone.

He felt a sudden and absolute sense of relief. It was like returning home after a blow-out meal, undoing the top button of your jeans and just being able to let go. But guilt followed swiftly. His brain mumbled through a succession of apologies and promises to his kids, to any potential god or being that happened to be listening in. He would make it up to his children for this new life that he had imposed on them. He'd do whatever he could to make it up to them.

They came thundering down the stairs only seconds after the opening, clunking bar of the ice-cream van's tune. Almost as if they'd been waiting for its arrival.

The children had appeared yesterday evening. Abbie had watched them through the spyglass. They each wore a rucksack on their backs – the boy's was blue and orange, the girl's pastel and cranberry pink. The girl also carried a pink handbag. They had looked frightened, lost. Their father had hurried them upstairs. The girl went first. The father's hand hovered behind the boy. It was the boy he was concerned about.

Abbie moved to the living-room window. She was in time to see the man striding down the path, the children behind him, like enthusiastic ducklings with identical bouncing, fluffy, brown hair.

She found it difficult to guess the ages of children; they looked, with their grown-up clothes and hair, like clones of their parents. The girl was the oldest; perhaps eleven or twelve. Her body lacked the defined form of a teenager. The boy must have been at least a couple of years younger.

They were soon back again. The father was shepherding them up the path. Fussing. Why hadn't he let them go on their own? That had been half of the excitement of the ice-cream man. She had loved running out to the van with Becca. Becca used to tease her because Abbie always took the longest time choosing but ended up buying the same ice-lolly every time. Kids were mollycoddled these days, prisoners in their homes.

The father touched the top of the boy's head but he was quickly shrugged off; the little boy's face was savage with a scowl. Abbie saw the recoil, the shadow of hurt in the man's eyes. Her sympathy washed against the feeling that he deserved it for being neurotic.

Walking past the front door on her way back into the study, she couldn't stop herself looking through the spyglass. She didn't expect to see the girl staring straight back at her. Lips pursed, poised over the tip of the ice-cream twirl she looked right into Abbie's eyes, as if she could see through wood.

Abbie was mesmerized. She watched as the man's fingers cupped his daughter's bony shoulder, watched her turn reluctantly away. Abbie half-anticipated that the girl would look back but she didn't and Abbie was glad. There hadn't been any children in the house before. Not in all the years she'd lived here: always adults – a lot of DSS, or students and single people sharing.

Abbie collected the shawl and two shirts she'd finished earlier and took them to the living room. She folded and packed them into the bag with the rest of the batch of clothes. She needed to call Kate to make arrangements for the bag to be collected and for more work to be delivered.

Kate immediately picked up the phone. 'I'm so glad you

rang, Abbie. I've just had an urgent job come in for next week. Can you help?'

'What is it?'

'A sequinned mermaid costume which is practically bald. I can courier it over first thing tomorrow but you'll need to start work on it straight away. I've got to have it in two weeks' time, at the latest. I'll pay a premium rate,' Kate added when Abbie hadn't responded.

'What colour sequins?'

'Silver.'

'OK.' She was sure that she had plenty of silver sequins in stock.

'Abbs, you're a star.'

When Abbie opened the storage box to check the sequins she realized she'd made a mistake; there wasn't going to be anywhere near enough. She'd forgotten she'd used hundreds of them on the Pearly Queen outfit a couple of months ago.

She picked up the phone to tell Kate she'd changed her mind. It was already nearly two o'clock. Abbie couldn't just drop everything and go out. She wasn't prepared for it, she simply couldn't face it. Kate would understand, Abbie told herself, as she dialled the number. Kate knew how difficult it was for Abbie to get out at short notice, she knew that Abbie wasn't able to be away from the flat for too long. But tucked under the phone was the unpaid electricity bill from the winter; its red lettering reproaching her. She cut the call before it connected.

She went to the kitchen and washed up her soup bowl and plate, she collected her sewing box from the study, returned to the living room and sat down at the table. She got up again to fetch her notebook, address book and telephone from the side table. She tore out four pages from the notebook. On the first page she made a list of the supplies she needed, on the second she wrote out a note:

I'm out shopping but I won't be very long. See you soon!
Love your kiddo. xxx

She copied this onto the remaining two sheets and put the three notes in one pile, the shopping list next to them.

She picked up her address book, and looked at the back where she recorded the names and dates of her phone calls. She noted down those people she was due to contact. There were two. She cut a Post-it note in two and marked the pages.

'Um, is that Pete?'

'Pete who?'

'Pete, um . . .' The name wasn't in her head. Just Pete. That's all she'd ever known him as. Pete. She peered closely at Nick's cramped handwriting. 'Pete Harris?'

'Nah, love. No Mr 'arris here. Only me. Mr 'arris went months ago, love. In trouble is he?'

'No, not at all . . . it's just . . . I mean . . . I was hoping, well, for news of someone he knew, knows. That's all.'

'No news here, love. All quiet here.'

'Do you happen to know, to have Pete's – Mr Harris's – new number?'

'Nah, love. Funny. You're the second person to ask me that this week.'

Her heart jumped. 'A man?'

'A woman. Popular with the ladies it seems, this Mr 'arris.'

Abbie left her number with the man and noted down on the top of the Post-it: 'Pete — moved.' She thought for a moment. Who would be likely to know Pete's new number? Who else had he been friendly with? He hadn't been one of the theatre crowd. He was someone Nick had met one night, from a band or something. He'd supplied Nick with dope for a while. She wrote: 'Check with Maddie for new no.'

'Hello. Is Bill there, please?'

'Who's calling?'

'Abbie.'

'What's it about?'

'It's personal. Could I speak to him, for a moment? Please. It's important.'

There was a pause; a breath, a delay detectable only to the practised ear. 'Who are you?'

'Abbie Silva. He knows my husband, Nick.'

There was a hurried, whispered conversation.

'He says he hasn't got anything to tell you. He said there's no news on Nick. Nick is it or Mick?'

'Nick.'

'Well, sorry Abbie but Bill hasn't got any news. Sorry. Bye.'

She wrote the time, day and date on the Post-it note and then: 'Wife? Tricky.'

She tidied up the flat, leaving everything as you would want to find it, should you arrive home after a long absence. The cushions on the settee, welcoming, the made bed, tempting. She took the vodka out of the freezer and placed it on the work-surface with a glass, together with a bag of cashew nuts, Nick's favourite.

The last thing she did before leaving the flat was to put the notes out. She propped up one on the telephone table, placed one on the kitchen work-surface, a corner secured under the kettle, and the final one on the mantelpiece in the study. She stopped there for a moment, taking time to touch Nick's photograph. She glanced back as she was leaving the room, just to check that the note was plainly visible.

As she was locking her front door, she realized she'd forgotten the shopping list. She hurried back in. The open door combined with her haste into the living room created a draught which made the note by the telephone flop forward. She straightened it up and then felt compelled to check that the other two were properly in place. She returned to the living room for a final check on the third note when she spotted the bus going past.

She stood motionless in front of the window not daring to move for the next twenty minutes.

Leaving the house in the daytime was much harder than at night. The daylight, infiltrating the rooms, dissipated the energy of their home. Her notes seemed insubstantial – even the writing seemed paler, the paper bleached and flimsy – so that she didn't feel confident she could hold Nick there if he came back. She pictured him easily bored, wandering off after a short while in search of company like he used to do on the days when he was in-between jobs or waiting to hear about a role. She'd come back from work, looking forward to seeing him, picturing how they'd spend their evening but the flat would be empty. There would be traces everywhere of how Nick had spent his time: the unwashed dishes, the unmade bed, the floor leading from the bathroom to bedroom still damp from where he'd walked after his shower. But he'd been gone for hours.

By night time the air molecules in the flat felt denser. She pictured them accumulating like a gentle sleeping gas – enough to make him doze in his armchair or to settle in bed where she'd find him when she got back, watching a film on TV, the bottle of vodka on the bedside table beside him. She felt it herself when she returned in the early hours, the flat smelt of home.

There were three other people waiting for the bus when she walked over to the bus stop. She noted – almost by reflex – their height, build, posture and scanned their faces. She did the same for anyone who passed by: a girl in a tracksuit, an old man with his back bowed forward, a middle-aged couple holding hands. She was alerted to a man with dark shoulder-length hair who was standing several metres away. She strained her eyes, so hard she felt them buzz in their sockets. He started walking in the direction of the park and it was all she could do to stop herself running after him – to see his face. Nick could have grown a beard, shaved his head, dyed his hair – it wouldn't matter. She would still recognize that unique combination of sharp and curved: his thin nose, his high cheeks, his crystal blue eyes that cut through into the depth of her that very first time she saw him.

The man crossed the road to join a woman with a pushchair on the other side just as the bus turned into the street.

Abbie's nerves were sparking. She sat on her hands to stop them fidgeting. She tried not to think of the telephone left to ring out in the empty flat. She tried not to think that she'd made a mistake phoning those people this morning – jogging their memories only to then go out. What if they were calling her back right now?

'Abbie? Sorry, I meant to tell you—'

'Are you the woman who rang earlier? There was something, I don't know why I didn't think of it before—'

She told herself that no one had ever, *ever* rung her back before. She told herself that, in any case, her answerphone was on.

She noticed that demolition work had begun on the old snooker hall where Nick used to spend some evenings, but which had been boarded up for years. She had read in the local free paper that there were luxury apartments going up in its place and wondered what Nick would make of the area now where only pockets of the original remained untouched by development. He had loved living in London. He took to it immediately as he had always known he would but it grew slowly on Abbie who had, for a long time, missed the wide, tree-lined streets that they had grown up in and the feeling of belonging.

Boats were travelling rapidly in the choppy water. They said there were fish and otters in the Thames these days. Even a dolphin had made its home there but she couldn't imagine it. The opaque water seemed hostile – more likely to have monsters lurking beneath it.

She flew around the suppliers, eschewing help offered by a friendly shop assistant.

'I've been coming here for years,' she told the woman.

Left alone, she managed to find everything so easily it was almost magical. She'd step and turn and the next item on her list would appear virtually under her hand: sequins, tailor's chalk, braid, red velvet trim, pins, white cotton, fifty small black buttons.

It was as if a fairy godmother was waving her wand, time and time again.

The friendly assistant was at the till.

'Making a costume for your little girl?' she said, counting the twenty boxes of sequins. She smiled at Abbie. 'A fairy?' She had stopped putting the items through the till as if she was waiting for Abbie to reply.

'Mermaid,' Abbie muttered, blushing.

'Looks like a lot of work,' the woman said.

Abbie stared at the floor. She waited for the assistant to tell her the total and then handed over the money and took the bag without saying another word.

She walked rapidly out of the shop, ran to the bus stop and was back on a bus home in less than an hour of leaving the flat. The bus was warm and airless. It was hard to stop herself drifting into a doze. She jerked awake and clutched at her bag of shopping as it began to slide from her lap; the boxes of sequins rattled gently.

When I arrive, the theatre seems abandoned; the entrance is locked and the tall, wooden doors at the side are closed. A man in jeans and a donkey jacket is heading towards me, so I ask him how I can get in.

– I'm Nick's . . . I'm with one of the actors.

– OK.

I follow the man through a small, black-painted door and then along dark passages. My apprehension grows. Nick has asked me to come today but I am worried about what I will find.

– They're through there.

I hesitate outside for a minute before walking in. I'm conscious even of my soft step down the carpeted floor. The voices from the actors on stage sound thin and quickly float off into the ceiling; their actions are stilted, melodramatic. Nick is sitting on a far corner of the stage, leaning against the wall. He is following the lines from a script in his lap but he glances up as I take a seat a few rows back from the others who are present. He winks at me and then resumes what he was doing.

The actors skip and stumble through their lines with Nick acting as prompt and I feel my nervousness change to embarrassment as they are told to repeat the scene over and over again until suddenly something changes. It lasts only a few minutes but in that time everyone becomes caught up in a kind of expectant stillness. The people in the seats in front of me, who haven't stopped whispering since I arrived, are quietened. I find myself sitting forward, drawn to the actors. Nick, too, I notice is watching them, the script forgotten.

When the actors break off, a fervour remains in the air. Nick waves me over to the stage; his face is flushed, his gestures are agitated. I feel excited, too, as if I've shared something momentous.

'Come up.' He takes my hand and hauls me up. As I turn to face the scattering of people in rows below me, I feel dizzy with exposure and am glad to hurry off backstage where Nick leads me.

Pushing through swing door after swing door, we might be going in a circle for all I know; I have completely lost all sense of direction. Nick taps on the white painted door of what appears to be a large cupboard and then we go inside.

A woman, blonde, tall and curvaceous, is standing in the middle of the tiny, windowless room, which is full of costumes on rails and in plastic boxes, holding clothes aloft from each hand; like Libra weighing her scales. The room smells like a charity shop.

– Abbie can sew, Nick announces, pushing me forward.

– Can you? Kate drops her arms and hugs the clothes to her body making her breasts swell up from her low-cut top. She fixes me with a steady eye. – I mean, properly?

– Definitely. She's going to study clothes design when we've got my career sorted. I'm sure she'd be happy to help out.

– Then you must have been sent by God.

A call for the understudies comes over the box in the corridor. I turn to Nick. – That's you.

– You'll be OK, Nick says and I don't know if it's a question or statement but he leaves me with Kate, who begins to hook the clothes on the rail, swishing the hangers along as she does.

– So you're Nick's girlfriend.

– His wife.

I see the catch of surprise in her face.

– I didn't know he was married. He doesn't wear a ring.

– He'd only have to keep taking it off with each part he goes for, I explain to her as Nick has explained to me.

– Yes, there is that.

I feel uncomfortable about the way Kate continues to look at me as if she expects me to add something more, so I ask her, – What do you want me to do?

We wheel away two clothes rails and push aside a tattered screen to reveal an old Singer sewing machine and a chair in one corner. To start with I find it hard to settle. I can't stop looking around. At first my eyes seem unable to assimilate the chaotic colour and textures around me; in every direction there are new treasures: clothes and hats and scarves and even an area of shelving for shoes. After a few minutes, though, I see that although the tiny room is packed to capacity, there is order here and I have the feeling that it is Kate who has imposed it. No movement seems to be wasted as she goes around the room selecting pieces from a list that she holds in one hand. There are clothes suspended on a wire which runs the length of the room just below the ceiling and Kate skilfully takes a dress down from it using a hook on a long pole. She carries this over one arm and adds two white shirts from one clothes rail and a short, red jacket from another. There's a soft rumble of wheels as she pushes a set of short wooden steps along the floor at the bottom of the shelving and runs up them to reach a blue pair of women's shoes. I find her busy presence calming.

— You've got an eye for this.

I hadn't noticed Kate behind me, I've been concentrating so hard. The skirt I am working on has been altered so many times that the perforations from where it has repeatedly been stitched and unstitched are enlarged. I have been taking care to sew as close as possible to the seam lines I'm following without exacerbating these stress points in the garment.

— How about helping me out with the rest of the production run?

— I'd love to.

I feel a spell has been cast over me; I don't know if it's because of Kate, or the strange dusty air in the room, or if it's from touching these beautiful pieces of history, but I wouldn't miss seeing the costumes brought to life on stage for the world.

Abbie was jerked awake when the bus pulled up sharply. She blinked several times and licked her lips. She must have fallen asleep for a few minutes; she felt drugged with tiredness. The scene outside swam in front of her – two denim-clad kids were kissing; getting completely stuck in, clamped tight in the middle of the pavement. People were looking at them with amusement or disgust. As the bus pulled away, she felt herself falling into the memory of that kiss.

That bone-melting, heart-thumping, sweet, sweet kiss.

Her eyelids flickered, heavy. She had only to sink a little further and she would taste, smell, feel him.

Then she saw him. It really was him. Nick. Nick.

She was on her feet in a second but the bus was moving and she slipped, grabbing for the handrail with one hand, clutching her carrier bag with the other. She made a strangled sound which caused heads to turn. She looked past the curious eyes, keeping Nick in sight as she inched forward to reach the button, to ring the bell, to stop the bus, to get to Nick.

Then he turned and she saw it wasn't him after all.

Abbie knew what the sneaking sidelong looks meant. They were thinking: stupid bitch, probably pissed or on drugs. A crazy freak, smack-head lunatic.

A woman came up behind her, pressing shopping bags against her legs and it seemed easier to step forward, get off and walk the rest of the way home.

She watched the bus driving away from her. She guessed

she was somewhere in Pimlico as they hadn't yet crossed the bridge. Tears prickled. She warned herself not to be pathetic. She reminded herself that this was nothing to how Nick must feel, nothing to what horrors he must go through every day as he tried to figure out what was happening to him. She thought, if this is all I have to put up with then I'm lucky, then I can do it.

She drew up her head, quickened her pace.

Traffic rumbled and shuddered the bridge under her feet. The tide was beginning to retreat and there was an oily, gassy odour from the exposed mud banks. A flat tarnished metal platform holding a rusting crane and several metal containers sat in the middle of the water. It looked too heavy to be floating.

As she approached her flat, a new thought began to slowly take shape in her head.

The man she'd seen hadn't been Nick but it had been a sign. There had been other signs, too, which on their own might have been insignificant. Yesterday she'd twice heard the name Nick on the TV. Earlier in the week, she'd been looking through her bags of scrap material for something to patch up one of the costumes when Nick's favourite leather jacket had fallen off the top shelf and landed at her feet.

The certainty that this was The Day flowed through her like smoke unfurling inside her body; a warming, glowing golden smoke. She felt as if she could snort great plumes of it and watch it rise into the air, gilding the afternoon light.

Her hands were trembling as she opened the outer door and stepped inside.

There was a clatter and a scrabble and she watched, helplessly, as the children charged down the stairs towards her, squabbling and squawking.

'Wait Tom, Iz,' a deep voice commanded from above.

The little girl planted herself in front of her.

'Hi. I'm Izzy. This is my brother Tom.'

Abbie mumbled hello, sidestepping the girl in a hurry to escape before their father came down. She wanted to get inside to see Nick. Her heart was a squeaky ball of anticipation.

She dropped her keys.

'I'll get those.' The father picked up her keys, held them out. 'Hello. I'm your new neighbour, Owen.'

'Yes.'

She was conscious of all their eyes on her. 'Nice to meet you,' she said, remembering the correct words. Suddenly self-conscious about her teeth, she covered her mouth with her hand.

'Come on, Dad.'

'Excuse me.' Abbie grabbed the opportunity to turn away. 'I'm in a bit of a rush.'

'Oh, sorry. We are too, really. Off to the park.'

She glanced back at them. She didn't care what they were doing, didn't care one tiny bit that they were off to the park with their stupid yellow frisbee.

Anger turned the smoke inside her a malevolent grey, poisonous gas to breathe over the father and wipe that quizzical smile off his face, to make his girlish soft brown eyes sting, to trail over the children and obliterate that sickening, wondering look on the girl, that petulant baby pout on the boy.

'Well,' he said. 'I guess I'll see you around then.'

As soon as she had opened the door, she knew Nick wasn't back. That he'd never been back.

She started to walk down the hall. She looked at the floor. It seemed to swell and heave like deadly quicksand under her feet. She wanted to wait until the floor had stopped moving but she had to check the notes. She inched her way forward, fearful that her feet would be sucked down at every step.

In the living room, she sat at the table while she examined the note for any sign that it had been picked up, read, put down again. She scrutinized it for any greasy smudges on a corner, and finally, with her heart bumping, she turned it over in case a message had been written there in spidery, tight handwriting: 'Sorry I missed you, kiddo.'

Although she knew it was a waste of time, she still had to do 1471. She fumbled with the handset, misdialled the first time. She sat hunched forward on the settee hardly daring to breath in case it said number withheld because she knew she'd have to tell herself over and over again that it was just stupid, bloody stupid, sales people who won't take no for an answer. That it wasn't him, standing in a phone-box, standing in a pub somewhere, having finally plucked up the courage, finally managed to do it, to say, kiddo, I've been ill and it all went wrong but now I've remembered it all. I've remembered you and I want to come home.

It was Becca's number from when they spoke a couple of days ago.

Nothing had changed from when she had left.

The note was still in her hand and she began plucking and tearing at it until she let the final piece of paper fall to the floor on top of the pile of thumbnail-sized paper petals.

Then she remembered that this had happened before. In almost exactly the same way – the same certainty, the same reading into signs, the same disappointment. She felt her hope crouching inside her, like an ugly, taunting goblin, and she thought why did she fall for it again? Why?

So the woman Owen had seen the other night was his new neighbour. She hadn't exactly given them the warmest welcome in the world but he was inclined to believe that she had been in a rush as she said. She was obviously flustered and seemed even a little shy. He'd noticed that her hand had been shaking when she took the keys from him.

'What's that lady's name, Dad? The lady downstairs,' Izzy asked.

'I don't know, Izzy, I don't think she actually said.'

'She's pretty, isn't she?'

'Well,' he said. 'Yes, I suppose she is.' From the view he'd had of the woman heading off that night with her hood up and her hands thrust into her jacket pockets, he'd been expecting someone a bit tougher, with tattoos maybe, like warning signs, on wiry arms. He'd been disarmed to meet someone so delicate who only came up to his chest. He had noticed lovely brown eyes in the brief moment they actually met his but then his attention had been drawn to her rabbity teeth which she appeared to be trying to cover behind her hand.

'Tom, we're walking, so there's no point standing next to the car, looking hopeful.'

'But it's miles.'

'How do you know when you've never been before?'

'Oh, God!'

Tom went on ahead and Owen felt Izzy's warm hand slip into his. Owen called Tom back when Izzy stopped to look in a tiny front garden. It was rather overgrown and dark and full of stone animals. In the centre was an oversized mouse with a broken ear.

'What are you looking at that for?' Tom demanded to know.

'It's weird,' Izzy said.

'You're weirder,' Tom said but they carried on peering through the hedge until Owen thought he spotted some movement in the upstairs window and urged them to move.

The day was dry and not as cold as he'd feared. Owen felt cheered by the amount of people enjoying the park; not just families but couples and teenagers and people walking their dogs. There was grass as far as he could make out and plenty of trees. As they followed the path round, they walked past the tennis courts, basketball and football areas and then some formal gardens – hedged off from the main park – with beds full of bright flowers. They continued past a children's play area towards a small Tudor-style building, which as they approached, Owen could see was a café.

'Isn't this great?' Owen said, thinking they could easily spend a few hours here out of the flat. Once breakfast was over, he'd felt the boredom and tetchiness of everyone rising by the hour. He couldn't remember ever feeling so absolutely aware of his children's physical presence. The flat had seemed to shrink, the longer they remained inside.

Tom and he started a game of frisbee on one of the areas

of grass where several other families were playing games, but Izzy declined.

'I'll watch, thanks,' she said.

'Don't go too far,' Owen warned. He tried not to look like he was keeping an eye on her as she walked towards a tree a couple of metres away but Izzy wasn't fooled. Once she had sat down, she waved to him. He waved back, feeling caught out.

A few minutes later as he turned to pick up the frisbee he'd missed, he was struck by her distant, rather secretive air. It made him think of Fliss.

Tom's toe, Owen remembered suddenly as Tom took a spectacular jump to make a catch. Tom seemed to have forgotten all about it, despite having limped and dragged his foot around the flat all morning.

He was conscious of Izzy becoming bored and too cold so after about forty minutes, he took them to the café. Inside, it was much larger than it had seemed from the exterior. Laid out in a kind of 'U' shape, there were tables on each side and a huge three-sided couch in the centre opposite the counter. The couch was occupied by a group of four young mums with pushchairs and several babies and toddlers. One of the babies was crying loudly and it was only when it stopped, that Owen could hear some kind of African music playing softly in the background.

The counter was oddly bare except for a selection of cake slices in a small glass case. Instead, the menu of drinks and snacks was chalked up on two enormous blackboards on the wall behind. The cakes, though, proved too tempting for them all. They each chose a different kind and Owen ordered hot chocolate for the children and a chilled beer for himself.

They sat on a table outside.

A group of people stopped on the grass across from the café; Owen counted eleven of them. They stood talking and stretching for a few minutes before forming three rows and then began to perform some kind of martial art. The leader's movements were confident and flowing but the rest of the group wobbled and teetered as they tried to keep their balance on the uneven ground. It didn't look easy.

'What are they doing?' Izzy asked.

Owen took a guess. 'T'ai Chi.'

'What's that?'

'Some kind of martial art,' Owen replied and wondered if that was true. 'Sort of relaxation, too, like yoga.'

'They look stupid,' Tom said in a very stern manner which was at odds with the comical moustache the chocolate had deposited over his lip.

'Don't you do yoga at school?' Owen remembered.

'No. Not like that.' Tom looked mortified but as no more information was forthcoming Owen let it pass. Even though he took his time over the beer, it was soon gone and Owen was faced with the decision of what to do next. With the frisbee as the sole entertainment and the day getting colder, he decided that it wouldn't be fair to Izzy to stay so he suggested that they make their way home.

The phone was ringing in the flat as he was unlocking the door; as soon as it stopped his mobile started. It was Fliss.

'We've just got in,' he told her. 'They'll ring you back from the landline in a minute.'

Izzy headed straight for the phone.

'Where are you going?' Owen asked her.

'My room.' She stopped and they stared at each other as if both of them were unsure whether this was OK. Owen had to force himself to walk away.

'Don't forget that Tom wants to talk to Mum, too,' he said as casually as he could.

'I know. I'll call him when I'm finished.'

Owen got on with preparing the evening meal. He felt as nervous as if he were facing an interview panel. He could only hope that both the kids would give him a good report but as the minutes passed and he ran through the events of both days he couldn't imagine that happening. All too soon, Tom was standing next to him, holding out the phone.

'Well, they both sound fine,' Fliss said.

'Oh, yes. Everything *is* fine.' He felt buoyed up; almost giddy with love for Izzy and for Tom. 'I'm just making dinner,' he almost sang out.

'What are you having?'

'Spaghetti Bolognese.'

'Ah. Your signature dish.'

'You could say that.' The sauce was bubbling. He turned the heat down and stirred, slowly. 'So,' he said, suddenly aware of an awkward silence on the other end of the phone. 'I guess I'd better get on with the food.'

'Oh, right. Yes, of course.'

'Unless you want to talk,' he offered, tentatively.

'Not really.'

'But you're OK?'

'Yes, Owen,' she said. 'I wish you'd stop asking me that. I'm fine. Everything's fine.'

I was only asking, he thought, no need to bite my head off,

but he kept his thoughts to himself and executed another too-cheerful goodbye; grimacing as he put the phone down. He went to find the children for dinner. Both were in their rooms. He looked in on Izzy first; she was lying on her bed. She had arranged all her belongings and her room looked colourful and pretty.

'You've done a great job in here,' he told her.

'Thanks.'

'Dinner's ready.'

'OK. I'm coming.' She didn't move.

'Don't be long. I'm serving up, right now.'

Tom had tipped everything into a big heap on the floor in his bedroom.

'You'll have to tidy this up before you go tomorrow.'

'Aren't I taking it all back then?'

'No, I thought you knew that. These are the things that you'll keep here.'

Tom looked at him askance. 'But what if I need something?'

'You won't,' Owen told Tom but his reply sounded much more confident than he felt. In that moment the complications and difficulties of the situation seemed completely unworkable. 'Come for dinner, Tom,' he said hurriedly and left the room.

Later, when the kids were asleep and he'd grown tired of the TV, Owen stood at the living room window. The glow of lights in the sky arced over the city; below, a light from the flat downstairs played palely on the paving stones. Traffic passed endlessly up and down the road; anonymous cars driven by strangers. Nothing stopped. He was living, he realized, in a place where nothing and nobody did stop – it was a passing place not a destination. He thought of his old street where everyone would notice if a strange car was parked up, where he recognized his neighbours from the car they drove.

The next day, as he arrived at his old house, the contrast between the two locations seemed even more potent. In every direction he looked there was evidence of thriving, affluent and confident children and parents and homes. There was a group of children playing on bikes on the road, two young girls intent on picking daisies from a lawn, neighbours working in the long front gardens and washing cars on their drives.

When he opened the car door the scent of newly mown grass hit him. It even felt sunnier and warmer than when they had left London.

Inside the house, everything shone and the air was so replete with chemicals from air fresheners and polish and cleaning agents, it made him want to sneeze.

Fliss hugged the children too tightly, as if something terrible had happened. He saw them react against it; even Izzy pulled away from her quickly.

Owen and Fliss were left alone in the hallway.

'I missed them so much,' Fliss said softly. Her voice trembled with emotion. 'I promised myself that I wasn't going to make a fuss.'

He felt for her. Their children were growing up, getting harder to read. They tried on attitudes and personalities like ever-changing items of clothing, shrugging off some, huddling into others. It was hard to keep up, he knew, for both of them.

Although his intention had been to get straight off, it didn't seem very fair to leave Fliss so soon. 'I wouldn't mind a coffee, if that's OK?'

As Fliss waited for the coffee machine to finish, he noticed that she was rubbing the eczema on her hands; a sign that she was nervous.

'So was it really OK?' she asked him, bringing the jug of coffee and a couple of mugs to the table.

'It wasn't brilliant,' he admitted. 'But Izzy took it in her stride. Tom was a little . . .'

'Difficult?'

Owen nodded. 'He was a pain in the arse at times.'

Fliss laughed which he was grateful for. 'How were you?' he asked her.

'Lost. At first. A bit better by the end.'

She saw him looking at her hands and then she tucked them into her lap, out of sight. This action shocked him. He saw that this was the moment he'd been anticipating, the change he'd been both dreading and hoping for. Fliss often hid her eczema from other people but it was a long time since she'd been self-conscious about it in front of him.

He took a mouth-burning gulp of hot coffee. 'Everything will seem strange for a while,' he told Fliss and hoped that he sounded convincing. 'But a few months down the line, it'll just be normal.'

Fliss leant on the table and pushed her hair back behind her ears. 'I think I've forgotten what normal is.' She didn't look at him but from the way she was furiously blinking, he could tell that she was trying not to cry.

'Look,' he said gently, putting his drink down. 'I think it's best if I go.'

He waited for her to speak, instead she gave a brief but definite nod.

'I'll just pop and say goodbye to the kids.'

Owen would have liked to have taken some moments in the car before he drove off but he was aware of eyes on him. Izzy at the front door, Fliss from the living room, maybe even Tom up in his bedroom. He felt completely drained. I can't do this, he thought. This is awful. I can't possibly do this.

When he pulled up outside the flat, his neighbour was just leaving. He lowered the car window and shouted to her, 'Hang on.'

She hesitated before stooping down to look inside. He couldn't make out much of her face under the shadow of her hood – a shine of eyeball, a glint perhaps of those protruding teeth. He liked to think that meant she was smiling.

He got out. 'I wanted to apologize if I made a lot of noise moving in. It'll be quieter for a while now anyway as the kids are back with their mum. They'll be here every other weekend usually and my share of the holiday with them.' The words didn't feel right saying them out loud.

'It's been fine. I've, um, to be honest, I've hardly noticed.'

The way she kept fidgeting and shuffling from foot to foot brought on a desire in him to do the opposite – he slouched against his car.

'I'm Owen, by the way.'

'Yes. You told me before.'

'And you?'

'Oh. It's Abbie. My name's Abbie.'

'Nice name.'

'I've got to go. Sorry,' she said. 'I'm, um, late. I've got to—'

Why did he never learn? He'd worked in London for over thirteen years and he still expected people to be friendly. He felt compelled to prolong the conversation, to capture her against her will and keep her with him for a few more minutes. She pushed away hair that had drifted in front of her eyes and, in doing so, her hood fell back revealing her face. It was then that he saw her resemblance to his middle sister, Mae. Not in her looks – Abbie was much darker than Mae who had been teased terribly as a child for her ginger hair and white eyebrows and lashes – but it was the same expression of pleading desolation that stopped his mouth. Mae's frail defences had always made him want to hug her fiercely close. But he also knew that comfort was the last thing she could accept. Instinctively, he withdrew his attention from Abbie by turning towards the car, making a show of checking he'd locked the door, casually saying, 'Yeah, sure. See you around.'

He watched her walk away knowing it was kinder to cut her loose but inside the flat he stood for a while at the window, even though Abbie was out of sight. He felt shaken by the pressing protectiveness he felt for her.

The flat's silence rang in his ears. In the kitchen he let the tap run until the water was as cold as it was going to get and filled a pint glass. He drank down half of it, licked his lips, then drank down the remaining half. The phone was lying on the work-surface; he picked it up; pressed out Mae's number. He let it ring on as she was always slow to answer.

'It's me, Owen.'

'Owen! Hi! Oh shit, hang on.' Owen heard a crash, then Mae's faint voice and some clapping.

'Mae? Is everything OK? Mae?'

'Sorry, it's Gordon. He's just knocked something over.' She sounded breathless.

'Who's Gordon?'

'My cat. Remember.' Mae giggled and she sounded exactly like Izzy.

Yes, he did remember now. 'I thought maybe you'd got a boyfriend,' he teased.

'I have, actually,' she replied. 'But don't tell Mum. She'll interrogate me.'

'I won't tell,' he assured her but immediately the questions started stacking up in his head. Who was the guy? Did he understand what Mae needed? He allowed himself one question: 'Where did you meet him?'

'At the psychos' group.'

'So—'

'Yep, he's a psycho, too.'

'He sounds perfect!' he joked, mainly to cover his concern but Mae surprised him by giggling again. She always got his sense of humour. He'd forgotten that. So often he tagged her as someone to worry about, not someone with whom he could laugh.

'I'm sorry about you and Fliss. Mum told me . . . How are Izzy and Tom taking it?'

'Not too bad, in the circumstances.'

'And you?'

'The same, really, I suppose. It's—'

Mae cut in. 'I shouldn't have said anything about Malcolm. I wish I could un-say it. I've probably jinxed everything now.'

He recognized the panic in her voice. 'Consider it un-said,' he told her.

'I don't know what I was thinking. I'm not really a relationship kind of person.'

'See how it goes,' he advised.

'I don't think it was such a good idea, after all.'

'You never know,' Owen said.

'I've got to go now,' Mae told him abruptly.

He wished he could persuade her to stay talking to him for a few more minutes but he sensed it was futile. 'Give me a call sometime,' he said, then remembered he would have to give her his new number.

'I can't take that right now,' she told him. 'I haven't got a pen. Or paper.'

'Don't worry. I'll call again. Or you can get it from Mum when you next speak to her. I've told her.'

'OK. OK.'

He was relieved to hear her sounding a little calmer.

'Owen?' Mae said at the last minute when he was about to ring off.

'Yes?'

'Don't worry,' she told him.

'What about?'

'About everything. And everyone. You always worry about everyone. Except yourself.'

He changed into some jogging pants and a sweatshirt and put on a DVD of *The Office*. He regretted now, taking tomorrow off. He'd thought there wasn't much point in going in just for Friday but now, of course, he'd have to find something to do with himself for the day. Never mind the first weekend on his own.

He counted off the days on his fingers and then did a

recount as if he couldn't quite believe it was true. He would not be seeing his children for eight whole days. At that precise moment he was hit head-on by the realization of what he had done.

Tonight the study was the only place she wanted to be; in the restful dark with Nick's eyes upon her from the mantelpiece. Tonight the need for comforting memories was so pressing that Abbie reached down and took out her memory box from underneath the chair. She sat it in her lap on top of the mermaid costume and unlocked its precious contents.

The hot weather breaks on the day of our wedding. The clouds thicken and spew out the tepid warm rain they've been holding on to for just this very moment. Everyone keeps saying, oh what a shame, on your wedding day. What bad luck, how typical.

They think I care. But I don't. This day is already perfect. Nothing could spoil it.

I'm rushed under a tree surrounded by a posse of umbrella holders trying to keep me dry while I hold my dress up off the wet grass. My silk dress turns translucent in the spots where the rain finds me. The photographer wants the church to be in some of the pictures so I'm hustled back again, trailing the few still loyal in this deluge: Becca who has hardly left my side, our cousin Nathalie and two friends from school, Lily and Christine.

It's gloomy in the church porch which smells like earth. The photographer is trying to crowd all the guests inside but it's too small and people are sullen with cold in their thin, summer clothes. Nick strides across the churchyard. He looks so handsome; his black hair wet like ink. He takes one look at everyone shivering and says, – Fuck this.

He tells them to go ahead to the reception at the hotel. Everyone. He is only twenty-one years old but everyone listens to him. Within only a few minutes it seems we are alone except for the photographer who Nick instructs to stay behind and to follow us down to the church gate when everyone else has gone. The photographer is pissed off; he doesn't stop complaining about the rain – even though it's beginning to ease. He grumbles that his suede shoes are ruined from the long, wet grass which he has to stand in to get the shots we want. Nick pays no attention to him. – We've paid him, he whispers when I start worrying, – so he has to do what we want.

Abbie rested her head against the back of the armchair. Her brain felt swollen with fatigue. She was behind on the work on the mermaid costume. She had finished the fishtail and had begun on the left side of the main trunk but it was slow going. Each sequin, each loop, each catch of the needle into the material was laboured, as if she was a teacher watching the actions of a clumsy student about to ruin a precious piece.

Tonight the rhythm of the work, where time disappeared and progress happened effortlessly, was eluding her.

She held the wedding photograph in her hand – the only one she had left – and she was struck once again by how calm she looked, how peaceful. Her eyes were closed, almost as if she'd forgotten that the photographer was there. Her body leant against Nick's. She willed herself back into that moment. Her body ached to sink into the relief his presence would give. She was tired of holding herself up, of being strong. She wanted to abandon herself to the damp and the heat and the strength of his hands holding onto her waist where the jagged crystals and the bumps of tiny pearls on the wedding dress pressed into her flesh.

There is a strange quiet over the street as the taxi drops me off. I wave goodbye to Nick as my parents come out to help me with my suitcase and bags. The trees are in leaf, shading the pavement from the early evening sun but the heat still rises from the ground.

This is the first time I have been home since I left almost ten months ago. Although we have spoken on the phone, the only one of my family I've seen is Becca. When my parents hug me, their bodies feel unfamiliar.

It's a shock to discover my room has been kept exactly as I left it; as if they have been expecting me to return home any moment. I wish that they had repainted it, bought new bed linen, thrown every trace of my old self away.

When my parents are asleep, I go to Becca's room. She shows me clothes she's bought recently, her new make-up and jewellery. She puts on a CD and turns the volume down. I hug my legs to my chest and we talk, quietly, so as not to disturb Mum and Dad. We talk about old friends, Becca's college, we talk about everything except what is happening the day after tomorrow.

The second night, the night before my wedding, Becca comes to my room. I'm not expecting her and so she finds me putting the finishing touches to my dress. I have made it all myself; skipping on food so that I can afford to buy pearls and satin, crystals and silk. I have been making this in secret, waiting for any time that Nick is out.

When I'm sewing it, I imagine every stitch to be a minute of the life I am going to share with him.

– It's gorgeous, Abbie. Put it on, let me see it.

– No. I'm going to wait until tomorrow. When it's the right time.

We both look at the dress where I've hung it on the wardrobe door.

– Are you sure you want to do this?

– Have they asked you to talk to me? It seems that from the moment I arrived my parents have constantly been one breath away from saying something.

– No. I'm asking. Sometimes, Nick seems to, well, you know what he's like. He's very persuasive. I just want to know that you are absolutely sure this is what *you* want.

– You don't have to worry about me, I tell her. – I've never wanted anything more in my whole life.

We hug each other and then she gives a little yelp. – It's gone midnight, she says. – My God, Abbs. It's today. You're getting married today.

I take the dress down and Becca helps me into it. Before I turn to face her, I take a moment to think of Nick.

– Don't cry, Becca. This is the happiest day of my life.

\*

Like a blink of mercury in the darkness, a tear lay on the photograph in Abbie's lap. She wiped it away with her sleeve and dabbed at her face. Some tears were welcomed – like these that came from happy memories – but not those that fell fast and furious, that spun her out of control.

The happiest day of her life.

From outside the hotel, I look at all our family and friends who have gathered in the bar waiting for us to arrive. As we step inside the lobby, there's a murmur, then a hush as everyone turns towards us. Although my hair is damp and there is mud spattered up the back of my train I see in their eyes that at this moment, I am beautiful.

There are balloons surrounding the door of the room behind, which I know are Becca's handiwork. The tables, laid out with flowers, are where we will eat and where there will be speeches. I no longer fear what everyone will say because, as I reach for Nick's hand and we step forward to take the first dance, I know that they have seen it. Even Nick's parents, who have told Nick not to expect any help from them in the future, have a drink in their hands and a smile on their faces. Everyone, finally, has seen what our love is; deep and strong and so much more than anyone had ever imagined.

Darkness hugs the circle of ice-blue light where Nick and I move dreamily, wrapped together. I fear the end of the song. I want to shout to the DJ to keep that record on, to repeat it again and again and again so that we can stay here for ever. The darkness recedes as coloured beams of light play across the dance floor and other couples join us. Other arms replace his, other hands touch me, other lips place kisses on my face.

But it's OK to separate because now there's nothing to stop us coming back together whenever we want. We've done it. I'm married to him and he's the love of my life. Nobody can stop us being together now.

I dance with Becca and the old gang and our cousins and even my dad who is gentle and serious as he concentrates on guiding me around the dance floor. I dance until my feet feel so hot and scorched and swollen that I have to take off my shoes.

Eventually, people begin to leave, lights come on revealing the party debris: the soiled tablecloths, the spilt drink, the half-eaten plates of food. The last guests blink, self-conscious in the glare. I stand by the door and say my goodbyes. When it's Mum and Dad's turn, they hug me close and there are tears in Dad's eyes. – If you need anything, anything, you just pick up the phone or come over. Remember you've always got a home with us. Do you hear?

I see Nick coming out of the Gents. He staggers a little. His shirt is crumpled and bunched up by the waistband where it has come untucked. When he looks at me it's as if he's tugging an invisible string which is tied at one end to my heart.

The honeymoon suite is beautiful but it feels too large for us. We haven't been alone together for three days and I feel shy. I wish we were back in our flat where I would know how to act. We sit on the bed and I wait for Nick to take the lead.

He pulls his shirt off over his head without undoing the buttons as if he's been waiting all night to do so. He switches the TV on. He has his back to me. I look at his spine – a knobbly curve – as he leans forward.

He gets up, fetches the champagne and glasses and sits next to me. Over his shoulder I can see the old black and white film he's chosen; the sound is barely audible.

His hands are shaking as he pours us each a glass of champagne.

– That day, when I first met you, remember? You and Becca were sitting on the wall. I thought, wow, she's beautiful.

– Becca.

– No, not Becca. You. Becca's pretty but she's like all the other girls. You were different. There was, is something about you, something wild – and real.

I take only a sip of champagne before putting down my glass. Nick does the same and then he helps me out of my dress and my underwear and we lie down together.

– You want me, don't you? he asks, and there is wonder in his voice as if he can't believe it's true. I hold his head and look hard in his eyes, the blue tenderized from alcohol and tiredness.

– I've always wanted you.

– And now you've got me.

– And you've got me, I say.

He surprises me by pushing in sudden and deep. My breath catches. I cry out.

– Do you like that? he asks.

I can't take my eyes off his face. I think how lucky I am to have got this man for the rest of my life.

On Tuesday, Owen arrived at work feeling relaxed and in a good mood. Like yesterday, he had slept well, woken up feeling refreshed, even before his alarm went off. He was enjoying his walk to the station. He'd been lucky – although the sky had been consistently greyed over – both days had stayed dry. On Monday, he'd seen, on his route, a row of run-down mews houses, which were behind an ugly empty seventies block. He discovered today when he got a seat on the left side, that he could catch a glimpse of them from the train, too. He had spent most of the journey fantasizing about buying the whole row cheaply, doing them up and making huge amounts of profit. He had seen in an estate agent's window what you could get for places around here – three hundred grand just for some ex-council two-bed flat.

As he came into reception, Owen could see Steve installed by the coffee machine in the far corner. By the time he'd reached him, hot sludgy brown liquid was being fired into a plastic cup.

'On the house,' Steve said, handing it to him.

'You're early. What's got into you?'

'I couldn't get out of the house quick enough.'

'Why? What's up?'

Steve shrugged.

Owen wasn't sure if he was imagining it but he'd noticed that ever since he'd left Fliss, Steve's complaints about Julie had escalated. Hardly a day went by without him passing some comment on their marriage in a tone which could only be described as bitter and almost desperate. Owen watched his friend morosely eyeing everyone who came into reception. No wonder they had the coffee machine to themselves; Steve was keeping them off his territory like a cantankerous Rottweiler.

'Over there,' Steve said suddenly, nudging Owen and gesturing in the direction of a couple of women waiting by the lift who had caught his attention. They were attractive – young with sleek blonde hair, short skirts and tight blouses – but that's all they were – nice passing scenery. They were nothing to get worked up about. Owen glanced at his friend. He felt in that moment that he hardly knew Steve at all.

The number of people coming in was beginning to thin noticeably. Owen checked his watch. 'Got to go.'

They took the stairs at the back of the building. Steve pushed open the door to the second floor while Owen continued up to the next level. He stopped when Steve called up to him.

'How about a drink tonight? We could go straight after work.'

'All right.'

'Let's make an early start.'

'I can't leave before six.'

'Six it is then.'

Owen was relieved to have a plan for the evening. It was four days since he'd seen Izzy and Tom and he was missing them badly. He felt like someone pining for a lover. He decided to plunge himself into his work otherwise he'd think about the kids the whole day. As it was fragments of their previous night's telephone conversation constantly came into his head and his heart bumped each time he caught sight of the photograph of them that he had on his desk. By the time he got home from work yesterday, he couldn't wait to hear their voices but all too soon, the phone call was over. He managed to keep them talking for ten minutes at the max and then they had simply slipped out of his reach.

He'd been left to face the consuming silence which he was beginning to feel almost like a physical presence.

In the nightclub, Steve was being loud, much too loud. He was attracting both of them the wrong kind of attention and they were pretty conspicuous as it was in their work clothes. They looked exactly like a couple of sleazy businessmen out on the pull.

'How 'bout them? How 'bout those ones?' Steve yelled in his ear. He seemed to think that women were items in a shop just waiting to picked up and bought. Owen was of the firm opinion that it didn't work like that and the way the women veered away only confirmed it.

'Ladies! Let me buy you a drink!' Steve called out but before he had finished his patter they were well out of reach and didn't look back. Owen mentally applauded their instincts.

While Steve was getting the next round in, Owen tried to count up how much he'd drunk so far: three pints in the first pub, one each in the next two with a tequila slammer; one – or was it two – more in the pub before they came here. He remembered having a whisky as well at some point.

He went to the Gents more for a change of scenery than out of need. His legs felt loose at the knees when he walked. Under his feet, the black flooring shone wetly. He feared slipping and toppled against the wall which felt clammy through his shirt sleeve.

Coming out of the toilets, he discovered a whole series of other rooms each with different music playing. There were very few people in any of them. Without the crush of bodies, the club held no glamour. The surroundings were lacklustre with shabby furniture; there was thickly streaked black paint on the walls and you could see that the carpets were badly stained.

Owen couldn't remember why he had agreed to come here. He turned round and set off to tell Steve he'd had enough. Steve was alone at the bar. He looked just as Owen had feared: shifty and unattractive. For a second Owen was tempted to abandon him and make his own way home but at that moment of indecision, Steve turned in his direction and Owen couldn't do it.

'How about we make tracks?'

'The night is young. What else are we going to do?'

'Sleep.'

Steve threw Owen a disappointed look but when he staggered against him, Owen took hold of Steve firmly and led him towards the exit.

They joined the queue at a taxi rank near Marble Arch. Owen only turned his back for a second to discover that Steve had moved to the front and was deep in conversation with a woman, his hand resting intimately on her hip. He tried to beckon Owen over but the eager faces of the woman's two friends convinced Owen to keep his distance.

'I think I'm in here,' Steve said, returning to speak to him. He had taken out his mobile and was pressing keys.

'Are you sure?' Owen asked him.

Over Steve's shoulder, Owen looked at the woman. She seemed to be about forty; rather mumsy with short blonde hair, tight black trousers and a shiny silver blouse pulled taut across big tits.

'Are you kidding me? She's well up for it.'

'I meant . . . Forget it.' He'd meant was Steve sure he wanted to go through with it. Owen had no doubt the woman would oblige. She flashed flirty glances in their direction and applied lipstick in a little mirror while her friends huddled around her.

'Look, will you do me a favour and . . . hang on,' Steve was holding his phone up to his ear. 'Jules, love. Change of plans. I'm going to stay at Owen's tonight. Yes. We have. A lot. Drowning his sorrows. I know. Yes. I know, love. Look, I'll pass you over.'

Owen shook his head and stepped back but Steve thrust the phone into his hands.

'Hi, Jules.'

'So you're having a boys' night out.' He thought she sounded suspicious.

'Something like that.'

'Well, I don't want you leading Steve astray.'

'As if,' he said and grimaced at Steve who grinned back and gave him the thumbs up sign. 'We're on our way home, actually. We're at the taxi rank right now.'

'Is he very pissed?'

'Not too bad,' he lied. 'We've both had a bit.'

'You sound more sober than he does.'

'There's not much in it.'

'Well, you'd better take care of him. I don't want him getting into any trouble.'

'I think he can take care of himself.'

'I'm trusting *you*,' she said, sounding irritable. Look, he wanted to say, I'm not the one you should be annoyed with. He glared at Steve who was nodding away at him in idiotic encouragement.

'OK. Look, the taxi's here. We've got to go. Bye, Jules. See you soon.'

He ended the call without waiting to hear Julie's goodbye. He clamped the mobile into Steve's hand.

'Thanks, mate.'

'Don't ask me to do that again,' he told Steve but Steve wasn't listening. He was heading straight back to his catch. The last thing Owen saw was his friend's arse as he was manhandled headfirst into the taxi accompanied by boisterous laughter.

Half an hour later, Owen was sinking against a taxi seat, relieved to be on his own and finally on his way home. He half dozed, watching the city speed by. He caught glimpses of the names of streets and Underground stations and tried to place them – unsuccessfully – onto the patchy map of this part of London in his head. It was not until they were coming over the bridge that he recognized where he was.

There was a low glow from a light in the corner of Abbie's front window, which felt welcoming even though he knew it wasn't intended for him. It was darker, though, by the front door and as he stumbled up the step, putting his hand out to stop his fall, his keys scraped loudly across the metal letter box.

'Shush,' he told himself. 'Be quiet.'

He concentrated on feeling across the door frame for the location of the lock. When eventually he found it, fitted in the key and managed to turn it, he let out a short yelp of achievement.

Inside, he hit upon the light switch immediately. The tube above him buzzed, flickered then flared. He stood, slightly dazed in the light. Without thinking, he stepped towards Abbie's door but stopped a foot away. The flat was silent and no light shone out from under the door. He turned quickly away, suddenly feeling ridiculous and hurried up the stairs.

'Nick?'

She fought to stay down, deep in her sleep where she was safe, but she couldn't stop herself rising, rushing towards the surface, which she broke through in a panic. Reaching across the bed, her fingers found nothing but the cold, flat sheet.

The bedroom seemed to echo with the ghost of the sound which had woken her. On the other side of the muslin drapes indistinct shapes huddled and shifted. Abbie shrank down into the bed. There was a series of muffled thuds followed by silence. A shiver passed along the drapes in the second before she understood it was only her neighbour returning home. As if in confirmation, she heard the sound of footsteps above her.

She leant forward to see the digital clock: 3.21.

She pulled Nick's shirt out from under her pillow and pressed it against her chest – hard – as if she might drive it through the skin and muscle, splintering her chest plate, and use it to stuff the hollow that was widening inside her. She bit down on to the material, gagging her mouth against the force of the sound that was welling up; scared that once released she wouldn't be able to control it.

She pushed herself upright, threw the duvet off her, swung her legs round. She pulled aside the drapes, stared at, without really registering, the costumes which hung on the wall opposite. She remained there for a few minutes, the air chilling her bare skin, before getting up and beginning to dress.

In the living room, she picked up her notebook and pen from next to the telephone and sat at the table. She carefully tore out three pages and shuffled them into a neat pile. She held her pen over the top, poised. She was alert now. She knew there was a reason for her having been woken. She waited as Nick's energy padded closer, like a wary wolf.

'Where are you?' she whispered. 'Tell me where I can find you.'

Owen reached the window just in time to see Abbie outside the house. He'd woken her up, he was sure of it, with all the fumbling around with his keys. She stood for a few seconds on the pavement as she had the other night before setting off in the direction of the local shop. She was quickly out of sight. Owen paced to the door then back to the window before grabbing his fleece jacket and running out.

Outside, the night had lifted and the shadowed brilliance of early morning covered everything with a glossy silvered sheen. The vistas ahead were blurred and jumping as he half trotted, half walked but he didn't see Abbie until he reached the crossroads onto Kennington Lane. From behind, you might easily mistake her for a young man. She walked with her shoulders slightly hunched, elbows out, hands in her pockets. He was surprised how rapidly she moved. Whenever he'd seen her, she'd seemed so vague, almost dreamy but now he was struggling to keep up with her pace.

He had not been over this way before and was surprised by the sudden appearance of depots and factory buildings blocking the view to the river. Two lorries rumbled slowly out of a junction and manoeuvred out to the main road. They shielded him from Abbie's sight just as she turned to look behind her. He quickly stopped and leant against the wall of a building, breathing fast, anxious about whether Abbie had seen him. He remained there for a moment to give her the opportunity to get further ahead. It occurred to him that he should stop following her but when he stepped out and looked up the road, she'd vanished. Just like that. He walked on a couple of metres. A tall metal gate to his right side was swaying. He hesitated before pushing the gate. It swung open easily.

He was in an unlit yard full of recycling containers and tall garbage bins. There was a stink of rotten vegetables. To the left was a row of lock-ups; a line of shutters rolled down and padlocked. In the centre of these was a darkly painted door. Drawing closer, he could see that it was red. At head height a sign read PRIVATE.

His heart was beating fast when he tried the handle and it opened. Inside was a narrow corridor. The fluorescent lighting against the white-washed walls blinded him and he stood still for a few seconds letting his eyes adjust. He became convinced that he could hear voices coming from the other side of the door at the far end of the corridor.

He pushed the door open just wide enough to see inside and was surprised to find himself looking at the back of a tall rack of bananas. He stepped into the mess and noise of an enormous warehouse containing a huge fruit and vegetable market. He knew then that he must somehow have come through the rear entrance of one of the market halls of New Covent Garden market. He began to walk around. His breath fogged in front of him but he hardly noticed the cold. He was dazzled by the vivid colours of the produce and the echoing mash of voices magnified by the high open ceiling. He was amazed at the volumes of everything: tens of boxes of tomatoes; crates containing hundreds of cabbages.

He loved markets. They reminded him of his grandmother. Before he was old enough to start school, he'd go with her to the market in Southampton every Wednesday while his sisters stayed with his mum. He liked the way everyone shouted hello and made a fuss of them and how Nan was always laughing as they walked through the market. The red-cheeked faces of the men on the stalls loomed down with friendly smiles, giant hands gently patted his head. He liked watching the stallholders perform – throwing cardboard boxes or bundles of towels between themselves over the heads of the people whose hands waved fivers in the air.

Each stall held promise. He was often presented with small treats – a strawberry, a piece of fudge; once he was allowed to choose from a tray of power balls. He had picked out a clear one which had blue and red specks inside like a miniature galaxy.

This market was something else. It was the biggest he'd ever seen. Owen zipped up his jacket to hide as much of his suit as he could and tagged on to the end of a group. He quickly picked up the system of the business taking place. There was a flurry of fingers and nods, acknowledged by rapid, unintelligible noises from the bearded auctioneer who gave a final emphatic utterance before a man in a blue overall stepped forward. This man's job was to scribble numbers on a label on a stick, thrust his hand forward and push it into the middle of the box before the group moved on down the walkway.

Owen had almost forgotten that he was looking for his neighbour when he spotted her sitting on a high stool at the counter of a refreshment stand on the edge of the hall. She looked small and funereal amongst the riotous colour. Black clothes, dark hair hanging either side of a face as white as the moon. She lifted a mug up to take a drink. It almost covered her face, leaving all the focus on her eyes.

He couldn't think of anything better than joining her for a mug of hot, sweet tea but, as he took a step towards her, he realized Abbie was in a world of her own. He felt strangely insulted as if she had deliberately pushed up a barrier to keep him away.

He turned away quickly, suddenly conscious for the first time of what he was doing, hoping that she hadn't seen or recognized him. He checked his watch – it was getting on for five o'clock. He felt grubby and stale. His hangover was gathering strength like a sickening mould in his body, green and festering. He looked round for any exit signs and located one across the hall. When he took a final last glance at Abbie, he saw that the large, fat ginger-haired man who was serving behind the counter, was talking to her and wondered if it was her dad.

Abbie was relieved to see Owen walk away. It had been a shock to have him turn up like that, even worse to realize, from the eager way he had been looking at her, that he was there because of her, that he had probably followed her from the flat.

She had held the mug of tea that Eric had just poured for her in front of her face to hide the tremor of surprise and fixed her eyes at a point just to the left of him – a blanking technique she'd sometimes found useful for ridding herself of unwanted attention. It worked instantly. Abbie felt a flash of guilt as she watched his friendly expression implode to one of embarrassment.

'Who was 'e then, love?'

'My neighbour. I think he might have followed me here.'

'Is that so?'

'He's harmless,' she said, realizing that perhaps she had been too harsh in her handling of the situation. 'I think he might be lonely. He's divorced. Two kids.'

'He looks decent enough,' Eric said.

'Yes.' Decent, Abbie thought, and ordinary. Very ordinary.

'There's no news, love, I'm afraid. Nothing at all.' Nick had had a few cash-in-hand jobs in the market and Eric always asked around about him and kept the Missing poster up.

'Thanks.' She was grateful that Eric always volunteered the information about Nick so that she never had to gather her strength to find the right time and words as she did with everyone else. Eric's eyes held hers briefly. He had the kind of eyes that looked sad even when he was smiling. His daughter had run away when she was sixteen, so he understood what it was like for Abbie, he knew that you never stopped hoping and waiting. Even after six years. And he was living proof that a happy ending was possible – his daughter had eventually come back, nearly three years later.

She fingered the pile of flyers she'd put out on the counter. 'How many shall I leave this time?'

She didn't look up as she spoke, nervous that she was giving Eric the chance to say, none, there's no point. But, of course, he didn't do that. He knew about the goblin of hope, prodding at your heart and jabbing your stomach with its malicious, taunting fingers.

'The usual, love. There's no harm in that.'

Eric took away her empty mug, wiped down the counter-top with the grubby cloth he kept for the purpose.

'How have you been, love?'

'Up and down.' If there was anyone she could tell the truth to it was Eric. 'Sometimes it just seems harder. Some days I wonder how it will all end.'

'It only needs one day for it all to be different.'

She stayed with Eric for a couple of hours, moving to the far end of the counter out of the way and nursing the second mug of tea he gave to her. There began a constant stream of punters; many of the faces were familiar to her now. Some spoke to say hello, most acknowledged her presence with a nod or a smile. She felt protected by the haze of cigarette smoke that built up and by Eric's attentiveness and was, for the first time in days, able to relax. When there was a lull in business she asked after his daughter.

'Just got engaged to a nice lad,' he told her proudly, which was the best note upon which to take her leave.

Abbie hurried to open her front door and get into her flat. She was relieved there had been no sign of Owen. She opened the curtains in the living room and switched off the lamp. The pale light cast a dull glaze over the room. The mermaid costume looked grey and lifeless, hanging on the rail like a butchered animal. She ran her fingers across the ruffle of sequins, trying to encourage the flicker and shine. Another week's work, or maybe a little less, and it would be finished.

She unhooked the costume and carried the dead weight into the study. She laid it across her chair before returning to fetch her sewing box which she placed on the piano-stool.

She eased the costume aside as she sat down, arranging the bare area she was working on across her knees. She stretched over to turn on the lamp behind her and this gave the room an immediate sense of warmth and intimacy. Concentrate, she told herself. Concentrate. Before she had even counted to three, Nick's voice burst through.

– We need to talk Abbs. I'm out of money. I mean completely and there's this gig coming up. You know, a part. In a few weeks' time. Someone's given me the tip-off that I'm in with a good chance. I might need you to support us by working for the next few weeks, while I concentrate on preparing for the audition.

– My course starts in a fortnight.

– One of us will have to work. He looks apologetic. – And I just don't know how I can possibly fit it in.

I think of the portfolio I've been building, the sketches I've done. I've been filling my notebook with photographs and images cut from magazines. Recently I have been studying the structure of the bridges, how their curves are created out of straight lines. But even as I'm thinking about my designs I know that I am leaving them behind. My dreams will keep. A couple of weeks ago Nick was sacked for taking the afternoon off to attend an audition which he didn't get and ever since he's been looking tired and unhappy. I hold him close. His heart is heaving against his chest, beating against mine as if he's been running. I'll do anything to help him. He is my prince, my love.

The sequins shimmered like heat-haze in front of Abbie's tired eyes. She should have stopped to rest them ages ago, but it was addictive work. She'd settled into a rhythm she was reluctant to break: dabbing the flake-thin metal onto the wet tip of her finger, tasting the metallic tang in her mouth as she slid the needle in, giving the thread a quick twist and tug into place.

She closed her eyes.

He bursts through the door. – Here you are, he accuses when it is him who is late home and you've been here all the time, waiting. You are surrounded by metres of material – a froth-light, cream chiffon whose spirit you're impatient to bring to life. You know the dress will be beautiful.

He slumps onto the chair in front of you. – Had a drink with the gang.

– I guessed as much.

You can't stop your eyes being drawn to the mantelpiece. You've been holding onto this surprise for Nick all evening.

He springs up. – What the fuck?

He stands splay-legged in front of the fireplace and one by one picks up the photographs that you've had framed: his *Spotlight* entry, the one of him as a fairground hand in *Carousel*, the cast of the *Wizard of Oz* when he played the Tin Man and a reproduction of an old photograph of Nick as Sherlock Holmes for the drama club that you found in an old school magazine.

– Are you taking the piss?

You watch him knock the photos off, one by one. All of them. Onto the floor.

– A gypsy, a gamekeeper and a fucking tin man. You think I'm going to sit in here and look at myself got up in a fucking silver foil suit like a giant fucking turkey and be pleased that that is the highlight of my fucking career? He steps onto one of the photographs. There's a crunch of glass.

Your heart is banging inside you. You don't understand his rage. You speak softly to calm him. – But everyone starts somewhere, love, that's how it goes.

– Don't. He leans in and he's so close that you can feel his breath hot on your face. – Don't ever tell me how it goes.

You busy yourself while you wait for him to come home. You

remove the scratched and punctured photographs from their frames and you put them in your memory box, alongside all the notes and cards that Nick has ever written to you, a pressed flower from your wedding bouquet and all the tickets and mementoes that you have gathered. You wedge it under the armchair behind the sewing box so that it can't be seen.

And later, hours later, when he rushes back into the house, grabs you, holds you tight, you feel his body trembling.

– Someone else got the part. I don't understand. The audition went well; I had a real good feeling about it. You did too, Abbs, didn't you? I remember you said it sounded like the best one so far.

You turn away from his clouded eyes and promise yourself that you will never, ever again say anything to feed his hope and his dreams. You will temper your own enthusiasm when Nick is energized by feverish optimism which leaves him wanting to make love time and time again, or eager to walk for miles and miles around London. You will remind yourself when he's talking non-stop and in great detail about future plans – a road trip through America, a summer spent visiting the haunts of Luc Besson – of what happens when the inevitable rejection arrives.

– Jesus, Abbie, you don't know how hard this is. I've let you down. I'm always letting you down.

– You know that's not true. That can never be true.

When he turns to you in bed and makes love to you, it is as if he is trying to forget everything. He falls asleep, suddenly, his body slackening to a dead weight and that's when you talk to him, whispering softly while he's asleep. You tell him how you love him, admire him and that he will never let you down.

You whisper these words and many, many more so that they will enter his dreams, travel to his heart and later, when he needs to, he will remember them and believe.

After Owen had spoken to the kids, Fliss came on the phone.

'Can I ring you later?' she asked. She lowered her voice. 'When the kids are asleep, about nine or so?'

'Of course. Why? Is there a problem?'

'No, nothing like that. I just want to talk.'

After he'd put the phone down, he couldn't help worrying about why Fliss wanted to talk. Her request threatened to invade his whole evening. Everything he did – boiling up pasta, ironing his work shirt – became an exercise in wasting time until nine o'clock.

After he'd eaten, he lay on the settee, with his feet up on the arm, and watched TV. He got up to pee but found himself standing in the doorway to Izzy's room. At the house, he'd been in the habit of visiting the children's bedrooms at some point during the evening when they were asleep. He rarely went in. He simply opened their doors in turn, glanced at their sleeping forms and took in the hushed, obscured surroundings before pulling the doors quietly closed.

As he turned to leave, a triangular shape, which seemed to

be hovering in mid-air by Izzy's bed, shone out. He stepped forward, his eyes attempting to discern the source of the light but it wasn't until he was up close to the bedside table that it became clear that it was a light-reflective strip on the crown of the baseball cap on Izzy's teddy bear.

He held the bear for a minute before replacing it in the same spot as carefully as he could. Izzy was particularly alert to any movements of her possessions.

After another half an hour back on the settee, Owen abandoned the pretence that he was relaxing. He opened the curtains and stood by the window. As he looked out at the darkening view, it seemed as if the whole city was covered in hundreds of thousands of light-reflective shapes.

He needed to get out. He needed a pint. He remembered seeing a pub just down the road; it would be good to get on first name terms with his local.

From the outside, the Greyhound didn't look very inviting. There was a half-barrel by the door containing a sad-looking, sparsely leaved bush with a clump of grass and other straggly weeds growing at its base and a weather-beaten bench table chained to the drainpipe. The paintwork was dirty and the bunched lace curtains at the windows obscured the interior as Owen tried to see what sort of clientele were inside.

Warily, Owen pushed open the door and after hesitating about whether to go into the lounge or the bar, he chose the bar. Inside was much better than he'd anticipated. The old-fashioned dark furniture and flock wallpaper were a bit shabby but otherwise clean. The barman greeted him in a friendly manner but didn't attempt to strike up a conversation which Owen was half relieved, half disappointed about. There were a couple of old men in one corner but otherwise Owen had the pick of the tables. He sat on one near the window and although he felt a little out of place, it was good to be out.

A swirling cold draught preceded the entry of a tiny, elderly woman. She struggled out of her coat and, even though she was wearing high heels, she had to stretch on her tiptoes to hang it on the coat-stand, which Owen hadn't noticed behind the door. She was quite elegantly dressed in a neat plaid skirt and a long string of pearls over a beige jumper. Her hair was pinned up at the back in some kind of elaborate plait and then brushed upwards on the top of her head, presumably to give her the illusion of height. It was like a net of finely spun glass dusted with tiny beads of moisture from the damp air.

As she passed Owen she fixed him with a keen eye, and he was reminded of his Aunty Bea who had reached the stage in life where her face had thickened and slackened to resemble that of a man in drag. He always found it vaguely disturbing how proud his aunt was of her lost beauty, almost as if the person in the photographs that she freely passed around were of someone else entirely. Fliss had hated looking at them. She always said the thought of what might lie ahead horrified her.

With some difficulty, the woman hoisted herself onto the tall bar stool, her heels clattering against the metal strut. The barman produced her drink swiftly and they exchanged some words which Owen tried and failed to catch. When he went to the bar for a second pint, the woman shifted on the stool to face him.

'Drinking alone?' Her voice was so surprisingly deep that

he couldn't help checking out her neck for an Adam's apple. Instead, he saw the pleated, drooping skin of an old woman. 'Escaping the wife?'

The question took him by surprise. 'No, I'm, well, I'm separated. I live on my own.'

'Quiet too loud for you, duck?' She winked at him and sipped her drink. The ghostly imprint of red lipstick kisses lapped the rim of her glass.

'Something like that.'

'I've been a widow for fifteen years and I still can't get used to it.'

'No . . . It's not easy.'

'Sylvia, by the way.' She extended her hand.

For a moment Owen felt as if the only proper thing to do was to bow over her hand and kiss it but instead he shook it; her small fingers rested lightly in his palm like a child's.

'Now,' Sylvia said. Her firm tone and the brisk way she lit her cigarette suggested that she was about to get down to business. 'Guess how old I am.'

He supposed she must be in her late sixties, perhaps just tipping seventy but it was difficult to tell; she looked like a heavy smoker and they age faster. Her mouth crinkled badly as she inhaled. He didn't want to go upsetting her. He gave her face another quick glance; her make-up was applied thickly, her eyebrows were unevenly pencilled on and her red lipstick was too bright. Her hair which had appeared white from a distance was actually an insipid yellow with a darker streak of what could be a nicotine stain over the right temple. Suddenly she looked at him in an appealing manner, her head tilted up, as she might have done once to a lover. Her eyelashes were fake, too, he saw now. There was a dab of glue at the corner of one eye, like a tear hardened there.

'Fifty-eight,' he offered, knocking several years off what he really thought.

She laughed at him. 'Come on, ducky. A proper guess.'

'Sixty-four.' He wished she'd put him out of his misery.

'Eighty-three,' she said. 'I'm eighty-three years old.'

He found it hard to believe and said so, which delighted her as they both knew it would. She giggled like a girl.

'Divorced then, are you, love?'

'Well, yes, um, I guess I am.' Owen didn't bother to explain, that he was only separated. After all, what difference did it make? He felt a creeping tiredness come over him. He leant on the counter; a beer mat slipped under his elbow.

'Kids?'

'A girl and a boy.'

'Shame. For them.'

It took an effort to swallow a mouthful of his pint. He pushed the glass away from him.

'Pay no mind to me. I'm just a stupid old woman.' She gave him a sly, measured look. 'Aren't you going to finish your drink?'

'Actually, I need to get off. I'm expecting a phone call.'

'Oh, well,' she said. 'Don't let me keep you.'

He shrugged and mumbled his goodbyes. When he reached the door he looked back and because he thought he might have been rude, he waved. Sylvia waved back, her small hand regally curving in the air.

It was raining. The wind blew it straight into his face. He was momentarily disorientated about which way to go. He felt more stupefied and unsteady than he should for a pint and a half. He stopped after a few steps and turned his heated face up to let the cool rain fall on it for a few moments. Then he walked quickly, with his head down, and almost went straight past his flat.

At about ten to nine, the phone rang.

'Fliss. This is a surprise!'

'I said I'd phone. You said—'

'Sorry. I was joking around.' Now he felt completely stupid and mean for having teased her. 'You wanted to talk?'

'I did say that, didn't I?' There was a nervous undertone to her laughter. 'Maybe it's not such a good idea.'

He found that he was hunched over the phone, his shoulders tense. He tried rolling them to relax and leant back on the settee. 'What isn't? Is something wrong?'

'No. Not really. Not at all, I mean. We don't get a chance to talk properly on the phone when you ring the kids, that's all, and I wondered how things really are. I mean, you always sound fine, but you must get lonely. You must miss Izzy and Tom.'

He was surprised that Fliss had asked. 'I do miss them – very much. But I'm not sure I could tell you how I really am. I'm not sure I know myself,' he told her in an effort to be as sincere as possible. 'Everything feels so different, Fliss, I'm just trying to get used to it all.'

'I was thinking that nothing much has changed. Except—'

'Except?'

'Well, except that you're not here but everything else is the same. Same routines, same house. Well, just the same, really.'

She sounded disappointed. In fact, she sounded amazed *and* disappointed. What had she expected, he wondered, when he left? What had she hoped for? Or dreamt of for the reality to already be falling short less than three weeks later. She had kept those thoughts so private – from him at least – that he didn't know what he could say to make her feel better.

'It's early days,' he said eventually and his words seemed to drop like stones into nothing.

Everything has changed since our first kiss. When we walk along, it's as if two sticks are being rubbed together; any second we're going to catch fire and burst into white-hot flames.

Air from the open window drifts down my bare legs but it is warm and gives no relief from the stifling evening. Sweat prickles at the backs of my knees and at the base of my throat. Becca comes to find me. She wants to talk. She sits on the end of my bed and tells me the latest about Si, who has been behaving like a pig since he dumped her a couple of weeks ago. She shows me a picture she's cut from a magazine of a new hairstyle she's considering.

– I want to look good, she says. – So that Si will regret what he's done. What do you think?

The model pouts from beneath a heavy fringe. She is sexy in a brooding way that Becca, with her pretty, sweet face, could never be.

– Why do you care what he thinks? You said you were bored with him, anyway.

– That's not the point.

She falls quiet then and my thoughts escape happily back to Nick. I wonder what he is doing and the idea that he might be thinking about me, right at this very moment, shoots hot blood through the length of me.

Something strikes my head and falls onto the bed beside me. It's Becca's slipper. I touch the towelling material, warm from her foot, before I look at her.

– Why are you so shut off?

– What do you mean?

– It's like you're thinking all this stuff and you don't talk to me any more, you don't share it. I am surprised to see how upset she is. Her lips quiver as she talks. For the briefest moment the desire to hug her close to me is huge but for some reason I resist and it passes.

– There's nothing to share.

– He wants you all to himself and you're letting him do it. You're letting him take you away from me.

– That's stupid.

I have to hide the smile which presses my mouth. I am no longer the baby of the house, the younger sister who is quiet and shy and who people like to tease. Nick has made me special. And strong. You're no longer in her shadow, he tells me, and it's true.

– What will you do if he finishes with you?

– He won't.

– Don't be so sure. Boys promise a lot of things but they're usually thinking something else.

– Not Nick. He means what he says. The spiteful twist of her mouth provokes me to spill my secret. – We're going to get engaged.

Becca laughs loudly. – Don't be daft. You're not even thirteen.

The next day, when I confess my slip to Nick, his scorn is comforting.

– Don't worry, Abbs, not everyone is capable of great love. Not everyone understands passion.

We're in his bedroom where we come every day after I've finished school. Nick's parents both work so we have the house to ourselves for a few hours as his sister is away at university. I love this chance of being alone without fear of being disturbed. I wait impatiently for Nick. I've removed my cardigan, shoes and the white school socks I wear pushed down to my ankles; I pull my blouse free from my skirt. I want to rush ahead to that moment of lying down together, to what I've been thinking about all day but Nick likes to take his time.

The first thing Nick always does once he's placed his keys, his cigarettes and wallet on the bedside table is kneel on the bed to reach the window. I see the dirty undersides of his trainers – the tread with the blue arrow insert in the centre and the right heel which has worn smooth. The air is cool but we have to leave it open so we won't miss the sound of his mum's car pulling into the drive.

Nick's room is packed with film and theatre memorabilia. Posters of films and plays cover the walls: Tom Cruise, James Dean, Terence Stamp in *Poor Cow*, *On the Waterfront* and his prize possession a framed programme of *Henry V* autographed by Kenneth Branagh. The shelves are full of catalogued videos, CDs and books and Nick spends a few minutes choosing which film to put on while we're here. It's important to catch the right mood, he tells me, but I often forget there's anything running. It's only when Nick hushes me in the middle of our conversation that I remember. He turns the volume up and we wait for the piece of dialogue he admires. He says, neat, or clever, when it's finished. Sometimes he'll ask me what I think and if I say I don't know, he pushes me to discuss it so that I'll understand. Even then, I might not get it, but there are times when I pretend I have otherwise he'll get up and waste our precious time by searching for a passage in a book or selecting another film which he fast forwards until he finds the clip he wants to show me.

Face to face, my skin prickles with the heat of his hand under my top. He strokes his thumb back and forwards against my nipple until I want to put my hand down and make myself come; I'm so close but I'm scared to let him see me. We've talked about sex. We are going to do it on my thirteenth birthday, which is soon but seems like ages away. I'm ready to do it with him now, but Nick says there's something about waiting which makes it extra special.

He pushes my hand against his crotch where I feel the swelling of his penis.

– Rub it, he tells me and I do. I smile when he groans out, – Fucking hell.

For Nick everything must be brilliant or fantastic or gross or the worst. Nice is for nobodies he always says. Nice is for people who don't have the soul to feel with. But I like the word nice, it hums like the heat of our bodies; it's sweet like our kisses.

Nick's hand grips my shoulder, his other my wrist, as he shudders with the fever of our passion and becomes pillow soft as he relaxes.

*

Abbie's fingers worked fast. She twisted her head to meet Nick's eyes. 'Prince, my prince,' she cried out as the deep pulses of her orgasm arched her back and released her to a long, gliding plummet to consciousness.

When she opened her eyes to Nick's photograph she felt his presence ebbing quickly, too quickly. She tried to hold it back, began again to work at herself until the desolation of his absence swamped her and she turned her back and curled up on her side.

Some time later, she heard Owen moving around upstairs, getting ready for work. She hadn't seen him for a few days now; not since the morning he'd appeared in the Buyers' Walk. She hadn't seen anyone. She pulled out Nick's T-shirt from under the pillow and laid her face on it. It was warm and soft as skin.

'You're working late.'

Owen turned his chair quickly. He hadn't heard the woman approaching. He glanced around the office and was surprised to find that everyone else had left for the day and that it was already dark outside.

For the last couple of hours, he'd been completely absorbed in his work. For almost a week now, he'd been fixated by a problem with his program and after hours of performing what he thought of as a meticulous finger-tip search of the lines of code, he believed he was finally nearing the possibility of an answer. He felt as if he'd come upon the end of a line where he knew, by the promising weight and tugging twitch, the solution was attached to the other, as yet invisible, end. His brain buzzing, it was a delicate balance between allowing himself to be pulled towards it and at times teasing it in. He had to be watchful of maintaining the right tension so that the line didn't break and the solution tumble away into darkness.

He'd seen the woman around the building a lot but Owen

couldn't for the life of him remember her name. He swivelled his chair as she walked round to the front of his desk. Considering it was the end of the day, she looked incredibly fresh and smart in her white shirt and short black skirt. Her dark hair was also very neat; cut short with a straight fringe and sharp sides. She stood slightly knocked-kneed, the light catching her tanned legs, making them gleam.

'This your family?' She picked up the photograph. Her long nails clacked against the metal frame. 'Your children are sweet.'

'Yes,' he said. 'But we're separated. My wife and I.'

'I heard.'

He attempted to cover his surprise at being gossip-worthy in the company. He was curious from whom she had heard the news. It seemed unlikely that Steve would be spreading the word and only a couple of other colleagues from his department were aware of his situation. Then he remembered that Fliss was still in touch with some of the women from the time that she'd worked here all those years back and the thought of what might be being said about him amongst her friends started up a mild panic.

He watched as she replaced the photograph onto the desk, leaving it to face towards him so that he was confronted by the chubby faced images of his kids from four years ago. For the first time he noticed that Fliss looked tired and rather miserable.

He braced himself for some hostility but she leant forward and asked, 'Would you like to come for a drink after you've finished here?'

The mix of cigarette-voice and Essex vowels was a curious but attractive combination. 'I don't know. Who's going?'

She put a fingernail in her mouth and smiled. 'Me. And if you come, too, then it'll be me and you.'

She was obviously flirting with him but he didn't know how to take it. He glanced around expecting to discover that he was being set up but the office was still empty. 'Oh, well, then. Great. Thanks,' he said, trying to sound casual.

'How long are you going to be?'

He looked at his screen knowing that it would be impossible to concentrate on his work now but suggested half an hour, anyway. He felt he needed to buy himself some time. He waited until she was out of sight and then accessed the staff listing on the Intranet. He scanned down a couple of departments on the floor where he remembered seeing her and then tried another on the level below his. Her name jumped out at him. Lisa Stuart. Lisa.

He felt sweaty and stale so paid a visit to the Gents where he splashed his face and, at the last minute, washed his armpits with the pink liquid soap dispensed in a glistening worm onto his hand. Back at his desk he realized he'd better ring the kids before he went to the pub. Tom answered.

'How's things, Tom?'

'I've done my homework and Mum said I could watch TV now.'

'OK. Good. And Iz?'

'She's sleeping over at her friend's. Mum said me and her are going to have popcorn and watch a film when she's finished.'

'Finished what?'

'Dunno. Ironing or something.'

'Is she there?'

'She's in the kitchen. Do you want me to call her?'

'No. Don't disturb her.'

'Are you . . . at . . . in the flat?'

'No, I'm still at work.'

'Why?'

'I was trying to solve a problem.'

'Then you're going back to the flat?'

'Yes. Later.'

'Is Uncle Steve there?'

'No.'

'Are you on your own then?'

'Yes. But I'm leaving very soon.' Owen spun round in his chair to see if Lisa was approaching. The guilt of not quite telling his son the truth made him rush. 'Look, Tom, I'd better go. I love you, big man, and tell Izzy I love her, too. Tell her I called, won't you?'

'OK.'

'Speak to you tomorrow. OK?'

'Yeah, bye, Dad.'

He rang off just as Lisa began walking the long length of the office. She must have used the stairs at the opposite end of the building. He watched her unhurried progress, swinging a tiny bag in one hand, her coat hooked over the other arm.

'Finished?'

'Yes.'

He logged out, pushed his papers into a messy pile and shoved them in the top drawer.

Lisa chose the lift instead of the stairs and although Owen stood at what he deemed was an appropriate distance considering the confined space, Lisa moved closer.

'What do you do exactly?'

'Programming,' he said. 'I write computer programs.'

'Oh, a nerd.' She nudged against him with her hip, just as the doors jerked open, startling him.

He had to adjust his pace to Lisa who walked slowly while keeping up rapid, wide-ranging chatter. They went past the pub favoured by people in their company and turned into a side street to one which Owen hadn't been in for many years.

He suffered a momentary crisis of confidence once they were seated at a table when Lisa turned towards him and every single conversation opener was wiped from his mind, but he needn't have worried. Lisa was easy, good company and he was flattered by the way she twisted in her seat to focus on him when she was talking and leant in close when he spoke.

When Lisa returned from a visit to the Ladies, he could have sworn that she had undone a button on her blouse. He could clearly see the black lace and pink silk of her bra edging her inviting cleavage.

He gently accused her of being a gossip and asked how it was that she seemed to know everyone and everything that was going on at work. He was surprised to hear that she belonged to the company social club. Both he and Steve had long been of the opinion that the club was an outlet for misfits and sad losers.

'I've met Felicity,' Lisa said suddenly.

This shocked him. He remembered her picking up the photograph earlier and wondered why she hadn't mentioned it at the time.

'I couldn't think where from earlier,' she explained. 'But then I remembered that she was on Seline's hen night.'

'Fliss used to work here. We started at the company together, straight out of university.'

'No way. When was that?'

'Over ten years ago. More like thirteen years, I suppose.'

'You old man,' she teased, taking the sting out of her comment by momentarily laying her hand on his thigh. 'Why did Fliss leave?'

'She was unhappy. We were in different departments but both on a fast track graduate training programme. It was tough. A group of us used to come here, actually, most evenings. We'd get pissed, moan a lot, talk about quitting. It was only Fliss who really meant it but then she got pregnant anyway. With Izzy, my daughter.' He remembered Fliss's frightened face when she'd shown him the pregnancy test but almost immediately he'd sensed a change in her; a few days afterwards, she resigned. Eight months later Iz was born. Six months after that, they were married.

'Change of subject?' Lisa asked, looking at his face.

'Please,' he replied quickly, appreciating the offer.

'Or perhaps we should go back to my place?'

Like Lisa, her studio flat was all clean lines and colours. The walls were painted a faint blue and a large white leather settee dominated the space. There was a plasma TV, a PC with flat screen, a stacked music system. Everything was silver coloured; even the fridge and washing machine that he could see in the kitchen area. He wondered when it was that Fliss and he had stopped buying themselves all the new things. When had people younger than him started to become better off than he was? He felt crumpled and old in a home which was as immaculate as Lisa's clear, unlined skin.

He followed her across the living room, trying not to stumble. He was more drunk than he'd realized. Lisa gestured for him to sit on the settee and he sank gratefully onto the leather seat, which was surprisingly unyielding and slippery. He sat immobile, watching as Lisa's skirt rode up as she leant forward over a low shelf of CDs.

She disappeared from the room and his attention turned to the ceiling which revolved slowly above him. The ceiling and all the walls were painted the same pale blue. It was like being inside one of those bird's eggs whose fragile cracked shells he used to find lying on the garden path when he was a child. He became aware of a rhythmic chiming noise rising above the sound of the music. Over in the kitchen, Lisa was expertly cutting out lines of coke on a glass chopping board.

'You do want some, don't you?'

'No, thanks.'

She looked so disappointed that he couldn't refuse when she offered a second time and it was worth the smile she gave him. Brilliant white teeth, small and perfect.

She had taken off her shoes and he liked the leisurely way she walked to and from the kitchen area, bringing a bottle of Bacardi and a couple of cans of Pepsi, the board with the lines of coke and finally some glasses and a bowl of ice-cubes. Each time she set them down on the coffee table in front of him, he enjoyed the show of the shiny curve of her breasts as she leant forward.

'Have you got any notes?' she asked him, kneeling on the floor at one end of the table. He stared at her for a moment, uncomprehending.

'To use.' She gestured towards the coke.

He shifted awkwardly to reach into his back pocket for his wallet.

'Why don't you join me down here?'

He passed her a ten-pound note and tried to get comfortable on the floor. He ended up with his back against the settee and his legs stretched out under the table.

'You first,' he said to be polite but also so that he could watch how she did it. He didn't want to mess it up and look like a complete idiot. She snuffed down a line, handed the note to him. He copied her and was surprised to feel nothing in his nose, just a brief bitter taste at the back of his throat.

Lisa bent forward and took another line. She looked up, placed one finger delicately against a nostril and inhaled deeply.

'Go on,' she told him.

He shook his head. 'Maybe later. Thanks.'

Lisa began to crawl towards him. At that moment, he realized that she was definitely going to let him fuck her. She had brought him here to fuck.

'Do you like me?'

'Oh, yes. Very much.'

'I've always fancied you,' she told him. 'When I heard you were single again I thought Felicity doesn't know a good thing when she sees one.'

'Oh, well,' he said, as she gently pressed her fingers against his chest so that he sank back against the sofa. She unzipped his trousers.

'You've got a great cock.' She began licking around the tip and when she covered it in her wet, warm mouth, he closed his eyes and surrendered to the pleasure. 'Show me what else you can do with it.'

She sat astride him and pushed his hand between her legs. She wasn't wearing any knickers and his fingers immediately encountered the smooth pleats and puckers of her hairless pussy. He withdrew his hand quickly. He felt the desire to stop rush forward with an intense clarity but when he opened his eyes and saw her looking down at him, the need seemed to pass straight through and out of him.

'You're a free man,' he caught himself thinking. 'A free man. A free man.' He clamped his hands tight on the cheeks of her tiny arse and helped them lift and drop, over and over, the rhythm gaining pace until he was past the point of stopping.

'Hey,' Lisa said first thing in the morning after a shrill alarm had shocked his heart into palpitations. 'That was good stuff, wasn't it? God,' she said before he could unglue his tongue from the roof of his mouth to respond. 'I've got a meeting this morning. We'd better get a move-on.'

He was sitting on the loo feeling terrible, trying to get his guts under control when Lisa came in. He stared at her in shock but she didn't bat an eyelid. She simply walked past him, got in the shower and immediately began to chat.

Owen felt completely floored and exposed. He remained sitting on the loo until enough steam had built up for him to risk wiping his arse and getting the hell out of there. He dressed quickly and sat numbly in the living room until Lisa was ready to go.

On the Tube, Owen watched Lisa efficiently apply her

make-up, switch on her mobile, squirt some perfume on her wrist, mark her diary at the day's page with its gold ribbon. She did all this while maintaining a near-constant chirpy conversation and directing a series of happy smiles his way. She did seem genuinely happy. She also seemed as comfortable with him as if they had known each other for years. Owen, though, found the journey interminable and with every minute that passed, he felt increasingly uneasy about the fact that she was hardly more than a stranger to him – he didn't even know what job she had in the company. He considered asking but decided against it for fear of insulting her.

'I'm going to Costa's first,' Lisa said as they exited the Underground. 'I'll catch you later.'

'OK, I'll just go in.'

'I don't suppose you can stand out here all day,' she teased.

In the open daylight, he was struck once again by her fresh face. His skin felt taut and the joints in his body ached as if he'd aged twenty years in one night.

'Thanks,' he said.

'For what?'

'For last night,' he replied, embarrassed at her question.

'You're very well mannered.' She seemed to be amused at his discomfort. 'I like that.' She stood on tiptoe and kissed him on the lips. 'Thank *you*.'

Steve arrived at the coffee machine a few minutes after Owen.

'I hate fucking mornings,' Steve said, viciously stabbing out the code on the coffee machine. He glanced at Owen. 'Hey mate, you looked wrecked. No sleep?'

'Not a lot.'

Lisa came into reception, blew Owen a kiss before continuing up the stairs.

Steve's head swivelled. 'I didn't know you knew Lisa.'

'I don't, really.'

'She's hot.'

'Yeah.'

'She's fucking hot.'

Owen felt his nerve going. What had he been thinking? Steve knew Lisa. Lisa knew Fliss. Lisa knew people who knew Fliss.

'Mate, you stink of booze. What did you get up to last night? Did you go out?'

'Yeah.'

'Why didn't you call me? I could have done with a beer. The missus was in a right one last night.'

'It was a last minute thing.'

'You could still have phoned, you fucker. Who did you go with?'

'Listen . . . look . . . I went out with Lisa.'

'Huh?'

Owen watched Steve's face physically attempt to absorb the brief summary Owen provided about the night – his face reddened, his mouth hung open; his eyes screwed up as if the idea was too much to bear. It would have been funny if only Owen hadn't come to the conclusion that last night had been a really bad mistake.

'Fucking hell . . . Fucking piece of . . . Fucking hell.'

'Jesus. Keep your voice down.'

'Did you?' Steve hissed. 'Oh for fuck's sake of course you did. She's fucking game on that one. Fuck's sake, mate.' Steve slopped coffee down his trousers and on to the floor. 'I don't fucking believe it. I tell you what. I fucking hate my life. I fucking hate it.'

'Look, it wasn't all that—'

'You had booze, coke and fucked a hot chick. I argued with the wife and wanked in front of the TV while she went to bed at nine to sulk. Where's the comparison?'

Wincing at Steve's graphic description, Owen rubbed at his throbbing temple; it wouldn't surprise him if he had an aneurysm in his brain. 'It was all kind of unexpected. I don't know what I was doing. I feel a bit, you know, uncomfortable about it right now.'

'Uncomfortable? Jesus. Are you crazy? If you think about what you've just said for a second, you'll see how wrong you are.'

'I mean, I'm not sure I was ready. I'm a father for fuck's sake.' He felt his hackles rising. 'And me and Fliss go back for ever. I still feel sort of married. Or responsible. Or something. I don't know. You must understand a bit how I feel. I can't believe that when you do that kind of thing, like the other night, you don't feel bad about Julie.'

'What kind of thing? What other night?'

Owen put out his hand to quieten Steve. A short, rather plump woman was crossing the foyer, a plastic coffee holder dangling from one finger. Steve spun round and barked out: 'It's out of order, love.'

'But—' She looked pointedly, in turn at the drink cups they were each holding and continued to approach but veered off sharply as Steve stared her down.

He turned back to Owen. 'Where were we?'

'We were talking about the woman from the taxi rank that you pulled.'

'I didn't pull her.'

'Well, she pulled you then. Whatever. What I'm talking about is afterwards. How you felt. Guilty, for instance?'

He shrugged.

'Well?' He couldn't let it go, even though Steve was looking incredibly uncomfortable and shifty. He didn't see why his private life should be the only one under scrutiny.

'I didn't feel anything because I didn't do anything, all right.'

'What?'

'I got out of the taxi five minutes down the road.' Steve shot Owen a look which was half defiant, half dismal. 'I couldn't go ahead with it.'

Owen took a moment to digest Steve's revelation. He really wanted to ask what had changed his mind but Steve appeared to have retreated from any further conversation. He was slouched against the coffee machine pressing the drink codes randomly, avoiding eye contact. Owen felt himself soften towards Steve. 'It's probably a good thing, really,' Owen said quietly.

'I know,' Steve acknowledged. 'Sometimes I think I'm just a complete, fucking idiot or just completely fucked up.'

'Or both,' Owen offered, touching Steve lightly on the arm.

Steve nodded. 'Or both.'

The mermaid costume was complete. Abbie pitied whoever was going to wear it under the hot stage lights; it was stiffer and heavier than she had thought it was going to be. Abbie's arms ached from manhandling it onto a hanger and the weight of the costume caused the clothes rail to bow. The tail was sticking out across the floor so Abbie tucked it under the telephone table out of the way.

She had arranged with Kate for the mermaid outfit to be picked up at around three together with the work she finished the previous week. Afterwards she planned to spend some time at the library checking the Internet and making some more photocopies of Nick's flyer as she was down to the last dozen or so.

Abbie had just finished lunch when the phone rang. The sound of her mother's voice instantly destroyed the calm of her day.

'Darling? How are you?'

'Fine, thanks.'

'So, what have you been doing? Rebecca says you're keeping busy with the theatre work.'

'Yes, I've been really busy this month.'

'I hope you're looking after yourself and not overdoing it.'

'Of course.'

'And you're eating properly?'

'Mum, please—'

'I worry about you.'

'You know there's no need to. Is Dad there?'

'He's out in the garden. Out of my hair for a few minutes, giving me the chance to have a nice chat with you.'

Abbie felt the slow sink of disappointment. Her mother's brittle concern and tactless questions never failed to set her nerves on edge but her father's easy manner was comforting. She lost concentration listening to a run-through of the itinerary for her parents' recent holiday to Ireland. Discovering the mermaid's tail next to her feet, she played gently with the pleasing ruffle of sequins under her toes.

'It sounds great,' she said when she became conscious of a silence. Her mother sighed loudly.

'I wished you'd have come with us, Abigail. I'm sure you'd have loved it. You must promise to come next time.'

'If I'm not so tied up, I'll try,' she lied to keep her mother from going on.

She was struck with a sudden desire for home, for her father, even for the fussy attentions of her mother. It must be nearly two years since she'd made the journey to see them, travelling back the same day, pretending to have something else on because they wouldn't understand that she couldn't stay away from the flat for that long. It was almost six months since their last, difficult visit to her.

'Good, that's settled then.'

In order to change the subject and because Abbie hadn't got any news she told her mum about her new neighbour.

'Another new one. What are they like this time?'

'It's just a man, on his own. Well, he's got two kids but they're only here some weekends. He seems OK but I haven't really spoken to him. He's quiet, though. Much quieter than the last lot.'

'Oh, Abigail. He sounds nice.'

She was suddenly suspicious of her mother's enthusiasm. 'What do you mean?'

'I'm just saying that it sounds promising. That he sounds like a nice young man.'

She put the phone down, slowly. She didn't want to be rude, but she simply couldn't continue the conversation. She felt sick at the thought of her mother rushing out to her father, misinforming him with the report that Abbie's met some nice, young man upstairs and maybe Abigail might . . . and maybe and maybe.

Sometimes it seemed as if it was so easy for everyone to forget about Nick that they expected her to forget about him, too. She found it astonishing how conveniently people ignored the fact that she was married and acted as if Abbie was being difficult when she reminded them. It was as if her marriage vows, their promises to each other counted for nothing.

She knew that most of her family, his family and their friends presumed Nick was dead. A few – not many – believed that he was living somewhere else, by another name. The only other people besides Abbie who still kept faith were Ken, the police liaison officer who came every year in October to give an update on Nick's case, and Eric in the market café. They were the only three people in the whole world who hadn't given up on Nick coming home.

— Abbie, having these photos all over the place, is just plain morbid.

— They're of Nick.

— But he's—

You dare your mother to utter the word 'dead' and though it remains unspoken, it chills the room. Your parents have been here less than two hours but already the morning has been thrown off balance and you feel invaded and tense. You can't imagine how you are going to get through the next couple of days of their visit.

You explain about the mental fugue — the escape route of forgetting that the mind may take when you are under stress. You remind them that Nick is just lost in his head for the moment. You press home the point that as soon as he remembers, as soon as he is well again, he'll come back.

— And besides, it's my home. I can do what I like.

Your mother sighs. — You don't have to be so fierce, Abbie. We worry about you, that's all.

— That's not what I need.

She jumps in immediately. — What *do* you need, darling? Tell me. We only want to help.

She gestures at your father, who is shadowy in the corner of your living room as if he has been greyed out in the background while your mother brims with unfocused energy. You wonder whether you'd get a shock, if you touched her, like static electricity. What you need is someone to share this living hell with but your parents can't do that. No one can understand what you are going through.

— It doesn't matter.

Later, when you have escaped to the kitchen by offering to make yet another round of tea, your father finds a brief moment away from his wife's watchful eye, to hand you money.

— Thanks, Dad.

— I wish there was something else I could do.

You kiss him on the cheek and he takes hold of you, briefly but firmly.

You know that if he could, he would tread softly into your room late at night and sit on the edge of your bed like he used to do when you were a child. He'd ask what fears were keeping you awake and, as you spoke, the fears would fly out of your mouth and scoot around the room. He'd jump up and catch them one by one and hold them tight by the scruff of their necks. He'd wrestle them until he'd trapped them under his invisible cloak and then he'd make them disappear.

Abbie was surprised to see Kate and not a courier at the door. It was rare that Kate could afford the time away from work and it set Abbie's mind racing about the reason behind her personal appearance. She was so intent on trying to see if there was a clue in Kate's demeanour that she forgot, momentarily, to invite her in.

'Would you like a cup of tea?' Abbie could remember when she and Kate had been close enough to make time for chats.

'I wish I could, love, but I promised I'd drive the mermaid straight round on my way to a meeting. They need it today.'

Abbie turned quickly to hide her disappointment.

Kate followed her into the living room. 'It's so good to have someone to rely on. You wouldn't believe how many people miss deadlines and spoil the damn things.' She took the large bag with the gloves and soldiers' trousers and all the other small items that Abbie had packed ready.

Kate returned with another, identical full bag. 'Nothing urgent, this time. Just give me a ring when you're done.' She turned to the mermaid costume on the rail and ran an admiring hand over it. 'Nice job.'

Abbie helped her sling it over one shoulder like a carcass. Kate pulled her long blonde hair free and stood with a hand on her hip to counterbalance the weight of the costume. She looked strong and beautiful. Now, Abbie thought. Now I have to ask. Her palms began to sweat, her mouth felt dry. What was worse than asking? Hearing the answer 'no' even though you've heard it so many times before.

'Any news?' Abbie blurted out and there it was – that flick of the eyes away, the embarrassed pause as they contemplate their feet when they realize that the awkward moment they hoped they'd escaped has now arrived.

'No, sorry, nothing,' Kate said and Abbie was grateful that she did, in the end, meet her gaze. 'I haven't, I mean no one's heard anything. There's no news, Abbie, I'm sorry.'

'It's OK, I didn't imagine ... I know you'd ring me if ever—'

'Of course I would. Immediately. The very second.' She placed her hand on Abbie's arm and squeezed it gently. Her thumbnail was incredibly long, the other fingernails were trimmed short. 'You look tired. How are you doing?'

'The same as ever.'

'You should take care of yourself.'

Abbie nodded. 'Yes, I do, really, you know.'

From the window, Abbie watched Kate walk out to her car. She was a bit flat-footed and her buttocks shuddered as she strode away.

Look after yourself, take care of yourself, how many times has Abbie heard those words? Each time you know that they're saying it because they care and they want to be kind, but they don't realize that it's tearing another chunk off your heart. Take care of yourself they tell you because they know that there isn't anyone else that will. You are on your own.

You know that, too.

Abbie stared out at the front garden. A chocolate bar wrapper drifted across the paving stones and was lifted for a second before being dropped by the wind against the foot of the front wall. Abbie was thirsty but the idea of moving, for the moment, seemed an impossible act.

You go over everything. You can't stop yourself. Everyone does the same. You relive the weeks and days leading up to the day he went missing. You scrutinise the evening before and the two hours of that morning – the last time you saw him. You pick each memory apart, piece by piece. You unstitch every moment until each one is laid out flat in your mind, like the flayed skin of an animal, and you examine both sides of the splayed result minutely for a flaw, a slub, a tear or pull, opening out the curled edges to reveal anything which is hidden there. You look for anything you may have missed and anything you did wrong.

It would be easy to glance up when he passes down the

hall as he's leaving but you don't. You could even wave him off at the front door, but instead you shout 'bye from the kitchen because you're too busy making your breakfast and you're relieved that he's finally going.

Since your alarm went off, he's been holding you up while you've been trying to get ready for work. Everywhere you've needed to go, in the bathroom, in the bedroom, there he's been and you can't afford to run late now that you're thinking about going for the supervisor position. Now that Nick doesn't have any money coming in.

In the bedroom you impatiently watch him trying to match a pair of his socks in the feeble lamplight when the light switch is only an arm stretch away from him. He steps back into you just at the moment you pass behind him and neither of you laugh. Another time you might have grabbed hold of each other, fallen together onto the bed to giggle and mock-fight and let the day take its own direction.

This morning, you hold a hand out in warning so that you can get over to the dressing table and while you're spraying your deodorant, you watch him in the mirror. He looks tired and nervous. He stayed up late learning his lines, practising the piece for the audition and you fell asleep to his soft murmuring from the study next door.

You say, – Break a leg, and hate the way he instantly brightens. Ever since he told you that the part he was auditioning for was a nineteen-year-old, you've wavered over whether to tell him that you don't think he stands a chance.

Perhaps it was the light, perhaps it was a day when he was more tired than usual, but a few days earlier, you caught yourself seeing him as clearly if he were a stranger and you realized that somewhere and at some point he had lost his youthful energy. He looks worn down and although his beautiful eyes still touch your heart, their dullness makes you sad.

This morning, he comes straight out with it. – Hey, kiddo. I look younger, right? I'll easily get away with it, won't I? Everyone always says how much younger I look than I am.

In the brief moment before you have to reply, you decide to take the easy route, to save the hurt and to avoid the rage being brought down upon yourself. You tell yourself that it will be easier for him to hear it from strangers at the audition. You tell yourself that he deserves only to hear good things from you, the things he wants to hear.

Before you leave the bedroom, you say, – I'll be late tonight. I'm meeting Becca, remember? Just for a couple of hours. I'll stop off for a takeaway on the way home, shall I?

– Well, let's wait and see what happens. Let's wait until tonight to see what we feel like doing.

And that's where you went wrong.

If only you had stopped and held him close, you would have imprinted yourself on his body, like an image left on the shroud of his skin. If only you had locked your eyes onto his, you might have burnt your love against his retina like the blinding sun, leaving a smudge, a tiny spot sealed on his sight for him to remember when the hole was blasted through his memory. You would have helped him find his way back home.

It was dark when Owen came out of the station, but he couldn't face going straight back to the flat. It was a crisp, clear evening and so he decided to take a walk to the park and enjoy some real air instead of the stuffy, recycled kind which had been pumping round his office all day. He entered the park through a side entrance which was near the café. The outside tables were surprisingly busy. Tall patio heaters hissed out warming blue flames. He carried on past, in the direction of the sports courts.

He walked alongside the tennis courts. He sometimes watched Wimbledon on TV but he'd always felt that tennis was the kind of sport where it was impossible to appear any better than you were and, unless you were good, it was boring to watch. He bypassed the empty basketball court and headed to the five-a-side football area where he could see there was a game going on. There was a group of spectators on the front benches of a short section of tiered seating. He sat at the back and picked the side which was wearing blue to support. The players were teenagers and the game was quick paced and occasionally flared up with the boys shoving and posturing at each other. He watched until the end of the match; neither team had managed to score.

When he stood up, he changed his mind about doing another loop round the park. He felt chilled and the pad of his left foot felt tender from walking in his hard-soled work shoes. He'd go home instead, dig out his sports stuff and come out for a run.

His enthusiasm for activity disappeared the moment he shut his front door. He changed, made a cup of tea and then settled on the settee to ring the kids. As his call went to the answerphone, he remembered that it was Izzy's dance class after school. Fliss used to take her while Owen stayed home with Tom but these days, Tom would have had to go along with them. He checked his watch. They probably wouldn't be back for another quarter of an hour so he left a message asking them to call when they were home.

No sooner had he put the phone down, when his mobile rang. It said 'Steve house.'

'Hi, mate.'

'It's Julie. So I take it he's not with you?'

'No.' Owen hesitated before asking, 'Did he tell you he was coming over?'

'Not really. He left a very confusing message on my phone and I can't get hold of him.'

'I expect he's at work. In a late meeting or something.'

'I don't usually try to track him down,' Julie said. 'But he sounded strange, as if he was upset. Have you noticed that he's been acting weird lately? Or am I imagining it?'

'He does seem a bit wound up,' Owen conceded, hoping

that his comment didn't get passed on to Steve. He could imagine Julie telling Steve later: 'Owen agreed with me.' 'Maybe it's work,' he suggested. 'I think they're pushing deadlines hard at the moment.'

'I'm sure you're right,' she said.

'Anyway, I'm glad you called. I was wondering if you've spoken to Fliss lately?'

'Yes. Why?'

'I wondered how she is. You know Fliss, she keeps a lot to herself and I thought you might have a better idea.'

There was a short silence. 'I feel uncomfortable about this, Owen. Whatever Fliss says is in confidence, really.'

'I wasn't asking for you to reveal anything private; just give me a general idea about whether she's coping OK.'

'I'm sorry. I don't want to be put in the position of having to take sides.'

'I don't think there are any sides to take, are there?' He felt confused and rather offended. 'And didn't you just ask for my opinion on Steve?'

'That's different. We're not divorcing.'

Not yet, he said in his head. She was one irritating, obstinate woman. 'For God's sake, Jules. I get that your loyalty lies with Fliss but I'm concerned about her, that's all.'

'Well, you've no need to be, she's getting on perfectly fine without you.'

'Good,' he said but thought, fuck you. 'Well, Julie, it's been a pleasure but I'd better let you go as I believe you have a husband to find.'

She deserved that, he told himself as he cut her off and threw the phone onto the settee. All the same, five minutes later, once he'd cooled down, he regretted allowing himself to have been so hostile. No doubt he'd hear something about it when he went to pick the kids up for the weekend.

Abbie lay flat on her back, settling her arms tight at her sides in another attempt to fall asleep. Like the princess with the pea, her skin felt sensitized and alert to the tiniest irritant but if she could remain motionless for a minute or so she knew that she might just trick her body into sleep. After only a few seconds she felt the desire to shift her legs creeping up on her, then an itch on her arm started.

The first signs of daylight were beginning to filter into the bedroom. Through the fine muslin drapes the shapes of the dresses on the wall were just becoming visible. She knew it would be better to simply bring the day forward a few hours and take a nap later in the afternoon but as each wakeful hour had passed her willpower had become increasingly baggy, pulled out of shape by unrestrained thoughts and the drag of lethargy. She repressed the desire to scratch but no sooner had the itch faded than a hair tickling her face became impossible to ignore. She passed a hand over her forehead and moved to lie on her side. Her skin felt irritated. She turned the pillow over, seeking the cooler material as relief. A mattress spring was digging into her rib. Finally, she forced herself to get up.

She went first into the living room where, perhaps from the warming effect of the lamp or maybe her own dazed mood, she experienced a brief affectionate pleasure at the tidiness of the room and the neatly stacked and labelled supplies on the shelves.

The bag containing work that Kate had brought over on Thursday sat unopened on the floor. She hadn't felt like sewing for the last couple of days and had remained uninterested in the contents. Now, as she lifted the bag onto the table, the anticipation of what she would discover inside began to grow. She unzipped the bag and took out the top item. It was a smocked blouse, in a flowery material, reminiscent of some curtains she remembered from her parents' dining room when she was growing up. Underneath were two pinstripe suits. Digging down, she pulled out a small cotton sack which, she read on the inventory, contained material for making cravats. She loosened the drawstring slightly to look inside at the nest of colourful scraps. Leaning forward, she delved further into the bag. The instant her fingers touched the cool gloss of silk, she prayed it was going to be beautiful. Drawing it out, she wasn't disappointed. The dress was a dull silver colour with a detailed embroidery design in gold thread. On closer examination the design appeared to be honeysuckle. It climbed the length of the front of the dress and blossomed extravagantly on the bodice.

Abbie checked the instruction details on the inventory. The seams on the bodice were worn and the eyelet fastenings had become loose; they needed sewing on more securely. She held the dress up to look at the back. As she did so, she caught a glimpse of herself in the mirror above the fireplace.

She made it a rule not to play around with the costumes but before she could stop herself, she was shrugging off her dressing gown and pulling the dress on.

At some point, the bodice had been relined with a rougher, denser material so that the stage lights didn't shine through; the seams had been left raw to allow for easy resizing and netting had been sewn inside the skirt in a crude but reasonably effective way of creating volume. All these cheap additions didn't detract from the fact that the dress was made from exceptionally good quality silk and that the embroidery was faultless. They didn't stop her taking pleasure in the way the bodice hugged her torso and the skirt gave a soft shape to her hips. If it were not for the length of material piling on the floor around her, it could have been made for her. She gathered the skirt in her hands and walked around the living room with a swish and a twirl, enjoying the sound and movement of the fabric. She turned on the radio and a Sugar Babes record burst out mid-track. She began to dance, a fast waltz, kicking her feet out, her head back.

She danced her way up and down the hall and into the bedroom. With a final twirl she tripped over the hem and half fell, half dropped onto the bed. She lay there puffed and glowing.

– Try it on, Nick says. – I'd like to see it on you.

It has been pouring with rain all day. Nick got up late, went back to bed and for the last hour since he woke up, he's been trying to decide what we'll do later. I would be content to spend the evening in. We'd sit together in the study, chat, read, I'd sew for a while, then we'd go to bed to watch a film, cuddle up together with some vodka, slowly sink into drunkenness. It's the kind of closed-in feeling I like. It's the kind of evening which Nick can talk convincingly about enjoying when he isn't actually experiencing it. I tease him about his incapacity to remain still for long; I joke that it's his genes or his body chemistry which always makes him restless.

I tell him that I can't possibly put the dress on. It's an antique, a piece of history.

– I know, he says. – That's what makes it even better.

He pulls me up from the chair and unzips my jeans. He removes my bra, gathers the dress and then drops it over my head. His face is gentle but absorbed as he adjusts the seams to lie correctly. I know from his expression that I look nice in it. He turns me round and zips up the back.

The skirt has settled in a pool at my feet; a shifting, shimmering ice-blue pool which has spilt over my toes.

– How many women have worn this? he wonders aloud. – What stories would it tell?

– Parties, a proposal, one midsummer night of lost love.

He places a kiss on my forehead, on my neck, on my breastbone. – Affairs, unbridled lust for her beauty. He kneels in front of me. – Take your knickers off.

The material shivers as I balance on one foot, then the other. I kick my knickers aside.

– Don't move, just don't move one bit.

He disappears under the skirt and all I can see are the frayed hems of his jeans, a ruff of black hair above his ankle bones, the creased, dirty soles of his feet. All I can feel are his hands, cold at first on my skin and clumsy but soon he's gentle. His fingers play incy wincy spider up my legs and I feel his hot breath on them. He plants kisses on each thigh and curls my pubic hair in his fingers. His hands hold my buttocks, hold me steady while his tongue finds my pussy; he licks and sucks and pushes his nose against me as if he's burrowing up inside me.

– Wider, he says. His distant voice is croaky and full. He repeats the word and pushes against my legs. I set them further apart but he eases them even wider so that the muscles in my thighs are quivering with the effort. He's sucking and sucking and his fingers are still working their magic but I can't hold the position any longer and I lose my balance.

He pushes the dress off him, pulls me to kneel on the floor, bends me forward and throws the skirt of the dress over my head. I am shrouded in dove-grey light. My face is warm, my bum cold, exposed to the air. Nick tries to hold me by the waist to stop me sliding across the carpet but my knees burn as Nick's force pushes me forward. He stops and guides me so that I am sitting backwards in his lap, his chin on my spine. The dress glides across my shoulders, falls onto my hands. Everything slides and shifts and I come harder than I ever have before.

We drop to the floor together and Nick says – Oh baby, that was so . . . oh baby.

We lie in each other's arms and it is Nick who remembers about protecting the dress; he takes off his T-shirt, folds and pads it underneath me with such care that sorrow flashes through me. I touch his face. He grips my hand, kisses the tips of my fingers.

– I don't know what I'd do without you, Abbs.

– It's nothing you'll ever have to worry about, I tell him.
– I'll always be here for you.

He holds me close and rocks me. I touch the damp nape of his neck, stroke his back and rock him, too.

On the way back from the loo, Owen looked in on Izzy. She was fast asleep, lying on her back as usual; the duvet hardly disturbed. There was nothing more peaceful than watching your child sleep, he thought, pulling the door to and walking towards Tom's room. Even if the child slept in a chaotic tumble of duvet, with limbs everywhere, like Tom.

He stepped into the bedroom, not quite believing the evidence of what he was seeing from the doorway. The duvet had been pushed to the end of the bed, exposing the deserted mattress. The monkey must have got up when Owen was in the bathroom.

He expected to find Tom, arms defiantly folded, in front of the TV but Tom wasn't in the living room. Neither was he in the bathroom. Owen's heart was already beginning to thump. A growing panic threatened to push all sensible thoughts out of his head. He returned to Tom's room. He looked in the wardrobe, on the windowsill behind the curtains, tested the locked window and then searched under the bed. As he hoisted himself up off the floor, he placed his hands on the bed for balance. The cool temperature of the sheet sent a strong pulse of alarm through him. He felt across the whole area. Tom hadn't been in the bed for a while.

Owen began to look systematically through the flat in all the possible places and some of the impossible places where it would be hard for a cat to hide never mind an eight-year-old boy.

'Tom!' The word came out sharp, like a bark. He stood in the kitchen with all the cupboard doors open around him. 'This isn't funny,' he called out. Tears sprang into his eyes, his voice wobbled like a child who had been tricked in a game of Hide and Seek.

'Dad?'

He had woken Izzy. 'I can't find Tom.'

Iz helped him look. They went through each room. Nothing.

'I think I'd better ring your mum.' His hand shook as he punched in the number.

'Fliss.'

She knew immediately that something was wrong. A mother's intuition. Fliss was a good mother. And he was a bad father.

'Owen? What is it?'

'I can't find Tom. Iz and I have looked everywhere in the flat and we can't find him.'

As he talked, he continued to work his way through each room, opening and closing doors that he'd opened and closed a dozen times before, peering under, behind, above. Izzy followed closely in his wake. She had begun to cry. He stopped and pulled her against him, leant down and kissed the top of her head.

'He must have gone out. Jesus, Owen, it's fucking *London* out there.'

'He can't have gone out. I would have heard him.' But despite his denials, Owen knew as soon as Fliss had said it that this was what Tom must have done. He walked up to the door and tried the key. It was unlocked.

'Tom?' His call echoed feebly around the stairwell. He heard Fliss gasp in his ear.

'Perhaps he's in the garden,' Izzy said.

'What garden?'

'Down there. He's been talking about getting in it. He told me that there's a secret passage into it.'

'Fliss? Izzy thinks she knows where he is. I'll call you back in a minute as soon as I've got him.'

When Abbie woke up the air in the bedroom felt damp and her bare arms were chilled to ice. The alarm clock said 10.14 but the solid darkness in the bedroom confused her. She considered the clock for a few seconds until the meaning of the tiny letters p.m. next to the number finally imposed itself. It was hard to believe that she'd been asleep for so long.

She became aware of her stomach griping from emptiness and decided to make porridge. It would be warming. She would bring it back to bed and watch one of Nick's old videos. She could keep the silver dress on, she promised herself, running her finger along an embroidered tendril; just for the hell of it.

She was halfway through eating her porridge when the noise of feet running down the stairs filtered under the sound of the TV. When a firm knock on her door came, she lay her spoon down in the bowl and quickly switched the TV to silent. She waited for her neighbour to go away but the knocking resumed, louder and persistent.

She walked slowly, hoping that by the time she got to her

front door, Owen would not be there. She looked through the spyglass just as his face rushed towards her. The spyglass went dark. She jumped as he thumped heavily on the door. She opened it on the third thump.

'It's Tom,' Owen said, sounding breathless. 'My little boy. He's gone missing.'

She didn't know if she spoke. The word missing vibrated in her brain. She felt disorientated by the fluorescent light in the lobby reflecting off the white walls behind Owen.

'What time is it?'

He looked annoyed. 'Nearly quarter to eleven.'

Eleven. Eleven was late for a little boy to be out.

She focused her eyes on Owen. He looked awful. His face was grey and he repeatedly licked his lips. He seemed angry, with her, Abbie realized, and it made her wonder if he'd said something that she'd not heard or if he was waiting for her to reply or do something. She felt sick.

'Can I . . . we thought . . . Izzy said that he was probably hiding in your garden. Can we *please* take a look?' She noticed that he spoke to her as if she was stupid and put an aggressive emphasis on please but she was still unable to respond.

'He's run away.' The girl, Izzy, appeared from behind her father. She was dressed in a large, navy-blue fleece jacket – presumably her father's, over a long, pink nightie with a yellow cat design on the front. She was barefoot in trainers, their pink laces hanging loose.

Abbie remembered that she and Becca had once run away, steamed up with indignation over their punishment for eating all the ice lollies in the freezer. They didn't get far. It was a part of growing up, asserting yourself. *It wasn't the same kind of thing at all.* She wanted to tell Owen that lots of kids do it and that Tom would be back before he knew it but the words stuck in her throat.

'Jesus,' Owen said. 'Look, it won't take a minute.' He moved towards her as if he was going to walk straight in. She put her arm out, barring the doorway.

'I'm sorry but it's impossible. The only access into the back is through the flat. And I think I'd have noticed something.'

Owen glared at her as if he didn't believe that she would. She found herself blushing.

'There's a secret passage at the front between the hedge and the wall. You can see it when you come down the path. He's been talking about it; getting into the garden. Dad didn't know.' Izzy glanced at her father and then at Abbie. Her eyes and lips looked reddened and puffy as if she'd been crying.

Of course, Abbie thought, of course she's been crying. She stood aside to let them in. Once the door was shut, the flat dropped back into darkness. She heard the girl gasp, her father mutter irritably.

'Wait here,' she told them and shuffled along, the dress bunching around her feet, until she located the hall light.

When she turned round, they were right behind her; Izzy first, with Owen's hands on her shoulders guiding her along.

The key wasn't in the back door. Abbie could almost feel Owen's impatience surging forwards and hitting her in the back as she tried to remember where she'd put it. After a moment, she reached up and felt along the top of the door frame until her fingers located it.

She didn't argue when Owen stepped forward, took the key

from her and unlocked the door with a loud clunk. He stepped outside.

The bulb for the outside light had blown ages ago and it took a moment for Abbie's eyes to adjust as she stood in the doorway. The lumps and bumps gradually presented themselves as objects: the carcass of an old kitchen unit, a broken washing machine that the landlord had dumped out there before she and Nick had moved in.

'Tom?' Owen called. 'Tom, are you out here, son?'

'The shed,' Owen said and started picking his way towards it before she could speak. 'You stay there,' he ordered sharply. It wasn't clear if he meant his daughter or Abbie, but they both remained where they were and Abbie felt a warm hand slip into hers.

Owen had some kind of miniature torch which looked like a tiny moon-beam dancing in front of him.

'It's locked,' she called out when she found her voice. 'It's kept locked. Nobody's been near it for years.'

But the door swung open with a creak and she stood there holding her breath when he stepped inside. He emerged alone.

'No,' he said. 'He's not here.'

When the door of the shed opened so easily, Owen had thought the nightmare was over. He'd stared disbelieving into the four dark corners while the feeble light from the LCD torch on his key-ring played illusory, hunched shadows in front of him before he had to accept that what he was seeing was true. The shed was completely empty. There was literally nothing inside.

He felt a surge of anger at Abbie. What kind of person kept a shed absolutely fucking empty? His anger grew as he stumbled on a broken paving slab and something soft squashed under his foot. What kind of person allowed a garden to go to waste like this? In London of all places. What a waste of precious, fucking space.

He glared across the darkness to where Abbie and Izzy were lit up in the doorway. He squinted. He could see Izzy peering out at him, her eyes alert and anxious, but it looked like Abbie was – yes, she had her eyes closed as if she was bloody praying!

He marched over and tugged his daughter's hand roughly away from Abbie. Pulling Iz behind him, he strode across the kitchen and was halfway down the hall when his mobile rang. Fliss.

'He's at Sam's; at his friend Sam's house,' Fliss said, the moment he answered. Her voice was tearful with relief. 'Sam's mum, Tina, has just rung. How the hell he got there I don't know but I'm off to get him now.' Owen heard her huffing as she walked through the rooms, finding her bag, keys, coat. He could picture it.

'He's been found,' Owen announced. He held Izzy's hands as she jumped up and down shouting 'Hooray! Hooray!' and grinning idiotically up at him.

When he remembered Abbie, he was shocked to see that the blood had drained completely from her face; she was white as a ghost.

'Are you OK?'

She sagged against the wall as if she was about to faint.

'I just, I'm sorry, I just ... please ... I just need to ... sit down.'

There was nothing to her; she was almost as light as Izzy. They edged their way down the hall, Abbie propped against his side and Izzy walking backwards ahead of them; about to burst with all the excitement.

Owen helped Abbie onto a settee in a room lit by a single lamp over in the window. It was so crammed full of stuff, it felt claustrophobic. It looked like a living room-cum-some type of dressmaker's. There was a pile of clothes on the table and a long rail of garments of the kind you'd see in a fancy-dress shop. In one corner sat an ancient old black sewing machine. On two of the walls there were shelves containing material, bundles of wool and whole rows of identical, white plastic boxes, clearly labelled on the front in large black letters. Owen read: 'braid – white, black, red', '19c silk/brocade,' before turning to look at Izzy whose eyes were popping out of her head. He asked Izzy to fetch a glass of water.

'Can I get you anything else? Is there some medicine you need?'

He thought of epilepsy and a mild panic started up in his stomach. He didn't have any experience of dealing with situations like this. He was relieved when she responded with a shake of her head. He squatted in front of Abbie so he was at her eye-level and pressed the glass into her hand.

'Are you sure?'

She managed a feeble smile but her voice was firm. The colour was beginning to return to her face and, a little unsteadily, she raised the water to her mouth and took a sip, her teeth hooking the rim of the glass.

'I just felt dizzy. I'll sit here a few minutes and then I'll be fine.'

He stood up.

'We'll be off then.' He lingered for a moment but Abbie didn't look up. 'I think we've had enough excitement for one day, haven't we, Iz?' He said Izzy's name sharply, to stop her touching a white lacy dress that was pinned on the wall. She lowered her hand and looked at him. Owen shook his head in warning.

'Thanks for letting us look in the garden, Abbie,' he said gently and, this time, he was relieved when she turned her head and raised her eyes, albeit briefly, to meet his.

'I'm glad Tom's safe,' she said, before looking quickly away.

The moment they were out of the flat, Izzy burst into questions.

'What's wrong with her, Dad? Is she very ill? Did you see everything she had, like in a shop? And all those clothes? I loved that white dress. I liked the one she had on, too, but the white one was prettier. Where do you think she was going?'

'Don't shout, Iz. "She" has a name which you should use please, and it's not really any of our business what she was doing,' he reminded her although he'd been wondering pretty much the same thing. 'It was very good of her to let us in, especially when she had a touch of flu,' he told her, half believing his story himself.

Upstairs, he put the TV on for Izzy thinking that, like him, she would be too buzzed to go to bed. He was heading into the kitchen when Fliss rang again.

'I can't fetch him, Owen. I wasn't thinking straight when I said I could. I even got in the fucking car and drove down the road before I remembered that I've been drinking. Not loads but too much to drive.'

'Oh, shit.'

'He could stay there, at Sam's. Just for tonight, maybe if Tina—'

'I don't think so, Fliss, I don't think it's a good idea.'

'Of all the nights.' She was crying. 'It's because I went out, it's because I had a laugh, it's because . . . I knew I shouldn't have, I just thought it would be nice to go out and not have to worry about—'

Owen cut her short. 'I'll pick him up. Give me the address and then ring Tina, tell her I'm on my way, explain the delay.'

It was only when he put the phone down that he remembered Iz. He was very reluctant to take her with him. It sounded as if Fliss was in a right state and God knows how Tom was going to be when Owen picked him up. He thought Izzy had had more than enough upset for one evening and wondered if he could ask Abbie to babysit her for a few hours until he got back.

When he went into the living room, the decision to ask Abbie was made easy. Izzy was asleep, curled up on the settee, her thumb in her mouth like she used to do when she was tiny.

As Abbie had watched Owen walk around the garden, she had felt the weight of Nick's desperation suddenly descend on her, squeezing her so hard that she thought she would split wide open. The only thing she could think of to stop the pain was to offer the little boy up. She had offered Tom up to anyone or anything that might have had the power to give Nick back to her in his place.

Abbie wriggled and twisted around until she was wrapped in a tight roll of duvet. She would have enclosed her head, as well, if she could have managed without breathing. She clenched her fists and felt her fingernails biting into the palms of her hand. She felt so ashamed. How could she have wished such a thing on a little boy and that terrible, terrible waiting on his family? Owen and Izzy were *nice* people who didn't deserve to suffer.

No good could come from it, she decided, unless she made a promise, right this second, to make amends.

She was not prepared for the tread of feet, the gentle knock on her door coming so soon to test her resolve. She hesitated for several seconds before dragging herself free from the duvet.

Owen was a better colour than earlier but he seemed agitated, stumbling over his words. 'I'm sorry, I really shouldn't be asking this but I don't know what else to do. I've got to go and fetch Tom. Fliss, my wife, my-um, ex, she can't do it. She thought she could but she can't. Look, I wonder could you possibly sit with Izzy? It would only be for a couple of hours, three maybe. I'd take her with me but I think it would be better if she stays here and I'd much rather she got some sleep.'

Abbie tasted the souring of her best intentions in her mouth.

She couldn't possibly walk out of the door at a moment's notice. It simply wasn't feasible. She visualized the preparations she would need to do: the notes, setting out the vodka, making the bed, plumping the cushions. With every heartbeat another pressure was added until her head was spinning and her blood rushing to keep up.

Anything, she wanted to say, ask me anything but that. 'I'm sorry, no.'

'I'm sorry, I don't know what I was thinking, you're ill and . . . I'm sorry to have—'

'It's not that,' Abbie began to say. 'It was a headache, that's all. It's just—'

She was horrified to see that before he turned away, he had begun to cry.

'Owen?'

He began to climb the stairs, his head erect, his shoulders stiff; his attempt at dignity made her feel even worse.

'Can you bring her down to me?' she called out to him, electrified by a sudden idea, without pausing to think it through.

'I'm more than happy to look after her here if that would be OK.'

'Oh Jesus, thanks. Yes. That would be great.' He beamed down at her.

Minutes later, Izzy and Owen reappeared walking slowly, hand in hand, down the stairs. Izzy was flushed and half asleep. She had her thumb in her mouth like a baby.

'I thought Izzy could have my bed.'

She moved some of the cushions off it and slipped Nick's T-shirt out from under her pillow. It felt warm in her hands.

'I'll just let you get Izzy settled. If you need anything give me a shout.' She hovered in the hall outside the bedroom in case she was needed.

Owen came out after only a few minutes.

'I can't tell you how much I appreciate this,' he whispered, pulling the door to but leaving a big enough gap for him to keep glancing in at his daughter. It seemed to take him several moments before he was able to turn his full attention to Abbie. When he did, she felt suddenly self-conscious under his soft gaze as if she had become the recipient of overspill of love for his daughter.

His demeanour quickly changed as he turned practical. 'I'll ring, once I get there, to let you know what time I'll be back,' he said, as they walked to the front door.

'I'll just go and write my number down.'

He took something out of his back pocket. 'No need, just put it straight in here.' He held out his mobile phone towards her. It was a tiny, sleek, black and silver one which she didn't dare touch.

'You do it,' she told him. In her embarrassment she stumbled over her number and had to repeat it once more to make sure she'd given the correct one.

As soon as Owen had left, Abbie thought of everything she hadn't asked him. What should she do if the girl didn't go back to sleep? Keep her in bed? Let her watch the TV or get up and have a drink? She peeked into the bedroom. Izzy was fast asleep.

She sat gently on the edge of the bed. She leant close and caught Izzy's flower-fresh clean scent. She touched her face, brushed aside a hair that lay on her cheek. Her rose-pink face was warm. A sleeping beauty.

In the car, Owen groaned out loud when he recalled how he'd almost cried in front of Abbie. The only consolation for him nearly making a complete fool of himself was that Abbie had visibly softened and then come up with Plan B.

He'd been worried that Izzy might feel uncomfortable at Abbie's but she had seemed delighted about it when he asked her.

'Can I ask about the dresses?' she immediately wanted to know, even in her sleepy state.

'OK,' he relented. 'But be polite.'

Abbie had waited anxiously at the foot of the stairs for them. She led them down the hall. From behind, her hair was a messy tangle and the zip of her dress was partly undone. She stumbled a couple of times as she dragged and heaved the long dress around her.

'I thought Izzy could have my bed.'

Abbie had opened her bedroom door and that was when Owen had been confronted by the sight of an enormous four-poster bed with curtains draped around it. He hadn't known what to say. He just kept staring. And the more he stared, the stranger it seemed. There were things draped on every piece of furniture: scarves hung down from the wardrobe and the handles of the chest of drawers; necklaces dangled off each corner of the mirror; dresses hung from a wooden rail on the walls.

'I'm sure Iz would be fine in your spare room.'

'We don't have a spare room,' Abbie told him.

'I want to be in here, Dad, please?' Iz looked like she'd discovered heaven.

He couldn't see there was any other choice. 'Well, that's very kind, Abbie. Say thank you, Iz.'

'Thank you, Abbie.'

For some reason, as he was leaving, the word frippery came into his head. He supposed the décor was meant to be romantic but it was more like one of the illustrations in Izzy's old book of fairy tales than something an adult would choose to live with. No wonder Izzy had instantly loved it.

Owen apologized the moment Tina opened the door.

'It's OK,' Tina said. 'Felicity explained your situation. It's tough for the kids, the changes. Tough on everyone. How are you doing?' Her hand briefly touched his arm and with that gesture he knew that Tina was one of the club: the Divorcees' Club.

He didn't know her very well. In fact, he hadn't been absolutely sure he had the right woman in mind until he'd seen her, so he was taken aback by how emotional he felt talking to her.

'Sometimes you wonder if you really are doing the right thing. It seems so – well – destructive.'

Tina regarded him for a moment. 'I'll tell you one thing – no one ever died from a divorce.'

'Dad?'

It was Tom calling him.

'He's in there. I'll leave you to it.'

Tom was sitting on a settee which dwarfed him and Owen's heart went out to his son. He was dressed in a pair of pyjamas – presumably Sam's – and when Owen leant forward to hug him, he was struck by the strong scent of a stranger's washing powder. He pressed his nose against Tom's hair and breathed deeply.

Tom's mood was subdued. He only spoke when urged to, politely thanking Tina for having him and to say goodbye.

The moment they were alone together, though, he asked where they were going in a tone which took Owen by surprise; not quite sullen, but somehow fierce.

'Home.' Fliss, he knew, was desperate to check out Tom in the flesh.

'Like home, with Mum? Or to yours, like the other place?'

'To the house. To see Mum. Not the flat. We want to have a talk with you.'

Tom sank into silence and Owen saw there was no point in forcing conversation; it was better to let Tom mull things over.

Fliss looked dreadful with eyes red and swollen; she'd obviously been crying non-stop. The instant she saw Tom, she burst into tears, which set Tom off snivelling.

Seeing him wrapped in a hug with Fliss, Owen recalled what a terribly clingy toddler he'd been. Fliss had been about to enrol on an OU course in Interior Design when she discovered she was pregnant with Tom and she had struggled to come to terms with having another baby. Owen had often wondered whether his son had picked up on this in some way; Tom was more sensitive than they often gave him credit for, just because he was quieter about it than Izzy.

The last thing anybody wanted to do was to have a 'talk' but Owen knew that it had to be done. They took him to bed and sat either side of him.

Tom was not very forthcoming on the details of his escapade except to confirm that at no point did he get into a stranger's car and to say that he'd remembered the journey home from one of their day trips to London. Owen felt overwhelmed by the resourcefulness of his son and with the relief that he was safe. But now that Tom was safe, he wanted to forget about the whole incident; the picture of his son – anyone's eight-year-old son – on the streets of London at night-time was almost too terrible for his brain to retain.

'The separation – our separation – is for good, Tom,' Owen said, glancing at Fliss who didn't meet his eye. 'There will be a divorce and we will have to deal with it, all of us, me, your mum, Izzy, as well as you. If you're upset or worried about anything then you must please talk to us, either of us. We all have to help each other.'

'I see,' Tom said and gave a sharp nod, like a wise little man.

'It'll work out, sweetheart, you know. In a little while it'll all seem like normal,' Fliss told him and Owen remembered that he'd told her almost exactly the same thing not that long ago.

He rang Abbie who sounded surprisingly alert.

'How's Tom?'

'He's fine. I think we're more upset than he is.'

He was amazed when she suggested that Iz stay with her if he didn't want to drive back that night. He looked at Fliss, who seemed completely at sea, and thought that it wasn't such a bad idea.

'It's getting late,' Abbie said. 'Iz is sound asleep – I've just looked in on her. I'm sure she'll be fine here until the morning.'

'That would be great. I'll just check with, um, see what, um—' He turned to Fliss. 'Abbie's offering to keep Izzy with her, if I, we, want—'

'It makes sense,' Fliss said and, in a lowered tone, added rather dryly, 'I take it this Abbie can be trusted.'

'Absolutely,' he told Fliss, feeling a little defensive on Abbie's behalf. 'She's just checked in on Izzy and she's fast asleep. Are you sure you wouldn't mind?' he asked Abbie. 'It would be great but I'd hate to impose if you've got other things you need to—'

'No, no other things. Nothing that I can't do here, anyway.'

'I'll come over first thing in the morning.' He looked for confirmation to Fliss who gave a sharp nod, exactly like Tom had done earlier. Owen smiled to himself. 'That's settled then. And, Abbie—'

'Yes?'

'Well, just, thanks.'

No sooner had he put the phone down than Fliss went to prepare the bed in the spare room. He anticipated them settling down afterwards with a bottle of wine, finally being able to relax and talk over Tom's 'adventure', and so he felt rather put out when about fifteen minutes later, Fliss put her head round the door and said: 'Your bed is made. I'm off. I'm exhausted.'

The guest room was depressing. They had decorated it several years ago in a bland colour and with furnishings that neither of them really liked but which they'd considered inoffensive. Although it was tidy it had a rather neglected air about it. He opened one of the wardrobe doors and was shocked to discover some of his personal things – books, a squash racket, some old winter clothes – heaped haphazardly inside. He couldn't help feeling a little affronted about the unceremonious way Fliss had shoved them in there.

The bed-settee was hideously uncomfortable, the stuffing in the mattress so thin that the springs felt as if they were drilling their way through his flesh. He felt a retrospective guilt about any visitors upon whom they'd ever inflicted this discomfort and a huge regret that he'd chosen to stay the night. He thought affectionately of his own bed, back in the flat. The way it rocked when a freight train was passing; the exaggerated silence once the train had gone by. He had even grown to appreciate the bold turquoise curtains he'd inherited and which gave the room a Mediterranean wash in the early morning light.

The longer he lay awake, the more he missed the flat and the more irritable he grew. He turned and turned again, endeavouring to hollow out a more comfortable position to lie in. His mind was completely alert now and awash with bitterness. He'd put himself out for Fliss because he felt sorry for her and thought she'd need some reassurance but now she was sleeping comfortably, peacefully, in the king-size bed.

He saw, too, that staying overnight would only serve to complicate things for Tom in the morning. How would they explain the presence of his father stuck away in the spare room as if he were a guest even though he was family? Owen vowed never – *never* – to stay in the house again.

Owen checked his watch. It was five o'clock. He fell asleep shortly afterwards, feeling that some kind of decision had been reached, that he'd regained a degree of control. He would draw a clearer line from now on, stick to those boundaries and not let himself drift out of line.

He woke to hear Tom giggling with Fliss in the bedroom and instantly felt swamped with feelings of isolation and jealousy but he stayed put and was glad when Tom put his head round the door.

'Mum says are you coming down for breakfast? She'll make you eggs. Are you coming down?'

'You bet I am,' he said in the fake hearty voice which he hated but which was all he could manage.

Abbie was woken up by Owen phoning and although she lied when he asked her, she heard from his apologetic tone that he hadn't been fooled.

'Is Iz awake, too?'

She cleared her throat. 'I'll check.'

Izzy was sitting up in bed. Her eyes were watchful and she didn't speak into the phone until Abbie had almost left the room.

Abbie had not slept very well on the settee – although she'd fallen asleep almost immediately, she kept waking up throughout the night. She had never had a child visiting before and she was conscious of the girl's presence all the time; as if Izzy's breath was a constant susurration in her ears and the atmosphere pulsed gently with each of her heartbeats. In the slow stretch of the night, Abbie had visited the child several times, mindful that she might feel afraid if she woke in a strange place, but each time Izzy was sleeping soundly and Abbie had left the bedroom with a feeling of peace. Now that she knew Izzy was awake, she was feeling increasingly tense about having a guest in the flat.

She didn't hear Izzy enter into the kitchen; it was her placing the phone on the work-surface which made Abbie turn round.

'Hello.'

'Hello.' Izzy, with one foot on top of the other, wobbled, slid forward, then stood up straight. 'Where's your dress?'

Abbie couldn't think what she meant; she looked down at the T-shirt and pyjama bottoms she was wearing. There were several greasy stains on one leg and she rubbed at them self-consciously.

'The silver dress.'

'Oh, it's not mine; I was only trying it on because I was . . . I was repairing it.'

Izzy's face dropped so Abbie took her into the living room where she'd hung the dress back with the other costumes on the rail.

'Can I touch it?'

Abbie hesitated but what harm could it do when she herself had spent several hours in it? 'OK.'

'I thought it might have been part of a dream. It's lovely.' Izzy fingered the material tentatively. 'The skirt sticks out.'

Abbie showed Izzy the netting used for the underskirt and pointed out the repairs that needed to be done. She noticed that the bottom was looking grubby, which she would have to attend to later.

'And it's really not yours?'

'No. It's a costume. They get hired out for actresses.'

'Like on TV?'

'Yes, and the theatre, too.'

'Like a panto? I've been to a panto.'

'Well, um, yes. And other plays, too.'

Abbie took down some of the storage boxes of beads, buttons and sequins and hoped that looking through them would keep Izzy occupied long enough for her to make the 'milky coffee' which Izzy had said she'd like.

Abbie put sugar in the wrong mug, dropped the spoon and hovered over the kettle for a while before she realized that she hadn't switched it on. She felt the morning unravelling out of her control and, as the panic rose, she knew that she needed to go into the bedroom to start the day back on track.

She sat on the bed and picked up Nick's photo from the bedside table and ran her finger gently across his face. 'Good morning, my love.'

I sneak out to meet him at night. I drop from my bedroom window onto the flat roof of the front porch. I do it night after night. Week after week. We walk the streets and sit in a bus-shelter whose fly-posted sides provide cover. We stay there for hours, talking and kissing. I am hardly sleeping but I don't feel tired in the day. I feel electrified and capable of anything as if I'm plugged into a special energy source. I grit my teeth in irritation at how slowly everyone around me seems to move and talk. I'm amazed that people don't notice that I'm different.

The old cow from across the road comes round and tells my parents what I've been doing. We're in the middle of one of our family meals at the big table in the kitchen and Dad swears when Mum gets up to answer the back door. For some reason, she steps outside and then shortly afterwards she calls Dad out to join her.

– Get on with your meal, you two, she says before pulling the door closed.

Becca and I are desperately curious about what's going on, deciding, when our parents fail to return after several minutes, that they have been abducted by aliens. I don't for a moment think it has anything to do with me and it still doesn't click when they come back in wearing strange expressions and bringing with them an expectant, serious atmosphere which makes me nervous. Even when I hear them speaking, even with the noise of raised voices and the hundred questions being fired at me, it takes a while for it to sink in that I've been caught. When I see Becca's shocked face, there's a clear space in my head which is happy that I've done something which Becca would never dream of doing in her life.

– You can't go out at night on your own, Abbie. It's dangerous, Mum tells me.

– I'm not alone. I'm with Nick. He looks after me.

– For God's sake, Abbie. The fact that he encourages you to do this tells me that this boy hasn't got an ounce of sense.

I react to this comment of Dad's with what I aim to be a scornful look and I'm surprised to see how angry he is. I expect it from Mum, but Dad's anger is rare and frightening. I no longer feel so confident.

– What about this boy, Nick? Is he at the same school? Mum asks.

– He's at college, Becca tells them.

– How old is he? Mum asks immediately.

– The same age as me, Becca says, quickly, before I can even open my mouth. I stare at her. For some reason, she's acting like she's on our parents' side.

– He's too old for you, Abbie, Mum tells me.

– Why?

– You should have friends your own age.

– He's not my friend. He's my *boy*friend, I shout. – And you can't stop me seeing him.

– Yes we can, Dad says. Now I feel the force of his fury. Behind his glasses, his eyes are stone-hard. He is white-lipped. – You are grounded every evening and weekends for three months.

– But—

– No arguments, Dad says.

I glare at him but I'm thinking of Nick and the hour after I finish school which we spend together. Dad can't take that away from me. Our precious time. It sustains me more than sleep, more than food. I never would have believed sex would be like that; that when he fits inside me, he becomes part of me.

– What are you smiling at, young lady?

– Nothing.

As if he has pulled out my heart and stamped on it, Dad says, – And you'll come straight home from school, even if I have to pick you up myself. Do you understand?

I scream until my ears ring. I can hear them shouting at me, I can feel them shaking me but I can't stop. A slap on my face makes me collapse onto the table. My breath is coming out in rapid, dry heaves. I try to fight off Dad, who is pulling me up. He carries me upstairs and lays me on the bed. I keep my eyes closed while he covers me over. At that moment I hate him with all my soul and wish him dead.

Alone in my room, I fall prey to my worst fears: what if Nick forgets me? What if he finds someone else? These fears are the first words that spew out the moment Becca enters my room. I make her promise to go round to Nick's that evening when she goes out to see Si.

Later, I watch from my bedroom window as she heads off. I can't even shout down to her because Dad has already been up with his drill and his toolbox and fixed the window with a padlock so it won't open. I can't move away from there even hours later, long after Becca is back and has gone through the conversation she had with Nick. I had pressed her over and over for more detail, how did he look, what was he wearing. I find it hard to believe that he spoke only two short sentences when he never shuts up talking when he's with me. Becca says she's repeating what he said word for word but it sounds so unfamiliar that I find it hard to accept. Right, he'd said. How long for? And, how did they find out?

It's a horrible wet, dark night and I'm sure that the witch over the road keeps spying on me. I'd like to flick the Vs at her but she'd only tell and then I'd be grounded even longer. I wait, believing that he might still come, just to see me, because that's what I would do. I would just want to see him even if I couldn't talk to him or touch him. I wait until my feet are blue with cold and my legs won't hold me up any longer but I can't sleep.

A long day at school passes with nothing to look forward to. Becca has been given the responsibility to make sure I come straight home. We walk in silence, both of us unhappy, both of us annoyed with each other.

Another day crawls by. I feel so drained that I can't keep my eyes open. My head rocks when I'm eating my dinner and my mother accuses me of putting it on but I know that I must look awful because she tells me to go to bed straight after the meal. The room is light, even with the curtains drawn, but it's not that which stops me from sleeping. It's the fear contracting my stomach, it's my heart booming in my head. I want to smash my hand through the window so that I can breathe again.

On the third day, when Becca comes back from seeing Si, she brings me a note from Nick. He has waited outside Si's house, and from then on, he makes arrangements to meet her, every day. I think it bugs her a bit but she never says so. One time I ask her if she reads the notes but she shakes her head.

– They're private, aren't they?

In his notes he quotes from films and plays but the ones I prefer are those in his own words. 'I can't wait for these weeks to be over.' 'Remember who we are.' 'I miss kissing you.' My favourite is the first note he sends. Written on blue lined paper, folded six times because he knows that six is the most times a piece of paper of any size can ever be folded. I almost tear it with my clumsy, trembling fingers. There is a single sentence but it is all I need. He has written: 'I miss you.'


'What are you doing?'

'Nothing.' Abbie blushed and hurried to set the photo back on the bedside table.

'Is that your boyfriend?' Izzy's voice came out in a squeak, her eyes looked furtively shy. She made a movement as if she was going to pick up Nick's photo but Abbie was quick enough to guide her hand away. Abbie angled the frame so that only she could still see his face.

'It's my husband.'

'Where is he?'

'Away.'

'When's he coming back?'

'I don't know. Soon. He'll be back soon.'

Perhaps Abbie snapped at her, perhaps it was just the odd way she replied, whatever it was Abbie didn't care that Izzy's face had crumpled and her eyes were shimmering with close-by tears. She stood up quickly, snatching the photograph which she held pressed to her stomach as she strode past Izzy to the living room. She was shocked to discover that the lamp was still on and the curtains drawn. She hurried to rectify the order of things and as soon as the daylight was allowed inside, she felt calmer. She turned to contemplate the costumes on the clothes rail which were waiting to be worked on and she could feel the day beginning to settle around her. Abbie took a deep breath. Now, she could deal with the girl.

Izzy had followed her into the living room and was leaning against the table. Her mouth was clamped shut, her face pink. She pushed a button across the surface with her finger and didn't look at Abbie.

Abbie sat down at the table. 'We could make something,' Abbie suggested, tentatively. She smiled, she hoped, in an encouraging way as the girl cast suspicious glances at her. Izzy scooped up a handful of the buttons and let them trickle through her fingers onto the table. As she watched, Abbie could imagine the pleasing slippery sensation of them in her own hands. The rattle and patter as they landed on the table made the only noise in the room.

The girl finally spoke. 'Like what?'

'A bag perhaps. A little evening bag, you know, for when

you go out to parties?' She wondered then, of course, whether Izzy was at the age of going out.

Izzy shrugged and said, 'OK.'

Abbie took a box of small scraps of material down from one of the shelves and they sat at the table while Izzy went through it to choose a piece. She chose well – a violet square of satin whose patina had softened with age. Abbie fetched a dinner plate and showed Izzy how to draw around it with tailor's chalk on the reverse side before carefully cutting out the circle. Abbie hovered as discreetly as she could – fearing some dreadful accident – and then quickly hemmed the edges on her sewing machine while Izzy watched.

Abbie took down two more boxes. In the one containing laces and cords and ribbons, she hoped to find something suitable to use as a drawstring. The other held a selection of small beads sorted by colour. She gave this to Izzy to choose something to decorate the outside of the purse.

Abbie found a thin silky twist of lead-grey cord, and Izzy decided, after some hesitation, to form the outline of a star using tiny, silver beads. Abbie tacked the outline of the star on the material to give Izzy the lines to follow.

'Am I doing it right?' Izzy asked, holding the material towards Abbie. There were just two beads attached.

'That's great,' Abbie told her, thinking it was going to take for ever at this rate. 'You're doing fine.'

She pretended not to watch as Izzy began on the next bead. She was hunched over the material, her face intently concentrating. Abbie realized that the size and slippery coating of the beads were making them difficult to manipulate, but Izzy was actually surprisingly skilful at it.

'Is it OK so far?' Izzy asked, twenty minutes later. She had completed almost half of the star. She held the purse out to Abbie, as she had before, but this time, Abbie could tell she was pleased with what she'd done.

'It's going to be lovely.'

Abbie smiled at her before continuing to sew a large fake pearl like a rain drop to one end of the cord.

Izzy straightened her back and pushed her hair irritably away from her face. In the daylight, a patch of pale, smudged freckles had become apparent and there was a smear of palest lilac under her eyes where the skin looked almost paper-thin. Abbie felt a jolt at the sight of her fragility.

'How old are you, Izzy?'

'Eleven.'

Abbie had been twelve years old when she met Nick. Not much older than this girl. Twelve years old and she'd known then that she wanted to be with him for the rest of her life. She lifted her hand to her mouth. She hadn't been pretty like Izzy but Nick had seen something in her, too.

Bone-melting, heart-thumping, sweet, sweet kiss.

He pushes me against the fence and holds me there, hips pressing, hands tight around my wrists until he knows I won't move. He places his finger to my mouth. – Ssssh. As if I would shout out, as if I would want to call the rest of the gang back. Even in my most secret dreams, I would never have dared hope for a moment like this. It is cool in the passageway and I have goose-pimples. I'm too nervous to look at him but he tilts my face up to his and although I lower my eyes, I know he is taking in everything about me. For once, I can't cover my mouth to hide my teeth, I can't even shake my hair back in front of my face. The only thing I can do is open myself, my true self, up to him. My skin heats from the graze of his ice-cold eyes. I wish for only one thing: that he will kiss me.

– Look at me, he says and when I do, my heart almost stops. He isn't smiling.

– I've been wanting to do this for a long time, he says and then his lips are on mine. The first time. My first kiss.

Abbie lifted her head up. The room seemed brighter. She blinked hard several times to make her eyes focus. Izzy was still sewing.

'How are you doing?' Abbie asked.

'I'm on the last one,' Izzy told her without looking up. 'There.' She snipped the end of the cotton and smiled broadly.

'Now,' Abbie said. 'If I do the next bit on the machine while you tidy up the table, all that's left to do is thread this cord through for your handle.'

The cord was the easiest part. Izzy pushed it through quickly and Abbie sewed the final pearl on the other end before handing the finished bag to Izzy. She swung it from her fingers.

'It's really cute. I love it,' she said just as they heard the bang of the outer door. Almost immediately there was a knock on Abbie's door.

'That'll be your dad,' Abbie said and stood up.

Owen presented Abbie with a bunch of freesias as soon as she opened the door. 'To say thank you.'

'You didn't need to,' she told him but she couldn't resist breathing them in deeply. They smelt of muddy fields in springtime.

'She's in the living room,' she told him but Izzy was behind her, hovering in the doorway.

'Look, Dad. We made this bag.'

'It's beautiful, Iz.' He examined each side and then tried to hand it to Abbie.

'It's Izzy's.'

'Well,' he said. 'In that case, you know, I should really pay for it.'

'Oh, Dad!'

Izzy looked embarrassed. Abbie reassured Owen that it was only leftover material and a few beads. 'And your daughter put all the hard work in.'

She risked a glance at Izzy, who returned a conspiratorial look. They waited for Owen to speak, like a king about to pass judgement. Finally, he handed the bag over to Izzy who clutched it tight against her chest.

'It's very generous of you.'

'Not at all. I've enjoyed it.' As she said it, she realized it was true.

After they'd gone, Abbie arranged the flowers in a vase and set them on the side table in the study. She would enjoy breathing in their scent as she worked. She went to the living room to select the work for the rest of the day, but running her fingers over the rail, she became conscious of the boxes still out on the table. She looked inside. Izzy had done a good job of tidying; only the button box needed her attention. Once she had rearranged the buttons and put everything away, she was in the right frame of mind to begin work.

She carried her sewing box into the study and placed it on the piano-stool beside her chair. She was going to alter a cape to make it – in Kate's words – 'more fancy' by cutting it shorter, adding some ribbon detail and replacing the hook and eye fastening. She had a paste bead bigger than a ten pence piece which would be perfect to use for the new fastener.

She rested her gaze on Nick's chair to focus her mind but kept being distracted by a glimpse of purple haze from the flowers on the other side. She told herself that they were a lovely addition to the room and yet she couldn't help feeling uneasy about their presence. It seemed as if they were agitating the atmosphere somehow. At last, she decided to remove them. She carried the vase first to the living room, then the kitchen, then to the bedroom. She simply couldn't find a place where it seemed right to leave them. She returned to the living room, placed the vase in the middle of the table and sat down.

It was now midday and she decided to break the day and start refreshed with her work in the afternoon once she'd been to buy some food. Her notebook was lying open on the table and she pulled it towards her to write the notes.

On the right-hand page, in her own handwriting – although she had no memory of doing it – were the words: 'Back soon.' They'd stolen from her head, like slippered ghosts, to crouch on the page; ready to shout 'Boo' when she least expected it. She covered her ears and felt everything go dark.

Every new hour promises to be the hour he comes back, that he'll roll up steaming drunk, slurring his apology. You'll bite your tongue from relief and after he's slept off his hangover, you'll ball him out for worrying you. You'll tell him that it's not that you want to stop him staying out with his mates, it's not that you want to stop him doing what he wants, it's about communication, that's all. It's about letting you know that he's safe.

— This is a marriage not a cage, you'll say and he'll smile, plant a kiss on your nose and say, — I get it, sweetheart, it's just sometimes, like tonight, it becomes one of these networking, male bullshit things. You know what it's like, kiddo. Jon knows this assistant director who's working on this film and they've got a part going; the other guy got kicked off. So, Jon says to me come out and meet this bloke. The one who can actually get me this job. And the thing is, Abbs, this is a young, free and single kind of part and, well, you know what that means, don't you? It's not about acting these days — I can do that standing on my head — it's all about appearances and lifestyle. This bloke expects me to behave like a young man, like a single man and so I'm stuck there. I can't be the guy to break up the party. Not if I want to stand any chance. I can't be the only one who has to ring home and check in. This bloke won't expect to find out I've been married for over four years.

And you'll say, — Of course, I know all that. I'm not saying I don't understand but just next time if you could possibly, you know, either warn me that it might happen or somehow sneak away for a minute and let me know. Because I worry. I worry that you're hurt or worse because I don't know what's going on. I mean now you've explained it to me, I can see, in future, perhaps not to panic so much. I won't, I promise, in future, if it ever happens again but if you could try, somehow, just to let me know so that I don't . . . I don't worry so much.

It's five in the morning and you ring Becca.

— I'm sorry, you whisper, though you don't know why you're bothering to do so now that you've already woken her and

Chris up. It's just you couldn't wait any longer. You've thought about nothing else, weighing up how long you can bear to hold on against a decent time, well, a reasonably decent time, to ring.

— Abbie? What is it? What's wrong? Her voice is thick with sleep, threaded through with alarm.

It has crossed your mind that she will be annoyed when you explain to her why you're ringing. She'll tell you, sharply, that you're making a fuss about nothing, you're being crazy, you're letting your imagination run away with you. In a way, you look forward to her anger which will replace the ache in your heart because that will mean that there's nothing wrong. There's nothing terribly, seriously wrong.

— He's not come home.

— Who? Nick?

— He left this morning and he's not been back since. He's never been out this late before without phoning.

There's a pause, followed by the low rumble of Chris's voice in the background. You picture their confused, sleep-hollow faces. Your leg is trembling so hard it's bouncing up and down and you press your feet into the carpet to try to make it stop.

— He'll be at some mate's house and got too pissed to ring. Or forgot until it was too late to call. Don't worry, Abbie, get some sleep. He'll be OK. I'm sure he'll be OK.

You thought you only needed to hear someone else say that everything's going to be fine but it turns out not to be enough. You see how light changes as dawn approaches. You feel your heart flickering into hope at every noise as you sit there and wait. You wait and wait and wait and all you can do is have cups of tea and go for a pee and drink more tea which tastes like nothing in your mouth. It's just wet and that's it. Each time you take a sip you're thinking, in one end and out the other.

It's two the following morning. Nick's been gone for over thirty-six hours. You ring again.

– Becca, he's still not home. I'm worried, seriously I am. I've rung his mates and no one knows, nobody's seen him and I don't know what to do.

She says, – I'm coming over. There's some shuffling and whispering and then Becca speaks again. – We're coming over.

– Should I ring the police?

There's a short pause and then she says, – I think you should.

It feels like your stomach's been torn out of you and you're shaking so uncontrollably now that when you speak it sounds like you're gargling. You say, – Please come, Becca, please come and be with me.

Becca and Chris stop talking when you return from the bathroom.

– What is it? Is there some news?

Becca shakes her head. – No, none.

There is a mountain of mugs on the coffee-table and a plate of curling, cold, soggy toast. When you open the curtains, you feel embarrassed to have the daylight show up all the dust and messiness. You are about to tidy up when you spot the phone and you have to check that it had been replaced properly from the last time you picked up. You hold it to your ear, just to check that it's working and then you sit down, forgetting to do anything about the mess. By the time you've remembered about clearing up, you can't face doing it.

Chris clears his throat. Chris looks at Becca and it's obvious they've discussed what they're about to say.

– You should try to sleep, Becca says. – You didn't sleep all last night either. You must be exhausted.

– I'll make coffee, a nice, fresh pot and there are biscuits if either of you would like one.

– We need to sleep, too. Chris has got work today and the police are coming at nine. We should all get some rest. There's nothing you can do for the moment.

– That's a good idea. You smile at them. – I'll get some rest and then I'll be in a good shape to do whatever I need to do when they find him. I'll be fit to nurse him. I do hope he's not too badly hurt. I'll nurse him back to health. I've done it before. Remember that time when he crashed his mate's car and got whiplash and broke his finger. I looked after him really well, didn't I, Becca? Who would have believed I could do it. Chris, Becca will tell you how useless I am around illness and blood but I did OK, didn't I, Becca? Didn't I?

Becca helps make up the airbed for you in the study and you find clean towels and a clean sheet for her and Chris.

– When we get up in a few hours' time, you tell her, – the day can start properly. And then we'll find Nick.

Before she closes the bedroom door, she hugs you close and you don't let her see that you're crying because you don't want her to worry. Except that, as soon as you are alone, you can't help thinking how Nick was always getting into scrapes. He was always attracting trouble because he was different and you can't stop imagining him, bloodied, knocked out on the hard, cold ground. You would give anything for magic wings so you could fly down, press your ear to his mouth and hear his soft breath. You'd gather him up and bring him home safe.

The image of him being out there somewhere – out of your reach – is so awful that you can't lie there any more. You tread softly past the bedroom door so as not to wake Becca and Chris. You stand in the living room for a moment and then you get out your button box that you've been meaning to sort. You empty all the buttons onto the table and wipe the dust out of the bottom, picking the fluff out from each corner with a needle. You retrieve some strong cardboard from under the sink that you've been keeping for this purpose. It's as thick as balsa wood and you measure out and cut eight interlocking strips to fit inside the box to form twenty-four small compartments. It is logical to organize the buttons by colour but you also decide to segregate metal and pearl and you cut a piece of foam padding to line one of the compartments for the fragile cloth buttons that you love with their rosebud pattern and tiny puckered behinds where the material is gathered.

Chris leaves for work just before a police officer arrives. Becca stays with you. When you are all sitting down together, you read in her face what you had most feared seeing. It is now very real and very serious and you have to run to the toilet to be sick.

The officer wants you to call him Ken. He wears jeans and a shirt and jacket. He asks you lots of easy questions – Nick's name, date of birth, height, whether he has taken any money with him, if he owns a mobile phone and credit cards. He writes it all down.

You tell them that Nick is white, with medium length, black hair. Ken wants to know whether you mean collar length and you agree. You tell him that Nick's thin and tall. Becca interrupts.
– No, he's not tall, Abbie.

You realize that she's right. Nick's taller than you, but he isn't a tall man, not like Chris.

– Five ten, maybe, you say and Becca says – Something like that. Five nine. Maybe.

– He's thin though.

– Yes, Becca says. – I can't argue with that. He's skinny.

And we smile at each other because she has always called him skinny from the first time we saw him.

– No facial hair?

– No.

– And eye colour?

You are shocked that you didn't mention Nick's eyes before you said anything else because, of course, it will be the very first thing anyone notices.

– His eyes are blue, as sharp as crystal.

There's a short pause while Ken hesitates. He looks at Becca. – Blue, quite intense blue eyes, she tells him.

– And what was Nick wearing the last time you saw him?

This question throws you. For some reason it's difficult to grasp the image of him as he left that morning. You try and picture Nick as he walked past you but he slides out of your head as if the inside is coated in ice. As if he'd gone so quickly it was impossible to keep him in focus. No matter how hard you try, you can recall only a vague, composite picture of Nick leaving the flat over the days, the weeks, the months before.

Ken suggests – to help jog your memory – that you take a

look around the bedroom, to see what of Nick's isn't there. He goes with you. Becca has made the bed but she hasn't tied the drapes back and, while you do this, you sense that Ken is taking the opportunity to look around for clues.

You stare into the wardrobe and finally you say, – Jeans, I think, and definitely trainers and his black blazer.

Ken looks at me as if he doesn't know what I mean.

– It's a kind of wool jacket.

– Can you see or think of anything else that is missing?

Nick, you want to shout. Nick is missing.

Back in the living room Becca's face is white and worried but she squeezes your hand. The questions are getting harder: where was he going? What was he going to do? Who was he going to meet?

– How did he seem – in himself?

You look blankly at the man.

– Was his behaviour unusual in any way? Was he down at all?

You don't want to answer but Ken jumps in as if your hesitation means more to him than words. – It's really important to tell the truth, he says.

You whisper, – Yes, he was down. A little.

– Was there any particular reason that he might have stayed away? Did you have an argument, perhaps, love?

– No.

You're not lying. You hadn't quarrelled that morning although there had been plenty of rows recently. You suddenly see your life as clearly as if you're watching an actor playing you on the stage.

You have a meal ready for Nick but he comes home over

an hour later than he said he'd be, so you plunk the plate down in front of him and start eating without even saying hello. All this anger tumbles inside you – the hassle about the rent being late, the fact you've had to ask for extra shifts at the supermarket and that you could have treated yourself to *Craft & Design* magazine if you hadn't blown the money on a bottle of wine and these nice ingredients which are now spoilt.

You notice that Nick says nothing about the meal. He just picks away at it, stabbing his fork in and swallowing so quickly that he probably isn't even tasting it properly.

You would wait for ever for him to actually notice the effort you've made.

You curl the knowledge up inside you and you think, sod him, I don't care, but then it gets the better of you and you end up sounding like you're begging for attention. You say, – I've tried a new recipe, do you like it?

He looks up, startled, as if he'd forgotten you were there and says, – Yeah, it's really nice, kiddo, well done.

You feel sorry for him then, because his face says it all. He is tired and fed-up and he shouldn't have to deal with shit from you, too, so you push all the horrible feelings back inside and ask him to tell you about his day. As you wait for him to speak, hope begins to rise that today, he will actually have some good news. That today will be the beginning of the rest of your lives.

He sighs and says, – The usual stuff. But almost immediately brightens and your own mood lifts as he tells you how he saw Jaz and that she's working on this great TV series.

– It's going to need extras, walk-ons, if nothing else. It's young stuff, modern, you know. My kind of thing. She says she'll let me know when she hears for sure and, you know, she was pretty confident she'd be able to get me something.

– That's great! You fetch the bottle of wine you've been withholding now that there is something to celebrate and be happy about. Nick seems to relax, too. He uncoils – that's how you see it – he stretches and leans over and touches your hand as you pass the glass to him. That touch is enough. Enough to remind you why you love him.

So you keep quiet about the bills, and the extra shift and your slimy manager who stuck his hand on your arse, and you remember to remind Nick about the auditions coming up that a woman at work has told you about.

– What were they doing again?

– Miller, I think, you say and you don't notice, at first, that Nick's face has tightened, his mouth is clamped down. – It's an amateur theatre group but they've got a really good reputation.

– Yeah, well, I can't afford to do am-dram.

– Why not?

– Because I'd never be allowed to climb back out of that hole again. Because it's best if I just wait until something real comes up. I've been thinking a lot about this and I've got to be strong and not let anyone distract me from my goal.

– Are you sure? Because I've heard quite a few people, quite a lot of them – Jessie for one – say that it looks good when you show you're willing to put yourself out, that you're versatile and keen to take on anything.

– What does she know about it? She's a bloody nobody painting scenery, for fuck's sake. It might look like a brilliant idea from where you're fucking sitting but I'm telling you now that there's no respect in the industry for the ones who go down that route. That isn't how it works at all. You just end up looking like a desperate sad cunt that nobody will touch.

You watch the anger boil up. He's beside himself. That's what it is. You wonder how it feels to be him, at this moment. What it must be like. You think of this rage as a noise. You picture it like a whistling in his head, high-pitched and savage.

You watch things you love flying through the air, you see the pretty blue bowl you bought together smashed to the ground. You know better than to say anything because if you ask him to stop, or intervene to save any of your possessions, or if he sees you cry, it will only feed his rage. You just have to sit still and wait for it to blow over.

Once he's stormed out of the flat you immediately start picking up the broken pieces otherwise you'll end up walking over them and cut your feet. You parcel them up in newspaper, layer after layer, so no shard can escape and pierce a dustman's eye. But you feel something in your own eyes. It makes them water. You blink as you sweep up the last tiny fragments and the sprinkling of blue dust and the tears seep out and drop onto the newspaper. You have cut your finger and you watch as the blood soaks slowly into the paper.

Ken and Becca are staring at you.

– Abbie? Becca says loudly as if you're deaf. – Are there?

– Are there what?

– Any money worries?

You shake your head. – No more than anyone else. We get by.

– Or is Nick in trouble at all?

This question puzzles you. – What kind of trouble?

– Maybe, Ken says, looking rather uncomfortable as he speaks, – maybe he got in with the wrong sort, a criminal element perhaps?

– No.

Ken wants to know where Nick might have gone if he had changed his mind about attending the audition.

– He would definitely have gone.

– Maybe there was some place or person that he might have been to see instead. Perhaps just to take a break from everything. If he'd been down, as you said.

– No. He wouldn't miss an audition unless he ... unless ... Acting meant everything to him. Only something really important would have stopped him.

You don't expect Ken to understand but he does listen and he makes a note and then he passes you a blank piece of paper and Becca goes to fetch the telephone directory for you to lean on. You stare down at your hand resting on the paper and you can't remember what you're supposed to be writing.

– Family? Friends? Ken says.

– Helen, his sister, Becca coaxes. – And what about Neil, his best friend?

You write down both their names with the address details like Ken has asked. You do the same for the Windsor in Barker Street, Dave, Nick's parents, Jaz, Ben, Sadiq, Frank, Birdie, the Anchor, Coombe Arts Centre, the snooker hall and Cliff. Then, finally, you write the name you least want to give and the one you fear the most.

When Ken and Becca have left, you fetch a new piece of paper and a pen and you sit at the table in the living room and you write down all the names of people and places that you just gave Ken and then you continue with the list. At first it's slow-going, but it gives you something to do while you're waiting for news and soon you remember everywhere and everything: the market, the Crown, the Old Moviedrome, the Lastman theatre, Camberwell Art House, Andy, Mandy, Leigh, the Hallway, Dover docks, Greiner hotel, John, Bill, Alison, Rich, Julie, Justin, Callum, Ian, Paul, Elif, Dan; a couple of places where you went on holiday in the first two years when everything seemed possible. You picture the cafés and restaurants you used to go to and walks you used to take. Whenever you can't remember a name of a place, you write down a description.

If you could shatter yourself into a million pieces then you would. You'd send each fragment off on magic wings with a kiss good luck to search for him in every corner, in every place on this planet.

The next day, you forget about going to work and eating and washing. The only thing that stops you continuing with the list is the phone ringing. Each time you pick it up it gets harder to speak and you're sick of hearing people – even Becca – ask you if you have any news.

But as a few days go by and the phone calls begin to lessen, you feel as if you're teetering on the edge of a void which threatens to suck you in.

Ken rings to arrange to come round. He has a gentle face which reminds you of your father, who came over a couple of days before and who has offered to come back if you want him to, whenever you want. You just have to ask.

You try to concentrate on what Ken is saying because all you can think of right then is how badly you want to have your father with you. You'd lay your head in his lap like you used to do as a child and he'd stroke your hair while you slept.

Ken tells you that no one on the list you gave him, as well as several others that he's also spoken to, has seen Nick. He didn't show for the audition and he didn't meet a friend that he'd arranged to see afterwards. Ken doesn't say which friend, neither does he name the people who have told him that Nick was unhappy and really quite depressed.

Ken says he's becoming concerned right now. For Nick.

Ken says, – Look, love, several people have said he was getting obsessed about the fact that he wasn't getting anywhere with his acting.

– You have to be driven, you tell him. – Nick tells me that all the time. You have to want it so badly that it hurts otherwise it isn't authentic and it's just not worth it.

– Do you think Nick could harm himself?

– No! Oh my God, no. Then you speak on into the silence of Ken's response. – I don't know.

Ken says it would be really helpful to have a photograph, a recent one, because it will be circulated and it will go on any posters should the need arise. You hesitate because you know you should give him the one which most resembles Nick. That's what they need it for, after all – so that anyone passing him in the street, or in a hospital or on the Tube will recognize him. But you can't help thinking that this is the moment Nick's been waiting for all his life – to see his face plastered all over the place, on every wall, in shop windows. For the first time in his life, he's going to get what he wanted. His name and face out there for everyone to see. Even maybe on TV, even if it is only the local station. So you hesitate because it's a chance in a million and if he comes back — when he comes back — you think he might reproach you because you didn't give them the one he likes the best.

— This was my best chance, you imagine him saying. — And you had to use the one where I look like a serial killer.

When you hand the photograph over, you tell Ken, for no particular reason, — I am his kiddo. He is my prince. We love each other.

Later that night, when you're lying in bed, you put your arms inside his T-shirt and hold it to your face. You remember one night when he came back, remorseful as he always was after your arguments. You think of him sliding into bed beside you, pressing his freezing body against your warm one, his burning forehead against your face.

— I'm sorry, kiddo, I'm so sorry. It's getting to me, that's all. I wish I could have a bit of luck and then it'll be great. Life will be great. I want us to have this amazing life together.

You remember hurrying to brush over his worries, and didn't pay attention to the cold that passed through you like a bitter wind when he cried into your shoulder and his grip tightened so hard you felt dizzy. You were eager to tell him we'll get through it; we'll get our piece of luck. You buoyed him up and yourself, too. You reminded him that everyone thought he had talent and that it was only a matter of time and a bit of luck.

In the secretive dark of the bedroom, you couldn't see his face but you knew that he was listening and the trick was to use the right words, the words he wanted to hear. You waited for the slowing of his breath, the softening of his body against you as it had done so many times before.

Except this time, instead of keeping quiet, instead of keeping your own fears inside you and letting him sleep, you sought the chance to quell the trembling in your stomach and you asked him to tell you that everything was going to be OK. In that question, in that desire for reassurance he heard the note of doubt and he understood the betrayal of all that you'd said before.

You thought that you fell asleep like babes in the wood, wound together, keeping each other safe. Except it was only you who believed you were safe. He wasn't feeling safe at all.

After a couple of desolate weekends on his own, Owen had decided he needed a better coping strategy for when he didn't have the kids.

On Saturday afternoon, he walked to the park and had a coffee sitting outside the café. In the evening, he had to choose between returning to the park to watch whatever game was on or a stroll down to the pub. He chose the pub. He exchanged a few words with Sylvia but stayed only as long as it took him to drink a pint, standing at the bar.

This morning, he took a longer walk to the road which he and Steve had discovered the evening he moved in. He bought a paper and took it to the bistro to read over a couple of coffees and treated himself to a doughnut.

Now, late on a Sunday afternoon, feeling quite content with his efforts, he was ambling around the tightly packed shelves of the local shop in search of inspiration for his evening meal.

A scent of spice lured him to a dark, slightly mysterious alcove which he didn't remember investigating before. He discovered huge bags of rice and flour and packets of curry mixes and the most diverse number of spices he'd ever seen. He spent ten minutes poring over the jars and packets but didn't put any in his basket. In the vegetable section, he selected an aubergine for its shiny purple plumpness and a handful of okra which was an inspired choice, he thought, to add to the ready-prepared stir-fry vegetables and chicken he'd already picked up.

He spotted Abbie at the opposite end of the aisle to him by the bread counter and quickly approached. He'd only seen Abbie in passing since the weekend of Tom's adventure a few weeks ago and he was buoyed by the opportunity to speak to her – to speak to someone he knew. It wasn't until he was less than a metre away that he began to feel awkward. She looked so lost in thought that Owen felt reluctant to break in.

When Izzy had told him that Abbie made and repaired theatre costumes, it had seemed an old-fashioned but oddly appropriate way to make a living for someone of her other-worldliness. In fact, it seemed stranger seeing her now – dressed in jeans and a boyish sweatshirt and jacket – than in the silver dress she had worn that night.

He remembered another thing that Izzy had told him – that Abbie was married but her husband was away. He hadn't really believed Izzy but now he spotted the gold band on Abbie's wedding finger and he wondered where her husband was. She must be lonely on her own all the time, he thought. He knew what that felt like.

He walked closer. Abbie's posture was loose, her arms hung by her side, a sliced loaf dangled from one hand. It looked as if she had simply forgotten where she was.

'Hi, Abbie.'

She turned dark, alarmed eyes up to him; her face was very pale. She had an air of sadness that turned his heart over.

'How are you?' He spoke softly as you might to gain the trust of a shy child.

'OK.' She gave a wan smile and then passed a hand across her mouth. Her eyes remained suspicious.

'I just have to tell you, Iz is over the moon with the little bag. It's her favourite thing.' He wasn't making it up, Fliss said she took it everywhere with her. 'All her friends want one.'

Abbie's face brightened. 'She did a great job. Are the children with you this weekend?'

He shook his head. 'The next one. I feel at a bit of a loss without them, to be honest.'

'It must be difficult,' she replied.

Like you wouldn't believe, he wanted to tell her. 'It's definitely quieter,' he said lightly but he saw that he'd already lost her attention. She stared at the floor and said something which he couldn't make out.

'I'm sorry?'

'I said, would you excuse me, please?' She looked at the loaf in her hand and suddenly thrust it back onto the shelf beside her. 'I have to get back.'

He tried not to take it personally as he stood aside to let her pass. He followed her up to the front of the shop but Abbie was already out of the door by the time he reached the cash desk. He watched her charge up the street, like the house was on fire.

'Poor thing,' the woman at the till said. She had an intense look in her eyes that told him she wanted to pass on some gossip. Owen found that he was just as eager to hear it.

'She's my neighbour,' he said. 'I've recently moved into the flat above her.'

'Years it is now,' the woman said and indicated a notice-board to the side of the counter which was covered in white postcards and the colourful flyers of takeaway restaurants. In the centre of the board was a small poster showing the photograph of a young man's face. Underneath the picture, in large bold red type, was the word: MISSING.

'Her husband. She replaces it every year with a nice new one, poor love, and tidies up the board every month, so that nothing gets pinned over it. Did a runner, I reckon, that one. Not a peep from him. Cruel it is, a cruel thing to do.'

Owen couldn't take his eyes off the man. He was in his early twenties, shoulder-length hair with striking eyes in a very thin face. He felt that instead of the word MISSING, there could equally have been written: WANTED. He looked a desperate kind of man.

After paying for his purchases, he went over and read the details in smaller print. Nicholas Silva, known as Nick. Missing since 2000. That was shocking – the fact that he'd been missing for six years.

He was swept with a sudden sense of guilt remembering Abbie's reaction the night that Tom ran away. At the time, he hadn't known what to make of her behaviour but now it made sense. It must have brought it all back when he blundered down there, stamping through her house and garden like he owned the place. She must have thought him an insensitive, thoughtless prick. But he hadn't known. He looked up the street as if willing her back so that he could tell her. He hadn't known.

For the rest of the evening, Owen couldn't get Nick out

of his mind. He stood in front of the mirror in the bathroom and contemplated his own image. He hadn't shaved since Friday morning and his face looked more contoured and older with some stubble. Think how different you can make yourself look if you really want to. Think about how time changes you. Owen tried to picture how he'd look bald or with hair grown long and a big bushy beard. He grimaced into the mirror. With many more wrinkles. Maybe fatter or thinner. He blew out his cheeks, sucked them back in.

After six years you could walk past someone in the street and not recognize them, couldn't you? What good could that photograph do? Abbie's husband looked like a boy. It seemed crazily ineffectual to be trying to find a man with an image so out of date. A photograph is a record of an instant and then it's over. Never mind after six years.

He couldn't stop thinking about Abbie either. Now he got it. Now he saw why there was this lost feeling about her. It must be like living your life in limbo, like permanently waiting for someone to arrive except that they never do. The poor woman. The bastard. He felt angry at the thought of Nick doing that to her. Of anyone doing it to anyone. It was a truly shitty thing to do.

On Monday morning, he pressed the snooze button on his alarm too many times. He rushed to get ready for work then charged to the station, feeling harassed. The sleety rain was the icing on the cake. The *Big Issue* seller was in his usual spot by the entrance but instead of walking straight past as he usually did, Owen found himself hooked by the man's cheery, '*Big Issue*, mate?'

The seller was standing with his back right up against the wall in an attempt to shelter under the shallow eave of the building but his hood was dark from the rain and wet clumps of hair hung in front of his eyes.

Owen handed over a couple of quid.

'Thanks, mate. Good luck to you.'

'You, too.'

On the train, when he opened up the slightly damp magazine, the first page he landed on showed four rows of photographs of missing people. He studied their faces. Most of them looked bright and happy, only a few looked troubled and, he felt bad for thinking it, a couple had rather vacant expressions. There were all sorts of race, age and sex. It was horrible to think that anyone could just up and disappear at any time.

Steve was in a meeting that ran into lunchtime so Owen ate a sandwich at his desk and logged into the website that had been given in the magazine. He read profile after profile, skipping the ones of children. They were far too hard to read.

He began to see a pattern in the information given about the missing people. There were oblique or actual references to them being under some kind of pressure or depressed or even mentally ill at the time they went missing. It seemed unlikely that Nick had abandoned Abbie simply to start a carefree fresh life, like the woman in the shop had inferred.

He felt incredibly sorry for Abbie and for all the other people like her who had been left behind. He read their humble messages and saw how carefully they were worded. 'Just let us know you're safe.' 'Your brother would love to hear you are safe and well.' Heartbreaking.

He continued to search the entries determined to find Nick. When his face finally appeared, Owen felt freshly shaken. The profile provided a little more detail than the poster. It said when Nick was last seen, where he was thought to be going, what he looked like and what he liked to do. He was an actor which, for some reason, Owen found astonishing. Then came the message, so similar to all the other messages he'd looked at that it sounded, at first, almost glib and impersonal: 'Your wife, sister and parents miss you and would love to hear that you are safe and well.'

He checked no one was watching what he was doing and then he enlarged the image so that it filled his screen. There was something elusive about Nick which took Owen a while to put his finger on. It was his eyes. They had an intensity about them but their focus seemed to be turned inwards not out at whoever was photographing him. Owen got the impression that Nick already had leaving on his mind when the picture was being taken.

Owen sat back. He felt annoyed with himself for reading far too much into the life of someone he knew absolutely nothing about. He closed down the connection and tried to get on with his work.

At home, Owen changed out of his work suit, drank a can of beer while he watched the news, and then phoned the kids.

Izzy answered on the third ring and squealed with delight when she heard his voice. Owen's heart swelled with love.

'What are you doing, Iz?' Izzy's voice had turned whispery and muffled.

'I'm in my top.'

'What?'

'I've put my head down in my top, like I'm in a tent,' she explained. 'With the phone inside.'

'Why?'

'Because of Big Ears!' The last two words were shouted. 'Big Ears,' she whispered again. 'I mean Tom. Might be listening.'

He laughed silently in case she became offended. 'You'd make a great spy, honeybunch. Now tell me a secret.'

'OK,' she said and was evidently giving this great thought as a short silence followed. 'I know. The secret is I love you best, Dad.'

He would have loved to have hugged her then and there. 'Well thank you, Iz, that's such a nice thing to say. And I love you, too.'

'The best?'

'You're my best girl. The girl I love best in the whole world.'

'Good.'

'So, how was school?'

'Bor-ring!' she declared, quickly slipping into 'teenage mode'.

'What? The whole day?'

She sighed heavily. 'I really don't want to talk about it, Dad. God!'

'What about your dance class?'

'That was yesterday.' He caught the sulky tone in her voice.

'I'm sorry, Iz. I forgot. So, tell me now, how did it go?'

'It was OK.'

'At least that's better than boring,' he joked but it was met with silence. He gave up. 'Do you want to give Tom a shout for me?'

'Tom!' she bellowed. 'Come and talk to Dad.'

'Guess what? I got picked for Football Team B today and I nearly scored a goal and I'm playing next Wednesday, too.' Tom's excitement was heartening.

'That's great. We'll—'

'Oh, Mum says she wants to speak to you.'

'OK.' There was rustling, then a thud. 'But . . . hang on . . . Tom. Tom?'

'Hello, Owen.'

'I hadn't finished talking to Tom.'

'Hadn't you? He's gone up to his room now. I won't keep you long anyway. I was only checking whether you were still OK for this weekend? Or if you wanted to change the times or anything?'

'No,' he told her. 'We'll stick to the same as usual.'

He looked at his watch. He felt cheated. The whole thing was over in fifteen minutes. He had nothing else planned or to look forward to for the rest of the evening.

'Abbie. Abbie.'

A face from the past loomed out of the crowd on the pavement.

Abbie was plunged right back to a moment years ago, when she and Nick were out with their friends. They'd been to someone's opening night and they were pushing and jostling to get into this very pub before last orders. Most of them were drunk already, some of them high. Nick's hot hand clasped hers, keeping her close to him.

Jim muscled his way towards her, pushing past a couple of women who had stopped to wave down a taxi. Now that he was closer and illuminated under the slanting street lights, it was startling how much older he looked. He had always reminded her of an oversized baby with his round face, plump body and disconcerting podgy hands but now, even though he was still overweight, there was a hefty power to his torso under a very well-made suit; and those soft cheeks were covered in the rough, dark bristles of a man.

He greeted her warmly. 'Hey, what are you doing round

here? I haven't seen you for ages.' Before she could properly catch her thoughts, he had taken her hand and was pulling her towards the pub she had just been in, handing out flyers. 'Let's have a drink. We've got a lot to catch up on.'

As she followed Jim inside, she remembered that Nick had never really liked him. He maintained that Jim was a user, always trying to screw what he could out of everyone and never giving anything back. But Abbie had thought, quietly to herself, that Jim was no different from the rest of Nick's friends. It struck her that the whole lot of them were so desperate to be successful that they would do anything to anyone to make it.

Here, though, was a golden opportunity to revitalize an old link to Nick, so she let Jim buy her a drink and followed him through the densely packed pub. Everywhere she looked, she caught a flash of red from Nick's flyer. She nearly knocked into someone when she saw a man pick one up off a table and read it. Jim was waving her over. Somehow he had managed to secure them a table. There was only one of those high-backed benches free so Abbie went in first and Jim squashed himself in after her. The table scraped the floor as it was pushed forward to accommodate his bulk.

'So?' Jim said, picking up her hand and twisting the wedding ring around on her finger. 'Who's the lucky guy?'

'Nick, of course.' She couldn't help feeling shocked. After all, when Jim had seen her, wouldn't he automatically have thought of Nick?

'I thought . . . I just thought he'd . . . well, Abbie, I'm sorry but I thought he died.'

'No, don't you remember? He went missing. About six years ago.' She fingered the flyers inside her jacket pocket briefly before drawing one out and handing it to Jim, who stared at it for several seconds before giving it back.

'And you're still wearing your wedding ring.'

'Well, I'm still married to him.'

'Yes, I suppose technically, you are. But can't you do something about that?'

'Like what? What would I want to do?' She watched Jim closely.

'What would you want to do?' Jim looked astonished, then puzzled. He took a long drink. 'So,' he said, eventually. 'What does that mean? You're kind of like, waiting for him?'

'Yes.'

'That seems very, um,' he looked at Abbie and he seemed to gulp the next word down with the rest of his drink.

'Very what?'

'Sad?' he offered and he looked so concerned she had to smile. 'Same again?' Jim said abruptly and stood up.

Abbie pushed the flyer back into her pocket and hurriedly started drinking the first one that she had hardly touched.

'Thought we could do with large ones this time,' Jim said on his return, sliding the glass towards her.

'Thanks.' Abbie felt flustered by the sight of a second large gin lined up before she was even halfway down the previous one.

'So, what do you do, Abbie? For work?'

'I work for Kate.'

'Kate?'

'Kate Spencer. Wardrobes. You remember?'

He shook his head. 'Not really.'

'Tall. Long, wavy, blonde hair.'

'Big boobs?' he asked. Abbie nodded. 'Yeah, I remember her.'

They both picked up their drinks as a silence fell over them.

'So you're still in touch with all the old crowd, I take it?' Jim asked.

'Just Kate mainly. I speak to some of the others from time to time. How about you?'

He shook his head.

'What about Ben?'

Jim shook his head.

'Jaz?' A shake of his head, again. 'Sadiq? Frank? Birdie?'

'No. None of them. To be honest, I gave up on that whole acting thing a long time ago. Thank fuck. Can't you tell?' He indicated his clothes. 'Best thing I ever did was get into property. You're not looking to buy anything, right now, are you?'

Abbie noticed he was one of those people who got spit in the corner of his mouth when he spoke. She looked away. Coming in with him had been a complete waste of time.

'No,' she told him. 'But thanks, anyway.'

'Got to shake the snake,' Jim said, standing up.

Abbie was grateful to have a few minutes alone. Now she had to work out how to get away as quickly as possible.

When Jim returned, he hooked his jacket on the back of the bench. Abbie could see rings of sweat on his shirt armpits and there were drops of water on his hairline as if he had just splashed his face with water in the sink.

'So poor, sweet Abbie,' he said. He picked up her hand and held it against his chest. 'Waiting all this time.'

Abbie felt embarrassed by his sudden, rather ridiculous gesture but also quite moved as he smiled sadly at her. She eased her hand away. Jim leant towards her.

'Now, you know, you're an attractive girl—' He moved closer and Abbie, trapped by the table, pressed herself against the end of the bench. 'What do you say to a little loving between friends?' One hand began to grub around near her crotch, his fingers wheedling clumsily at the top of her thighs. 'Nick would understand. You can't live like a nun for ever.' She tried to push him away but this only seemed to excite him.

'There's no need to go all prim on me,' he told her. 'I know you were in that swingers' crowd.'

She closed her eyes.

'And, anyway,' he said. His words felt hot against her ear. 'Weren't you two already at the end of the road? Wasn't he with that redhead?'

'No!'

He held her wrist tightly on the seat and laughed as she struggled.

'Here mate.' A man placed his pint heavily on the table. 'Give it a rest. She don't look interested.'

Abbie sprang up and pushed with all her strength against the table. Then she ran. She didn't stop running even when she was out of the pub, though she doubted Jim would follow her. She just wanted to be as far away from him as possible.

She threw up over the low wall of a petrol station forecourt, then sat down further along the wall and watched the cars pull in and out. The smell of petrol burnt in her nostrils. She could taste the vomit in her mouth. She would have liked to have curled into a ball and rolled down the road, on and on until she dropped into the river and sank. She couldn't stop thinking of Jim's groping hand, the foam in the corners of his mouth.

She rubbed at a tender spot on her wrist where he'd gripped her.

She waved at a cab on the other side of the road which performed a wide, rapid U-turn before pulling up next to her. She sank into the back seat.

'You all right, love?' The cabby had an Eastern European accent and a wrinkled face. A face that told a thousand stories as Nick used to say. There was a cross dangling from the rear-view mirror like you saw in pictures from other countries.

'A bad night.'

He nodded as if he understood. 'Boyfriend?'

She shook her head. 'I'm married. I've been married for eleven years.'

'Ah, husband. Good,' the taxi driver said. 'So, husband at home. Waiting for you.'

She took out a flyer, passed it through the screen to him. 'He's missing.'

He held it against the steering wheel with his thumb. He whistled. 'Six years.'

'Could you take it, please? With maybe some others? If you could pass them around to the other drivers. He used to come to this area a lot, so it's quite possible someone will have seen him.'

The driver spoke softly. She caught his eye in the rear-view mirror. She thought he'd said something about being dead.

'No. No, he isn't, you're wrong.' They drove past a fish and chip shop, a kebab house, an Indian, Chinese, Lebanese. The street was busy with people hurrying with food bags back to their cars. The cab stopped at a crossing to let a group of young men over. They had skateboards hooked over their arms. One of them was eating chips out of a paper bag. He threw the empty bag onto the ground and the taxi driver gave a tut-tut of displeasure as he pulled away.

Somewhere out here, she knew, Nick was still alive. 'And I'll never give up on him.'

The man shook his head. 'But maybe it's time you let him go.'

'If there was this person, hanging from a cliff and you had hold of them. If you were their only chance, would you let go? Would you let them drop?'

She met his eyes in the mirror again. In the cab light they looked black. The cross swung wildly as he took a corner sharply. He shifted in his seat and shrugged. She thought that he had said all that he was going to say and so she turned her attention back to the streets. All it required was one day to be in the right place at the right time.

Several minutes later the cabby spoke. 'It's maybe right, what you said. But it's been a long time. Maybe he's tired of hanging on. Maybe he wants to be let go. Maybe you're tired, too.'

Abbie requested the taxi driver stop a couple of streets away from her flat. She handed over a twenty-pound note and didn't give him back any tip from the change. His face was sour but she didn't care. Fucking cabbies, they think they know everything but he didn't know Nick, he didn't know that he was worth ten thousand times the waiting. She slammed the door in protest and began to walk quickly away.

She walked past the flat, glancing at the upstairs window which lay in darkness, and went straight to the corner shop. She wasn't alone. Everyone was buying alcohol before it closed at midnight. The woman at the counter was friendly, asking her how she was.

'Great. I feel great,' she said as she paid for the vodka.

Back in the flat, the first thing Abbie did was check the notes. All were untouched. She threw them in the bin. She changed into her pyjamas, cleaned her teeth and took the cold bottle of vodka out of the freezer replacing it with the one she'd just bought. On the plastic chopping board, she carried the vodka, some ice in a bowl and a glass to the bedroom. She put the TV on, arranged cushions in a bank behind her pillows and got into bed.

She picked up Nick's photograph from the bedside table and sat it in her lap. Her stomach flinched as she raised the glass of vodka to her mouth but as soon as she had downed the first shot a warmth spread through her. How good it would be if Nick came back now; they would laugh about Jim, they would curse all cabbies, they would get drunk together.

– Hey babe, he says. He holds you for a moment, looks deep into your eyes and you let yourself believe that something has changed. For so long now he's seemed anxious and snappy and you've been waiting for this moment. You've been waiting for him to forget his troubles and come alive again.

– I've invited some friends over tonight. You'll like them.

That's all he says before going to lie down and rest. You creep out of the house to buy some drink and nibbles. When you come back, you tidy around, quietly so that you don't disturb him. You make sure everything is ready for when they arrive.

Nick gets up and showers. He puts on black jeans and a

white shirt that is one of your favourites. You see the V shape of chest hair at the base of his throat. You fancy him like mad. You just want to grab hold of him and have him clasp you tight and bite into his shoulder.

A young couple arrives. You keep wondering when the others will get here but nobody mentions anyone else. Nick pours out drinks, he offers them the food you've prepared but they decline it. They're only interested in the drink.

Something feels strange. You feel like the odd one out, as if the others are in on something together. The talk is oblique, and you keep thinking you catch looks passing between them. Between everyone but you. You realize that you haven't ever heard Nick mention these people before.

Nick follows you into the kitchen.

– Do you like them?

You are careful with your words, trying to gauge Nick's reaction. – They seem quite nice.

– They really like you.

– How do you know?

– They've told me.

– They're just being polite. Don't you think they're a little, well, strange, Nick?

– They think you're sexy.

– Now you're just being stupid.

– They do.

Nick is clearly excited. You know then. It settles in your head, the knowledge.

– I think you're sexy, too, he whispers, licking your ear, round and round. – Come on, kiddo. How about it?

– OK, you say. – OK.

– Come on, then. He's already gripped your wrist as if he can't risk you changing your mind but you ease yourself away.

You say, – I'll be in, in a sec. You sound OK even to yourself and when you hear Nick's voice talking to your guests, you quickly go to the bedroom where you know there is some vodka left in a bottle on Nick's side of the bed. You drink it straight down, gulping it quickly, as much as you can bear without gagging.

Before you leave the room, you catch your image in the mirror; you are wearing your favourite skirt and a pretty top. You were dressing up for Nick, you didn't realize you were dressing up for others, too. You can't wonder about how the evening's going to unfold, you have to just get on with it.

They all look at you and, for a second, you hesitate. You are tempted to turn straight round again but they're waiting for you. They say, relax, just relax and somehow you manage to because Nick is the one kissing you, Nick is the one whose eyes you look into and you feel the familiar twist in your heart. You take a deep breath and give yourself up to the vodka and to the night and everything is going fine until you happen to turn your head and see Nick with the woman, kissing her, pulling her towards him.

The scream burns through you as if someone was tearing the artery from your heart out through your throat. The rushed noise of your guests leaving barely registers, only Nick's stone-cold silence penetrates your consciousness.

He gazes down at you from the doorway with eyes which are not his eyes; turned dark with whatever he has taken. He takes a step towards you – this person who is not quite Nick – but he suddenly stops. Something like fear travels across his face.

Before he turns away, before he leaves the room, he speaks.

– You used to be such fun, Abbie, but now, you don't seem to want to do anything, you just want to sit in this fucking flat, doing nothing all the time.

You see what he means but there was a time when what he wanted to do were things with you. When the flat which he now calls depressing was his castle. When you were his princess, and the world was your oyster. Now nothing satisfies, nothing is good enough.

Abbie sat up slowly. She inched her way to the edge of the bed and remained there for several minutes until she thought she was able to stand. She walked towards the door. With each step, it felt as if her feet were striking the ground so hard that shockwaves were shooting up through her body and striking the vein on the side of her head. She dug her fingers into her temple to try to stop the throbbing.

She sank onto the loo and let her head hang down while she relieved herself. A strong stench of urine rose towards her. When she stood up to flush she saw that her pee was amber.

The daylight in the kitchen scorched her eyes. She covered them over while she let the cold tap run. There was a dirty glass on the draining board which she rinsed and then filled. She felt her lips and mouth soak up the water but her stomach heaved. She drank only half the glass.

As she was passing the living room, she noticed that her address book was on the table instead of in its usual place by the phone. She went in and picked it up. She looked around. Everything else seemed to be in order. She felt dizzy. She sat down heavily, landing awkwardly on the chair. She dropped the book. It landed open at the back pages. She picked it up. All the entries on the page were neat and legible except at the bottom. She couldn't make any sense of her handwriting but there was a large asterisk by the name Tony that she didn't remember writing. She found the 'T' pages and found one entry for Tony.

She stretched across for the phone and dialled Tony's number. She put her elbow on the table, leant her head on her hand and closed her eyes.

'Hello?' The speaker sounded male and young.

'Tony?'

'Nope. Try again.'

Abbie couldn't think clearly. 'Tony?'

'No! I thought we'd established I'm not Tony,' he said, and laughed. 'Hey, you're not that woman who phoned yesterday, are you?'

'No.'

'It is you! I recognize the voice now. We were talking for ages, don't you remember? You were telling me about your husband. All his naughty stuff.'

'No.' Abbie felt weird. Her hands were trembling.

'You sounded pissed but you said you weren't.'

'I don't know you,' Abbie said.

'You mean you don't remember. I'm hurt.' The man's voice was teasing. Abbie felt sick. 'You lied about being pissed. I thought you were lying. Naughty girl.'

'I don't know you,' she repeated.

'Well, I know all about you, now.'

She cut the call. She stared at the phone in her hand. She

was shivering. The phone rang and she threw it on the floor. It landed on her toe. She pressed her other foot down on top, to stop the pain. The phone carried on ringing. She grabbed it and yelled, 'Go away!'

'Goodness, Abbie, that's not a very friendly way to answer your phone. What on earth is going on?'

'Mum. I thought it was someone else . . . It was just someone joking around.'

'You sound very faint.'

Abbie sank onto the floor. 'It's the phone. I've been having problems with the line.'

'Have you rung them? You have to keep on at them, you know. It took us three weeks to get someone to come round, that time.'

'Mum,' Abbie said, lying on her side. She drew her knees up towards her stomach. 'I'm sorry, I don't have time to talk. I'm literally on my way out.'

'Oh, right, love. Where are you going? Anywhere nice?'

'Just out, with friends,' Abbie said, then added in a moment of inspiration, 'The usual Thursday night out.'

'You mean Friday.'

'Friday?' Abbie was confused. She wondered for a moment if she'd used the same lie before but on a Friday.

'Today's Friday, Abbie.'

'Yes, of course. Did I say Thursday? I meant Friday. I'm in such a rush.'

'Well, you'd better go then, love.'

'OK, Mum. I'll call you soon.'

Abbie got up. She walked straight to the kitchen, took out the cold bottle of vodka from the freezer and went into the bedroom. The glass she'd been using was on the floor. She picked it up and poured in a large measure. She held her nose and drank it down quickly, with her head back. She poured out some more and drank that in one go. She put the vodka bottle and glass on the bedside table and got into bed. She pulled the duvet up around her shoulders. She pressed her eyes closed and hoped for sleep.

He says, – I need some space, my head is fucked. I need to have some time alone and you say, – OK, although your heart is splitting in two. He leans over, holds onto the back of the chair and peers into your face. – I knew you'd understand, kiddo, that's what I love about you, that you really understand.

When he squeezes your knee you are filled with the warm fizz of love.

– So. Do you think that you can stay at your sister's for a couple of weeks?

Your smile freezes because you didn't realize it was you that had to go away. You don't want to leave your dear little flat. You say, – What about my sewing? We need the money. And he replies so quickly that you are in no doubt that he's been planning the arrangements for a while.

– Kate can drop it off there. It's easy enough. Becca's place is as close, if not closer than here.

Nick helps you sort and pack everything. You leave just two days later.

Becca has recently met Chris and so you'd think that she would understand why you always want to talk about Nick, why you never stop thinking about him but it seems to annoy her. She arranges not to see Chris for a couple of days so that she and you can spend time together on your own, even though you tell her not to. You try really hard to make an effort but your heart isn't in it.

Nick rings you every day and he always says he misses you.

One night – the ninth night – he says, 'I can't wait to see you. Maybe this isn't such a good idea. Maybe two weeks is too long.' So the very next day you go back to surprise him, although you suspect he will be half expecting you, anyway.

You arrive around lunchtime when you assume he'll probably still be in bed. When he isn't working he always seems to drift into an upside-down way of living, going to bed in the day, waking up in the evening. The house is quiet but it breathes life and so you know he's there. You know he'll be pleased to see you. He said it made him happy to hear your voice over the phone and you can't wait to see his reaction.

You take off your clothes outside the bedroom and tiptoe inside. The curtains are drawn and although the sun is bright outside, in here it is like dusk. You hear him stir, so you freeze. Your breath is held, a smile rises. You creep closer. The drapes aren't down but it is still hard to make sense of the shapes on the bed: Nick, cushions, pillows. It isn't until you are up close, your legs pressed against the mattress that you see there are two people in the bed.

A red-haired woman lets out a shriek. She scrambles upright, shakes Nick.

She says, – Who the fuck are you?

On the floor, to the left of you, is her open suitcase, clothes lie half pushed in, half hanging out and you know then that she's been here all the time that you've been away, that she's probably been here from the moment you left.

You sit down on the bed and you look at them sitting up at the other end. The woman's hair looks greasy and her eye make-up is smeared towards her temples. She keeps glancing at Nick as if she's expecting him to say or do something, but you can see that Nick is waiting for you. His eyes cut deep into you. He doesn't blink. It's as if he's urging you, willing you towards something. You hold his gaze and search in your mind for what it is that he wants.

You say to the woman, – I'm his wife. Get dressed and get the fuck out of my home.

When she scrambles out of bed, her hot skin skims close to your iciness. You move up and take your place next to Nick. You pull the sheet up to cover yourself. Her dark muff and the line of hairs which travel almost to her navel show that she isn't a real redhead. Her breasts are pendulous, there's a visible vein running up the back of one of her legs, like a snaking purple string. She is older, much older than you. You don't look at Nick but you know he is also watching the woman as she hurriedly pulls on clothes and snatches things from the floor and on top of the chest of drawers, throwing them haphazardly into her suitcase.

She picks up the case. – Fucking psychos, she spits out as she is leaving but she is shaking and nearly in tears.

As soon as the front door closes, Nick leaps up and dances on the bed, throwing his arms up as if in victory. His prick flaps and swings. You look at the sinews in the dip of his groin creasing and at the matted pubic hairs and feel sick.

Nick drops onto the bed, sits cross legged in front of you. His face is flushed from his jumping around; he talks excitedly. – God, Abbs. You were brilliant, thank God you came back.

Petra's such a bitch. Seriously, I think *she's* the psycho, she gave me a real pack of lies, leading me on saying I'd get this great part. When I realized nothing was going to come of it, it was too late; I didn't know how to get rid of her.

Even though your heart is beating so hard that you think it might burst out and fly around the room like a crazed bird, you say, – Don't ever bring another woman here, to our home. Don't ever do that again.

All the colour in his face leaches out. He drops his head and his voice is small and pleading. – She was just using me.

When you touch the top of his head, he looks up eagerly and grabs your hand.

– You know, there was nothing in it. It was physical, purely physical. Nothing like what we have, you know. What we have is special, deeper; a connection of souls.

Abbie propped herself up on her stomach. She felt across the bedside table until her fingers located the glass and nestled it against her chest. Her fingertips discovered the vodka bottle. She coaxed it towards her until it was close enough to get a firm hold.

'Yes,' she said out loud when she planted it on the mattress in front of her. She held the bottle by the neck, hooked the glass up with her thumb and rolled over onto her back. 'What we have is special,' she said, as she filled up her glass. 'Deeper. A connection of fucking souls.'

You think you have seen the last of that woman but you haven't. You go to meet Nick at The Swan and Petra is there. You couldn't miss her.

All evening, her loud, deep laughter rises above the noise in the pub, all evening no matter where you look, her cheap red hair catches your eye. Every time you see her, she is hugging or kissing someone different.

Nick sees you watching her. – She's such a bitch, he whispers, close to your ear. – Look at her.

She doesn't come near Nick. And she doesn't come near you. But you can't stop thinking about how everyone turned round when you came in and it makes you feel ashamed.

Abbie missed her mouth. 'Whoops.' She wiped her fingers across her chin and licked them, then wiped them across the sleeve of her pyjama top. She checked the level in the bottle. Halfway down. Half to go.

He says, – I'll love you forever. When you look in his eyes, you believe it's true.

– Don't leave me, he says.

– Never.

– No matter what?

You wonder why he needs to ask you that. You ignore the quivering that starts up in the pit of your stomach. You turn on your front to look at him but his eyes shift away as if he's been caught out and so you drop your gaze. The mattress dips and rolls and his head suddenly appears on your pillow. His eyes, so close. They lock onto yours. You see that there is definitely love in his eyes; there's no faking that. He tucks your hair behind your ears.

– No matter what, kiddo?

– No matter what.

You make love then, gently, slowly and it's only afterwards, when you are almost drifting off to sleep, that you find the courage to ask him what's wrong. You speak out to the room, your back against his front. You have your eyes open and you can see through the drapes a spear of light on the floor coming from the hallway.

– What is it?

There's a pause before he replies but his body immediately tenses. He says, – I've done something bad.

You whisper, – What?

– I slept with Petra again. I was drunk. I'm so sorry. He rests his head against your shoulder blades and pulls your waist tighter into him. – It won't happen again, he says. – I promise. That's the last time.

Owen woke early as he always did when Izzy and Tom were with him. He laid the breakfast stuff out on the dining table and sat down with a coffee. The flat felt peaceful. Happiness simmered inside him.

Owen calculated that this would be the fifth time he'd had the kids. The first couple of weekends he'd fought for normality but what he ended up doing was battling against everyone's boredom – and losing. He'd quickly given up on trying to have a 'normal' weekend in the flat, with the lack of garden, the absence of friends and everything else which constituted the children's normal life missing. So now he made a point of doing something special. During the week prior to them coming to stay, Owen had taken to studying *Time Out*, the Leisure Pool times, cinema listings, family entertainment in the *Evening Standard* and even his company's Intranet. He always marked out several possible events they could go to and a few other ideas just in case. It seemed to work; hanging around the flat without a plan didn't.

Outside the sky was a dull grey. He pulled *Time Out* towards him. Rain would cross some of the possible activities off the list.

Izzy was up next. She made a dash to the bathroom, locking the door decisively. Soon, he could hear the shower running and, above it, Izzy singing in her high, pleasant voice. Steam and fruity scents drifted towards him, misting the window. Tom appeared from his bedroom. He stared down the hall at the bathroom.

'She won't be long,' Owen told him. 'Come and have some breakfast.'

Tom slouched across the room, slumped on the chair, sighing theatrically as he poured cereal into a bowl. His head jerked up as if he'd just been struck by an amazing idea. 'Can I put the TV on?'

'After breakfast.'

Tom sighed loudly again. There was no sign of the sweet little boy who last night had pressed his hot body close against Owen on the settee while they watched the TV.

Izzy appeared dressed in a long jumper over a pair of jeans which finished mid-calf. The outfit looked unbalanced to Owen although he didn't mention it. Instead he voiced his admiration for the way she'd put her hair up – with a series of clips and cute plaits.

She beamed at him. 'Thanks, Dad.'

'So,' Owen said brightly, once Izzy had brought her toast to the table. 'What shall we do today?'

'Why do we have to always do something?' Tom moaned.

'So you'd prefer to stay in?'

'No,' he said flatly. He tapped his spoon repeatedly on the side of his empty bowl. Owen chose to overlook his son's behaviour for the moment. 'Do you want me to read out some of the things we could do?'

'Yes, please,' Izzy chimed out.

'Tom?'

He took Tom's shrug as a yes.

'OK. How about we go to the cinema and see *Chicken Little*?'

'Seen it,' Tom said.

Owen fought to keep the frustration out of his voice. 'Don't lie, Tom.'

'I'm not lying.'

In what seemed like a single flowing, high-speed movement, Tom threw himself away from the table onto the settee and turned the TV on.

'Tom, would you come back to the table, please. We're in the middle of a conversation.'

Tom continued switching from channel to channel, his chin pressed down onto his chest.

'Tom. I'm warning you.'

'I'm not listening. You don't listen to me. Last weekend, I went with Sam for his birthday. I *told* you.' He stormed out.

For a moment Owen and Izzy sat in silence looking at each other.

'I didn't know,' Owen said. 'Or maybe I'd forgotten. Anyway, I'd better go and talk to Tom.'

Izzy got up. She put her arms round him and pressed her face against his.

'Don't be sad,' she said, which made him feel even worse.

'I'm not, honeybunch,' he told her. He tweaked her nose and she told him off. 'Love you, Iz.'

'I love you, too,' she replied without hesitation. In a strange moment, she took his hand, pressed his palm to her forehead, before going to her room. He felt her absence physically, like a loss of heat. Sometimes she was such a mystery to him, sometimes as open as a book. How did he get to deserve such a sweetie? How did he get to have such a wonderful girl?

Tom was sitting on his bed hunched over his PSP, pretending to be absorbed in a game. He threw out a furious look. Owen could tell he was on the verge of tears.

'I'm sorry, Tom. I must have forgotten about the film.'

'You're always forgetting,' Tom said, seizing any opportunity to accuse.

'Then you'll have to be more patient with your old forgetful dad. Tell me everything twice so that I remember next time.'

Tom hesitated, sensing a way out of the quarrel but suspicious about taking it.

'Will you do that for me? So my poor old brain won't forget.'

'I suppose.'

'That's settled then. So, now, how about we go to the London Eye today?'

'Can we have a pizza afterwards?'

'All right. Agreed.'

They bought advance tickets for the Eye. There was an hour to kill before their turn came round. They walked along the river and stopped to eat ice creams.

'They're waving, Tom,' Izzy said, waving back at the people on a passing tourist boat.

'So?' Tom was fascinated by a group of boarders behind them who had set up an enclave in a dark corner under the bridge. The walls were covered in graffiti.

'Did you see that jump?' Tom said, but neither Owen or Izzy had been watching.

'I thought it would go faster,' Tom said when they were in the Eye.

'It's so you have time to look properly,' Owen told him, pointing out several famous landmarks to them both.

'Everything looks so small from up here,' Izzy said.

'How far up are we, Dad?' Tom wanted to know. Owen took a guess. 'And how far when we're right at the top?'

Owen took another guess and hoped that he was somewhere in the ballpark.

'Which is Big Ben again?' Tom wanted to know. Izzy went to stand next to him and pointed it out. Owen looked at his two children – Izzy with her peculiar outfit and Tom with unbrushed hair at the back of his head – and thought how lucky he was.

It was nearly half past three and they had just been seated in a restaurant when Izzy announced that she had a party to go to back at home. After Owen had pressed her for an answer, she told him that she thought it began at six.

'Didn't Mum tell you?'

He shepherded them back out of the restaurant, past the scowling waiter, with Tom in whining protest, and phoned Fliss to establish exactly where and when.

Fliss frustratingly said, 'I thought you knew. She's been going on about it all week.'

'No, I don't remember either you or Iz mentioning anything about it.' It felt like a conspiracy. Either that or he was going mad.

Izzy was hanging onto his arm. 'See, I told you.'

'You have to tell him twice,' Tom informed Izzy. 'Otherwise he forgets.'

'She's got her clothes with her,' Fliss said. 'It's six thirty until eight thirty.' She told him the address.

'This is ridiculous,' he said, lowering his voice and taking a couple of steps away from the children. 'I'm going to have to drive all the way there and back again. I'm literally going to have to drive past the house.'

'I know,' Fliss said.

'And I'm going to have to drag Tom along. I can't leave him in the flat.'

'I know, Owen. That's why I asked you when you rang on Thursday whether you still wanted to keep to the same arrangement this weekend. You were quite definite that you did.'

'But that was because I didn't know about Izzy's party. Oh never mind.' He turned to the kids. 'Well,' he said, much more enthusiastically than he felt, 'let's see if we can get Izzy here to her party in time.'

It was nearly seven o'clock by the time they dropped Izzy off. He leant forward on the steering wheel and waited to make sure that Izzy was welcomed in. A group of girls appeared at the door and Izzy was swallowed up inside. Owen felt exhausted, as if he'd just accomplished Mission Impossible.

'We've got an hour and a half to kill, Tom. Any ideas?'

'We never had the pizza,' Tom said and, unprompted by Owen, climbed over to the front seat.

'You're right. We could go over to the pizza place on the High Street.'

'Or we could have a Chinese,' Tom said.

'A Chinese.' Owen was amazed at his son's choice. 'Whatever made you think of that?'

'We had some at school,' Tom told him. 'For Chinese New Year.'

They chanced upon a small, very brightly lit Chinese restaurant which flooded Owen with misgivings the moment he stepped through the door. The décor was quite elegant but seemed more appropriate for someone's living room with its cheesy still-life paintings and dusty plants and low padded seats around coffee-tables. There appeared to be many more staff than customers. Several waitresses were standing beside the tiny corner bar, all of them wearing beautiful dresses. Rather incongruously a flat screen TV was showing a martial arts film. Tom seemed happy enough. He couldn't take his eyes off the large, stuffed armour-plated creature in a glass box. They were led to a small table by a tiny woman who dipped and nodded her head at them but didn't speak.

'Do you think they dress like this normally?' Owen wondered to Tom quietly when she had left them with the menus.

'Yeah, why not? But don't ask them, Dad, OK?' Tom flashed him a look and Owen had to hide his amusement.

'I like the crispy roll things,' Tom said when pressed for his order. Owen requested a selection of dishes for them to share.

Tom gamely tried the chopsticks to the delight of the waitresses, who seemed to find him irresistible. He didn't seem fazed by their attention, though, and even laughed with them when they presented him with some cutlery to use.

They ordered a strange-sounding dessert and politely spooned up most of the unusual custard-like dish under the watchful eyes of the women. The jasmine tea arrived with great ceremony: one woman to carry the pot, another to set out the cups in front of them. Their constant bowing and nodding and smiling was beginning to wear a little thin.

'Do you drink the bits?' Tom asked. He took a sip. 'I don't like it.'

'Leave it then.' Owen wasn't keen on it himself but he felt obliged to empty at least one cup and have a refill. He checked his watch and was surprised to find that an hour and a half had gone by. 'It's time to pick Iz up.'

'That was great,' Tom said as they were walking back to the car.

The word 'great' vibrated in Owen's heart. 'Yes,' he agreed. 'Yes, it was.'

Abbie woke with a lurch. Flailing around to dislodge the pressing weight on her chest, her hand knocked against the glass lying there. A sticky patch of liquid was pooled at the base of her throat. She pushed aside the glass, mopped herself down with the sheet and burped. She rolled over, her head spinning. The darkness in the room rose up around her like spilt oil riding the waves of her nausea. She struggled to sit upright and then gave in as it folded over her head like a doughy oil slick.

People come, people go. A stream of them. Every day; someone. Becca, of course, and the police, Detective Ken Higgs, Nick's mother sometimes, friends, your parents, more friends. The weeks go on and the stream begins to dry up until the visitors are reduced to a trickle by the summer months.

None of them have noticed. You hide it from them. This constant jumping in your stomach which means you can't keep anything down.

You think you must be frozen inside because even though these are the warmest days of the year, you can't stop shivering.

Your fingertips are tinted an eerie blue and when you touch them against your face they feel like ice. You wear lots of layers. His T-shirt, worn to softness, next to your skin, then his sweatshirt and your jumper sandwiched between another sweatshirt and maybe another. You forget how many. You just keep piling them on top because you can't get warm.

Becca discovers you, ill in bed. The frozen part, right in the middle of you, has finally thawed. Your tender skin feels as if it's blistering under a searing heat and you've clawed and torn all your clothes off to ease the pain.

When Becca sees you, she says, – Oh my God, Abbs. You're a fucking skeleton.

You wince at the sound of her voice, shrill in your ears. You screw up your eyes against the blaze surrounding her in the doorway.

You hear her talking to the doctor who she has called in to examine you. You have no say in the matter, she told you, and you have no strength to protest. They are standing right in the room but it's hard to concentrate. You latch on to parts of their conversation whenever you remember to listen. The doctor says there's pills to help this and pills to help that. You watch his elbow moving as he writes out line after line on a pad and watch as he rips off a page and hands it to Becca.

When he's gone and Becca sits on the bed beside you, you ask, – Is there a pill which will bring Nick back to me?

She catches her breath in anger. – For God's sake, Abbs. She gestures at your body, cooler now under a smooth, clean sheet. – For fuck's sake, what if he did come back and found you like this? And then she adds, – I don't even want to say that because I want you to be well for yourself and not for that bastard.

Your heart is like a slab of roadkill and Becca's words are huge, black, squabbling birds. They tear and peck and jab away at it with their big, dirt-grey beaks and gobble it down, their gullets bobbing. You curl up and pray that the birds will fly away because it hurts so much.

Later that day, when you wake up, your first thought is that Becca is right. It would be awful if Nick came back and found you like this.

When Becca looks in and sees you're awake, you say, – I think I'd like some mashed potato. Soon the chalky scent of potatoes cooking reaches the bedroom. By the time Becca brings in the bowl, you're salivating. There's a big mound of mash with a golden curl of butter on the top. It looks beautiful but so sickly that just looking at it makes you feel a little nauseous and nervous. Becca is watching so you know you must at least try. You scoop up the mash from the side, avoiding the butter. You close your eyes so that you can't see the spoon approaching your mouth and after the first mouthful you feel a sudden hunger. You're starving and you eat quickly although your hand is trembling and you think how much easier it would be to put your face into the bowl and suck it all up in one go but, of course, it isn't something you would do even if you were on your own and Becca wasn't there. She says, – Is it nice? Do you want something else?

You shake your head and say, – That was lovely, thanks, Becca.

After that, you eat like you've forgotten how. You put weight back on, but it settles in odd places not evenly like before – a swell on your stomach and a bulbous padding on the backs of your thighs.

But he doesn't come back. And part of you understands why.

It has become really clear to you how hard it had been for Nick.

You see, now, that he'd been tired and scared and worried all along. He was just trying to hold on to his dream as it drifted away.

To be told all the time no thanks, you're too old, too thin, too tall, too dark, too posh, too rough, too clean, too scruffy, too eighties, too nineties. I'm afraid you're not what we're looking for. Sorry, but we didn't think you were right for this part. Thanks for calling but we've gone with someone else now.

You can see how that would chip away at the shell.

It chips and scrapes and wears away every layer until there's only one wafer, crisp-thin layer left on the surface. Underneath lies the softest, most vulnerable part of you: the tender quick. Maybe not the next time, but the time after that, their words expose it and strike home and the pain is incredible.

You kick yourself for being blind to the danger, for not giving Nick the nourishment he needed to harden the shell, for not doing enough to help him regrow those layers. You see that Nick had never meant to hurt you – he was desperate. A prostitute he called himself once. I hate myself, he'd say sometimes when he was drunk and he'd cry like he was never going to stop.

Becca, on the phone, says, – Of course you did enough, you did more than enough. How do you think he'd have survived if it hadn't been for you? If you hadn't worked at the supermarket and then sewed for hours every evening? If you hadn't sacrificed things that you wanted to do? Like your course, for one. Your clothes designing which, Abbs, is *your* talent, a *real* talent. Not an imaginary, fucking pie-in-the-sky wouldn't-it-be-nice-to-be-an-actor kind of thing. Not to mention you never having any holidays or going out somewhere nice and, I mean, for God's sake, when did you actually buy yourself some decent underwear? Let's face it, everybody else has to get out there and work rather than just sit on their arses and wait for fame to come along. There are swathes of actors being waiters and barmen and holding down all sorts of jobs. When did Nick ever really put himself out?

– You have to be dedicated. They're the only ones who make it.

– No. I'm not going to let you take me down this road again. I want to hear about now and the future. Those are the words I want to start hearing from now on. They're the only words I'm going to listen to.

You keep falling asleep all the time. Sleep slices through the hours leaving you only a few that you have to deal with head-on.

After a few days you discover that you need only move when you really have to and that this, too, can be drawn out so much that you need never surface beyond a half-daze. That way getting through another week seems just about bearable.

If the phone rings, you pick it up and wait until the person on the other end speaks. Then you end the call. There is only one person whose voice you want to hear and that person never phones. You don't talk to anyone else.

The landlord comes knocking for his rent which you're late paying. He peers past you into the flat saying, – Is everything

OK? It smells a bit damp in here. Are you looking after the place?

You tell him that you've been ill and because he's always had a bit of a soft spot for you, he crinkles his forehead and says, – Yes, dear, you don't look so very good.

– I'm on the mend now, you tell him. I'm sorry I haven't been able to get out of the house for a while but I'll sort the rent money out in the next couple of days.

– By Friday?

You nod and as soon as he's left you ring up Becca.

– Of course I'll give you the money, Abbie. I'm so glad you called, I was getting worried. Do you know there's something wrong with your phone? I keep getting cut off.

– Loan not give.

– OK, a loan then, but on one condition.

You hardly dare ask what.

– You get some work in from Kate. Start to get yourself back to normal.

On Friday morning, Becca comes over with the money and she helps you clear up the flat. Although you're expecting her to say something about the mess, she snaps on the Marigolds and says, – I'll do the bathroom.

Soon every window is opened wide and there's a smell of polish and lemon and pine and everything sparkles so bright it makes your eyes smart.

The landlord arrives in the afternoon and when Becca answers the door he says, – You must be Abbie's sister. You look just like her.

You find this funny because sometimes when you catch a

glimpse of your face in the mirror you see a Becca expression and yet sometimes when you look at your sister, she could be someone you don't even know.

Becca stands over you while you phone Kate who says, – Thank God, Abbie, I've been lost without you. You don't know what a mess some people can make of the simple job of sewing on frigging buttons.

On Saturday, she brings over two full bags of work and says, – Do as much as you can but I'll pay you double, though, if you get it all done in a week. I've just taken on a big, new contract.

Your fingers are stiff and your eyes feel out of focus when you begin. But you soon realize how much you've missed it. You fall in love with a lavender-blue forties dress and matching scarf which you are decorating with mother of pearl. You rest your face on the soft grey fur of the children's mice costumes and imagine their faces peeping through. You sew ball-bearings to weigh down the hem of a Spanish skirt so that it will fan out but not rise too high when the dancer spins. The radio is on. Sometimes there's music, sometimes news, sometimes a play. Time is not important.

Kate is astonished that you have finished the whole batch and flatters your workmanship, too. She counts out the double pay onto the kitchen table while you make a cup of tea. It's hard to concentrate on her chatter because you're waiting for the right moment to ask her.

– Have you heard any mention about Nick?

– No. I'm sorry, Abbie, Kate says, – but I promise I'll let you know immediately if I do. She repeats I promise, as if she thinks you don't believe her.

She leaves you another bag of work and as soon as she's gone, you open it. This time when you take the clothes out, they smell musty and look unappealing. You check the inventory of work but nothing really sinks in. Suddenly you have to walk away. When you go into the kitchen you find that it's all messy again with dirty plates and cups piled in the sink and crumbs and scraps of food on the work-top and cooker. The floor is splashed in places with something dark, like tar.

You run a bath but when it is only half-filled and you are sitting on the edge looking at the bowl of bath balls that fizz in the water and the bottle of oil that Becca gave you, washing seems pointless.

Instead, you see long day after long day with no news and no hope. Just your life flat-lined in front of you. You go to the bedroom and slowly take off all your clothes and put on Nick's Rolling Stones T-shirt and then you get into bed. In the middle of the night you wake up and you understand where you've been going wrong. You've been looking for Nick in the wrong place.

You count up the pills and place each to form a line on top of the duvet. In the lamplight, they're like tiny, phosphorescent pebbles marking the pathway through the wood. You know that you're on your way home. For the first time in a long time, longer than you can ever remember, you feel happy.

You are pulled roughly into shocking, glaring light and noise that hurts your ears. You feel red-raw, scraped and desiccated inside. You make out shapes at first – blue, blurred figures that are busy around you. The second time you open your eyes, your parents and Becca are sitting on chairs beside the bed. Mum is red-faced and teary, Dad's face is grey like pumice stone and Becca looks beautiful, as pale and composed as a nun.

Although they greet you with words of love, their eyes are watchful as if they are scared of you. You see Becca's face change. Her lips begin to quiver, her chin trembles until her face collapses into tears.

– Oh my God, Abbie, I thought I'd lost you.

Her choked words are all that you need to know. Her love for you is precious but it is as heavy as gold and you are already so tired that the extra weight is almost more than you can carry. You push your strength to its very limit just to be able to squeeze her hand and to say you're sorry.

Becca holds on to your hand tightly. – Promise me that you won't ever try this again.

And you make the promise, knowing that no matter what happens, no matter how tempted you are, no matter how difficult it may be, your promise can't be broken.

Abbie sat up tentatively, keeping her head bowed and her eyes cast down. She remained like that for several moments as she took in the two empty vodka bottles, the disarrayed bedclothes and her creased and sticky pyjamas. She looked at the time. 8:15 a.m.

She heard a faint high-pitched noise which she believed to be inside her head at first but which, as it persisted, became clear it was the sound of a girl singing. Izzy. The singing stopped abruptly.

She raised her head. She felt incredibly thirsty. Her stomach rumbled. A mild headache lurked ready to pounce. She took a deep breath and discovered that the pressure on her chest seemed to have lifted. She took off her pyjamas and put on her dressing gown. She would have a bath and then make some tea and toast. She would get back in bed and watch children's TV for an hour as she and Becca used to do, every weekend for years, and as, for all she knew, Izzy upstairs might be doing right now. Sitting on the floor, her pink nightdress stretched over her bent knees, her smooth, unblemished feet planted firmly on the floor.

As she was passing the living room, the phone began to ring. She felt the blackness ooze forwards and touch the fringes of the white, calm space in her mind. She steeled herself for something horrible. Something unknown.

It was Becca. 'Thank God, you're there, Abbs. I was beginning to worry. I've been trying to get hold of you for days.'

The fear retreated. Abbie sat on the settee. She tucked her feet up under her dressing gown, to keep them warm.

'Abbie? Are you there? Are you OK?'

'I'm here.'

'Are you sure you're OK? You don't sound it.'

'It's been a bad time, that's all.' A tear landed on her hand.

'Oh, love, I'm so sorry. Why didn't you ring? I could have come over. Do you want me to come today? I could be there in a couple of hours or so.'

'No, I'm OK now,' she said. 'Really.'

There was a short silence. 'Mum said you'd been out for the evening with some friends?'

Abbie couldn't think what Becca meant. She didn't remember talking to their mother recently.

'On Friday night?' Becca prompted.

A memory descended, making her shiver. Jim. In the pub.

Jim pushing closer. Jim putting his hands all over her. 'I saw someone from the old days. Someone Nick used to know. But that wasn't Friday.' Or was it. She felt confused. She wanted to ask Becca what day it was but didn't want to alert her sister to her confusion. Abbie gripped the phone and tried to think. Today must be a weekend day because Owen's children were here.

'Who was it?'

'Jim. Nobody you know. Nobody I want to know. He was horrible, Becca.' She heard the panic in her voice and struggled to stay calm.

'Do you want to talk about it?' Becca's voice was soft.

Abbie shook her head.

'Abbie? Do you?'

'No. Not now,' she said. And she felt something deep inside her crack open. 'Not ever. I want to forget him. I want to forget I ever saw the stupid man.'

On Sunday morning Owen left Izzy in charge while he went to buy a paper from the local shop. He was sweating with fear by the time he returned less than ten minutes later, but no harm had come to them. They seemed surprised that he'd been so quick. They leapt on the almond croissants he'd bought as a treat. Both of the children stayed in the living room with him; Tom on the settee playing his PSP and Izzy lying on the floor reading a magazine. Owen allowed himself a small moment of happiness as he settled to reading the paper, with a cup of tea made by Izzy.

At just after eleven, the phone rang.

'Oh good, love,' his mum said. 'We were hoping to catch you in. Are the children with you?'

'Yes, they're here.'

'Can we have a chat with them? It's hard to get to speak to them these days, now that we can't ring them at the house.'

'Don't be ridiculous, of course you can ring them at the house.'

'You say that but Felicity didn't sound very happy to hear from us the last time we did.'

'I'm sure you're imagining it.' He walked into the kitchen out of earshot of the children. 'Fliss is more than happy for you to talk to them.'

'Well, we don't know what to say to her.'

'Say what you usually say, just behave as normal.'

'But it isn't normal, Owen, is it?' His mother's voice was sharp, accusatory.

'Well, you're just going to have to figure it out for yourself,' he told her. 'Because I can't help you. I've got enough on my plate.'

He walked back into the living room and handed the phone to Izzy. 'It's Granny Renshaw.'

Izzy squealed down the phone. 'Gran!'

Owen didn't stay in the room. Instead, he went into his bedroom and stood by the window. In an hour's time, he'd be driving the children back to the house. Then he wouldn't see them for another twelve days. His life consisted of counting. Twelve days without. Two days with. It seemed to get harder not easier.

On Tuesday evening, Steve came over bringing a computer game with him. Almost immediately Owen began to lose, but he didn't care. He felt buoyant. He found himself grinning at Steve who took advantage of the moment to make a killer move.

'You've been practising.' Owen threw aside the controller in mock disgust and declared a beer break. He fetched the cans from the fridge. While they were drinking Owen told Steve about Abbie and her missing husband.

Steve pulled a face. 'So? What do you care?'

Owen was surprised to discover he couldn't explain why. 'I don't know, I just do.'

'You've got the hots for her! Is she nice looking, then? You never told me that.'

'She's all right, quite pretty, but it's not that. She reminds me of my sister.'

Steve howled his disbelief. 'Yeah, right. Which one?'

'Mae, the middle one.'

'Oh, OK.' Owen could see Steve was being careful. He knew how protective Owen was about Mae. 'But she's *not* your sister, so perhaps it's best just to keep out of it.'

To get off the subject, Owen admitted that Steve was probably right, but that wasn't how he felt at all. Ever since he'd learnt about Nick, he'd been trying to think of ways he could help Abbie. And he thought that he'd finally come up with something. He was pretty sure that she didn't have a computer. It struck him as far too modern an item for her to possess. He certainly couldn't picture it among all the frills and froth anyway. He'd almost decided to offer her the use of his whenever she needed it and had wanted to float the idea past Steve before he actually mentioned it to Abbie. After Steve's comment, though, he decided to keep the idea to himself for the time being.

They resumed their game and, at the end of it, when Owen had again lost woefully, Steve suggested the pub.

Sylvia was sitting in her usual spot at the bar. Owen introduced Steve. 'Sylvia has lived round here for her whole life.'

'OK, right.'

'Even through the war,' Owen added, attempting to compensate for Steve's rather dismissive response. 'When virtually the whole of this area was destroyed.'

'Do you know what my grand-niece says? She says, Sylvia, you don't know how lucky you were to live in such a time: the romance! The passion!' Sylvia laughed her deep man's laugh. 'She sees it differently from me, of course, but she's a historian. She lectures in history. You'd like her. She's a lovely girl. I'll introduce you to her sometime. She comes over to see me a lot.'

'I'm going to sit down,' Steve said.

'What's up with him? Another one like you, is he?'

'What do you mean?'

'A new divorcee.'

'No, he's definitely married.'

Sylvia let out a peal of laughter then grasped Owen's wrist. Her eyes sparkled with mischievousness. 'Well, he won't be for long, you tell him that. Unless he bucks his ideas up.' She giggled. 'Women don't like a misery-guts.'

'Jesus, house of horrors,' Steve muttered when Owen brought over the drinks. 'What is this dump?'

'I like it,' Owen said defensively. He looked behind him and Sylvia winked. He couldn't help grinning back.

'Are you crazy? And why did you have to go talking to that old bat?' Steve sank his nose into his pint. 'Fix you up with her grand-niece – Jesus – what kind of troll do you think she'd turn out to be.'

Owen glanced over again, hoping that Sylvia was well out of earshot. Thankfully, she had her back to them and was talking to the barman.

'You never know,' he told Steve. 'She might be all right.'

Steve pulled a face. 'Hey, talking of pussy,' he said and Owen flinched, knowing what he was going to say next. 'Anything more happening on the Lisa front?'

Owen shook his head. 'And I'm sure there won't be either,' he said, firmly.

'Yeah, yeah, I know.' Steve hunched even closer to his pint. 'Guilt. Responsibility. Being a mature adult. You don't have to say it.'

'Good,' Owen said. He thought he'd better keep it to himself that over the weeks since he had slept with Lisa, his guilt had dissipated and she occasionally made an appearance in his dreams.

The next day, Owen sat dazed in front of a particularly tedious piece of code, suffering from an afternoon energy slump, when Lisa leant over him from behind and whispered close to his ear: 'Long time no sleep together.'

'Sorry,' she said when she made him jump. 'I thought maybe we could go for a drink?'

'Yeah, great,' he said. He had meant to say no but he'd been distracted by a sudden mental image of her smooth, bare arse.

'I'll see you in reception at six thirty.' She pressed her hip against his arm before moving away. He watched her little arse swaying on top of her slim legs, on top of those high, high heels and he knew she knew that he was watching her. He looked around to see if anyone had noticed but everyone was gripped by whatever was displayed on their screens. Thank God he worked with a bunch of nerds. He rocked his chair further under his desk, and concentrated on ignoring his burgeoning erection. This disappeared immediately when he remembered his conversation with Steve in the pub the night before. It wouldn't surprise him if Steve had put Lisa up to playing a joke on him.

But when he turned off his PC at six twenty-seven and went down to reception it was Lisa who was waiting for him. She suggested that instead of going to the pub, they go straight back to her place. They took a long cab ride over, which he knew was going to cost him at least forty quid but he didn't care. They ordered a pizza en route from a menu card which Lisa produced from her handbag. The pizza arrived shortly after they'd begun on large glasses of rum on the rocks. They sat on the floor and chatted easily while they ate. Lisa went to get a refill of the drinks and just as Owen began to think that perhaps he'd got it wrong and the evening wasn't about sex at all, Lisa sat on the floor directly in front of him with her legs yoga crossed, her skirt pulled taught across her lap. She wasn't wearing knickers again and he couldn't keep his eyes away. He kept remembering the way her bald pussy felt under his fingers. Lisa drained her glass, crunched an ice-cube in her mouth and crawled towards him. She sat on his lap and kissed him, her lips ice-cold and wet. She lifted up her skirt.

'It's called a Las Vegas,' she told him.

Where her pubic hair would have been, there was a silver glitter heart with a red glitter arrow shot through it. He ran his fingers across the surface; it was rough like sandpaper.

'How long does it last?'

'Only one night.' She pushed his fingers to where she wanted them. 'It's only for special occasions.'

*

Not guilt but something far worse hit Owen the moment he woke up next to Lisa. A terrible panic that everything was wrong overwhelmed him. He couldn't remain in bed. He left Lisa sleeping and took a shower. Slowly the hot water calmed him.

Lisa came in the bathroom as he was drying himself and sat on the loo to pee.

'I've got a boyfriend.'

'OK,' he said, wondering where this was leading.

'He wants me to, you know, just be an item – him and me. I've never felt like it before.'

'But?'

'But now I think I do. I guess I kind of missed him last night. Oh,' she said, 'no offence to you, Owen.'

'None taken,' he assured her. He thought he understood what she meant. Last night he, too, had missed not someone, but a kind of substance, a gravity to the experience. Despite their physical intimacy, he felt closer to Lisa now.

On the Tube she suddenly turned to him. 'You're not comfortable doing this kind of thing, are you?'

'No,' he admitted. 'I don't think I'm really a casual kind of person.'

'There's nothing wrong with that,' she told him and patted his arm as if she was consoling him. 'I won't say anything, you know, at work, if you were worrying about Felicity getting to hear.'

'I would prefer if she didn't know,' he said, carefully. 'I don't want to upset her.'

'My lips are sealed,' she said and smiled. Owen smiled back. Lisa really was a very sweet girl. He allowed his gaze to linger on her long, smooth legs for a moment before she wagged her finger at him in mock rebuke.

'Do you think you'll get back together again?'

'No,' he said and he was surprised by how certain he felt. 'No, definitely not.'

On the train that evening, he decided that he was going to call in on Abbie. It was a good time to do it. With his work clothes on and his briefcase in his hand it would signal that he had just arrived home and wouldn't be expecting an invitation in.

Abbie opened the door with a defensive look which threw him. He was suddenly tongue-tied. How on earth did he expect to suddenly bring up the subject of her missing husband without seeming perverse?

'Abbie,' he began, attempting the honest approach. 'I just wanted to apologize about that time when Tom ran away. I didn't know about your husband, I didn't know that he was a missing person.' He pronounced 'missing person' as if each word began in capital letters. 'I wouldn't have asked you to look after Izzy, if I'd known. I saw you were upset but I hadn't realized—'

Even if Abbie's face was unreadable, her silence spoke volumes. He was making a complete hash of it. He blundered on, anxious to get to the good part of why he'd called round, fearing as he neared that point that his offer wouldn't be enough.

'I was thinking, if I could do anything to help, I'd be more than happy to. You haven't got a computer, have you?'

She shook her head.

'Well, I thought, if you ever needed to use one – for the

Internet – or whatever, you're welcome to come up and use it. Any time.'

He was about to walk away when Abbie spoke. Quietly at first, shyly looking at him through the strands of hair in front of her face. He would have liked to reach out and brush them away so that he could get a better look at her eyes. You could tell more about what a person was thinking when you saw their eyes.

'Most people,' she said, 'when they find out about Nick, pretend it isn't real. Most people who *know* Nick, don't want to talk about him. Even his friends and family avoid talking about it.'

'Oh.'

'So, thank you, Owen, for not ignoring Nick and thanks for your offer.'

She shook the hair away from her face and smiled. For once she didn't cover her mouth and he saw her real, full smile which made her eyes light up and her face look pretty.

He went up the stairs feeling content. He was glad to have done it. It had been the right thing to do.

The phone rang just after seven in the evening. Abbie picked it up and heard Kate apologizing for ringing even before she'd told Abbie why she was.

'I wouldn't dream of asking you – particularly at such short notice – unless I was desperate. And I am, Abbie. Absolutely desperate.'

Abbie had to laugh at the drama in her voice. 'Kate. What are you talking about?'

'I need somebody tomorrow for a wardrobe fitting. The whole day. Practically everyone has gone down with the flu and I've got the whole cast for a regency play booked in.' She paused briefly. 'It'll be good money, Abbs. Double what you normally get.'

Abbie felt the tug of excitement at working with her favourite kind of costumes: lush materials, beautiful, detailed accessories. Before she could stop herself, she said yes.

'You mean it? That's fantastic. I can't tell you how relieved I am. It'll be like old times, Abbie,' Kate said. It was heart-warming to hear the pleasure in her voice.

Later that evening when Abbie was lying in bed, thinking of the day ahead, she suddenly realized what she had agreed to. What had she been thinking? She never left the flat empty in the daytime for more than a few hours. She saw the flimsiness of her notes, the bottle of vodka, the sandwich, the comfort of the living room, their cosy bed, the peaceful study, exposed under the harsh, mocking daylight. She saw their power to detain Nick flood out of the door as he walked in.

She reasoned with herself that it would be a terrible coincidence for Nick to return the one time she was out all day, but as soon as she permitted entry to that thought, she felt as if she had betrayed him. As if she were wishing him to stay away.

Before going to sleep, she made the decision that it was simply impossible for her to go. She convinced herself that Kate wouldn't really have believed that Abbie would turn up. Not after all these years. She hadn't imagined the sceptical tone in Kate's voice when Abbie had said yes.

In the morning when the alarm went off, Abbie didn't ring up to cancel. She ate breakfast and then went about preparing to leave the house. She kept the writing of the three notes as the final act. On each of these she wrote her location and Kate's business number and then sat for a while with them laid out on the table in front of her.

If Nick became bored waiting for her return, what could be better than to offer him somewhere to go? A familiar place with friends who would welcome him back? She felt a thrill at the rightness of it.

She resisted the towering panic as she closed the door. A

frail sun was making an appearance and people were hurrying on bus, on boat, on foot, like her going to their place of work.

The theatre was at that stage of total disarray before an impending performance. There was scaffolding, tarpaulins, enormous tubs of paint and nests of wires everywhere. As she passed one of the dressing rooms she saw a group of musicians crammed inside. The drone of strings echoed through the labyrinthine passages of the backstage where Abbie followed Kate. They walked past the green room, the production office and several other unnamed, closed doors. It became quieter and calmer the longer they walked. Finally, as if they were emerging into a sun-lit clearing, Kate swung open the final door to reveal the wardrobe department. High windows let in the light and gave a view from the back of the theatre to the red brick walls of the building behind.

Kate introduced her to the two women she would be working with – Beryl, a seamstress and Tilda, a cutter – before giving her a tour around.

The room had been extended since Abbie had last been there. The layout was unrecognizable. There were new cutting tables, two modern sewing machines on tables fixed against one wall; a corner screened off as a fitting area, and a desk with a computer. Behind the desk, Abbie spotted the new laundry room with two launderette-size, top-loading machines.

'The kettle and microwave are in there, as well,' Kate told her. 'I'm afraid it's going to be a pretty busy day but grab a drink or food whenever you can. I've scheduled breaks for eleven or so and then at two but you know what it's like – we'll be lucky to get them.'

A clothes rail had been wheeled into the centre of the fitting area and Abbie's first job of the day was to unload the clothes from the rigid cardboard wardrobes that they'd been transported in. Kate explained that most of their costume stock was now kept in off-site storage which explained why they felt colder than Abbie was expecting when she touched them; like a coat does on a winter's day.

Abbie had to hang the clothes onto the rail next to the fitting area and sort the outfits for each actor according to the listing that Kate had provided. She worked as quickly as she could and was just finishing when the first actors arrived.

Kate had allocated some of the actors to Abbie. Her role was to show them their costumes, measure and fit them. Kate was doing the same with the others but she was also supervising and making notes about any accessories or additional costume pieces that were going to be required. Tilda and Beryl were busy at the sewing machines and cutting table.

Abbie's second fitting was a brittle young woman who was physically trembling as she stood in her underwear. The woman was playing a teenage girl and her very thin body was childlike but her sallow face showed the wear of her real age. Abbie crouched down, tucking her hands in the folds behind her knees to warm them up before she took her measurements. The woman hadn't yet spoken a word but when Abbie brought over the dress selected for her she shrieked, 'Yellow? I can't wear yellow.'

Abbie stopped still. She felt the colour rise in her face. She looked around for help but Kate was already there.

'But, Colette, it suits you. Look.' Kate turned the woman to face the mirror, holding the dress up against her. 'Not many people can get away with it, but with your skin, it looks just perfect.'

Colette sank back into silence and as Abbie was helping her into the dress she glanced up at Kate, who grinned and gave her a wink.

Abbie found herself grinning back. She slid dress shields under Colette's armpits and began pinning in the back, working more confidently now.

In a moment of silence, Beryl's sharp voice rang out, 'And so I said he was not going to get into bed with me, dressed like that!' There was a short pause and then everyone started laughing. 'Oh, God!' Beryl said. 'Did you all just hear that?'

Her embarrassment made everyone laugh more. Abbie had to sit back on her heels and wait until she was composed enough to continue her work but it kept her smiling for several minutes afterwards.

During a lull, in the early afternoon, Abbie slipped away and found herself backstage. She stood in the wings. The stage was bare except for a roll of paint-smeared tarpaulin but it wasn't hard to imagine it full, to imagine herself looking round and seeing Nick, his face intent, ready to step in if the understudy was needed. Ready, always, over the weeks of rehearsals and performance; hopeful, every day; happy, even though he was never called for in the three-month run. The happiest she had ever seen him.

She heard someone approaching. It was Kate.

'Are you OK?'

'I think so,' she said but she was grateful when Kate didn't ask any more questions. She put her arm around her and gave her a hug. They walked back to the wardrobe department in silence.

Once the last member of the cast had been fitted, Beryl

made tea for everyone and they settled around one of the cutting tables as if they were going to be there for some time. Abbie politely drank hers but she was impatient to leave.

Kate offered her a lift home if she could stay for half an hour or so but Abbie didn't want to wait.

'Thanks, but I'll walk and get some air,' she told Kate.

'If you ever decide you want to join the team, permanently, I'd take you like a shot, you know that,' Kate told her.

'I've enjoyed it. I really have,' Abbie said, feeling shy as Kate gave her a quick hug.

She caught the first bus that took her within walking distance of the flat. She got off by the river. The sky looked steel grey. The air was freezing. It looked like it might snow. She stopped for a minute to work out the quickest route back and then set off.

As she came nearer to the flat, she deliberately slowed her pace. She had to keep one step ahead of herself. That's how she saw it. She felt quite dizzy with defiance but emboldened, too. She had to defy the hope that was growing. She pictured herself sitting on the goblin, pinning him to the floor. His legs – in black and white striped stockings – flailed furiously, trying to kick at the inside of her stomach.

She passed through the flat with business-like efficiency, checking the notes, the phone, the unlaid in bed, the unsat on settee. She put away the untouched drink, threw away the uneaten snack that she had prepared. Once this was done, she changed into her pyjamas and sat down to ring Becca. She heard laughter from someone passing the window as she waited for the phone to be answered. There was no reply, so she hung up without leaving a message.

She put on the radio, turned it up loud enough for her to hear it in the kitchen where she made herself tinned spaghetti on toast and a cup of tea. She hummed along to the songs as she prepared her meal. The toast popped up done exactly as she liked it; the spaghetti smelt delicious.

As she waited for the toast to cool she tried Becca once again and this time left a message: 'Becca, it's me. I just wanted to say hello and to let you know that I've been working at the theatre today – I'm exhausted but it's been great. I wanted you to know that . . . well . . . that it's been a lovely day.'

'What's so interesting?'

'Nothing. It's my neighbour.'

Owen heard Sylvia's heels clip across the floor. As soon as she was beside him he could smell her perfume and a strong musty undertone which he had never noticed before and which made him turn towards her as if he expected to see a visual source of the odour. Sylvia's clothes were as neat and clean as usual but the light from the window was harsh on her face – her skin was so wrinkled and pale it was as if someone had left her soaking in the bath for days.

'Your new paramour?' She gave him a searching look and even when he denied it, he felt flustered by her attention; as if she was determined to scoop out the truth from inside him.

He tried again. 'No. She's . . . I couldn't . . . she's too fragile . . . And she's married, anyway; she's very in love with her . . . her husband.'

'Fragile?' Sylvia flung out and then suddenly banged on the window, making him jump. 'She looks fine to me.'

Owen stared, helpless, as Sylvia pushed aside the grubby

net curtain and began tapping on the window and beckoning to Abbie, who had stopped still. Suddenly Abbie caught hold of her hair and pushed her head forward to peer across the street. He backed away, out of view.

'Is she a little simple?' Sylvia glared at him. He shook his head. 'Well, what you waiting for? Go and fetch her.'

He crossed the road. Abbie didn't greet him. She showed neither recognition nor annoyance. 'I think Sylvia would like to talk to you.'

'Sylvia?'

'She's a . . . um . . . elderly lady in the pub.'

Abbie did a kind of jump-start. She took a step forward then twisted back; her voice sounded urgent. 'What did she say? Why does she want to see me?'

'I think she just wants to say hello,' he replied but Abbie was already on her way and he wasn't sure she'd heard him. He caught up with her and they entered the pub together. Sylvia was back on her bar stool attempting a poised pose except one foot kept sliding forward and so she had to hitch herself more firmly onto the seat. He made the introductions.

'Charmed,' Sylvia said.

'Nice to meet you.'

'Is Abbie a shortening? Are you an Abigail?'

'Abbie's fine.'

'I hope you don't mind,' Sylvia said. 'I fancied some female company. All I ever get in here are men and we women like to have a bit of a chat about things, don't we, dear? And he said you were a lovely girl.'

Sylvia shot Owen a mischievous glance. He felt his mouth flap mutely in confused protest. He half-turned to Abbie but she seemed to be refusing to look at him. There was a short, potent silence during which Owen wished for the ground to swallow him up.

'I love your shoes,' Abbie said suddenly. 'Are they from the nineteen forties?'

'They are, my dear, they most certainly are. How clever of you to spot them.'

'They're beautiful,' Abbie breathed, surprising Owen by the softness of her tone. She bent down to look closely as Sylvia elegantly raised her foot and pointed it like a dancer. She met Owen's gaze and held it as if she was trying to convey him some kind of message. He felt giddy somehow as if he'd done something right, as if something good was going to come of this instead of something awkward as he'd feared.

'Sylvia,' Owen caught himself saying rather proudly and grandly, when Abbie stood up, 'Sylvia is eighty-three years old.'

'Wow,' Abbie said, which reminded him of Izzy. 'I'd never have guessed. You look incredible.'

Sylvia bowed her head in gracious acknowledgement.

'What can I get you both?' Owen offered.

'I'm not stopping,' Abbie was quick to say. 'I only came in to um ... to say hello—'

'Of course she's stopping. Don't listen to her. What do you have to do which is so urgent, my dear, that you can't even stay for one drink? I'll share a secret with you. The secret to a long life is a little daily drink.'

'I'm sorry, I have to ... I'm supposed to be back.' Abbie looked first at her watch then up at Owen. She was obviously appealing to him for support.

'Another time,' he said and Abbie's relief was visible, but Sylvia waved her hand in the air. She touched Abbie's shoulder. 'Not so fast.'

Abbie flinched. 'I can't. I'm sorry. I left a note for my husband. I told him I'd be home in an hour. I can't stay longer, in case he's back.'

Abbie ran. Literally ran away. The door from the bar flapped noisily behind her, like a saloon in a Western. Owen hesitated before following her out. He called after her but she didn't stop. She didn't look round. She just hurried in a half run–half walk down the street away from him.

'Come in, lad,' Sylvia called. 'You're making me cold.'

He returned to the bar and picked up his pint.

'Good Lord,' Sylvia said. 'What dramas.'

Owen felt winded from the events and Sylvia wasn't helping. He had warned her about Abbie, and she must have seen she was getting upset. Old people could be so obstinate. They were so intent on telling you the way of the world and how it all worked that they didn't listen to anyone else.

'Her husband's been missing for six years.' His voice sounded sharper than he'd intended. 'I think she has every right to be upset.'

It was a few minutes before Sylvia spoke. 'In the Second World War, a lot of men went missing in action. They were presumed dead. Two weeks before my fiancé was due to come back, he went missing, too. We were going to get married on his next leave. He sent me this ring.' She wriggled a finger at him. It was badly stained with nicotine. 'My engagement ring. He bought it in France and sent it over with one of his pals who was brought home injured. He wrote a beautiful love-letter, a proposal of marriage. He had his friend swear that he was wearing a ring, too.'

'I'm sorry,' Owen muttered. Now he really felt bad.

'Back then, you didn't know whether they were alive or dead. There was a shortage of men, of course, so the French women got their claws in some of ours before we had the chance.' Sylvia patted a cigarette out of the packet. 'I waited two years then I married his cousin. I've never regretted that. We had a good marriage until he died. Life goes on. Six years he's been gone, you say?'

'Yes.'

Sylvia lit the cigarette, inhaled. 'She's wasting her life,' she pronounced.

'I don't think she sees it like that.'

'I know. But she is.'

They were both silent for a few seconds until Sylvia spoke again. 'And what's your story? What went wrong between you and your wife?'

'It fizzled out,' he said. 'Our marriage was, I don't know, we just kind of drifted into it. We both, I think, felt that we never chose each other for the right reasons.'

'Fall pregnant before you married, did she?'

'Yes, how did you know?'

Sylvia laughed, throatily, then coughed. 'It's the oldest story in the book, my love.'

Abbie scolded herself as she hurried back to the flat. She should never have let herself be drawn in. She should know by now not to wake the goblin of hope; not to set his fingers poking at her insides. It was just that her expectations had been raised when Owen appeared out of the pub. His voice had sounded urgent and he had looked as if he was holding back something when he'd said: 'I think Sylvia would like to talk to you.' Why would anyone want to talk to her, except to tell her about Nick?

But as soon as she got in there, she knew that it was nothing to do with Nick. Sylvia just wanted to make small-talk so Abbie had to get through all the pleasantries and politeness until she could get out of there.

As she left, she'd turned back towards the door, and seen that the poster she'd asked to put up only a few months ago had disappeared. They were always being taken down, or stuck over with posters of gigs and DJ nights. No one in that pub had ever taken Nick seriously.

They had never been welcome. You would have thought

they would have been grateful for the amount of custom their crowd brought in, but instead they were constantly being asked to keep the noise down. One time Nick had been refused a drink at the bar because the barman had said he'd had enough. It had been an old guy then who walked with a stick and was incredibly slow to get drinks. For all Abbie knew it might have been some relative of Sylvia's. She was just as ancient and had that same suspicious look about her, as if she was sizing up Abbie all the time, as if Abbie was the strange one, and that it was perfectly normal to be wearing clothes from another era and to dye your hair blonde and wear make-up in an attempt to make yourself look forty years younger than you were.

It had been a frustrating night all round. Abbie touched the flyers inside her jacket pocket. She hadn't been able to give many away. People stayed at home on rainy Monday evenings. She had been in two minds whether to go further afield into Central London but there didn't seem much point.

The bottoms of her jeans were soggy and the inside of her trainers felt damp. She pulled up her hood. She comforted herself that she would soon be home. You never knew, that was the thing. You never knew what a wonderful surprise there could be there. Waiting for you.

If you had three wishes, what would they be?

— You first.

— You, a house by the sea somewhere wild, like Scotland, a dog.

— You've already got me. You've wasted one.

— Just in case. Just to make sure. Now you say.

– Fame, fortune and all that it brings.

– That's only two.

– I'd keep the other one for when I needed it.

– That's cheating.

– That's prudent, Nick says and he looks pleased with himself.

Abbie unlocked the outer door and stepped inside. The darkness billowed around her. She rested her cheek against her front door.

If she had one wish, or a hundred wishes, it would always be the same. To push open the door and to find her wish come true would be amazing. It would be the best thing in the whole world. Her heart would leap ten thousand feet and she would never come down. If she had ten thousand wishes, they would all be the same. Just to make sure.

The flat felt cold. She turned the thermostat up and the boiler in the kitchen woomped into action. She hurried around the rooms, turning on lights, collecting the notes up. In the kitchen she put away the vodka into the freezer and threw Nick's cheese and pickle sandwich in the bin. In the bedroom, the bed was undisturbed. In the living room, though, the telephone showed she had a message on the answerphone. She dripped rain onto the handset as she stood over it.

The message was from Kate. She was just wondering, she said, whether Abbie had given more thought to her suggestion to work a day a week at the theatre; perhaps a couple of days when there was a cast dressing. 'It's just, if you do, there's a really nice job coming up in a few weeks' time. Very modern, no holds barred, very creative stuff. I'm sure you'd love it. Give me a call whenever. Take care. Bye-ee.'

Kate's breathy, happy voice filled the room returning Abbie instantly to that busy, happy day. But scattered across the picture, like a flock of birds scared into flight, came the thought of the preparation involved.

She went through it, one by one. Step by step. Gradually, as her mind settled, she discovered that the idea of working there again did seem to be a possibility. She would ring Kate tomorrow to check the date to make sure that it didn't clash with Nick's birthday party.

Owen was surprised but pleased to see Abbie standing at the door.

'You said I could use your computer.' She spoke in the abrupt manner of hers, her hand held up against her mouth so that it muffled her voice and drew attention to her eyes. They looked black and were unreadable through the mesh of her hair. Owen wondered if it was a trick of hers; that she shook her hair in front of her face on purpose, to hide. She blinked and averted her gaze.

'Sure, yeah, of course. Come in, come in.' He hurried her over to the PC so that she might not see too much of the mess of the place, which he suddenly felt ashamed of. What, he wondered, did he do with all his time? She sat down and he turned the computer on and logged on to the Internet for her.

'I'll leave you to it. Coffee?'

'Thanks.'

When he handed over the mug, she barely looked up.

'Managing OK?'

'Yes. Thanks. I usually go to the library.'

He wasn't quite sure where to go with the conversation after that. He watched her hunched forward towards the screen as if she was shielding it from his sight.

'Look,' he said to her back. It seemed almost easier talking to her that way. Easier for her, anyway, than face to face. 'I'm sorry about the other day with Sylvia. I mean, old people, God. They can be a bit strange, can't they?'

He wasn't sure what she said in reply – something about being used to it.

'Is it OK if I put the TV on to catch the headlines?'

'Oh, please.' This time she did look round. 'I don't want to stop you doing what you usually do.'

'Not cleaning, obviously,' he joked into empty air as she immediately turned back again. He zapped the TV into life and tried to concentrate on what the newsreader was telling him but he couldn't help glancing round the room. He couldn't blame the kids for the mess. Their stuff was mainly in their bedrooms. It was his newspapers, office papers, odd items of clothes, even, he cringed, a pair of dirty socks just left on the floor at the end of the settee. Not to mention the two glasses and one, two, three mugs distributed randomly around the room.

What did he usually do in the evenings? He often found he was bored and restless; that time seemed to expand limitlessly in front of him when he got home from work but somehow had magically evaporated by midnight when he began to think he should go to bed. Unlike the weekends he had failed to settle himself into any kind of routine or activity. He hadn't even been for a run yet, even though he'd got his kit out ready weeks ago.

Abbie's presence was unsettling. He was intensely curious about what she was doing. He wondered if she was on the Missing People's website. He checked it himself at least once a week, he didn't know what for. It had become strangely addictive. Perhaps there was a separate special area for those people whose loved ones were missing. He found himself feeling, illogically, a little cheated at the idea.

'I've finished. Do you want me to switch it off?'

'No, it's OK. I'll be using it myself in a minute. Do you want a top-up of coffee before you go?' When she hesitated fractionally, he saw his chance. 'Take a seat,' he told her.

As she approached the settee they ended up performing one of those awkward step-side-steps before Owen put a hand on her arm to stop her moving and slipped past her to the kitchen.

He glanced behind him to check that she was actually sitting down. It looked as if she was watching the TV. He didn't trust her not to disappear, to rush away suddenly as she seemed prone to do. He half expected to hear the clunk of his front door closing and to find her gone before he'd finished making the drinks. He slopped spoons of instant coffee into mugs and barely let the kettle come to the boil before he yanked it off the base.

'I'm a programmer,' he said as he walked towards her. She looked confused. No wonder. He was plucking things randomly from his brain just for something to say. 'A computer programmer. It's quite creative really. You're making something, piece by piece. You're looking for patterns, connections and also where the holes might be.'

'A bit like my sewing, I suppose.'

Her grin was sweet; a flash of her prominent teeth before she pulled her lips over them and hovered her hand in front of her mouth. Her eyes were watchful. He could tell that she wasn't quite comfortable with him.

'You work somewhere at night as well, though?'

'What makes you say that?'

He felt caught out. 'I've heard you,' he said. 'Going out, coming in late.' He blushed furiously, remembering too late the one time that he had followed her.

She shook her head. 'I go looking for Nick.'

'Do you? Where?'

She shrugged. 'Everywhere. It's the best way to do it. I take flyers and talk to people that might have seen him. I go to places he used to go, or where he might be drawn to, instinctively.'

'Instinctively?' He wasn't quite sure what she meant.

She set her face as if she was tired of explaining this, but he was interested. He really was. He wanted to understand.

'If someone loses their memory, they lose all their past references, but they're still the same person. Nick might still have the same urges, the same likes and dislikes. So I go where I know he would like to go or where he used to go.'

He didn't know if that was true. It sounded plausible but he vaguely recollected reading somewhere that amnesiacs basically had to reinvent themselves. That they created a new personality. He felt bad thinking it, but he was inclined to believe that Abbie's theory was just wishful thinking. He felt, suddenly, terribly sorry for her.

'And you go looking for him on your own? Isn't that rather dangerous? It's a bit dodgy round here, don't you think?'

'It looks worse than it is, mostly,' she said. 'And anyway I can take care of myself.'

Perhaps he had her all wrong, after all. Perhaps she was tougher than he gave her credit for. Certainly the idea of Abbie out on her own at night, approaching complete strangers, was at odds with the shy, nervy woman that he'd seen so far.

'How did you and Nick meet?' He saw that he had startled her with the question. She flushed but then brightened.

'You really want to know?'

'If you don't mind talking about it?'

She smiled; another rare smile which she let flourish and fade naturally without obscuring it with her hand. It struck him that it was only when she was talking about Nick that she forgot to cover her mouth.

'We were teenagers, well younger, really. I was twelve. Nick's nearly three years older than me. The same age as my sister. We hung around in the same gang.'

Twelve. Not much older than Izzy. He felt appalled at the idea of his daughter falling in love with someone so soon. Or ever, for that matter.

'It was love at first sight. I couldn't take my eyes off him,' she said. 'He was different to everyone else. Special. Everyone thought so. There was just something about him which made him stand out. I couldn't believe it when he chose me, although I'd wished for it a thousand times. I always knew that I never wanted to be with anyone else.'

He felt humbled. He had never experienced such complete,

unconditional passion for Fliss although he had often wished he could.

'People tell me I should forget about him, but I don't want to. He was the best thing that ever happened to me, so why would I want to forget that?'

'No, why should you,' he agreed but he couldn't help wondering why people would say such a mean thing to her.

'I know he'll be back,' she said, suddenly. 'When he gets his mind sorted, when his memory returns. I never doubt that.'

He looked at Abbie in alarm. There was something odd about her. She was flushed and her eyes had glazed over, as if she was drugged or brainwashed. He felt wariness shiver through his body. The hairs on his arms prickled.

'Abbie?' he said softly. 'Are you all right?' It took a few seconds before he felt that he had her attention again.

'Oh, dear, I'm sorry.' She looked incredibly embarrassed. 'I go a bit over the top, I know.'

'That's OK.' He sounded lame. He was back-pedalling in his head. Had he imagined that strange moment earlier? Abbie looked fine. She seemed perfectly normal as she sipped her coffee.

'Are the children coming this weekend?'

'They were supposed to but they both have things on. They have a life of their own, if you know what I mean – clubs, friends, social stuff – which they miss out on if I drag them all the way here. I'm going over to see them tomorrow. I'm not sure the arrangement is working too well,' he added and felt himself grimace. Recently, this uninvited thought had kept cropping up and its persistence made him very uncomfortable.

'Perhaps it would be easier if you lived closer to them.'

'Yes,' he said, rather surprised at her insight. 'I've been thinking that, too. It's the obvious solution—'

'But?'

But what? He'd gone over this in his head so many times that he'd given up trying to understand what he should do. He knew that it would probably be better for the children if he wasn't so far away, but it also seemed to him that a retreat in a physical sense would somehow prove to be a backward step for himself. And for Fliss.

'Things are muddled right now,' he said evasively.

'Are you on good terms with your ex?' Abbie asked. She dropped her head a little and her hair fell forward.

'Yes. Very.'

'Do you still love her?' she asked in a rush.

'No,' he said. 'Well, yes, but as a friend.' His answer came out rather sharply. He wondered how much time would have to elapse before people stopped asking him that question. Before people accepted that Fliss and he would not be getting back together.

'They say men don't like to talk about love but Nick did. He'd talk about it all the time; he said it is the most important thing in the world no matter how much people try to deride it.'

Owen felt tiredness sweep over him and a desolation that made him sigh. 'I don't think I've ever loved someone properly. I don't think I've ever allowed myself to.'

He must have closed his eyes because when he next looked, Abbie was standing up. Her stomach was at eye-level and he had a sudden desire to pull her towards him and briefly rest his head there. Just long enough to feel her warmth. He looked up at her and she held his gaze.

'I hope you will,' she told him. 'Because it is the most wonderful feeling in the world.'

He accompanied her to the door.

'Where do you work?' she asked him at the front door.

'The big Sceptre building off Heligan Road in SW10. Do you know it?'

'Yes. If I bring up a few posters, do you think you could hand them round to people? Or stick one or two on the notice-boards? There's a theatre near there that Nick sometimes used to go to.'

'Well, sure.' He thought it would be unlikely he'd be able to help. They had strict rules about putting up personal things but he would give it a try.

After Abbie had left, Owen was surprised to find it was only eight o'clock. He felt as if he'd been in a time warp. He went to the kitchen to make some food but discovered a three-quarters full bottle of wine which diverted him from his culinary intentions.

He found a rerun of *Only Fools and Horses* on the TV which gave him a few welcome laughs but he was still grateful when his phone rang at nearly nine o'clock. It was Izzy. Late home as usual after dance practice. He knew immediately she had some big news and he was chuffed to bits that she had thought to ring to tell him.

'I *know*,' he heard her say irritably to Fliss. 'Dad?'

'Baby cheeks.'

She giggled. 'Don't be stupid! Guess what? I've been picked for the choir in the school show!'

'Honey, that's brilliant.'

'It's called "Singing in the Rain".'

'What is?'

'The song, the song I'll be singing.'

He sang the first line.

'You know it!' She sang the line back to him and he thought his heart would break.

'That's stupendously fantastic! That's brilliant!'

'Are you mucking about?'

'No, sweetheart. I'm proud of you. You have a wonderful voice like your mum.'

'Mum can't sing.'

'Can't she?'

'No! Don't you remember, Dad, you were always telling her to shut up.'

How mean of him, he thought, to have crushed someone's joyous moment when they burst into song. He poured the last inch of wine into his glass and drank it straight down. 'It was only a joke, Iz, but your voice is better. It's the best one out of all of us.'

She sang another part of the song then stopped abruptly. 'Mum says it's time for bed.'

'It is. Sweet dreams, my love.'

'Night, Dad.'

Love. He might not have felt passion for their mother, but he was filled with it for his kids. They say children will change your life for ever and you hear these words; you even believe that you can prepare yourself for them but all you're doing is preparing for the practical changes, the physical presence of a child. What you can never guess at is how overpoweringly real and amazing they are. How suddenly everything has a meaning and a centre. It becomes impossible to do anything without referencing that fact in your life.

Owen would do anything for his children. He would tear his body to bits for them, if he had to.

The next evening when the entrance buzzer sounded in the flat, Owen's first thought was Abbie and her posters. His heart sank. He'd remembered to make some tentative enquiries at work but had achieved nothing other than some strange looks from Office Admin and the discovery of an ambiguous and unhelpful page in the Staff Handbook.

He was making his way to the front door when he suddenly realized that Abbie wouldn't need to press the buzzer. She was already inside the building. He had a visitor!

He rushed to the living-room window prepared for the disappointing sight of a salesman or a Jehovah's Witness but it was Steve. He shifted uncomfortably from foot to foot and when he looked up and saw Owen, he gesticulated frantically to be let in. Seconds later, Steve was stomping up the stairs, breathing heavily and cursing Owen for taking so long.

He stopped in the doorway. 'Nice jammies, man.'

Owen was wearing a set of Wallace and Gromit pyjamas, of which he was very fond, that Tom had given him for Father's Day. He didn't, he decided, have to explain himself to Steve. 'Bit late for social calls, isn't it?'

'I've walked out. I couldn't stand another fucking minute.'

'You've what?'

'Fucking walked out. I've had it—' He stomped across the room and jabbed his hand out at neck height. 'Up to fucking here.'

'Keep the noise down,' Owen warned. 'Remember Abbie.'

'Abbie?'

He pointed. 'Downstairs. Neighbour.'

'Yeah, right, OK.' Steve began taking off his coat. 'So what do you think, mate? Can I stay here?'

'Sure. You can have my room.'

'I don't mind bunking in one of the kids' rooms.'

'No. Take mine. It's fine.'

Owen wasn't being generous, he simply wasn't happy allowing someone else in either Tom's or Izzy's room without asking them first. It didn't seem right.

'Thanks, mate. It'll only be until I get myself sorted.'

Get himself sorted? Owen had assumed Steve had only been asking about staying overnight but this was beginning to sound a lot more serious. A worrying thought occurred to him. 'You do intend to go back, don't you?'

Steve shook his head. 'No way, we're done.'

'Are you sure about that?'

'Uh-huh.'

Before Owen had a chance to pursue the matter, Steve slumped onto the settee and took possession of the remote control. 'Have you got a beer? I could murder a beer.'

'I'll go and get some,' Owen said, glad to escape. 'Won't be long.'

He was halfway to the shop when his mobile rang. Fliss.

'I was going to ring you,' he told her. 'Guess who's just turned up on my doorstep asking to stay?'

'I think I know. I've been talking to Julie on the phone for the last half an hour. She's in a right state. She blames you, you know.'

'What have I done?'

'She thinks you've been encouraging him.'

'That's crazy. Why the hell would I do that?'

'Don't worry, I've almost convinced her that you haven't been. What *are* you doing, Owen?'

'I'm on my way to buy some beers. Just arriving at the shop – now.' He pushed the door open.

'So what has he said?'

'Not much. Just that it was over but I took that as Steve's dramatics. I've told him he can stay.' He put a couple of four-packs of lager into his basket and then added a third.

'Oh, great. What did you do that for?'

'What else was I supposed to do? I couldn't exactly turn him away.'

'I suppose not,' she said, rather grudgingly from her tone of voice. 'But you are going to talk to him, aren't you?'

'I'll try. He didn't seem in a very chatty mood, though. Maybe these beers will help.'

He nodded and smiled at the woman on the till. He put his card in the reader and tapped in his PIN while she packed the beers into two bags.

'You've got to get him to go home.'

'I can't make him,' Owen protested. 'And I certainly don't think it's likely he'll go back tonight.'

'What makes you say that?'

'I don't know – maybe the way he's made himself comfy on my settee with the remote control.'

'I don't think you're taking this seriously, Owen.'

'I am. What do you want me to say? I am going to talk to him, all right. I'm just saying that I don't know if it will do any good.' He stopped outside the shop and put the bags down. 'I've got to go, Fliss. I can't carry all this with one hand.'

'What am I going to tell Jules?'

'I don't know. Not to worry. Give him a couple of days. Something like that. You know better than me.'

'I'll ring you tomorrow. Oh – and Owen – if you need to talk about anything – I'm here, you know. If you need me.'

Abbie cut off the final piece of cotton, laid the shirt aside and stood up. She brushed her clothes down then packed everything away into her sewing box. She took the box and the shirt into the living room. Holding the shirt by the shoulders, she shook it out, to rid it of any bits of loose thread and the worst of the creases before hanging it up on the rail.

She picked up her notebook and pen and sat the table. She tore out four pieces of paper and laid three of them aside. On the fourth, she wrote the heading, 'Nick's party' and underlined it three times before starting the list of food and drink that she needed to buy from the shop. When she had thought she was finished, she went through the list several times more before she was satisfied that she hadn't forgotten anything.

She wrote out three notes. *At corner shop. Back soon. xxx.* She added the time in the bottom corner so Nick would know when she had left. She put the notes out, locked up and then hurried down to the shop.

She took her time, buying the items in the order they appeared on the list so that she didn't miss anything. She wished she had brought the pen with her so that she could have crossed them off to make doubly sure. The only thing they didn't have were cake candles but she only needed one and she thought she probably had some left over from last year.

The woman on the till offered to help her pack, but Abbie preferred to do it herself; the shop assistants always used far too many bags which made it awkward to carry. Abbie managed to fit everything into two, keeping the weight evenly distributed.

Abbie had taken two steps towards home when she realized that the woman coming down the street was Sylvia. Before Abbie had time to think, Sylvia saw her and called out. They walked towards each other. Sylvia moved slowly. Out of the pub, she looked tiny and frailer; as if she might fall over if you blew on her.

'I thought it was you. Owen's friend.'

Sylvia's deep, strong voice caught Abbie off guard. 'Well, not really his—'

'What you got there then?'

'Sorry?'

'In the bags, dearie.'

Abbie didn't know what to make of the woman's interest in her shopping. She held the bags behind her legs and didn't reply. Sylvia looked at her. Abbie found her eyes as unnerving as the last time they'd met.

'Tell me, is Owen your boyfriend?'

'No!' Abbie was startled. 'He seems nice, but—'

'But?'

'But nothing,' Abbie responded firmly, catching Sylvia's challenging tone. 'He's my neighbour.'

'So you don't have your eye on him?'

'Perhaps you got the wrong impression but I hardly know Owen. He's my neighbour; he lives in the flat above me. I thought I'd told you, I'm married.'

Sylvia gave a knowing smile. 'Yes, yes. Your husband's been gone, though, a few years.'

'Six.'

'My fiancé went to war and never came home.'

Abbie felt the lurch in her stomach. She searched Sylvia's eyes; her own filling up. She thought here is a woman who has survived this. A woman who has lived until she is eighty-three.

'When he didn't come back after two years, I knew he was dead. I married his cousin.'

Abbie felt confused. Sylvia was watching her. A malignant smile was spreading across her face. Abbie flinched when she felt the weight of Sylvia's hand on her arm. She wrenched her arm away and dodged past the old woman, out of her reach.

'You can't wait for this man for the rest of your life, dear; you might as well just get on with it.'

Abbie carried on walking. Her skin was crawling where Sylvia had touched her. She shook her sleeve as if she could still feel her presence there; as if one of the maroon coloured nails had snagged on it and attached itself. She felt the hairs on the back of her neck prickle. She looked behind her but Sylvia seemed to have vanished.

Owen could see Steve behind him in the reflection on his PC screen. It was nearly ten o'clock and while Owen had been surfing the Internet for the last two hours he had been watching Steve on and off. Over the past five days he'd been amazed at his friend's seemingly inexhaustible capacity for watching TV, combined with his ability to remain completely immobile for long periods of time as if welded to the settee. He had reached the conclusion that either Steve could sleep with his eyes open or he had an unnaturally large bladder.

The phone rang. Steve's head shot round. So, he was alive at least.

'Hello.'

'Owen, it's Fliss. Where are you?'

'I'm at home. You just phoned the landline, Fliss.'

'I meant, where in the flat? Is Steve around? I need to talk to you about him.'

'OK.' He stood up. 'It's for me,' he told Steve.

'I take it he's there, then?'

'He's always here,' Owen said once he'd shut Izzy's bedroom

door. 'The whole weekend and every night since. Once he comes in from work, he never leaves the flat. In fact, he never leaves the settee. He just watches the TV all night. It's driving me nuts.'

'Has he said anything about going home?'

'No. Not a thing.' Owen moved his work clothes off the bed and hung them from the hook on the back of the door. He sat with his back against the padded headboard of the bed. The padding was thinner than it appeared and a piece of wood pressed into his spine. 'He doesn't seem to be in any rush to leave.'

'You've got to make him, Owen. Julie's frantic.'

'I can't. I've tried. He won't talk to me. In fact, I can barely get a word out of him.'

'But you two talk about everything.'

Owen gave this some thought. 'I don't think we do, really,' he said. 'But, anyway, he doesn't want to talk abut this. Look, Julie's quite welcome to come round here and have a go herself because I'm certainly not getting through and, to be honest, I'm sick of trying.'

'How can you say that? These are your friends.'

'Frankly,' he whispered, 'I would have thought Jules would be glad to be rid of him. He's a real messy bastard. And boring. Why would she want him?'

Fliss giggled. 'She loves him. You put up with all sorts when you love someone.'

Even after they'd said goodbye, this phrase of Fliss's stayed with him. Of course it was simplistic but that didn't stop it from being true. The fact that Julie was willing to put up with Steve and all his shortfalls counted for something. For a lot, even.

Owen returned to the living room.

'There you are, mate,' Steve greeted him. 'I made you a tea.' He indicated the mug on the coffee table. 'It might be cold now.'

'Cheers,' Owen took a swig. It was warm and weak. Steve always made the tea milkier than Owen liked it. 'Listen, Steve, it's my turn for the kids this coming weekend.'

'Nice one.'

'Except there's a bit of a problem—' He left the sentence hanging to give Steve the chance to cotton on. After a few seconds in which Steve's attention switched from him to the TV and back, Owen told him: 'We haven't got enough beds.'

'Oh, OK.' This time, Steve made it quite plain that the conversation was over. He turned back to the TV, changed channels and sank further down on the settee. Owen sat beside him for a few minutes and then returned to his web surfing, feeling defeated.

The next night, Steve came home later than usual. Owen heard him dragging something heavy up the stairs and went to let him in. Steve pushed a tall cardboard box into the hall.

'A Z bed,' he announced but Owen had already gathered what it was from the packaging.

'I'll put it up in Tom's room,' Steve said. 'We'll be bunk buddies.'

At about ten o'clock on Thursday night, Fliss rang.

'It's Fliss, for me,' Owen said.

'For people that aren't supposed to get on,' Steve remarked, 'you don't half talk a lot.'

'Yes, mostly about you,' Owen half-joked as he headed to Izzy's room for some privacy. It was true. Since Steve had arrived at his flat, Owen had spoken to Fliss about him every single day.

'I'm not sure it's appropriate for the kids to come this weekend, Owen. Not with Steve there.'

'He's bought a Z bed. He can go in the living room or Tom's room.'

'I'm not talking about the sleeping arrangements. I'm worried about the kids. First you and me split up, then they find out their Uncle Steve and Aunty Julie might be about to, as well. It's not going to make them feel very stable, is it?'

'So, they don't know anything about Steve being here?'

'There didn't seem any point if the situation was going to blow over.'

'I'm not sure that it will.'

'It's not looking good, is it? I don't suppose Steve's said anything yet?'

'Nothing. Look, Fliss. I've got to see the kids. I've been looking forward to it for days. I'll tell them Steve's staying with me for a holiday and I'll make sure he doesn't say anything else. If I don't think it's working for the kids, I promise I'll kick Steve out immediately.'

He held his breath in the pause while Fliss considered his suggestion. He knew he couldn't argue if she didn't agree. He'd been worrying about the effect Steve's presence might have on them, himself. He just didn't want to admit it. He needed to see the kids so badly.

'OK,' Fliss replied.

Owen mouthed 'Thank you' to the ceiling.

'But see how it goes, Owen. If there's any chance of them getting upset, promise me you'll either bring them home or get rid of Steve.'

'I will.'

'Maybe they'll drive him away with their squabbling. God knows you're obviously making it much too comfortable for him there.'

Tom raced towards Steve with a burst of enthusiasm that Owen would have given a limb to be on the receiving end of.

'Uncle Steve!'

'Tomahawk! Give me five.'

They struck hands and whooped while Izzy and Owen looked on.

'Play you?' Tom shouted leaping towards the Xbox.

'Yeah, Tomahawk. I'm in the mood for winning.' Steve grabbed hold of Tom and they began to mock fight. Tom was almost hysterical with excitement and Steve wasn't much calmer. It never ceased to amaze Owen how electrified his son could become about computer games.

Izzy gave Owen a look that he could only describe as bemused despair. 'Can I go to my room?'

'Of course, Iz. You don't need to ask.'

After half an hour of watching Tom and Steve playing on the Xbox and feeling like a spare part, Owen wandered down the hall. He was pleased to see that Izzy had left her door open as if inviting him for a chat. She was lying on her bed, her legs waving in the air, writing in a notebook. She had one headphone in, so the sound of music from her mp3 was just discernible. He knocked on the door.

She folded her arm across the page of the notebook. 'Hi, Dad.'

'Mind if I come in?'

'OK.'

'I hope you're not feeling left out in a house full of males.'

'It's all right. I just wanted to get my homework out of the way.'

'Good girl.' He touched the top of her head lightly.

'Dad? Are Uncle Steve and Aunty Julie getting a divorce? I mean, you can tell me now that Tom isn't here.'

'What makes you say that?' In the car, both Tom and Izzy seemed to have readily accepted Owen's explanation for Steve staying with him.

Izzy had applied some blue eye shadow. It looked like a woman's act on a girl's face. Her expression was the same, a mixture of the child and adult, with neither one of them sitting true. Izzy's pen rested against her bottom lip. 'I heard Mum talking to Aunty Julie the other night.'

'I don't know,' he said honestly. 'Uncle Steve and Aunty Julie feel they need a few days apart to help them think about things a little more clearly.'

She started chewing on the top of her pen. 'Is that what you and Mum are doing?' She wouldn't look at him; she continued to chew her pen. He knew that she was trying not to let him see that she was hoping – really hoping – that he was going to say yes. It took every ounce of his strength not to lie to her. 'No, sweetheart. Your mum and I have already made our decision.'

'I thought so, really,' Izzy said flatly. 'I was just checking, in case.'

There was a commotion in the hall and then Tom burst in with an ear-damaging yell. 'I won, Dad. I won!'

Steve appeared in the doorway. 'I let him,' he said, mock-seriously. 'I'm lulling him into a false sense of security.'

'What does that mean?' Tom asked.

'It means you need to watch out in the next game, mate.'

'Look at what I've got.' Tom held out his clenched fist to Izzy. She sat up, closed her notebook and pushed it behind her, under her bum.

'What is it?' She shrank back. 'It had better not be a spider. Dad, tell him it had better not be a spider.'

'It's not. Cross my heart.'

Izzy leant forward and Tom opened his hand. Izzy shrieked. Tom let out a howl of laughter. He held his hand up, his face glowing with triumph. A fat spider in black marker pen had been drawn on his palm. 'It's not real, you baby!'

'Grow up. And get out of my room,' Izzy said with a sudden fierceness which stopped Tom in his tracks.

'It's not real, Iz,' he said, looking confused. 'I'll draw one for you, if you like.'

'I think it's time we gave Izzy some peace,' Owen interjected. He bent forward and gave Izzy a quick kiss on her cheek. 'OK, sweetheart?'

He took hold of Tom's bony shoulders and ushered him out of the room.

At the door Owen stopped and glanced back. Izzy was back to lying on her stomach; she had her chin propped up on one hand and the ends of her loose hair hung down onto the notebook which was open in front of her. She didn't look round.

Abbie saw Owen and Izzy approaching the house. She stepped back from the living-room window but they had already seen her and waved. Abbie waved back and then, after hesitating for a moment, she walked to her front door and opened it.

'We've been to the shop,' Izzy said. 'To get a DVD. I'm bored. Uncle Steve and Tom have taken over up there.' Izzy curled her lip, disapprovingly. It made her sweet face look rather comical.

'Why don't you come down, later? I've got some hats that I need to decorate and I could use your help.' The offer was out of her mouth before she had thought about it.

'Can I, Dad?' Izzy pulled on her father's arm like a young child.

'Are you sure?' There was no mistaking the hope in Owen's voice.

'Yes, I would love to have some company.'

Izzy came down an hour later. It amused and flattered Abbie that Izzy had thought to put on some eye shadow and a glittery top with her jeans to visit her. She dangled the little violet bag from a wrist.

Abbie asked Izzy to sit at the table and placed the hatbox in the middle of it. Inside were five plain ladies' hats. The instructions on Kate's inventory were to 'tart up in the style of an Edwardian boating party and picnic. White and pastel colours only, please.'

'OK,' Izzy said. 'Are they in there?'

Abbie nodded. She really hoped Izzy would enjoy working on them with her, otherwise she was soon going to be as bored as she was upstairs.

Abbie opened the box and laid the hats out.

'I think I like that one.' Izzy pointed to a bleached white hat with a floppy rim at the front while Abbie chose a soft cloche hat to start with.

'What are we going to decorate them with?' Izzy asked, looking round.

'Oh, yes. I forgot. Can you put the other hats away, please, Izzy?' Abbie pulled a large box of scraps of material out from under the table. She scooped up a heap of them in her hands and dropped it onto the table; she added another handful.

'Use whatever you like,' she told Izzy rashly, thinking that she could always undo Izzy's work if it was too awful.

Izzy began to sift through the pieces; she picked some up and put them down. Abbie watched Izzy's fingers hover over a piece of sepia rose-printed chiffon which she had her eye on. She was relieved when Izzy didn't choose it.

'Can I have this?' Izzy asked, holding up a wide sky-blue ribbon. 'I could put it round the hat.'

'And leave it hanging down the back perhaps?' Abbie gently suggested.

'OK.'

'That sounds great. I'm going to use this.' Abbie held up the chiffon.

'That's pretty,' Izzy said.

Abbie first showed Izzy how to sew the ribbon in place without the stitches being visible then she cut the chiffon into eight circles of decreasing size to make a flower. She attached this to a beige headband she had secured around the bowl of her hat.

For several minutes neither of them spoke.

'Do you miss your husband?'

Abbie was startled by Izzy's question. 'Yes, very much.'

'What does he do?' Izzy wanted to know.

'He's an actor.'

Izzy's eyes widened. 'Like a film star?'

'Well, not as famous but yes, that's what he does.'

'Wow.'

'It's his birthday on Tuesday,' Abbie told her. 'But he might not make it home. I'm holding a party anyway. His parents are coming.'

'But he might miss it.'

'He'll know we're thinking about him, though.' Abbie was surprised how happy that made her feel. She smiled encouragingly at Izzy who was looking upset. 'And that's what counts.'

– Happy Birthday.

He makes me sit on the bed. He hands me an envelope – my birthday card – and a tiny wrapped present.

My hands are shaking. I don't know why. I open the card first. It's a black-and-white photograph of a couple kissing by a French photographer called Doisneau. Inside it says, 'I love you.' Just that.

Nick is watching me keenly as I begin to open the packet which is flat and crackles whenever it's touched. It takes a few seconds to realize that it's a condom.

– We talked about it.

– Yes.

It's my thirteenth birthday. The one which I've been waiting for ever for, except now I can't stop trembling and if my limbs would only work, I swear I would scrabble upright, stand, panting, with my hand on the door handle and dare him ever to touch me again.

– Where? I ask him.

– Here, of course.

He eases me to lie back on the bed. He removes my blouse, he tries to unzip my skirt but he can't do it so I have to. I take off my bra but I've still got my knickers on. Nick has removed his shirt and I try not to look when he takes his jeans off. Under his blue check underpants, I see the swell of his penis. I put my hand on it, like I've done before. He takes off my knickers and then his underpants.

His penis springs up. It butts wetly against my leg like the nose of an insistent dog.

I've thought about this moment so many times and each time it's been different. Except for one thing. The room is near dark, with hazy, warm light which softens and blurs. It has never been like this with the daylight so fierce that even with the curtains drawn, it will be as if a spotlight is directly upon me.

– It's OK, he tells me. – Just relax.

He plays with me and then I begin to forget where we are. I begin to feel all that I imagined I would feel, as I do when I play with myself in my bedroom when I think about him. He reaches across me and picks up the condom.

– Do you know how to put it on?

– Sure, he says. Only afterwards does he tell me that he's been practising doing it all week. So he'd get it right. For me. On my birthday. His face is serious as he sits up, leans over himself. I'm scared but I want to giggle.

Then Nick is ready. He lies on top of me and pushes my legs apart. I immediately try to close them but I can't. His weight is too much for me. I struggle then for a minute but he holds my arms.

I become conscious of every sound our – my – body makes. If I could only turn the volume up on the TV where Nick's favourite video: *The Prince and the Showgirl* is playing. The remote control has just fallen off the bed and I can't reach it. I ask Nick to close the window but he says he can't, of course. We need to hear in case anyone comes home early.

– It'll be OK, he tells me. – No one is coming. It's just in case.

There isn't a lock on his door and this thought makes me feel sick.

– Open your eyes, he tells me. – Open them, Abbie.

When I open them, he pushes inside me. I feel it shocking and real. He starts pushing in and out and his face is different to how I've ever seen it before. It's frightening because he no longer looks like Nick. It's over, quickly. And as soon as it's over, I know that I want to do it again and again.

We can't stop, whenever we get a chance, we do it. In his

room, twice, three times a day, hurried and rushed. We even do it when his mother is driving up to the house. I can hear the car but I don't say anything because I want him to finish. I want to feel that shudder of him. I want to feel that he has done something with me. I want to feel him hold me roughly, pull me close, kiss me gently. All these things I can't get enough of. But more than that, it is as if we have reached a different level, accessed a different part of ourselves and each other. A private, deeper part which will stay with us for ever. Which will bind us together, for ever.

'That was your door.'

Abbie looked up in surprise at the sound of Izzy's voice and blushed when she met the girl's inquisitive eyes.

'I expect it's Dad checking up on me.'

Abbie stood up quickly and rushed to the door. It was Owen. He looked worried. 'You have still got Iz here, haven't you?'

Abbie blushed again. 'I'm sorry, it's my fault. I completely lost track of the time.'

'Not to worry. This young lady knows the rules. She must just have forgotten to mention them, isn't that right, Iz.' He hugged the girl, who had come from behind her. Izzy giggled.

'Has she been OK?' he asked quietly, hanging back while his daughter went up the stairs ahead of him.

'She's been fine,' she told him, already beginning to close the door. She returned to the living room where she examined Izzy's work. The trim was a little lopsided and the stitching was showing through in places but the blue against the white perfectly suited a day by the water.

Abbie closed the curtains and turned on the lamp. She took

her sewing box to the study along with Izzy's hat and began to unpick the ribbon.

Later that evening, on her way to the kitchen, Abbie discovered a card pushed under the door. It was from Izzy. A big apple-green tree dominated the centre and the sky was covered in silver and blue glitter. Inside she'd written: 'Dear Nick, Happy Birthday, Love Izzy.'

Everything was under control and yet Abbie still felt nervous. She was watching out of the window but kept turning round to check that the room looked all right. She wondered if the 'Happy Birthday' banner hanging across the shelving was off-centre then made another adjustment to the position of her and Izzy's cards which she had placed on the telephone table.

She returned to the kitchen to check that the cake still looked as tasty and tempting as she thought it did. She grated another square of extra chocolate onto the top because she knew Nick's mother was a big fan of chocolate and the topping of the shop-bought cake was a little stingy.

In the bathroom mirror her reflection looked unfamiliar. It could have been the make-up which she so rarely wore these days, it could have been the way she'd cut the sides of her hair so that they fell softly away from her face. It might have been the silver-frosted light from the small high window which cast a glow to her skin and a brightness in her eyes.

What she liked about the day was when Marion talked about Nick as a boy and Abbie could feel him, his presence solidifying in the time they were there. She could feel Nick's exasperated pleasure at his mother's childhood stories and the way he laughed off Roger's remarks. Roger who never missed the opportunity to tell Nick that he should get himself a proper job one of these days.

A birthday is a hopeful time. A birthday is a date that might stick in your mind, no matter what you've been through. She and Nick had always made a big thing about birthdays.

– Take your time, kiddo, he says. – There's no rush.

We're out shopping because Nick's money from a radio commercial he did has come through. I bite my tongue about the red bills piling up and the food we need. He's got the whole day – a special day – planned for my birthday. After we've chosen my present, we're going for a drink in the West End before buying a bottle of champagne and booking into a hotel for the night.

– How about this? he says and I pull a face at the top he's holding up.

– It's see-through.

– Exactly why you should get it.

I spot some earrings; they're long with blue stones, as blue as his eyes. They feel weighty in the palm of my hand. We buy them and I put them straight in. I move my head, ponderously from side to side and feel them swing under my hair.

Nick looks troubled. – What do you mean, no? A shadow has passed over his face. – What do you mean, you don't love me?

I am laughing so much that I can hardly speak and then I kiss him and tell him that I do. How could I possibly not? I watch the light burst into his eyes and I don't think I've ever been happier.

*

Each year they were always so precisely on time that Abbie always wondered if they sat in the car a little further down the road until it was exactly one-thirty. And each year their visit seemed to become shorter and shorter. Marion was getting a little frail and she fussed about Roger driving into London and travelling back in the dark. Last time they had left only two hours later to avoid getting caught up in the rush-hour traffic.

As soon as she saw the car draw up, she went to the front step. She always waited there to greet them because Marion needed to take her time getting out of the car and she became flustered if she felt rushed.

It wasn't Marion's bowed head or Roger's white hair which emerged first but a person whose profile and shoulder-length black hair made her freeze. The person turned to face her, but Abbie already knew that it was Helen, Nick's sister. They looked at each other across the top of the car and then Helen gave Abbie a quick wave before ducking down to help her mother.

The three of them were approaching her. Marion's movements were slow and stiff, Roger hovered beside her like an over-anxious terrier, tripping against the edge of the path in his distraction. Behind them – taller – came Helen. Abbie could hardly bear to look at her. But, when she did, she was surprised to see Helen's eyes were like Roger's – small and a sort of hazel-green colour. Meeting Marion's blue eyes, she felt the shard press against the flesh of her heart. She managed to kiss and hug them all briefly and even to get them settled in the living room before escaping to the kitchen to make tea and to compose herself.

Helen's voice sounded loud in the flat, Roger's was softer but deep. Abbie could even hear a gentle murmur which must have been Marion and yet, when she entered the room, nobody was talking. All three seemed startled to see her. She had a sudden sense that something was wrong. She stopped in the middle of the room tempted to let the mugs of tea tumble and spill onto the floor to break open up their silence.

Abbie sat down at the table. She raised her mug and toasted Nick. She watched as they all hurried to add their voices but the way they averted their eyes, made her stomach drop.

'What is it?' she asked them, her voice sounding strange. 'What's wrong?'

'Abbie, love—' Roger's tone was dauntingly sweet. 'There's nothing wrong, but . . . we have to tell you . . . we're selling up. We're moving to Spain.'

'Spain,' she echoed.

'Yes.'

It took a moment for it to sink in and in that moment, Abbie looked at each one in turn: Marion's face was pinched with pain and tiredness, Roger's was tanned and healthy. Finally, her eyes travelled to Helen whose unflinching gaze and half-smile jarred in Abbie's brain.

'But what about Nick? You can't abandon him.'

'It's not like that, love, you know,' Roger said. 'I'm afraid there's nothing we can do for him.'

'There is.' Abbie felt the confidence rise in her that she could convince them of it. 'You can believe in him.'

She heard Marion's gasp and turned towards her. A mother would never abandon her child, she thought, and saw in the way that Marion didn't stop looking at Roger that there had been coercion there.

'It was your idea,' Abbie accused him.

'It's what we both want to do,' he replied firmly. 'We can't live like this any more, Abbie. We've done all we can. All of us. It's time to let go, to look after ourselves. Marion needs the sun. It helps her arthritis and we're happy in Spain. We feel better there. Life is easier.'

Abbie looked at Marion's buckled fingers lying in her lap and the way she hunched forward, as if her body was curling in on itself. She was much worse than last year but Abbie still felt bitter. 'Easier to forget.'

'No!'

Abbie turned in surprise at Marion's voice. She was shocked at the strength in it and the defiance in her face. She looked like a headmistress about to tell you that the punishment is for your own good.

'We've thought long and hard about this and the decision hasn't been an easy one. But, it's done.' Marion's tone softened. 'We loved him, Abbie, but we don't believe he's still alive.'

'And besides, we're not abandoning him,' Roger said. 'We're passing our new contact details to the police and leaving them with everyone else we know. Helen will live in the house for the time being, so if he turns up, then—' He paused. 'And, of course, you'll be here.'

Marion cut in. 'But we don't believe that he will return and that's why ... we think ... well, we think you should stop waiting for him.'

'You're too young,' Roger added quickly. 'You're a lovely girl, who deserves more out of life.'

'You must be lonely, Abbie. No one would think the worse of you if you met someone else.' Marion's lip quivered as she spoke. 'I'm sure you must want to have a family.'

Abbie leant forward. 'Yes. With Nick.'

'Oh, Abbie, you know that's never going to happen.' Abbie turned away from Marion's look of pity and was confronted with a mocking expression on Helen's face. A face of ridges and curves, the mouth exactly like Nick's. If Helen hadn't come, if it had all gone on as before with Marion's stories and Roger's quiet presence then this wouldn't be happening. Helen was four years older than Nick and she had never really liked him. She always called him the spoilt brat.

'If he is alive,' Helen said, without taking her eyes off Abbie, 'which I don't believe for one second, then I have no doubt he knows exactly what he's doing. He'll be living the life of Riley he always did, in some country, living off some woman like he did with you. I know you think I'm a cow, Abbie, but the best thing you could do for yourself is forget about my brother and get on with your own life. You can bet he's doing just that, he's not killing himself worrying about you.'

'He loves me.'

'Not as much as he loved himself.'

'Helen.' Her father's voice was curt and firm. She flushed but it didn't stop her. 'Look at us. Even when he's dead, he's got everyone fussing about him. He always had to be the centre of attention.'

'No,' Abbie told them. 'It's not true. None of that's true. I know you never thought much of Nick's career.'

'Career. That's a joke.' Helen let out a derisive laugh.

Abbie ignored her. 'I'm sorry, but I think I'd like to be on my own now. I think I'd like you to go.'

She stood up and waited for them to stand up, too. She refused to look at them, she refused to speak. When Marion hugged her, Abbie imagined her body petrified, hard and unyielding. She would not cave in.

Her only thought was: how could you?

Fliss's ten o'clock phone calls were becoming worryingly regular and a little annoying. One of the few things he liked to watch on TV was the ten o'clock news and he was always missing it, stuck in Izzy's room, listening to Fliss giving him a countdown of how many days it had been since Steve left Julie (thirteen today); and telling Owen how he should be doing more to get them back together.

He drew the curtains and settled himself on Izzy's bed.

'Who is this Abbie that Iz keeps going on about?'

'She's the woman downstairs. The one whose husband has disappeared.'

'The man that's been gone for years?'

'Yes.'

'I thought so.' Owen could tell from Fliss's voice that there was more to come. 'To be honest, I'm not very happy about Iz spending time with her.'

Ah, yes. There it was. 'Why ever not?'

'Well, the thing is, Owen, this Abbie doesn't exactly sound normal. Did you know she told Iz the other day that her husband was coming home soon? And that she was holding some kind of birthday party for him? A man who's been dead for—'

'Missing. Nobody knows if he's dead.'

'Oh, come on. He's as good as dead as anyone can possibly be, without there physically being a body. I think the woman is seriously delusional.'

'It's a difficult thing to explain to a young girl. It's a complicated story. I think she did the right thing.' He was evading the truth. He knew that Abbie's motive for telling Izzy that Nick would be coming back wasn't really to protect his daughter, it was because Abbie believed it. She absolutely believed Nick was still alive.

'Except I get the impression this Abbie has actually bought into her own line which means that she's got to be mentally unstable,' said Fliss as though reading his thoughts.

'That's a bit of a leap. Iz had a great time. It was good to see her doing something different which she enjoys.'

'I'm just not comfortable about it and I can't see why you can't see it.'

'See what?'

'That it's inappropriate for Iz to spend time with her.' That word inappropriate again. 'Is there something else?' Fliss asked.

'I'm sorry?'

'I mean, is it really you that's interested in Abbie?'

Owen felt affronted. 'Not in the way I think you're implying.'

'Don't jump down my throat, Owen. I'm only trying to find out what's behind all this.'

'There's nothing behind anything. Iz likes Abbie and she enjoys going there. It's like a fucking giant dressing-up box in that place, what young girl wouldn't want to go there? And I think Abbie likes the company; she doesn't seem to have many visitors—'

'I'm not surprised.'

'I think it's a great combination.'

'And I think we're going to have to talk about this another time.'

'Fine, let's do that.' He said a rapid and curt goodbye and returned to the living room, where Steve was looking unusually animated. He had even, Owen noted, managed to turn his head a full hundred and eighty degrees away from the TV.

'Bit of a heavy one, was it? I couldn't help hearing you shouting.'

'I wasn't shouting, I was trying to get my point across. Fliss seems to think Abbie's some kind of psycho who I should keep away from Iz.'

'Well, Abbie is a bit strange, you've got to admit, but I don't think that's what's bothering Fliss.'

Steve had assumed a knowing expression.

'So?'

'So. I reckon she's jealous.'

'Who, Fliss? Of Abbie and Iz?'

'Of Abbie and you.'

'There is no Abbie and me.'

'Isn't there?'

'No, of course not. For fuck's sake, don't you start.'

'Ah-ha, so I was right. Fliss does think that,' Steve said sounding pleased with himself.

'She doesn't now. I've made it quite clear,' Owen said, failing to control the exasperation in his voice.

'Only trying to help,' Steve called out, sounding aggrieved as Owen escaped to the kitchen.

Owen ran a glass of water. He drank it slowly, standing with his back to the sink. He could hear the murmur from the TV in the living room. He could always hear the TV wherever he was in the flat. He gripped the glass tightly. He wanted quiet. He wanted to sleep in his own bedroom and wake up to the Mediterranean light. He wanted Steve out of his home. He didn't know how long he stayed in the kitchen. When he passed through the living room on his way to bed, Steve didn't bother to look up.

Abbie's anger was like a constant humming in her head – it spiked and dropped from time to time – but it never ceased.

She was angry at her home which had suddenly become claustrophobic. The last few days she felt as if she'd grown huge like Alice in Wonderland and was now so big she was stuck inside. She was angry at Nick's parents, who today had sent her a letter containing a photograph of Nick which they thought she would like to have. He was standing on a beach dressed in shorts and a stripy T-shirt. He looked about ten years old. He was very thin with sharp elbows and knees; the peak of a baseball cap darkened his face and obscured his eyes. They wrote that she must always think of them as being there for her if she should ever need help. She need only ask.

She almost ripped up the letter in her frustration at the way they failed to see that the only way to help her was to wait for Nick, to continue to believe in him. She didn't understand why they couldn't see that.

She was angry mostly at herself, for letting her search for Nick slide.

One evening when she was looking through the list of contacts and places, she realized that renewed and much greater efforts to search for him were required. She burnt with guilt because she had barely been out looking for him for over two weeks. She had let herself be distracted by too many things lately and she couldn't afford to be distracted any longer. Not now Nick needed her even more than ever. This gave her a jolt. Nick needed her more than ever.

She phoned Kate at home to tell her that she wouldn't be able to work at the theatre after all. Kate seemed surprised to hear from her; Abbie hadn't realized it was nearly eleven at night. Kate said she understood but there was disappointment in her voice which freshened Abbie's anger. She found herself speaking more sharply to Kate than she should have. When she put the phone down, instead of feeling relieved, Abbie felt both incredibly tired and restless.

In the fridge was Nick's four-day-old birthday cake. Abbie took it out and checked for any signs of mould. The chocolate icing was glossy from the cold; it almost looked plastic. She took a knife out of the drawer and cut into the cake; the top crisped under the knife but the sponge was soft and yielding. She ate a single piece where she was standing before throwing the rest of it in the bin.

In the bathroom, she found herself staring at a stranger's face; childlike with pale skin and big, dark eyes. She wiped a finger across the smear of chocolate on this face. She tasted the sweet, sickly taste of cake, sticky on her tongue, sticky on her finger. She leant over the toilet and threw up.

She watched another face, blotchy, streaked with tears as it brushed its teeth.

She undressed and walked naked to the bedroom.

If you could have three wishes what would they be?

She got into bed and turned to look into his eyes: Nick, Nick and Nick.

You are caught in a spiral which whirls you round then dumps you down into a landscape which is grey and white and flat and stretches as far as you can see. You don't recognize this place but there is somewhere, ahead of you in the distance, which clamours for your attention and you know it is important. That the most important thing that you have to do is to get there.

You walk, dragging your heavy feet with each step. You stumble and roll over a precipice and you are falling. The ground beneath you spins: greens and browns and a blue which makes you dizzy. Your descent slows and you are now running, swiftly, as if your feet are barely touching the ground. You can see nothing but ice-blue in front of you but you are sure that you are on the right track so you keep on going.

Something catches your eye. It's a shadowy figure to the left of you which is running, too, and you know that he is heading to the same place. Your feet are flying now. You look down and see them below you, moving so quickly it's as if magic wings on your ankles are propelling you forward. You understand that if you both keep on running, that you will reach the place where your paths converge and you will finally meet. You think how happy, how amazing that moment will be. Your heart will leap ten thousand feet and you will never come down.

You look across and your heart stops. The shadow is fading

and flickering as if the light is failing. You call to him. He's disappearing fast now and you try to slow down, to stop and reverse back to him but your feet are moving, flying of their own accord. Behind you, if you twist your head, you see that he is the one who is retreating; he is becoming smaller and smaller and dimmer and dimmer. You let out a scream which echoes around you and there is a whistling noise, so piercing that it sucks all colour into it like a collapsing star leaving only whiteness. And then he is gone.

Owen had stayed at work later than usual so he caught the tail-end of the chaos caused by a security alert. The Victoria line had been shut down for over an hour and although the trains were now running, there were severe delays.

The train he was on was packed solid and an unpleasant mixture of burger and BO scented the warm air. He was standing by the doors so that each time they opened, he was jostled and shoved as more people tried to squeeze on and others attempted to get out. He lost count of the number of times someone stood on his foot.

It was a relief to finally get off and Owen walked along the platform happy to go at the steady pace of the crowd. A few feet ahead of him, he spotted a tall woman whose thick, brown hair swayed gently as she walked. He caught a tantalizing glimpse of close-fitting jeans and a short cream jacket. He began to walk a little quicker to see if he could catch her up. He was filled with the urge to see her face. He had begun to gain some ground when he lost sight of her.

He almost walked into her. She was on her knees, picking up the contents of her bag which had spilt out onto the stone floor. The man who must have caused the accident was standing over her.

'Yes,' Owen heard her say loudly in a clear, precise voice. 'You can watch what you're bloody well doing next time. You're not the only person in the world, you know.'

The man turned abruptly away. She caught Owen watching. He held out his hand to help her up and she took it.

'Oh, dear. I was a bit rude, wasn't I?' She tucked her hair behind her ears and smiled. She had a nice smile.

'Maybe a little, but I'm sure he deserved it.'

She laughed. 'He did knock into *me*.' Her eyes were blue and lively.

'It's madness tonight,' she said, as they continued to walk towards the exit.

'Yes,' he said. 'Totally.'

Outside, it had stopped raining and the sky was lighter than he'd expected. The evenings were beginning to draw out.

'Well,' she said, pointing in the opposite direction to Owen's route home. 'I go this way.'

'And I go that way.' As he watched her walk away, he was filled with the regret of an important moment missed and yet, as he set off, his mood lifted. He strode out.

The next day, Owen had arranged to help Fliss take two of Izzy's friends on their monthly trip to the ice rink. It was their 'turn' in a long-standing arrangement with the parents of the other girls. He left work early and managed to secure a seat on the train so that he was able to give his thoughts over to the coming evening. He was looking forward to seeing the kids and particularly spending some time with Tom. It sounded as if his son would be in need of an ally. Fliss had told him that Tom had been complaining about being dragged along with a 'bunch of girls'.

Owen spent no more than five minutes in the flat. He changed, had a quick swig of juice from a carton in the fridge, cleaned his teeth, gave Fliss a call to say he was leaving and then went out to the car. The car badly needed a wash; it was filthy from standing on the street. Someone had drawn a face in the dirt on the door panel. He thought wistfully of the jet wash sitting idle in the garage.

The journey seemed to him much longer than normal. He had to force himself to concentrate on the road and not clock-watch but there were no serious delays and as he turned into the drive, he found he'd made really good time.

He rang the doorbell and, after a few seconds of waiting, almost fished his keys out of his pocket but then Fliss opened the door.

'You're early,' she said, looking flustered. 'Not that I'm complaining. The girls are in there. Would you mind checking on them? I'll be back down in a minute.'

As Owen opened the living-room door the excited chatter of three girls immediately ceased. Izzy flung herself towards him and draped herself limp and warm against him but he'd barely had time to hug her back before she'd recovered her cool and slumped down on the settee with her friends.

'Hello, girls,' he directed at the other two.

'Hello, Mr Renshaw,' they intoned at him, their eyes fixed to the TV. He watched the programme for a few seconds but quickly got the feeling that he was spoiling their fun so as soon as he heard Fliss coming down, he went to join her.

'They're fine,' he reported. 'What are their names again?'

'Charlotte and Kylie.'

'They never look like the same girls twice.'

'Charlotte's had highlights put in her hair,' Fliss said, 'which has set Izzy off on one as you can imagine.'

Tom came in looking miserable.

'Perhaps I should stay home with Tom,' Owen suggested, hopefully.

'You're not leaving me trying to look after three excitable girls on skates.' Fliss's tone was amused but firm. 'You never know, you might even enjoy it.'

'We'll sort something out,' he had time to whisper to Tom, giving him a wink. He was rewarded with an expression of pure gratitude from his son.

'Are you having a go, Tom?' he asked when they were buying the tickets.

'I'm not allowed.'

'What do you mean?'

Tom hung his head. Owen glanced at Fliss, who shrugged back. She shepherded the girls along while Owen paid for everyone except Fliss, who had declared herself exempt, and handed Tom his ticket.

'Iz said I wasn't to hang around with her and her friends.'

'I'm sure that she only meant she wanted some time alone with them, that's all. You and I can stick together and not even go near them.'

Owen and Tom hadn't even finished putting on their skates

before Izzy and her friends were away and skimming around the ice like a trio of pros.

It had been a long time since Owen had last skated and he was beginning to remember that he hadn't been very good at it back then. The girls swept past. He and Tom inched their way along the perimeter, clinging to the side. It seemed an age before they were back at their starting point where Fliss was established on the benches as custodian of bags and surplus clothing.

'You're doing great!' she shouted to them. 'How about letting go!'

'Easy for her to say,' Owen muttered.

'We could try.' Fear and hope played across Tom's face which set off an eruption of daring in Owen. He grabbed Tom's hand and they half ran, half skidded across the centre of the rink, gaining momentum until they slammed against the other side, intact, laughing.

Fliss waved at them; clapping her hands in the air.

It was a relief when after another couple of slow turns around the rink, Tom accepted Owen's suggestion of a refreshment break. Afterwards, despite a couple of offers from Owen, he seemed content to remain on the benches and watch.

Fliss was kept busy as the girls constantly required something from their bags: money for the vending machine, lip-gloss, a mobile phone to take pictures.

Izzy, flushed with cold and pleasure, seemed to grow with confidence over the hour. Owen noticed that she, out of the three of them, had the most elegant way of curving slowly into the side as she came to a stop.

'She's so pretty,' he remarked to Fliss, who smiled in agreement over Tom's head.

It was eight o'clock by the time they had dropped the girls off and arrived back at the house.

Owen stayed while the children got ready for bed and Fliss took a shower. Neither of the children was very talkative so he contented himself with wandering around Tom's room switching off anything that was showing a standby light. With Izzy, he hovered in the doorway while she unpacked her schoolbag. She handed him her lunchbox to take down to the kitchen.

Fliss came out of the bedroom. She was wearing a red kimono. Her hair, wet from the shower, looked dark, giving her a rather glamorous oriental appearance that Owen had always found attractive. She swished past, pausing only briefly to tell Izzy, 'Lights off in ten minutes.'

She stopped at the top of the stairs. 'Are you coming down?'

In the living room, at Fliss's invitation, he poured them both a glass of whisky.

'That was fun,' he said. 'Isn't Iz amazing?'

'Tom hated it,' Fliss said. They both laughed.

'At least he had a go, though. He always gives things a try.' Owen was about to tell Fliss about the meal at the Chinese restaurant but he kept quiet. It was a memory to treasure for himself.

Fliss stretched her legs out onto the footstool. Owen didn't remember her looking so relaxed for a long time.

'They're good kids.'

'Yes,' he agreed. He contemplated his whisky glass and reluctantly set the remains down on the table. 'I guess I'd better get going.'

'Why don't you stay?'

'No, it's OK. Thanks,' Owen said, thinking of the hideous guest bed.

'I mean stay with me. For old time's sake. That would be OK, wouldn't it? If we had one night together? It wouldn't harm anyone.' She was suddenly there, next to him, kissing him. He sat, paralysed, his arms pinned to his sides by Fliss's legs. There was a slither of silk and then she was standing in front of him. Her kimono gaped, revealing a breast and a glimpse of her stomach. She backed away, holding his hand and led him up the stairs.

At first Fliss's body seemed different to his touch, but his hands quickly recognized her familiar shape as he held her. She seemed more willing, more open than he could remember her ever being but their love-making was as silent and careful as it had always been. Slowly, stealthily, a sadness began to creep up on him until he could no longer deny its presence. He grabbed around in his head for something to take hold of to get him through and fixed on an image of Lisa.

Afterwards, he couldn't look at Fliss. He pulled her against him and they lay together, unspeaking, for several minutes. Her hair was still damp; several strands were sticking to his arm.

'Would you tell me, if you slept with someone else?'

If Lisa had lied, if she had betrayed him and told someone who had gossiped to Fliss then she would know it was true, just from the way his heart was thumping.

'After all, you are an attractive man. There will be women out there who would want to sleep with you.'

'Thanks. I think there's a compliment in there somewhere.'

'So, would you?'

'I think it would depend.'

'On what?'

He felt sure then that she didn't know about Lisa and the relief made him brave enough to test the ground a little more. 'If it was serious or not. If it was a one-night stand, or someone I wasn't likely to see again, then I probably wouldn't.'

'I'd tell you.'

'You don't know that for sure.'

'I do. I would.'

He thought for a few seconds and then said, gently, 'Well, perhaps you shouldn't. Maybe we've got to get used to not telling each other things.' He reached out to set the alarm. 'Better make it early, so that I'm gone before the kids wake up.' He left it hanging as if it was a question.

'Yes. Good idea,' Fliss said. She turned on her side and settled against him; her bum felt cold against his legs. He turned off the lamp and fell asleep, quicker than he would ever have imagined he could.

Discipline. Commitment. These words rolled through Abbie's mind as a constant reminder of what was required of her.

And yet, when the alarm went off at ten o'clock, she had to force herself out of the enveloping darkness by invoking a mantra: this could be the day. This could be the day that I find Nick.

Once the shock of the alarm had eased, she was pleased to discover that she was able to carry out her preparations to leave with greater efficiency and calm than she had managed the day before. She would, she determined, do better in every way than yesterday when somehow, she didn't know how – perhaps it had simply been a lapse in concentration – she had circled back on herself and was actually walking down a street where she had already been. She only became aware of it when a man shoved the flyer back in her hands and told her that he'd been given one of them an hour ago. Sure enough, when she had looked around, there were discarded flyers all over the place. She had started to gather them up but they were all spoilt, torn and dirty and screwed up.

On her way out, she thought she caught sight of the pale image of Owen's face at his window again but the wind was blowing her hair across her eyes and by the time she captured it under her hood and took another look, there was nothing there. She realized that she was mistaken.

There was a sharpness to the wind which sent a shiver through her. She put her head down and walked quickly. Her first call was to The Ship down on the river.

Once she was in sight of the pub, she pulled her hood down, shook her hair free and felt inside her jacket pocket to get the flyers ready.

She was blocked from going further than the top step by a bouncer. 'Hang on a minute, love.'

It was a square-jawed woman with white-blonde hair cropped short. The only make-up she was wearing was a very bright red lipstick which served only to make her small mouth appear smaller.

'Sorry, we have a weekend dress code. No jeans, no trainers.'

'It's OK, I'm not stopping, I'll only be in for ten minutes and then I'll leave.'

'No can do. Step aside, would you, and let these people pass.'

A hen-party of women dressed as nurses shrieked and laughed their way inside.

'But I have to. I have to get in there.'

'That's what they all say, love.'

'Hang on a minute.' The bouncer from the other side of the entrance approached. 'Don't I recognize you? Didn't you bring all those leaflets about that missing guy the other week?'

She turned away from the woman, smiling. 'Yes, that's me.'

'Bit soon to be giving them out again, isn't it, love? You'd be wasting your time.'

His eyes were kind but his face was set. Abbie knew immediately that he wasn't going to allow her inside. 'I don't think so,' she appealed to him. 'You never know, you see. You only need one person to—'

'I'm sorry, love.'

She turned away down the steps.

'Look,' he called after her, holding out a large hand, hairy as a paw. 'Give me a few and I'll take them in. That's the best I can do.'

She passed a small pile up to him.

'And don't come back for a while,' he said, suddenly sounding irritable. 'I mean it. OK.'

She didn't know where she was going. She walked and walked until her feet were aching and the salt of her tears was stinging the skin under her eyes. Remember, she told herself. Remember all the good things.

He comes home with flowers on Valentine's Day and a book that I've been wanting for ages, signed by the author. When I am paging through it several days later, I discover his kisses on the very last page.

He calls Becca and tells her that he loves me and that it is imperative she remembers that because it is of the utmost importance.

We bump into each other on the street when I'm coming out of the local shop. He sings several lines of 'When you're in

love with a beautiful woman' and when he's finished he stops
a couple who are walking past and says, – May I present to
you, the woman who I love most in the whole wide world.
Abbie – my wife.

Abbie came across an old iron bench on the pavement. Its
back was to a fenced-off overgrown area of land around a
dark, derelict building. The street was quiet and the bench was
intact so she sat down. She had been there barely five minutes
when a couple of policemen pulled up in a squad car.

'You all right, Miss?' the driver called out to her.

'Yes, thanks.'

'Not the place to stop at night. You'd better move on.'

'I'll be gone in a minute. I'm only resting.'

'Have you been drinking, Miss?'

'No.' She stood up and approached the window. Their faces
were obscured in the dark of the car but she knew they were
scrutinizing hers. 'Do you know where I can get a bus?'

'Back up the street, turn left.'

She set off. She stopped a few metres along and looked
over her shoulder. The car had remained stationary – no doubt
they were watching her progress in the mirrors. She carried
on, following their directions, and in two minutes she was in
Grosvenor Place.

The bus was full. There was a drunken couple who were
having a loud, heated argument and this seemed to be pissing
off the other passengers. They were certainly less receptive
than usual as she walked the length of the aisle, handing out
Nick's flyers. Someone pinched her bum and she stumbled,
almost falling over as she turned to confront the putty-coloured,

blank face of one young lad and the amused expressions of three of his friends. When the bus stopped again, the driver yelled out to her to sit down or get off, so she sat as close to the front as she could.

Each time someone passed her getting on or off, she tried to press a flyer into their hands. From her seated position she was witness to all sorts of intimate details which she would never have noticed otherwise: bitten fingernails, a broken zip, a lot of grease stains, the bulge of a belt under a tight jumper, the brown spots on an elderly gentleman's hand which clutched the head of his walking stick – a carved silver hare. He took the flyer, considered it briefly before handing it back, shaking his head solemnly. He mouthed something at her, but she was unable to make out what it was before he walked on.

Between the stops she closed her eyes.


He rings me up one day and says, – I just had to tell you I love you.

I say, – Is there something wrong?

Nick laughs and I can hear someone talking in the background. There's music. He must be in the pub or the snooker club.

– Nothing's wrong. Don't be silly. Can't a man tell his wife that he loves her?

They announced my name over the Tannoy system in the shop and I have had to come up to the manager's office to take the call. The manager is pretending to be busy with some papers but I can tell he's listening.

– Of course you can, I reply. – Thank you.

– Thank you! he shouts out. – She says thank you!

There is more laughter and someone claps. I am nervous for the rest of the day and when I get home Nick is there already.

– I've been waiting for you, he says and he takes me straight to bed. After we've made love, he says, – Thank you! Abbie, Thank you!

We shout – Thank you! Thank you! over and over again.

She opened her eyes. In the window, she saw her image smiling back.

If a hand were to touch her shoulder right here, right now – a hand heavy with love – she would keep still and let the warmth cascade down her body.

He says, – You are a much bigger person than me, and when I protest he shushes me.

– You must remember that you are a great person, Abbie, and I'm proud to be your husband and I think the world of you.

The alarm went off at five.

'Quick,' Fliss warned. 'Turn it off.'

They listened for a few seconds but there was no sound from the kids. Owen got dressed, feeling slightly nauseous and light-headed from lack of sleep. Fliss, tugging on her kimono, was first out of the room. She waited on the top of the stairs for him as she had the evening before, except now her face was tired and strained. He felt the complications swarming over him as he walked down the stairs behind her. She gave him a quick kiss goodbye at the front door. Once he had heard her relocking it, he walked to the car.

He drove up to the nearest burger place. He felt ravenous. He bought a giant coffee and a double sausage and egg sandwich which he ate in under five minutes.

It was only just after seven o'clock when he arrived home. Owen wondered if there was any chance Steve hadn't noticed his failure to come back last night. He parked, got out, glancing up at the flat. The curtains in the living room were still drawn. He walked down to the shop for fresh milk and bread.

When he went into the flat, Steve appeared almost immediately. He had on the baggy yellow T-shirt and pair of faded blue boxer shorts that he always wore in the mornings. He rubbed his arms as if he was cold, while he watched Owen put the milk in the fridge and the loaf in the cupboard.

'What happened to you last night?' he asked.

'I stayed over with the kids.' Owen waited for the probing questions and the knowing looks but was relieved when none came.

'Nice one,' Steve mumbled and wandered out, calling back, 'I'll have one if you're making one.'

Owen filled the kettle, took two mugs out of the overhead cupboard, dropped a teabag into each and picked up the sugar canister. Sleeping with Fliss had been a really stupid thing to do and the shame of his action hit him so forcefully that his hand jerked, sending sugar flying across the work-top. It was done, he told himself as he wiped up the mess, and he would have to deal with whatever he had set in motion. It was done and could not be undone. After a lunch of fish and chips and a couple of stupefying hours in front of the TV with Steve, Owen could think of nothing better to do in the afternoon than go to bed. When he woke up, he knew immediately that he'd been asleep for ages. As he walked through the flat, he felt disorientated. There were no lights on, not even the TV was on. He tentatively pushed open the door to the main bedroom. No Steve.

He discovered a note in the kitchen.

'Back later. Fliss rang.'

It was nearly half past nine. With a shock he realized that, for the first time, he had missed ringing the kids. He stared at Steve's scribbled writing and wondered how he was going to explain himself to Fliss; sleeping through the afternoon would sound completely lame.

There was a knock on the door. He rushed down the hall and then paused before opening the door, trying to make sense of who might be there.

'I brought these up. You said you'd display them.' Abbie thrust a pile of papers at Owen. Bloody hell! There were dozens. The building would be plastered in them. He became aware that Abbie was watching him closely.

'Great,' he said enthusiastically. 'Thanks. Do you want to come in?'

As she passed him, he caught a strong smell of alcohol. Following her into the living room he suspected that she might be drunk – she seemed to be having trouble walking although this could equally have been due to her cumbersome slipper socks which were designed to look like sheep. He remarked that Izzy had a similar pair, only cats.

'Becca gave them to me. I feel the cold.'

'Becca?'

'My sister.'

He put the PC on but she didn't go over to it, instead she hovered in the middle of the room until he made a point of asking her to sit down on the settee.

He scanned the room. 'Sorry, it's a bit of a tip. I've got a friend staying at the moment. He's just split up with his wife, so—'

'It's fine,' she interrupted. 'I hadn't noticed.'

She accepted his offer of a glass of wine and held it balanced on top of her knee. Her eyes were so wide and unfocused that he began to wonder if she was on drugs. The PC hummed away in the silence, which seemed to gather strength the more he struggled for something to say. Trust Steve to be absent the one evening when he could have done with him around. He suddenly remembered to tell Abbie that her costumes had recently inspired Izzy to join the local youth drama club.

This seemed to trigger something in Abbie.

At first Owen thought she had started to sing, which would have been strange enough, but then he realized it was more of a chant spoken in an eerily childish voice.

'If you had one wish, or a hundred wishes, it would always be the same.'

She took a long drink of wine, not noticing that her hair was dangling into it, and stared into space. He called her name but when he didn't get a response he leant forward to place himself in her line of vision. She barely raised her head except to drink some more wine. He saw clearly now that she had had far too much alcohol already. He would have taken the glass away if he had known her better, but he was worried about how she'd react.

She started to speak again. At first he thought she was addressing him, but he couldn't make sense of her words. He came to the unsettling realization that she was addressing herself.

'You think how amazing, how happy that moment will be. Your heart will leap ten thousand feet and you will never come down.'

He went into the kitchen to fetch water; his hand trembled slightly as he filled the glass. He charged into the hallway when he heard Steve coming in but he wasn't quick enough to stop him going into the living room.

'Um, Abbie's here.' Owen pushed past him and jerked his head in Abbie's direction. The expression in Steve's eyes as he advanced towards her was familiar; too late it came to him that Steve was also drunk. Abbie's head slowly lifted as Steve placed himself in front of her and thrust out his hand.

'I'm Steve.'

There was a moment when the two of them simply stared at each other before Abbie took his hand. 'Abbie. Pleased to meet you.'

Owen sat on the other end of the settee to Abbie while Steve pulled round the chair from by the computer, knocking the leg against the coffee-table. He groped around the floor and came up with a glass which he sniffed before sloshing in the remaining wine. Red drops splattered across the tabletop. Steve's clumsy actions confirmed what Owen suspected – he was definitely drunk. He glanced at Abbie who returned his look with a wary expression. She shifted in her seat so that she had both of them in sight.

Steve picked up one of Abbie's flyers. 'This your fella?'

'Yes.'

Steve whistled. 'It's been a long time.'

'Yes.'

'Don't you feel you want to—' Steve said, leaning forward, his eyes fixed on Abbie. 'Don't you wish you could forget it all and start again?'

She shook her head. 'Never! Never!' she repeated, sounding angry. Steve threw a panicked look at Owen.

'Is that what you're doing?' Abbie jabbed her finger towards the wedding ring on Steve's hand. 'Trying to forget?'

Steve's mouth gaped in an empty response.

Abbie stood abruptly. Owen stood, too.

'I'll tell you something,' Abbie said as she handed Owen her not-quite-finished glass of wine. She leant down towards Steve. 'I'll tell you what I think. I think how lucky you are. And—'

A nervous look flashed across Steve's upturned face; Owen felt his pulse quicken.

'I feel dedicated. To Nick. And to everything we shared.' Her voice dropped to a whisper. 'Dedicated.'

For a second Owen thought she was going to cry but she pulled herself upright and walked out of the room. The last word hung in the air behind her.

Owen followed her into the hallway and stood at the open doorway, watching her go down the stairs. She seemed to be walking more steadily but she took each stair gingerly; her feet turned out as if she was wearing flippers. Her hair fell in front of her eyes, which must have been obscuring her view. She didn't look round.

Steve had resumed his place on the settee, Owen took the chair. The light from the street lamp shining through a gap in the middle of the curtains angled into Owen's eyes.

'That was weird,' Owen said.

'Is she always like that?'

'She's always been a bit intense but—'

'What do you think has happened to Nick? He's got to be dead, hasn't he?'

'I think he might have killed himself,' Owen said.

'Why do you say that?'

'It's just a feeling I have.'

The image seemed to silence them both.

'It makes you think, though, doesn't it?' Steve said after a while. 'I mean we've walked away from our marriages and everything but at least Julie and Fliss know where we are, and they can get hold of us if they need us.'

Owen's mind had returned to the disquieting note that Steve had written.

'You know you said Fliss rang me?' he said to Steve.

'Oh, yeah.'

'Did she say whether she wanted me to call her back?'

Steve shrugged. 'Not particularly.'

'She didn't then?'

Steve gave him a quizzical look. 'I guess she probably does, mate. I didn't stop to ask. I thought she was going to harass me about Jules, so I said I had to go out. And then I was so fucking bored, I thought I might as well go out, seeing as I'd already said it.'

With every second that Steve was talking, the feeling that he should ring Fliss became more pressing. It was better to get it over with than have a sleepless night wondering what on earth he was going to say to her. He took the phone to Izzy's room, dialled the number and waited for Fliss to answer.

'Is it OK to talk?' Owen asked. 'I know it's late.'

'It's fine. I was watching the TV.'

'I slept all afternoon,' he told her. 'So I didn't get your message until nearly half past nine when I woke up. Then Abbie and Steve came.'

'Together?' Fliss's voice rose high in alarm.

'God, no. I don't know where Steve had been but Abbie didn't stay long.' He sat on Izzy's bed, reached over to the bedside table to pick up her teddy bear. He looked at it for a moment before sitting it on the bed beside him. 'I'm so sorry I missed talking to the kids, I could kick myself for that.' He wanted to ask if they had said anything but he wasn't sure he could take the answer.

'Don't worry,' Fliss said. 'One day won't do them any harm. Besides, you saw them yesterday.'

'That's why I was ringing. About yesterday. Well, about last night, really.' His pause was met with an unnerving silence. 'Fliss? Are you still there?'

'Yes, I'm here.' She spoke so softly, he could hardly hear her.

'I just wondered, I just wondered what we were doing.'

'I think we both know what we were doing.' She laughed an awkward laugh, which wrenched his heart.

'I meant why? Why now?'

'I don't know why,' Fliss groaned. 'Do we really have to talk about this? I feel embarrassed enough as it is. I shouldn't have drunk so much, I know, but I was emotional and . . . and it seemed like a good idea at the time.'

'Oh.' He felt a complete idiot and rather ashamed. 'I'm sorry, Fliss, God, I thought—' He was no longer sure what he thought. He stopped talking. 'Shall we forget about it, then?' he offered after a moment.

'Could we?' Fliss said in a quiet voice. 'Please.'

You go over everything. You can't stop yourself. Everyone does the same.

The night before the very last time you saw him, he never came to bed. In the morning, he looks hollow-eyed, old and ill. He says he slept in the study for a couple of hours where you'd left him earlier practising his lines and it's true that each time you woke in the night, you could hear him pacing to and fro, his voice a muttered hum. Except that you both know there have been plenty of other nights recently when the same thing has happened and there have been no auditions the next day.

You say, – Break a leg. You know from the state of him that he doesn't stand a chance but you can't feel sorry for him. He's been getting in your way all morning while you've been trying to get ready for work. You watch him in the mirror while you're spraying on deodorant but when he looks over, you avert your eyes and steel your heart because you can't bear to meet his which are tarnished grey from fear.

When he stops, briefly, by the kitchen door, you pretend to

be too busy with your toast and coffee and getting the milk out of the fridge to notice because you feel empty of all that you can say and you are too tired, simply too tired, to make the effort.

You only look over when he has gone.

But if only you had taken a moment.

If only you had locked your eyes onto his, you might have burnt your love against his retina like the blinding sun and left a smudge, a tiny spot sealed on his sight for him to remember when the hole was blasted through his memory. You would have helped him find his way back home.

When Owen got in from work he was disappointed to discover that Steve was already home. He'd been looking forward to at least an hour on his own. He called out hello and then went straight into the kitchen so that he didn't have to engage in conversation immediately. He was annoyed to hear Steve approaching and so he didn't turn round straightaway even though he could sense Steve eyeballing him from the doorway.

'I've been waiting to see you.'

Owen took in Steve's 'smart' jeans and shirt. He saw that he was holding his large sports bag in one hand, a bulging carrier bag in another. He could smell freshly applied aftershave.

'You off somewhere?' he asked casually. He felt a buzz in his stomach at the thought that Steve was leaving.

'Yes. Home,' Steve said.

'This is sudden, isn't it?' A thought occurred to him. 'Is Julie expecting you?'

'I went to see her yesterday. But I didn't say anything until it was definite.'

'Good for you, mate.' They stood nodding and smiling at each other like a couple of idiots. 'Really, I think that's great.'

In a rush of affection, Owen stepped forward. He gave Steve an awkward hug and finished the gesture with a friendly push to set Steve moving in the direction of the hallway.

Steve stopped at the front door. 'It was because of Abbie. I couldn't get what she said out of my head. I kept thinking how she didn't give up; even with the odds stacked way against her, she hasn't given up. It made me feel ashamed.'

Owen stared at him. 'Why? I mean—'

'I got thinking about how I'd feel if the same thing happened to Jules – if she just disappeared one day. And it would be terrible. Fucking terrible. And I think you should think about it, mate. Just think about it, like I did. How would you feel? And, you know . . . the grass isn't always greener. And what with the kids and everything.'

Owen continued to stare at his friend to see if he was serious. He was. 'Yes,' Owen felt obliged to say, 'maybe I will.' He opened the door. Steve stepped out and hooked the strap of his bag over his shoulder before holding out his hand to Owen.

'Thanks for letting me stay, mate, and everything.'

'I won't say any time,' Owen joked, shaking his hand. He watched his friend begin to descend the stairs and then closed the door.

He stood in the middle of the living room and waited to hear the exterior door shut before he moved. As soon as he did, he was released into activity. He stripped and remade his bed, taking care to get the sheet as smooth and tight as possible; he hoovered the bedroom and then the rest of the flat, sweating with the effort. He opened every window as he worked his way through. Everywhere he walked, he felt the brisk draught chilling his feet and purifying the air.

He took a long shower and then, as he was getting dressed, decided to go out for a pint to celebrate.

The pub was quiet as usual. He avoided a yellow bucket set in the middle of the floor. It had an inch or so of water in it.

'Burst pipe,' Sylvia told him cheerfully; the barman looked less happy about the matter.

Sylvia accepted his offer to buy her a drink so quickly he didn't even finish the question. She patted his hand as he passed her the glass.

'I have a surprise for you,' she told him.

'Oh?'

'My grand-niece is on her way here. I told you about her. She's a lovely girl, you'll like her.'

'I can't stop long,' he told Sylvia. He felt his good mood physically retreat, leaving him hunched sulkily over his pint.

'Don't fret,' she chastised him. 'She'll be here in a minute.'

Sylvia wriggled on her stool, tapped out a cigarette and winked when she noticed he was looking. He felt mean. She was only an old lady proud of her grand-niece. He reminded himself that he was exactly the same with his kids. Given half the chance, he'd tell anyone who would listen how utterly amazing and incredible they were.

'She's here, she's here.' Sylvia's heels clanked against the strut of the bar stool.

'Stay put, Sylvia,' a voice rang out.

Owen turned to face his fate for the evening and was dumbstruck.

'Oh,' he said.

Sylvia's grand-niece paused halfway across the room, the bucket perilously close to the tip of one foot. 'Oh,' she said.

Sylvia eyed them curiously. 'Do you know each other?'

Owen said, 'No', while she said, 'Yes'.

'Well, which is it?'

'We met briefly at the station the other day,' Owen explained and he held out his hand. 'I'm Owen.' Hers was cool and firm. He couldn't stop smiling.

'Anne.'

'Aren't you joining us?' Sylvia said, as Anne helped her down from the stool and over to a table.

'I wouldn't want to intrude.'

'Don't be a ninny,' Sylvia told him. 'Anne doesn't mind.'

He carried his drink over and sat down, hardly daring to look at Anne. When he did, he felt flustered to find that she was already looking quite openly at him.

She smiled encouragingly. 'You must live round here.'

'Just up the road. I've only been here a few months.'

'He's a new divorcee,' Sylvia said and Owen felt the blood rush to his face.

'And I wonder how long it took for you to pry that out of the poor man?' Anne said, looking affectionately at Sylvia. She turned to Owen. 'I'm sorry but she's terribly nosy.'

'Don't go apologizing for me, young lady,' Sylvia retorted. 'You're just as bad.'

'It's true,' Anne laughed. 'I admit it. I find people fascinating. I like to know their stories.'

'She's a history lecturer,' Sylvia said, proudly. 'She knows everything about London. You can ask her anything.' She leant towards Owen as if challenging him to do so.

'I specialize in London history,' Anne explained. 'But it's best not to get me started, I could bore you for hours.'

Owen knew he'd be happy to listen to Anne for as long as she wanted to talk. She had a lively, engaging manner, an expressive face. She drew you in, somehow; captured your attention so that it was hard to look away. Even when he tried. 'I'm sure you wouldn't be boring,' he said and was startled how earnest he sounded. He thought he caught a glance pass between the women and he wondered what his face looked like. He attempted to compose his expression into one more nonchalant than he felt inside.

'She knows things about the Second World War that even I didn't know,' Sylvia said. 'And I lived through it.'

'Sylvia's being modest. She comes in and talks to my students every year about the war. It makes the whole time come alive for them.'

'You don't forget the most exciting years of your life.' Sylvia's voice cracked and dropped away suddenly. A silence fell. Anne reached for Sylvia's hand and held it for a moment. Her face was thoughtful.

'I've got to go to the little room,' Sylvia said, getting up.

Anne pushed back her chair. 'I'll come with you.'

'Don't be ridiculous.' Sylvia waved her away. 'It's my plan to give you two time alone,' she said in a loud stage whisper before walking away.

They watched Sylvia until she had reached the door before turning to each other.

'I can't believe that it's you,' he said. 'I mean—'

'I know what you mean,' Anne told him and then added, a little shyly, 'Isn't it called fate?'

Their glasses were almost empty but he picked his up and held it towards her. 'Let's drink to fate.'

They made their toast, took a drink and placed their glasses back down on the table without breaking eye-contact. Owen's heart was booming so hard in his chest that he found it hard to swallow. Out of the corner of his eye, he could see Sylvia approaching. Too soon.

'We need another round,' Anne said. 'No, sit down, Owen. I'll get them.'

Anne and Sylvia exchanged a few words as they passed. He watched the barman laugh at something Anne said and he felt jealousy bolt through him.

Sylvia sat down, took out a cigarette and lit it. 'So, what do you think of Anne?' she asked, exhaling a long stream of smoke into the air.

'She seems very nice,' he replied carefully.

'Nice,' Sylvia tossed back at him as if he had just said something ridiculous, but he didn't have time to add anything further as Anne had returned with the drinks.

'Sylvia's tiring,' Anne whispered to Owen what seemed like only minutes later. She had brought her chair a little closer to his during the evening and his whole body was fizzing from her proximity. He looked at their table and saw they had all finished their drinks and that Sylvia was visibly drooping.

Despite her great-aunt's protests, Anne insisted on calling a taxi. They waited outside for it to arrive. It was a clear night and the air felt fresh and clean on his face. All too soon, the taxi came.

Owen opened the door for the women to get in and at the last moment Anne turned and handed him her business card. He fumbled for his wallet and leant in to pass his own one to her. Just before he closed the taxi door, she had held it up to the dim cab light.

'Thank you, Owen Renshaw,' she said. 'I look forward to speaking to you.'

It felt good to come back to a clean, empty flat. He lay on his newly made bed and felt the space and the quiet expand around him. His mind drifted back over the last couple of hours.

He took his mobile and wallet out of his pocket and extracted Anne's card. He had his mobile in one hand, her phone number in the other. He couldn't think of any possible reason for calling her – except for every possible reason.

'Anne? It's Owen.'

'Owen. Hello.' She sounded amused.

'I thought, I just thought that there was so much that I still wanted to say and now, well, to be honest, I feel a bit stupid because I can't think of a single thing.'

Her laughter filtered into his ear and ran riotously through his body.

'Well, how about we meet up again and see if you can think of something then. How does that sound?'

'That sounds great. That sounds more than great.'

Owen opened the door an inch or so.

'Hi,' Abbie said. 'It's only me.'

'Oh, Abbie, sorry. I've just got out of the shower.' He opened the door wider. 'You're welcome to come in and use the computer, though.'

She stepped into the flat before she realized what she was doing. He had only a sea-blue towel around his waist and his hair was wet, dripping onto his shoulders. Some drops glittered on the hair on his chest like dew on a web. Behind him, a line of wet footprints darkening the wood down the length of the hall showed his approach. He smelt of shampoo, a fresh scent of citrus.

'It's not convenient,' she stated.

'It's fine. I'm going out later, you see, so you might as well use it now.'

He stood there, it seemed, almost unwilling to let her leave and yet he didn't move to let her pass. He stood with his thumbs tucked into the waistband of the towel, one hand clasping where it was knotted as if he was urging her to look there; to take in the dark brush of hair running out of the towel up to his navel. Her eyes travelled back down, quickly past the line of hair which seemed to form an arrow to where she should not be looking, further down to his feet which were sturdy, planted wide apart, blocking her way.

'I'll come back,' she told him quickly. 'I'll come back another evening.'

As she turned, she slipped on the water he'd puddled there and his hands immediately clasped her waist, setting her upright. He kept holding her for a little longer than she needed but she couldn't step easily out of his grasp.

'Got your balance?'

She nodded.

'Thought for a minute there you were about to fall at my feet.'

He grinned at his own joke but Abbie's facial muscles refused to respond. She found, instead, that she was staring up at him as if there was something about him that she needed to work out. She wasn't expecting him to lean forward and kiss her on the cheek.

'Whoops.'

Abbie felt the air push out towards her as Owen made a sudden grab at his towel. She saw a spin of blue as the towel flapped free and seized her moment to escape. Her feet flew in a tapping gallop down the stairs, drumming out their speed so that she was back inside her flat in seconds, falling against her closed door, panting as if she had just been in a sprint.

When she opened her eyes the light in her hall seemed hazy as if visited by the river-mist.

It was not very long afterwards, when she was sitting on

her bed, that she felt a tremor as Owen slammed shut a sash window upstairs. She heard him walking slowly down the stairs and held her breath while she waited for the sound of him closing the outer door.

As he was coming down the stairs, Owen wondered whether he should knock on Abbie's door and apologize. She had seemed strangely freaked when his towel had come loose even though he'd caught it in time before anything was revealed. It was probably his kiss which had set her off; he wished he'd never done that. He'd forgotten that, like Mae, she wouldn't want to be touched. It was just that she had looked so startled and sweet, he'd acted instinctively.

He hesitated on the bottom of the stairs. The whole episode had been strange – the way she'd collapsed in his hands as swiftly as if someone had pulled the plug, and how she'd let herself slump even further the instant she felt him supporting her weight. It was shocking how light she was, almost as light as Izzy. Then had come that noise: 'Oh, oh, oh,' she went – the weirdest human sound he'd ever heard in his life.

He checked his watch. He didn't want to be late for his first date with Anne. He looked at Abbie's door once more and decided that, as he didn't want to risk embarrassing her still further, it was probably best to leave the matter alone.

He opened the outer door, relieved to be finally on his way to see Anne. Two days hadn't seemed very long when they spoke but they had been two tortuous days of worrying that she'd have enough time to reconsider and cancel.

They had arranged to meet in a pub near Russell Square close to where Anne worked. He found it without any difficulty – Anne's directions had been detailed and precise – the only trouble was, he was nearly an hour too early. He wandered around the streets and then sat in the park for a while. Time had slowed to an excruciating crawl. He felt dazed with nerves and excitement.

The pub had filled up in the last hour. Customers had come out onto the pavement and some were standing in the road, holding their pints. It had been a sunny week and even though the April air wasn't very warm, people were dressed as if summer had arrived. He pushed his way inside which turned out to be quieter than the outside. He worked his way round, trying to familiarize himself with the layout, trying to see if there was an upstairs or basement where Anne might be. He was terrified of missing her, or worse not recognizing her. He wished that they had chosen somewhere less busy.

He felt someone touch his arm.

'Looking for me?'

He kissed her on the lips without even thinking about it because he was so pleased to see her and it seemed such a natural thing to do. He was delighted that she didn't seem to mind. She gently squeezed his arm and pointed to a free table in the corner of the room.

Anne sat down while he went to order a pint and a half of the real ale which she had recommended. He kept turning around from the bar to look at her even though she had her back to him. While he was watching she unpinned her hair and it dropped free, falling to the middle of her back. It took his breath away. He glanced around the room, sure that everyone must be looking at her. The barman knocked loudly on the bar to attract his attention. Owen told him to keep the change just so that he could get back to Anne as quickly as possible.

'Great place,' he said.

'It's a good spot to wind down after a hard day before I travel home.'

'Do you go out in London much?' he asked, hoping she'd say no otherwise he might be driven to ask with whom.

'Not really. I attend a few work social events but most evenings I spend at home, working.' She looked apologetic. 'I live a quiet life,' she added, which worried him.

'I have kids,' he told her. 'They're brilliant but they're noisy and they tend to take over a bit.' He wasn't sure exactly what he was trying to tell her but she seemed to understand.

'I know what kids are like.' She touched his hand. 'And I never said I liked it quiet.'

'I'm not yet divorced,' he told her. 'I'm sorry if I gave you the wrong impression the other night. We're in the process of.' He grimaced.

'It's the hardest thing, isn't it, when relationships fail?' She paused for an instant. 'It must be even harder when you have kids.'

'Have you?' He hardly dared utter the words. 'Have you ever been married, Anne?'

'No, but I was with my last partner for six years. We broke

up a couple of years ago. We wanted different things,' she told him. 'He worked away a lot and I wanted to share everyday things with someone, to have someone to come home to. When we had the opportunity to make some changes, we realized that neither of us was willing to compromise for the other.'

'I'm sorry.'

'So was I,' she laughed. 'But not any more.'

Without thinking, he started to kiss her. At the exact moment when he thought that he ought to stop, he felt her hand on the side of his face and her mouth kissing him back.

That bone-melting, heart-thumping, sweet, sweet kiss. His hands on me. His hips pinning me against the fence. Finally. Pressed close to me. His crystal blue eyes make contact with the secret centre of me. I am all that he can see. I am the single thing in his vision; there is nothing to distract him. For this moment, I am his world like he is mine.

– I've been waiting to do this for a long time, he says.

Abbie woke with a start. The room echoed with the swelling silence of an aftershock from a loud crash or thunderous shout, and although she called out his name as she peered through the drapes to the empty room, it wasn't Nick's image which came to her mind.

She went for a pee then to the kitchen to get a drink of water. She found she was shaking.

Outside, a full moon hung low above the trees which ran along the railway track, its phosphorescence bleaching their leaves and rendering them ghostly images of themselves. She felt the shudder underneath her feet of an approaching train, something which she rarely noticed any more. It passed behind the trees, a blinking sequence of glowing yellow lights which suddenly disappeared, dropping the outside into darkness as a cloud cut across the moon.

Her half-formed reflection hovered in front of her. That she was without definition seemed appropriate. She felt as if she was walking inside a dream.

A light came on upstairs, touching the air like lights above a stage, deepening the shadows at the edges, chasing her reflection away. There was a rush of water from the pipes upstairs as the toilet was flushed.

Abbie raised her hand to her cheek to the spot where Owen had placed the kiss.

It had been the way he had stood there that had brought it all back. She remembered that arrogance. She remembered that chest, wide enough to lay yourself across it. She knew what the strength of arms like Owen's meant as he caught her fall; big hands which tightened around her; hands and arms strong enough to save you or to squeeze the sense out of you and make you do whatever they wanted you to do.

The moonlight had filtered even into the bedroom, silvering the light and causing the temperature to fall several degrees. She felt the chill as clearly as if she had been thrown outside and the door slammed in her face as she caught a glimpse of Nick's essence in the corner; a dejected wraith, curled up like a punished dog, fearful accusatory eyes waiting to see what she would do.

Nick had seen right through her, straight through her deceit and into her brittle soul which creaked under the strain like a pane of glass before it shattered and turned to sand.

'Tom?'

'Hi, Dad.'

It always pleased Owen inordinately when Tom showed he recognized his voice. 'How's it going?'

'Dad, there's this school trip and Mum said I had to ask you first. If I could go? Everyone else is going. I think.' Tom's words tumbled out of him, all mixed up in his eagerness to get them out. 'It's twenty-five pounds.' Tom gasped his concern.

'Where's the trip to?'

'A museum. With dinosaurs and stuff.'

'The Natural History Museum?'

'I think so.'

'I went there, too,' Owen told him. 'When I was about your age.'

'Did you?' Tom said with the disbelieving tone his voice always took on when he was faced with the idea of Owen ever having been a boy.

All Owen remembered about the museum was running through enormous rooms, one after the other, rushing to fill in a questionnaire. The coach trip had been more thrilling. He'd had a window seat and could hardly tear his eyes away from the scenery except to prematurely eat his packed lunch.

'OK,' Owen told him. 'Tell your mum, it's fine with me.'

'He said yes, Mum. Mum?' Tom yelled. Owen wasn't surprised when Fliss came on the phone.

'You've just made his day,' she told him.

'I was telling Tom I went there myself.' The microwave was beeping. Owen went into the kitchen, took out his ready meal of chilli and rice, gave it a quick stir and reset the timer for two minutes. 'I had a great time.'

'Well, they're asking for parent volunteers, if you fancy going again?'

'Yes,' he said carelessly, distracted by watching the seconds count down. As if catching an echo, he heard his own reply a second later and really liked the idea. 'Yes, Fliss, put me down. I'll do it.'

'Are you sure? It's a week day.'

'I'll take a day's leave. I'd like to go.' He had a sudden thought. 'You don't think Tom will mind, do you? I don't want to spoil his fun.'

'I'll test the water with him, but I'm sure he'll be pleased even if—' Fliss paused.

'Even if he doesn't show it,' Owen filled in for her and they both laughed at the thought of Tom's ways.

'You sound cheerful.'

'I do?' He cancelled the timer and, leaving the chilli in the microwave, he returned to the living room.

'I assume that you having rid your flat of Steve has a lot to do with it?'

'Yes,' Owen said, happy to agree, but it was Anne who had immediately come into his head. He lost concentration and had to ask Fliss to repeat her question.

'I was wondering what you'd said, in the end, to convince him to go back?'

'Nothing. It was Abbie.'

'Abbie?'

The mention of her name drew him over to the window as if he expected to find her standing on the street below. It occurred to him that for several days now, he hadn't seen Abbie or heard her coming and going in the night.

'It seemed to make him feel guilty.'

Fliss was quiet for several moments. 'It does make you think, I suppose.'

'Except you can't really compare her situation with Steve's.'

'Perhaps not but . . . Hang on—' He could hear a murmur of conversation. 'Tom's got a joke for you.'

Owen prepared himself to laugh. Tom's jokes were usually dreadful and he often screwed them up in his rush to tell them.

'What do you get if Batman and Robin get smashed by a steam roller?'

'I don't know, Tom, what do you get?'

'Flatman and ribbon.' Tom laughed loudly at his own joke. His high, lively laughter was infectious.

'Nice one,' Owen told him.

'Here's Mum back,' Tom said.

'OK,' he replied, but instead of waiting to talk to Fliss, Owen found himself pressing the button to cut the call off. He stared at the phone in his hand, amazed at what he'd done. He thought about calling straight back but the longer he left it, the harder it became to make himself do it. He went into the kitchen and took his meal out of the microwave. He turned the food out onto a plate but found that it now needed reheating so he put it back in.

He wasn't surprised when one minute and thirty-eight seconds later, the phone rang. But it wasn't Fliss.

'Owen?'

'Mum. How are you?'

'We're both fine, love. What's that noise?'

'It's the microwave, I'm just having a quick . . . jacket potato,' he lied.

'I won't keep you then. I was ringing about Easter. We wondered what you were going to be doing this time?'

Easter was only a couple of weeks away. So far, he and Fliss had simply agreed to split the holidays evenly. Owen had provisionally booked two weeks off until he knew which dates would be best for the kids. 'We haven't finalized anything yet, to be honest.'

'Oh.'

It was a short word loaded with his mother's disappointment. 'Why?' he probed gently. 'Did you have something in mind?'

'We haven't seen Tom and Izzy for weeks now. We feel like, ever since, well, Owen, – your father and I feel like we're being sidelined.'

He caught his sigh before it became audible and told himself to be patient. Does everyone, he thought, have to be this patient with their parents? 'Nobody's being sidelined,' he told her. 'It's taken us a while to settle into our new routines and everything, that's all. I'll tell you what. Why don't I have a word with Fliss and see about bringing them down to see you?'

'She won't be coming, will she?'

He chose not to respond to the mild panic in his mother's voice. 'Who? Fliss? No. I meant I would confirm which days I'm having them and then I'll get back to you.'

'I don't want to be . . . but when might that be?'

'I'll call you at the weekend,' he told her, firmly.

'Well, good,' she said, brightly. And he raised his eyes in mock thanks to God. 'I'll let you get back to that potato.'

Owen had eaten precisely one mouthful of chilli when the phone rang a second time. He considered not answering but at the last minute, picked it up.

'Hi, Owen. It's Anne.'

'Anne.' He couldn't have kept the pleasure out of his voice even if he'd tried. 'I was going to ring you later.'

'Is it a convenient time now?'

'Of course,' he told her, pushing his plate away.

'I just wanted to say I had a lovely evening, yesterday.'

'Me too.' He found he was smiling into the phone.

'And I've just arranged to come over to Sylvia tomorrow so I wondered whether we could see each other before I go there?'

'Yes,' he said. Absolutely. Definitely. 'How about if you give me a call before you get here and I'll meet you off the train?'

'That would be lovely.'

'I know a nice bar we could go to,' he said.

'Or, maybe, we could go back to your flat.'

After he'd put the phone down, he looked around, hardly able to imagine her there. Tomorrow. She'd be with him tomorrow.

Abbie's head felt like someone was slicing through her brain every two seconds and then sewing it up with a giant needle and thread. She was finding it hard to breathe as if the air had become silted up. She talked herself through each breath, counting as she exhaled and inhaled; one, two, three; one, two, three.

She got up, dressed quickly in jeans and a T-shirt. She looped each drape into a knot and tied them to the bedposts, plumped the pillows, folded the duvet down to let the bed air. In the living room, she switched off the little lamp and opened the curtains, turning before she had time to see what kind of day it was, and headed straight for the kitchen where she stopped quite still.

She returned to the bedroom, said, 'Good morning, my love' but she didn't dare pick up Nick's photograph. Instead, she hurried to collect her work for the day and her sewing box.

In the study, she checked several times that she had everything in its place, everything that she needed but still she was finding it hard to calm herself. Panic shook her hands, made her press trembling fingers to the spot at the base of her throat where it felt as if her rapidly beating heart would come bursting out.

She picked up the yellow skirt. The seam had come unstitched at the back. She would need to unpick the whole thing and pin it in place in readiness for sewing on the machine later. She turned the skirt inside out and angled the scissor point towards the first stitch. The blade flickered in front of her eyes. She squinted, paused, told herself: concentrate. Concentrate. She screwed her eyes up tight. Concentrate.

She felt the air leave her lungs in a rush as if she was falling.

He brings a friend home. A man you've never seen before. He's short and rather grubby looking with bovine-lidded eyes and curly hair which he has tried to tame with a brutally close, rough cut. His name is Carl. The way he stares at you is unnerving. You think that you should find him repellent but he is intriguing. He makes no pretence about how much he's staring and you try to catch Nick's eye to see if he's noticed but he's busy going through the CDs for some music. A frail spike of ash hangs on the end of his cigarette because he always forgets that he's smoking or because, maybe, you think, he can't bear to take it out of his mouth for even one second.

— I'll get some drinks, you say and you sense two sets of eyes following you as you cross the room but when you turn back, you realize that you're mistaken. Nick is still crouched over the shelf of CDs and Carl has leant back on the settee and closed his eyes. He no longer looks dangerous – you were just being paranoid and silly like Nick has told you off about before – and you feel light with relief, swamped with love for Nick.

When you return, Nick behaves the sweetest he's been to you for ages. He sits by you, kisses you and holds your hand and you wallow in it wondering all the time what it is about Carl that Nick likes because he doesn't join in the conversation except to tell a couple of dirty jokes; he pushes up his sleeves and looks like he's ready to fight.

You drink far more than you usually do. Nick keeps topping it up and the more you drink, the more you sink against Nick. He laughs and calls you a lightweight.

Somehow you end up on the settee between them and there is something good about having the hot weight of a man on either side of you. When you laugh, you let your head fall backwards and Nick kisses you on the neck.

When Carl goes to the loo, Nick pulls you down so that you end up with your head lying in his lap looking up at him. You feel his hands everywhere on you, stroking your breasts, your hair, your legs. You feel unable to move. Speared to the settee by the desire in his eyes, you let yourself forget about everything.

Nick slides to the floor to kneel at your head and you see that his hands are undoing his flies and you say, – No, Carl will be—

And then you realize that there are other hands, hands which have been rubbing and pushing between your thighs and which are now undoing your jeans. You try to move but Nick says, – It's OK.

You don't like it at first. You want to stop. You kick your legs, but someone holds your ankles. You twist your body, but someone holds your wrists. You catch your breath and in that moment, your body discovers a feeling which you've never felt before. It rises, it builds inside you. You are like an animal, an animal on heat, greedy to have them both, you want your body to open up and take them both. In your mouth, inside you.

You close your eyes and you can't tell which is which. You let yourself slide under the fingers, the tongues, the wet, the pushing. You hear the grunting and the moaning and some of it is coming from you.

It doesn't feel like it will ever stop and you don't want it to.

You open your eyes and you see Nick kneeling on the floor and he is watching with his hungry wolf eyes. You feel Carl's rough bristle on your stomach and hear the grunts he makes. There is a strong scent about him and he moves you around, like he knows you, like he owns you; like Nick used to do. You close your eyes and you don't know anything any more. You are not you, you are some animal, rutting and humping and rolling and you don't want it to stop. Ever. You know you should feel frightened but you're not. You feel safe, safer than you have done for a long time.

She couldn't escape them. They followed her from room to room. If she stopped suddenly and half-turned, Nick froze; his wary eyes burning into hers. When she stayed still, he crept closer, behind her. And the other one was there, too. His hot, dense smell was everywhere. Getting stronger.

'What are you looking so fucking happy about?'

'I don't know. It's just a Friday feeling,' Owen said. He knew that he was grinning like an idiot. Only ten hours to go before he would be seeing Anne. Eleven at the max. He was bursting to tell someone but he couldn't risk saying anything to Steve. It would be back to Fliss in a nanosecond.

'Well, fucking stop it,' Steve said. 'You're making me uncomfortable.' He held out the coffee cup to Owen and gave him a searching look. 'You're a dark horse,' he concluded as Owen took the drink.

'Am I?' He couldn't imagine what Steve was going to say but his heart was bumping already. He cast his eye around Reception to avoid meeting his friend's eye.

'You never told me you'd slept with Fliss that night.'

'Oh God. I'd forgotten about that.'

'That's a pretty major thing to forget, isn't it?'

They had reached the door leading to the stairs.

Owen turned to Steve. 'I don't mean forget, exactly. It just hasn't seemed important with everything else that's been going on—' It shocked and shamed him to think that the night with Fliss was only just over a week ago.

'What are you on about? What's been going on? You told me the other day you were bored in the evenings.'

'Jesus. What are you – the divorce police?'

They walked up the first flight of stairs in silence then stopped. Owen rested his arms on the landing rails. He looked down and then up the stairwell. The sun was coming in through the windows on the higher levels. They seemed to be on their own.

'It was only the one time, OK.'

'OK.'

He felt Steve join him at the rail. Steve's arms stuck further out than Owen's. He held his coffee cup loosely around the top as if, at any moment, he was going to let it drop. Owen noticed a blue pen mark scored across the cuff of his shirt.

'And we don't intend to do it again.' He took a drink of coffee. It was bitter. He didn't know why they continued to drink the stuff. 'Things have moved on since. For both of us.'

Steve turned and leant his back against the rails. 'So there's no chance of you getting back together?'

'No. Absolutely not.'

'Julie seems to think so.'

Owen met Steve's eye. 'I don't know why. There's never been any chance.'

'Actually, I told her that.' Steve drank his coffee in several loud swallows. 'This tastes like shit.' He squeezed the empty cup and the plastic creaked as it bent under the pressure. 'And I think Fliss has told her that, too. It's just that Jules wants everyone to be happy and everything to be like it was before.'

'I wasn't happy before,' Owen said. 'And neither was Fliss.'

'But you are now.'

'Yes.'

'So why was that again?' And Owen knew, immediately, from Steve's expression that he hadn't been fooled earlier but he still couldn't tell him. Not yet. Not quite yet.

Owen stood upright. 'Just a Friday feeling,' he said, glancing at his watch. 'A happy Friday feeling.'

The phone was ringing, shrill and insistent. Abbie opened her eyes. She was lying face down on the bed. Her eyes felt dry, unused. The creases on the sheet were like tiny white mountains in front of them. She widened her focus to the pile of pillows and cushions to the left above her head and then further out through the grey light towards the door which was open. She pushed herself upright. Her body was stiff down to the bones. She was dressed; fully dressed in jeans and jacket and socks as if she was ready to go out. Or as if she had recently come back in.

She thought the phone was ringing again but by the time she got to it, it had stopped. The red light was flashing though so she pressed play.

You have three new messages.

First new message. Wednesday, April fifth, eight p.m.

'Hi, love. It's me, Becca. Just phoning to catch up and to say I'm coming over on Friday evening if that's OK with you. Give me a ring if it isn't. Or if you fancy a chat. Take care. Hope you're OK.'

Second new message. Thursday April sixth, eleven fourteen a.m.

'Hi, Abbie. Only Kate. Could you give me a ring back about the pickup time you need? Thanks. Speak to you later.'

Third new message. Today, ten twenty-seven a.m.

'Abbie. Kate again. Um, I don't know if you got my last message but we need to arrange a pickup time asap. And I've got a good new batch of work for you – so give me a call. OK. Thanks.'

Abbie switched off the lamp in the window and opened the curtains. A pale light stole into the room. She found Kate's bag but she couldn't see the inventory anywhere. She went into the study. Lying in the seat of her chair was the yellow skirt that she'd been repairing – which she thought she had finished. She picked it up. It had been pinned on the seam but not sewn. The skirt slid from her hands as she felt her legs give way. She bowed her head as if to ward off what was coming next but it still hit her like a wave slamming against her chest and knocking her off balance. She dropped onto the chair, put her head between her knees. Breathe.

Everything has changed since that night with Carl and if you could go back in time, you would. You know you both would without a second's hesitation.

Each morning before you go to work you scrub so hard at your body in the shower that your skin stings and retains a boiled-pink colour all day until you come home when you shower and scrub again.

You are sick to your stomach for the first few days and don't manage to keep anything but water down and although you feel faint, you continue not to eat, finding some solace in your body's emptiness.

Now, just when you would welcome some time alone, Nick always seems to be there. He follows wherever you go; you experiment by walking from room to room for no reason other than to see how long it takes him to appear. The bathroom door is the only one which locks and you sit on the edge of the bath for a few minutes while his shadow pads to and fro outside.

When you come out, neither of you speaks.

You have nothing to say but when you are quiet, it seems to drive Nick crazy. He wants to know what you're thinking about and so you tell him about the shopping lists, reruns of conversations from work, the washing and cleaning jobs to do around the house. Nick doesn't believe you. Even when you tell him that these are the thoughts that you have stuffed your head full of, that these are the only thoughts which you want in your head, he still doesn't believe you. Because of his insistence, you end up thinking about the very thing you're desperately trying not to. That neither of you want to remember. That night, that man.

Every night you are flooded with the musky scent of Carl; you feel the way he moved inside you, the sandpaper roughness he scoured across your stomach. Your body is a palimpsest; you need Nick to remake his mark upon it and efface the clumsy, heavy presence of the last person who was there. But when you try to cuddle up to Nick, he feels insubstantial; the sparse kisses he plants on your hair evaporate quickly like the moisture left from a handprint on cold glass.

You need Nick to help you remove these memories because he is responsible for introducing them. You long for him to find a way to pick up the end of one and pull them out in a long, long thread, leaving your mind blissfully empty.

Except he doesn't seem to be able to do anything any more. He sits on the settee with his knees up, his chin propped on top and he doesn't move for hours so that you could almost forget he is there. One day when you walk past him you see salt tracks of tears on his face and you feel full of rage.

You want to slap him, punch him, scratch him. You spit red-hot words across the room at him and you don't even think of holding back. Your anger is unstoppable; it burns everything in its path.

– You made me, you tell him. – You asked him here. You made me do it. I was happy with you. I only wanted you.

He escapes by going out every evening and returning late, drunk.

One night, he comes home and gets into bed. He is rough with you, pushing your legs apart before you are even properly awake. You don't have time to block the thought that you wish it was Carl.

Nick is suddenly stilled.

– This isn't enough for you now, he says.

In the dim light of the room, as he sits above you, you struggle to fix your eyes onto his. What you're looking for is the crystal blue of his eyes, what you hope to feel is that sharp pain which pierces your skin and skewers your heart to him.

– You are my prince, you tell him but he is already climbing off you. – My precious love.

He lies next to you and holds onto you tightly, as if he is holding onto the edge of a cliff and only you can prevent him falling.

He says, — What are we going to do?

— We are going to forget that it ever happened. That's what we're going to do.

That is your decision. That is your promise to yourself and to Nick. You will sew the memory of that man in a pouch right at the very back of your brain; with twine so tough nothing can break it, with stitches so close that not a scent nor a breath can escape.

— I can't, he says.

— You are just going to have to.

— I can't.

— You must.

Abbie knew what she had to do. She sat still on the chair and waited, her breath so quiet, you might think that she was sleeping.

When she smelt him close enough, she caught him up and held him tight. Even though he struggled with all his strength, she was stronger. She pushed him inside the pouch and pinched closed the edges of the escape hole. She tacked it secure before covering it over with a leather patch so tough that her fingers hurt each time she drove the needle through. She tested the twine and knew that it was so strong it would last forever. She kept on sewing with stitches so close that not even a wisp of scent could escape and tugged tight the last stitch before biting through the thread.

She opened her eyes. She half-turned her head, ready to meet Nick's eyes, but the room was empty. She turned the other way and this time her eyes landed on Nick's chair. A grey, dead light lay upon in and she was filled with fear about what she had done.

Outside the house, Owen saw a woman whom, from behind, he mistook for Abbie. As she turned at the sound of his footsteps, he realized the woman was a taller, fuller figured and more robust version. She smiled in greeting and he noticed immediately her small, perfect teeth.

'Hi, I'm Owen, from upstairs. You must be Abbie's sister.'

'Yes. Rebecca.' She held out her hand. 'I think Abbie's mentioned you.'

'She comes up to use the Internet sometimes,' he explained. 'Have you been waiting long?'

'Ten minutes or so. I think she must have popped out. She is expecting me.' Rebecca pressed one hand into the small of her back and brushed at her damp temples with the other. 'God. It's warm today.'

'I'm so sorry. I wasn't thinking. I'll let you in.' He hurried to unlock the door. 'It's always cool in here.' He gestured for her to pass ahead of him.

'Thanks.'

He started to walk up the stairs, leaving Rebecca in the hall.

Glancing back, he realized that she hadn't moved. He stopped. 'God, I'm being completely useless today, I'm so sorry. You're welcome to wait upstairs if you want to. Or perhaps you'd like some water?'

She declined his offer, laughing. 'I must feel a lot better than I look.' She paused. 'I'll just try Abbie again, now.'

He hung back while Rebecca knocked on Abbie's door. As soon as it opened, he continued on his way. One hour, twenty minutes to go. He told himself off for being ridiculous, then looked at his watch again. One hour, nineteen minutes.

There was something dazzling about Becca which, at first, hurt Abbie's eyes. It was as if there was a silvery light surrounding her. As Becca moved, Abbie felt sure she could see sparks flying off from her sister. Some of these sparks landed in the corners of the flat and illuminated the empty shadows like tiny stars, others left a glittering, perfumed trail in the air behind her.

'Oh, Abbie.' Becca's face shone. 'I'm so excited. I can't wait to tell you—' Her expression changed to one of concern as she stepped towards Abbie. 'What's wrong? Are you ill?'

'A headache,' she said, quickly. 'That's all.'

'Have you had painkillers?'

'Yes. I think so.'

Abbie watched Becca pick up the photograph of Nick that Marion had sent and which Abbie, after some consideration, had propped up on the telephone table.

'Nick's parents gave that to me. They're moving. They're moving to Spain.'

'I know, you told me.'

'They've given up on him, Becca.' The words came unbidden and tasted bitter.

Becca had her back to Abbie when she started speaking. 'It's time they thought about themselves.' She turned round. 'If Nick were here, I'm sure he'd be pleased for them and for himself, no doubt — lots of cheap holidays!'

Abbie felt Becca's warm hand on her arm, encouraging her over to the settee. 'I should get us some tea,' Abbie said, but sat down with Becca all the same.

'He's a grown man, Abbie, you can't expect them to behave as if he's a dependent child after all this time. And they must be getting on a bit now, aren't they about the same age as our parents?'

'Older. Roger's been retired for years and Marion's not well.'

'There you are, you see.'

The despair that was coiled up inside her suddenly sprang out of her mouth. 'I'm not sure that Nick's here any more.'

Becca moved closer. 'What do you mean? Have you heard something?'

'I think I might have driven him away.' She looked at her sister's gentle face and it burnt in her, the desire to tell. 'I feel so terribly ashamed and unworthy.'

'You're worthy, Abbs. You're a bloody saint. I know you don't want to hear it, but you know, you shouldn't think it's wrong to move on. You can't wait for ever.'

'I have to. I owe it to him. Becca, I have to try.'

As Becca's gaze drifted away down to the floor, Abbie noticed that the silvery glow which had accompanied her when she came into the flat, had completely disappeared. Now she looked sad and tired. Abbie shivered. She couldn't think what to say so she, too, stared at the floor. The carpet was covered in thread as if hundreds of fine, coloured worms had been sprinkled on it. She couldn't remember the last time she had vacuumed.

When Abbie dared to glance up, she found Becca was directing a frail smile at her. Abbie quickly took her sister's hand. 'Let's talk about something else. What was it you wanted to tell me?'

Everything about Becca lit up; colour bloomed on her face, her eyes sparkled. 'I'm having a baby. Abbie, I'm having a baby.'

Abbie stared. 'A baby?'

'A little girl. So they say, but you know, it's never one hundred per cent definite.'

She had never for a minute, not a single second expected this news but as Becca spoke, she felt herself getting caught up in her sister's excitement. She felt almost giddy as they gripped each other's hands and laughed and laughed. As they both were wiping away tears, Abbie felt seriousness descending. Her voice wavered under the awesomeness of the moment. 'I can't quite believe it.'

'Neither can I,' Becca told her. 'Especially as we've been trying for a couple of years; I thought we'd never manage it.'

'I didn't know you'd been trying. You never told me.'

Becca shrugged. 'I felt a failure. I didn't want people to know. I didn't want to talk about it to anyone except Chris, and I've driven him up the bloody wall because that's all I've been able to think of and talk about for the last two years.'

'But, Becca, you should have been able to talk to me. You've always been there for me.'

'You have your own worries.'

There was no accusation or long-felt disappointment in Becca's voice but Abbie thought she deserved it. 'I haven't been much of a sister, have I?'

'What do you mean?'

'I should have been there—'

'Be there for my daughter. Your niece, Abbs. Be the wonderful, happy aunt that I know you can be.' Becca described them playing on the beach, going out for the day, taking her niece shopping. As her sister kept talking, Abbie could clearly see the shape of Becca's daughter's life and her own place in it. She felt the love ballooning inside her, lifting her up. But no sooner had the pictures formed than they popped and she saw that her real place was here.

Abbie twisted in her seat, looked behind her, and then to the side.

'What are you looking for?' Becca's voice was sharp. 'You're looking for him, aren't you? You're thinking how can I go on the beach with my niece when I have to sit in this sodding gloomy flat waiting for Nick. That's what you're thinking, isn't it?' Becca pressed her fingers into her temples. 'I knew it was going to be like this but I really hoped that it wouldn't be.'

Abbie watched, horrified, as Becca began to cry; a string of soft dewdrop tears which left dark patches on each leg of her jeans where they fell.

'I'm sick of it, Abbie, I truly am. Right from the very beginning, he took you over; he never left any room for anyone else in your life. It was always Nick first before you would dream of fitting anyone else in.' Becca wiped at her face, brushed at her jeans. 'And now that he's gone, it's even worse.

He's so large in your head . . . and demanding, there isn't enough space for you to love anyone else.' She smiled but it was a small smile and Abbie knew that she was to blame for Becca being sad.

'I love you,' Abbie said but it seemed as if her words dissipated in the air before they ever reached Becca.

Becca stood up. 'And I don't want my daughter to take second place to a . . . to a ghost. I want you to share her, to love her, properly.'

You think if only she would look at you, she would know, she would understand just how much you love her and want to share this with her; but she is leaving. She is leaning towards you and quickly pressing a warm cheek on your cold skin. You breathe in the sweet scent of her but she won't meet your eyes and you stand and watch, helpless, with all the love and wishfulness tumbling around inside you, as she walks down the path to her car. Left behind her is a dull trail of tears.

Abbie lay on the bed and closed her eyes. It wasn't true, she told herself, there had always been plenty of room in her life for others. Especially Becca. Just to prove it, she began to summon memories of her and Becca. Instead, she found she was pushing through a jungle of memories of Nick which sprang up in front of her, lush and vigorous. She was only able to catch glimpses of the other memories, the ones she wanted to find. They were spindly and stunted like etiolated plants struggling in the dark undergrowth.

The realization fell like a weight onto her chest. Her breathing quickened. She fixed her eyes to the ceiling and, with a force which gripped her whole body, began chopping away at the memories of Nick until she had cleared some space, and as the light began to creep in, weak, fleeting pictures began to form: Becca teaching her to tie her shoelaces, Becca teaching her to dive at the swimming pool; the first time she and Becca were allowed out on their bikes on their own together and Abbie fell off and cut her leg open and Becca got told off; a memory or a photograph of a snowy day with her and Becca bundled up warm, Becca's scarf and gloves yellow, Abbie's red, carmine red; sitting on the bed, talking, lying in the garden, talking; holidays in Suffolk with their long-dead great-grandmother who scared the life out of Abbie because she was deaf and she shouted loudly and couldn't understand what Abbie said so Becca would speak for her instead.

There had always been Becca, before Nick there was Becca.

Abbie got up. It was already dark outside, so she drew the curtains in the living room and turned on the lamp. She flicked the main light on briefly while she took the man's camel-coloured overcoat off its hanger on the rail. As she folded it over her arm, she felt its weightiness and the rough wool brushed against the back of her hand. She scanned the shelves for the box which contained leather buttons and had to stand on tiptoe to reach it.

She took everything to the study and returned to fetch her sewing box. Each time she left or entered the room, she glanced at Nick's photograph.

Abbie settled herself in the chair to work. She felt the chill of the deepening night and would have needed to put the heating on if it wasn't for the thick coat covering her like a blanket. Her fingers were cold, though, so she pushed them under her legs for a few minutes to warm them before she began carefully snipping off the chipped and discoloured ivory-coloured plastic buttons. She made sure that she picked out every last tendril of thread from the coat and off the buttons which, after inspection, she placed in a pile on the floor; none of them were in a good enough condition to keep. There were six buttons required for the front and two smaller ones on each cuff. She carefully selected them from her button box – laying each one out in a line on the arm of her chair, twisting the lamp so that she could see clearly the variations in colour of the leather to match them as closely as she could; dropping those she discarded straight back in the box. When the selection was made, she threaded the needle, took the first button and told herself, concentrate.

Outside the sound is muffled; there has been snow overnight. School has been cancelled and Becca and I are out in the back garden. It is freezing and the light glares, making me squint. Becca looks like a round blue ball in her padded anorak; her legs in her Wellingtons are like two short, red sticks. I have so many layers on it's hard to move. My mittens are matted with ice and when I pat them together they clunk hollowly. Mum calls us in. On the garden path, near the back door, I slip on a patch of ice where the drainpipe has been dripping. I land on my bum, winded. Becca puts out a hand to help me up but before I've found my balance she lets go and I fall back down. Before I can even thinking of crying, she pushes her arms under my arms and yanks me up. There is a rushed sound of our anoraks sliding against each other.

*

Christmas morning. Cold. Before the heating has come on, I creep into Becca's room and get into bed beside her. In only those fifteen short steps that separate her room from my room, my feet have turned to ice. She envelopes them in a scoop of her nightdress and I feel them warming from the heat from her legs. Downstairs I know there is a bike for me. We found it last week, hidden in the shed, when we went looking for presents. From the moment I saw it – its frame enclosed in sheaths of cardboard so only the wheels were visible – I have been worried because I know I will be found out and I don't know what will happen when I am. I think that they will take my bike back to the shop. I wish we had never gone into the shed.

– It'll be all right, Becca whispers when we hear the sound of our parents' bedroom door open; my heart is thumping.

The first thing I see when we go into the lounge is my bike. It rises above all the presents, wrapped in Christmas paper. I hang back but Becca pushes me forward and sends me a look which panics me because I don't know what it means.

– Don't you want your presents? Dad is smiling. – Which one are you going to open first?

– The b ... the big one, I tell him.

As soon as I rip the first piece of paper off, as soon as the first part of its shining grey and purple frame is revealed, everything is all right. It is better, bigger, brighter than I ever imagined. It has a tiny white bag under the back of the seat and a light at the front and a bell. I can't resist ringing the bell. A single, cheerful ring. I look round for Becca; she is smiling.

– Do it again, she says.

So I ring it again, twice more and everyone laughs.

\*

Every day coming home from nursery school, Mum and I walk past the shop with the tiger in the window. It's called The Chemists and sometimes we go inside where there's a funny smell and lots of old ladies who are sitting on chairs in the middle of the shop. They peer into my face and shout and sometimes poke me in the stomach. I am told to say hello, to say thank you, to tell the lady my name. And even though I don't want to Mum has that look on her face which makes you do as you're told. But I would do all that and lots more if only I could have the tiger. I imagine its fur is the softest fur I've ever felt and I know that I'd feel safe at night if he was in bed with me but whenever I mention it, just in case Mum hasn't realized that this is what I want most in the world, she doesn't say a thing. Today she tugs my hand sharply to pull me past and because I'm not expecting it, I stumble forward and fall on the pavement and suddenly there is bright red blood everywhere.

Mum picks me up and takes me into The Chemists where I sit on a chair while a woman in a white coat puts a plaster on my knee. She promises me a present and I wish and wish for the tiger but I'm given a lollipop which tastes like strawberries.

The next time we walk past, the tiger has gone. There's a basket of pink things in its place. I try to walk as slowly as Mum will let me, all the way past in case it's been moved somewhere else. But it's definitely gone.

When it's my birthday, Becca gives me a squashy present and when I open it, it's the tiger. He looks smaller out of the window but his fur is the softest fur I've ever known and I love him the best of all my presents.

*

Abbie opened her hand where the last leather button lay pressed in her palm. She held it between her thumb and finger as she looped the cotton through the metal ring on its base. She sewed the button quickly into place, testing that it was secure before cutting the thread.

She glanced down at the pile of buttons on the floor. The light under the door was playing upon them, making them glow prettily, like pearls in moonlight.

She thought, all of a sudden, of Becca's baby as if an age had passed since she had first heard about her. She reached down and dabbled her fingers among the buttons and saw how her skin became touched with silvery light; like the light which had surrounded Becca when she had arrived earlier that day to tell Abbie her news.

When Owen wasn't with Anne he lived in a state of suspended exhilaration, which developed into full-blown happiness at the drop of a hat. Or rather, at the arrival of a phone call, email or text from Anne, or simply at the thought of her. He couldn't believe that it was so easy to be that happy.

Whenever Owen was waiting for Anne to arrive at the flat, he had to set himself as many activities as possible to keep occupied otherwise he thought he would go mad. This evening he had put on a Pulp CD at full volume and was distracting himself from clock-watching through the last hour by giving the kettle a polish with some metal cleaner he'd bought to shine up the bathroom fittings.

He didn't hear Anne come into the kitchen. She slid her arms around him from behind. He caught the bottle of cleaner just in time before it went everywhere.

'I used my key,' she said, happily. The last time they had seen each other they had exchanged keys after a frank discussion about whether their relationship was moving too quickly.

'Who says it's too quick, anyway?' Anne had said, finally. 'I like this pace, don't you?'

He had had to agree that he did.

She held his dirty hands away from her and placed a kiss on his lips. 'I need a cup of tea,' she told him, stepping back. She eyed the half-finished kettle. 'And to get these shoes off.'

She left him to go and get changed and returned, barefooted, wearing some loose black trousers and a white T-shirt. She never wore slippers she had told him, not even in the winter.

She peered into the fridge and he was absurdly pleased when she discovered a bar of her favourite chocolate that he'd bought. She broke off a couple of pieces and fed him one.

'How was your day?' he asked her.

'It was a Ben Gilling's day.' Owen knew all about Ben Gilling. He was one of Anne's students who was serially late handing in his assignments.

'What was his excuse this time?'

'Someone stole his laptop.'

'Do you think you're supposed to believe him?'

'I'm not sure. But I don't.' He found the way she took everything in her stride refreshing. She wasn't phased by tricky students, or competitive colleagues, or busy days.

'And how was programming today?' she asked him. She had learnt more about computer programming in the last six weeks than Fliss had ever known in all the years they'd been together.

'Challenging,' he told her.

Owen was surprised when she reached behind him, picked up her mug of tea and left the kitchen without saying another word.

He followed her into the living room. She was standing in front of the window. Something about her posture was worrying him. He walked towards her.

'Is everything OK?' he asked.

When he saw her face, his first thought was, she's leaving me and he felt as if his whole body had turned into one giant heart, battering away. He let her take his hand; her skin felt cold against his.

'Owen, I've been thinking about this a lot,' she said and she pulled him to face her. 'And I really want to meet Izzy and Tom.' She paused. 'I know what I'm asking. I know what it means.'

He found that he couldn't speak.

'But I understand if you don't want me to—' She dropped her head.

He caught her chin to raise her face so that she was looking at him. 'Of course, I want you to,' he told her. 'Let's do it.'

'Are you sure?'

He could see how much she wanted to believe him. 'Yes,' he told her, firmly. 'It's time.'

As Abbie approached the house, she could see the shadow of a large envelope propped up on the ledge of the window next to the outer door. She knew instantly, even before she saw that it was addressed in Becca's hand, that this was no ordinary piece of mail, no circular or bill. She held the envelope between her teeth as she juggled keys and bags through her door and bumped and rustled her way down the hall into the kitchen where she dumped everything onto the work-surface.

She opened the envelope carefully and pulled out a piece of A4 paper. In the centre was a grainy black-and-white image; a blurred, curved shape, safe inside Becca. On a Post-it note stuck to the front, Becca had written: 'I've been meaning to send you this for ages.' On the paper, under the image, she'd written: 'Say hello to your niece!'

Just this day, only a few hours ago, when Abbie was looking through the bargain bin for offcuts of material she had come across a piece of yellow silk barely half a metre in length. It was a honey-gold colour like the secret centre of a flower, like the deepening sun of a late summer's evening. She had pictured a baby's foot and tiny toes with translucent nails curling inside a silken shoe; these very feet grown plump and pink.

When she had finished all the sewing for the day, when she had eaten and showered and was in her nightwear, instead of going to bed, Abbie returned to the living room. She took the silk out of the paper bag and cut through the stitch of the price tag which held the piece folded in two. She shook it out and laid it flat on the table.

She sat at the table and worked on a pattern for over an hour before she had it good enough to draw onto tissue paper. She cut out, then pinned the pattern on top of the material and fetched her sharpest scissors. The silk sounded crisp and clean as she sliced into it. The pieces were so light that they drifted across the polished surface when they were cut free. She put them carefully into a pile on top of a fresh piece of tissue paper and carried them into the hall. Here she paused for a moment. She looked over at the study door but she didn't want to sit in there; she knew it was the wrong place for her to be. Instead, she went into the bedroom.

Once her sewing box had been collected, she arranged pillows and cushions to prop herself upright and tuned in the clock-radio to the World Service. The poor reception crackled and buzzed but she liked the sound of the calm, confident voices in the background. She picked up the first piece of silk and began to work.

She worked steadily through the night, minute by minute, hour after hour. She didn't feel tired; she didn't even feel the need to move or shift or stretch. Time disappeared as her fingers worked, almost of their own accord, with barely a pause, and with each stitch she made a wish. A wish for the baby, her niece. For every stitch, a year of happiness.

No sooner had the final ribbon been threaded through, then she fell asleep exactly where she was and she slept solidly without dreaming or waking until gone ten o'clock the next morning.

It seemed only right when she had risen, dressed and made coffee that there should be a knock on the door and that when she opened it, there was Izzy.

'Dad said I could come and say hello but I wasn't to stop.'

Abbie let the girl in. They made their way into the living room and Abbie invited Izzy to take a seat at the table. Her face, Abbie noted, had lost a little of that young girl's softness. She was hardening, strengthening just like the baby who was growing inside Becca. Toughening herself up for the next stage in life.

Abbie brought in the pair of golden booties and placed them on the table.

Izzy cooed: 'They're beautiful. Can I pick them up?'

Abbie nodded and watched as Izzy reached out fingers with half-bitten, half-pink-varnished nails and picked the booties up, placing them on the palm of one hand.

'They're as light as a butterfly,' she said. 'Who are they for?'

'My sister's daughter. My niece.'

'What's her name?'

'She isn't born yet. Not for a few months.'

Izzy laid them carefully aside and Abbie took them and wrapped them in a piece of tissue paper. She clearly heard Owen shouting his daughter's name down the stairs, but Izzy didn't react at all. 'I think that's your dad calling you.'

Izzy got up. 'We're going out. We're going to see a film.

He's got a new girlfriend. We met her a couple of weeks ago. She's nice. It's OK,' Izzy said in a very grown-up voice. 'We're all OK about it.' She paused for a moment. 'Well, maybe not Tom, so much.'

'He's younger than you,' Abbie said. 'It'll take him a little longer.'

'Mum hasn't got a boyfriend, though.'

'Oh, well, there's plenty of time.'

'That's what Dad says.'

They were both looking at the tiny white package of the booties which seemed to Abbie to glow from within. Abbie picked it up.

'Does your sister live far away?'

'No. Not really. Thirty or forty miles perhaps. In Surrey.'

'Are you going to post them?'

'No. Once she's born, I'm going to take them, I'll take them to her myself.'

'So then you'll see the baby.'

'Yes, I'll go and see her. I've promised,' Abbie said before she could stop herself because it wasn't exactly true. The promise she had made was unspoken, made only to herself. It was so new it was barely there. As barely there as the weight of the booties in her hand.

It is a warm September day and I am here, at the train station. I have the ticket in my purse and I am waiting, along with others, many others, on the platform. I glance around at them and they stare down the track in the direction they expect the train to appear and across to the other side when one out of the city comes rattling noisily through. Everyone's mind is focused on the journey ahead. We are all impatient to be on our way. For one final time, I retrace the route back to the house, in my head: out of the station, up the main road, down the underpass, left across the road, follow it to the junction, down the street, up to the front of the house. I unlock the door and go in. The notes are there – one, two, three.

I have written Becca's telephone number and my new mobile phone number in black felt pen on large pieces of gloss-white, strong card. This tough card will not fall down or be caught by a draught from the door and drift to the floor, where it might lie hidden under the settee, under a chair, or beneath the cooker. This black ink will not fade in the daylight or evaporate in the night. These notes can't be overlooked or ignored should he return. They are my messengers while I am away. They will have to do.

Next to the one in the study, propped up on the mantelpiece are the postcards from Roger and Marion; a patchwork of scenes of ancient crumbling churches, unnaturally blue sea, people in summer clothes wandering through pretty narrow streets, terracotta pots brimming with brilliant-red geraniums; a pink sunset over a marina. They sound happy and I'm surprised how good that makes me feel. I look forward to getting their cards.

I thought that when Marion and Roger left I would feel more alone but Helen and I are in regular contact every couple of weeks now. I wouldn't go as far as to say we're friends, what connects us isn't often spoken about but she's someone I can trust which is a great surprise to me. She's taken over being the contact for the Missing People's website and together we've updated the message to Nick – something I'd been thinking about for a long time. When I finally made the decision to come away it was Helen I rang to tell first, even before Becca. I was scared of Helen's reaction, I suppose, but she didn't make a fuss about it. She wrote down the dates, all my contact numbers and wished me a good time.

Yesterday, Owen moved out. It's strange how no one ever stays in that flat for long. Perhaps by the time I get back there will be new faces around, new names on the entrance buzzer. It seems only to be me who remains constant.

Owen came down with Anne to say goodbye. They are moving in together; closer to where the kids live. Izzy likes Anne but Tom is taking longer to accept her. I'm sure, with time, they'll work it out.

Anne told me that Sylvia has had to go into a home. She'd

suffered a bad bout of pneumonia and it had left her too weak to manage for herself. I said, 'Poor Sylvia', because I could see the sadness in Anne's eyes, and Owen put his arm around her.

'It's not so bad. She's enjoying having lots of people to talk to,' he told me but his words were really meant to comfort Anne. I'm glad, I really am, that she's OK but when I think of Sylvia and the suspicious, searching way she used to look at me, as if she didn't believe anything I was saying, I can't help feeling relieved that I won't be bumping into her again.

The kids weren't with Owen yesterday. I'd said my goodbyes to Izzy last weekend. She's given me her email address for when I finally get set up. 'You can talk to people without having to leave the house,' she told me. 'There are websites,' she said, 'where you can make friends and chat to them without ever going to see them. I'll come and visit you, though,' she added quickly. 'I didn't mean that.'

'I'd like that,' I told her, but Owen and I caught each other's eye because we both know it will never happen. Time will pass, life will move on and I will be forgotten. I don't mind. She doesn't yet know how to recognize what is important and what is not, what is permanent and what isn't.

I touch the smooth, cold case of the mobile in my pocket but I won't take it out just yet; Becca has warned me that people will knock you down in the street to steal one so I'll wait until later before I take another look at the photos of Pearl she has sent me.

Pearl was born nearly five weeks ago, on the twentieth of August. It was a sunny day to welcome her arrival. She has a crease on her chin, and a tuft of dark hair. Sometimes she looks solemn, sometimes she looks surprised. I can see Becca in her mouth, Chris in the shape of her eyes but she is also herself, a little stranger.

The train comes in. I pick up my bag as everyone around me heaves suitcases and holdalls and adjusts briefcases and handbags, pulling them in tight under arms, holding them like battering rams ready to force others to yield as we all crowd around the doors. I have tried to pack selectively but the strap drags down on my shoulder and the full bag is unwieldy as I push through to an empty seat.

The train rattles along towards Waterloo.

There are so many faces getting on and off the train, there are many hundreds more arriving, leaving, standing on the station platforms. It is that bulge of humanity which is London. There is no point looking, I tell myself. It is better to let him come to me. If that is what he wants. So when someone bumps into me and the gypsy woman tries to make me buy a straggly bit of heather wrapped in a piece of tinfoil, I step aside and continue on my way, pushing through the crowd to get to the departure board. I am in plenty of time to make my connection. I buy a cup of coffee and a magazine that I know I'll be too excited to read and come back to stand in front of the board. I concentrate on the fact that I am one step closer to Becca and to Pearl.

In my bag I have Pearl's golden booties wrapped in tissue paper, placed inside a black velvet-covered box. I have spoken to Becca on the phone almost every day since Pearl was born and each time she has offered to drive over and bring Pearl to see me and, though my heart has ached to see her, I have always said no.

'I'm coming to you. I'm bringing her booties.'

'She is changing by the day,' Becca told me a couple of weeks ago.

'I can tell from the photos you've sent.'

'I'm afraid she'll get too big for them,' Becca said. 'She's growing awfully fast.'

And I knew, of course, that her real fear was that this day, the day I am going to see them, would never come.

'Soon,' I told her. 'I promise, I just need some time, a little more time.'

My train is in. I find a seat and squash my bag in on the floor under my legs. I don't want to let it out of my sight. The train isn't very busy. Nobody sits next to me.

I take out my mobile phone and I begin to look through the photographs of Pearl.

Last week, when I was sewing, a phrase of Nick's suddenly came into my mind. His voice sounded so clear and close, the breath froze in my throat. 'Everything that you wish for yourself, I wish for you, too.'

And I knew then what I had to do.

One of my wishes is to be with Pearl and so it is up to me to make it happen. It is down to me to live the life I want, that Nick would also want for me. I have to be brave enough to experience all that I can and to want even more, so that if he comes back – my God – I will have so much to tell him, I will have so much to share and I'll have so much to give.

I have missed precious time with Pearl. I have wasted time that I will never get back. I have a lot to make up for.

The train is slowing. The next stop is mine. I am off the moment the door opens. I can see Becca who is trying to catch sight of me; she is frowning. She looks anxious. I rush over and Becca tries to hug me but Pearl, strapped to her chest in a navy-blue baby sling, is in the way. Becca holds the sling out and I take my first look at my niece. Her eyes flicker open, she yawns and then her chin droops down and she is asleep.

'I thought you might not come.'

'I promised,' I tell her. But I know from the tears in our eyes, that we both understand that there was always the possibility I wouldn't be able to make it; and if I think about it too much, it is almost unbelievable that I have.

'I've still not got the hang of this,' Becca says, as she fiddles with the baby seat in the car while I hold Pearl. She is a warm weight against my arm and I feel terrified about dropping her. I'm just beginning to relax when it's time to hand her over.

'There'll be plenty of other chances,' Becca says, seeing my reluctance to let her go. 'It'll be great to have an extra pair of hands – or arms – around the place.'

We are quickly out of the town and into the countryside. We zoom along in Becca's little car which smells of lemon and pine. The hedges are high and thick and the fields are green.

I keep looking at Pearl who is completely absorbed by sleep. She doesn't move one bit.

'She's beautiful, Becca. She's amazing.'

'She's a dream come true.'

We look at each other across the car and we don't stop smiling for ages. Becca puts on her shades and she opens the window and shakes her hair out and I can tell that at this very moment, she is absolutely, purely happy and I feel honoured to be part of it.

Becca's house is full of light and air. She opens the French doors to the garden which is so enormous I can't even see where it ends. There are flower borders around a wide lawn and in the centre stands a big copper beech. It must be like owning a piece of your own countryside.

'We'll eat out on the table and chairs that Chris made,' Becca says and I hear the pride in her voice. 'But first I must feed the baby.'

We sit on Chris's furniture. It's handsome, generous and built to last. We don't talk while Becca gets Pearl settled. It's a bit of a battle at first. Pearl is damp and pink and she lets out a thin, anxious cry in her urgency for milk but she soon relaxes and I can hear her grunting and snuffling as she sucks. I watch Becca watching Pearl.

I'm glad of this slower pace. Things have been happening so fast that I need a moment to adjust. I can feel the sun on the top of my head, sending its rays right through my body.

The instant Pearl has finished feeding, she falls asleep. Becca puts her in the carry-chair from the car and we take her over to the beech tree. There is only patchy grass under the tree and the soil is like dust. It is cool though and restful on the eyes under the copper-coloured canopy where the sunlight barely reaches the ground. Becca fetches a blanket for me to sit on and then she leaves me alone with Pearl while she goes to prepare our lunch.

I lie down and Pearl's feet are in my line of vision. On impulse I lean forward and kiss the sole of one. Pearl curls her toes and suddenly opens her eyes and fixes me with her sweet, dark gaze which sets off a sunburst in my heart.

We both fall asleep and when I wake up just a few minutes later, the first thing I hear is the hush and sigh of Pearl's breath. It is the most wonderful sound in the world.